Dear Reader:

I hope you will enjoy the **last** installment of the *Pure/ Dark Ones* saga on the following pages (Book #13 in **Pure/ Dark Series**).

When I began Book #1, **Pure Healing** (also available in **Audible**), in 2010, finally published in 2012, I never knew how this fantastical world would unfold. I only had an inkling. And it all began with Sophia, the young Pure Queen trying to figure herself out, amongst a complex world of humans and Immortals. My first Pure hero, Valerius, the Protector, will always have a special place in my heart, and I hope in yours as well.

I realized as I was writing *Pure Healing* that the "bad guys" are not what they appear to be. What defines good and evil, light and dark, right and wrong, is so much more nuanced than "black" and "white." So, I couldn't resist putting myself in the shoes of Dark Ones and see the world from their perspective. Hence, Book #2, **Dark Longing**, was written. This one was close to my heart when it began, because the opening scene was taken right out of my own life when my mother was in the last days of battling her second cancer. After she passed, I stopped writing one-third of the way into the book.

When I picked up the threads of this world again, it was six years later. Though I always had some idea how the stories would unfold, new inspiration took over and swept me away in unexpected directions...it has been an unbelievably thrilling, addictive ride! ***Thanks to all my Muses and Addicts for being the wind beneath my wings!***

This final book is about one of my favorite characters in the series, who, from Book #1, has captivated me with his mischievousness, deviousness, multi-faceted personality, and ambiguity (in so many different ways). I've grown to love him whole-heartedly. I hope you have too.

Email me at **megami771@yahoo.com** to find out more. And follow me on **https://www.facebook.com/AjaJamesAuthor** and **https://aja-james.blog/**.

Also know that this is not the end. The world continues in my new series **Dragon Tails**, with **Book 1:** *Dream of Dragons.*

I love hearing from you!

Enjoy!
Aja James

Soundtrack for Dark Purity

Courtesy of the incredible Cecile! And thanks to Kate as well!

Apocalyptica, **Strong Enough**
Hozier, **Movement**
Golden State, **Wolves**
League of Legends (ft. Cailin Russo and Chrissy Costanza), **Phoenix**
Legends of Legends (ft. The Glitch Mob, Mako, and The Word Alive), **Rise**
Nothing But Thieves, **Holding Out For A Hero**
Bad Wolves, **Hear Me Now**
Through Fire, **Breathe**
Smash Into Pieces, **Burn**
Smash Into Pieces, **Boomerang**
Fivefold, **Til Death**
Bad Wolves, **Zombie**
Pop Evil, **Torn To Pieces**
Alter Bridge, **Broken Wings**
Pop Evil, **Next Life**
Adelitas Way, **Last Stand**
Adelitas Way, **Stay Ready**
Bad Wolves, **Crawling**
Breaking Benjamin, **Angels Fall**
Breaking Benjamin, **Give Me A Sign**
Alter Bridge, **Rise Today**
Alter Bridge, **Watch Over You**
Alter Bridge, **Open Your Eyes**
Bad Wolves, **Better Off This Way**
No Resolve, **Love Me To Death**
Radiohead, **Creep**
Nine Inch Nails, **Closer**
Citizen Soldier, **If These Scars Could Speak**
Five Finger Death Punch, **Bloody**
Five Finger Death Punch, **Wrong Side of Heaven**
Bad Wolves, **Video Games**

Glossary

Awakening: test of courage and strength of spirit which leads to the subject, who possesses a Pure soul, coming into his/her Gift, a supernatural power, if he/she passes the test.

Blood-Contract: Contract by which a human Consents to surrender his/her blood (and sometimes soul) to a vampire for a promise in return that the vampire must fulfill. The vampire has the choice to accept or reject the Contract. Upon acceptance, he/she must fulfill the bargain or risk retribution from the unfulfilled human soul in the form of a curse. See also Consent.

Blooded Mate: the chosen partner for each Dark One. Once the Bond is formed between two Dark Ones, it cannot be broken unless a third party has prior claim of blood or flesh. The third party can elicit a Challenge to one of the Bonded Dark Ones to obtain rights to the other. The Challenge is fought to the death.

Save in the case of a successful Challenge, the Bond cannot be broken except through death. Attempts to break the Bond by one or the other Mate will end in death or madness or something worse, depending on the depth and strength of the Bond in question.

Blooded Mates do not need to take the blood and souls of others to survive. However, they must take blood and sex from each other on a regular basis, else they will weaken and eventually go mad and/or die.

The Chosen: royal guards of the New York-based Vampire King, Alend Ramses.

Consent: a human's willing agreement to surrender his/her blood (and sometimes soul) to a vampire.

Cove: base of the New York-based vampire hive, with dominion over the New England territories in the U.S.

Dark Goddess: supernatural being who is credited with the creation of the Dark Ones. She is a deity to which Dark Ones pray. She is the twin sister of the Pure Ones' Goddess. See also The Goddess.

Dark Laws: One, thou shalt protect the Universal Balance to which all souls contribute. Two, thou shalt maintain the secrecy of the Race. Three, thou shalt not take an innocent's blood, life, or soul without Consent.

Dark One: supernatural being who prefers to live in the night and who gathers energy and prolongs his/her life by feeding off the blood, and sometimes souls, of others. Dark Ones are born, not made. Sometimes confused with the term *vampire*.

Decline: condition in which, or process of, a Pure-Ones' life force depletes after he/she Falls in love but does not receive equal love in return. The Pure One weakens and his/her body slowly, painfully breaks down over the course of thirty days, leading ultimately to death unless his/her love is returned in equal measure. Triggered through sexual intercourse.

The Dozen: see Royal Zodiac.

Ecliptic Scrolls: events past, recorded by the Keeper of the Dark Ones.

Ecliptic Prophesies: events in the future as foretold by the Oracle of the Dark Ones.

The Elite: royal personal guards of the Pure queen.

Eternal Mate: the destined partner to a given Pure soul. Each soul only has one mate across time, across various incarnations of life. Quotation from the Zodiac Scrolls describing the bond: "His body is the Nourishment of life. Her energy is the Sustenance of soul."

Fallen: Term used to describe a Pure One who Fell in love with the wrong person, endured the Decline, and chose to become a vampire at the end of it rather than death.

Gift: supernatural power bestowed upon Pure Ones by the Goddess. Usually an enhanced physical or mental ability such as telekinesis, superhuman strength and telepathy. True Blood Dark Ones also possess powerful Gifts. See True Blood.

The Goddess: supernatural being who is credited with the creation of the Pure Ones. She is a deity to which Pure Ones devote themselves. She protects the Universal Balance.

The Great War: circa 2190 B.C., the Pure Ones who had been enslaved by the Dark Ones rebelled against their oppressors en masse. At the end of decades of bloodshed, the Pure Ones ultimately regained their freedom, and the Dark Ones' empire lay in ruins with the members of the Royal Hive scattered to the ends of the earth.

Hive: society of vampires with typically a matriarch, the queen, at the head, with the exception of one Dark King in modern times.

Horde: small groups of vampires with no queen, typically composed of Rogues who band together for ease of hunting.

Nourishment: the strength that Mated Dark Ones take from each other's blood and body through sexual intercourse. Once Mated, they will no longer need others' blood to survive, only that from each other. Sexual intercourse is required to make the Nourishment sustaining.

Nourishment is also what Pure males provide their females as Eternal Mates.

Pure One: supernatural being who is eternally youthful, typically endowed with heightened senses or powers called the Gift. In possession of a pure soul and blessed with more than one chance at life by the Goddess, chosen as one of Her immortal race that defends the Universal Balance.

Rogue: lone vampire who does not belong to an organized vampire society or Hive.

The Royal Zodiac: twelve-member collective of the Elite, the Circlet and the Queen of the Pure Ones.

Sacred Laws (Pure Ones): One, thou shalt protect the purity, innocence and goodness of humankind and the Universal Balance to which all souls contribute. Two, thou shalt maintain the secrecy of the Race. And three, thou shalt not engage in sexual intercourse with someone who is not thy Eternal Mate. Also known as the Cardinal Rule.

Shield: referred to as the base of the Royal Zodiac, wherever it may be. Not necessarily a physical location.

Sustenance: the strength that Mated Pure-Males take from the Pure-females' spirit. Once Mated, the Pure-male becomes dependent upon the Pure-female for sustaining his life. If his Mate dies before him, he too will perish. In equal exchange, the Pure-male provides Nourishment. See Nourishment.

True Blood: a vampire born of Dark parents. See also Dark One.

Vampire: supernatural being who prefers to live in the night and who gathers energy and prolongs his/her life by feeding off the blood, and sometimes souls, of others. Contrary to prevalent beliefs (see Book 1: _Pure Healing_), vampires are both made and born. Some vampires are Pure Ones who have chosen Darkness rather than death after they break the Cardinal Rule. Some are humans turned by other vampires. Some are True Bloods that are born of a vampire mother or father, more accurately called Dark Ones.

Zodiac Prophesies: events yet to come, foretold by the Seer of the Pure Ones through the Orb of Prophesies.

Zodiac Scrolls: events past, recorded by the Scribe of the Pure Ones.

Prologue

Hiiiii!

I'm soooo excited to meet you!

My name is Benjamin Larkin D'Angelo. That's Warrior Angel to you!

Larkin means tough or fierce and it's Gaelic in origin. How cool is that? Uber cool, right? Combined with D'Angelo, my Dad's last name (his first name is Gabriel, so it totally runs in the family), I'm pretty badass.

At least my name is.

I don't know what to make of Benjamin, but...you can't win 'em all.

(Just don't tell my parents I said "badass.")

It's not every day an almost-nine-year-old gets to talk (in my head at least) to an ADULT! A "private tête-à-tête," as my uncle Ere would say.

Well, okay, I talk to adults every day. I'm surrounded by them.

Aside from my art teacher Clara's daughter, Annie, there aren't a lot of children around for me to talk to. Tristan and Ayelet's daughter Isolde (I call her Izzy) is just a baby. I like her and all, but I'm almost thrice her age. She has a long way to go before she can catch up to my *considerable* years of wisdom.

And, since I've been here in this hush-hush place where my Mom, Dad, Uncle Tal and Auntie Ishtar and I (and of course, my favorite Uncle Ere, but don't tell him or his head will get big) have been hiding out from bad guys for the past several months, I haven't gotten to see Annie and Izzy at all. Only on video chats.

Okay, so maybe I exaggerate. Uncle Tal tells me I'm prone to it.

Mom and Dad always look at Uncle Ere when they shake their heads and lament (yes, I know big words, I've read the Encyclopedia Britannica forward and backward five times already) at my bad habits because, apparently, I take after my uncle more than I do my parents.

Go figure.

I like it though. Uncle Ere is the coolest, the funniest (even when he isn't trying to be) and the weirdest.

I like weird people. They're *unique*.

Anyway, there are children here. I do go to school with them five days a week in town. But it's a really small "town," population under thirty-eight thousand, spread out over almost two hundred thousand square miles. That's bigger than California, which has almost forty *million* people.

Yes, I'm a "veritable fount of knowledge," as my Uncle Ere would say. I'm curious about EVERYTHING and I have a really good memory.

Even if it's selective. Another thing Mom and Dad lament about me.

I just don't have a lot of deep conversations with the kids at my school, is my point. There are less than two hundred children of varying ages in the whole town.

I mean, they're cool and all, but I don't have a lot to contribute when topics range from the latest video games and TV shows to toys and sports. I'm not very sporty per se. I don't like competition; I just like hanging out with people.

Mom and Dad tried to put me in some "regular kid's activities" like soccer, basketball, and swimming (all indoors these days since it's winter), but I always end up talking too much to the other kids or the coaches and not even notice when a ball has zipped past my defense, or a whistle was blown to signal the start of a race.

The other kids like me, but...nobody wants me on their team :(.

ANYWAY...what I mean is—it's not every day I get to talk to adult STRANGERS!

I'm not allowed to talk to any strangers, actually. But I never can remember the rule. I don't break it on purpose.

It's just... I LIKE people! I want to get to know EVERYONE!

People on the subway. People I pass on the street. People in the shops. Even the very bad dragon-lady who tried to kidnap me.

On this, I'm not exaggerating AT ALL. She really is a dragon-lady. Her name is Lilith. But I call her Lily (not to her face, cuz she doesn't like it, but in my head, I call her Lily).

And when I say dragon, I mean DRAGON.

She's a Hydra. She has nine serpent heads and is the size of a three-story building, maybe more. I think she can take Godzilla down without a sweat. She's like the *Kaiju* from *Pacific Rim*. Her heads spew different things, like hellfire, acid, poison, and other nasty stuff.

To be honest with you, it's hard to like Lily. She's awfully unattractive with those gaping dragon mouths with hundreds of teeth, lolling tongues and bad breath.

She's even harder to like when she hurts my family and friends. I'm so mad at her!

She hurt Uncle Ere most of all. I saw some of it before I closed my eyes and looked away when my friends rescued me from her clutches and spirited me away in a helicopter. I'm mad, mad, mad!...

Oh look!

There's a dragonfly chasing dandelion puffs! It's so pretty!

Like its wings are made of crystal prisms and its body is made of diamonds. Up, up, up it flitters, like it's playing flying soccer with the dandelion puff.

I wonder if it's lonely, playing all by itself. I'm going to run and keep it company, blow some more puffs in its direction...

Hmm, where was I?

That was so much fun! I love it out here! There are mountains, lakes, rivers, endless blue skies, grass, trees... a sea to the north and a gulf to the south. I've always lived in New York City before this, first with Dad and Olivia (my birth mother), then with Dad and Nana (my new Mommy as of three years ago, so not so new anymore), and then with all kinds of elves and vampires and vampire-elves.

I am NOT exaggerating!

They actually have names for their "Kinds"—the Pure and Dark Ones. But I think vampire-elves sound best.

There are also Beasts and Lesser Beasts, or Animal Spirits, which are humans or Immortals who have the spirit of an animal bound to their soul. They can transform into the animal version too. Really!

There are Elementals, who can command air, fire, water or earth. I've met a couple of those before—one of them was even in my rescue party—but I haven't met many. They are the rarest of all Immortals.

And of course, there are DRAGONS!! Hurrah!!

I've seen three dragons now, believe it or not. One is a heavenly jade-green dragon, who's actually a Pure warrior called Cloud. He can't turn into a dragon any more, no matter how much I begged him when I lived for a while at the Shield. But sometimes, he lets me into his mind and we go flying together in our imagination, using real memories that he has from the time he was a Celestial Dragon.

Then, there's the Hydra I already told you about. Let's not think on her. My chest feels like an elephant is sitting on it whenever I think about her.

Lastly, there's the obsidian dragon who fought the Hydra and saved me and my friends. He's the most beautiful dragon of all, just like the dragons I always dreamed of since I was a baby. With shiny black scales that sparkle fire in sunlight, pearlescent like moonstones in water. Gigantic wings that seem as wide as a football field. And glowing, sapphire eyes, same as the blue flame he breathes.

Best of all, I know who he is. I like to think of him as *my* dragon.

And the only reason I'm not madder at Lily is that he's safe and sound after their battle. He's here with me, Mom and Dad, Uncle Tal and Auntie Ishtar.

He's not himself though. That makes me sad.

He's wearing his "illusions" again.

Sometimes, he takes a young man's form, and we call him Binu. Sometimes, he takes a woman's form, and we call her Erena. But he never takes his true form—he's never my Uncle Ere.

I guess I understand why. After the awful battle with the Hydra, Uncle Ere is badly scarred.

He always wears clothes to cover as much of himself as he can, but his face is visible. It's like his face was a hard-boiled egg that got its shell crushed into tiny bits. Much worse than Humpty Dumpty. There are countless fractures in his skin, like he's a puzzle somebody pieced together the wrong way.

His hands look okay though. But they sometimes shake or twitch uncontrollably. He tries to shake them out when that happens, then tighten them into fists.

Like he wants to take on the world. Like he wants to tear down the skies. There's so much pain and vengeance in his eyes...

But then it's all gone in a flash. Only emptiness remains.

No one but me (or is it I?) can see the real him underneath his skins.

I'm glad it's only me. I think our family and friends would be really, really, sad if they saw Uncle Ere's scars.

We don't know how he got away from the Hydra. We all feared the worst. But one day, months after what happened, he just showed up on our doorstep, here in the middle of nowhere hush-hush place. He was wearing his Binu form that day, and when he twisted his lips into a smile that was meant to comfort us upon greeting, I thought his whole face would splinter apart like crushed glass.

He doesn't talk about it. We all asked. I might have needled him more than I should have. But he doesn't say. He's so good at changing the subject. So "glib" (I love that word!) and funny and snarky and cool.

But something is missing inside him.

Sometimes, I catch him looking into the distance as if lost. Not just lost in thought, but just plain LOST. Like he left something important behind. Or he lost it, maybe.

But if he lost it, why doesn't he go looking for it? I wish he would.

I wish with all my heart that Uncle Ere finds what he's looking for.

Chapter One

It was strange to have a job.

He'd never had a job in the whole of his existence. Which was a fucking long time. Over five thousand years, in fact.

Well, technically, he'd never had a job and got paid for it.

He'd been a spy, a whore, a lie, an agent of destruction, a criminal mastermind, but never received a penny for his troubles. He'd never owned anything of value, or even anything cheap. Everything he had, including the clothes on his back, belonged to other people, people he pretended to be. Or they were provided to him for a particular purpose.

Never were they provided to keep him warm or modest. More often than not, he was made to wear things that emphasized his shameful bits. What other people covered up, he'd learned to flaunt. To tempt and seduce.

In whatever form he took, he was always the most beautiful thing you'd ever seen.

Nor were clothes provided because anyone had pride in him. Not the good kind of pride anyway. The kind that everyone needed from someone important to them to build their confidence. A rare few might be born with poise and self-assurance, but alas, he wasn't one of them.

He owned nothing. After all these millennia, he hadn't a penny to his name before he came here.

Except a hand-made wood comb and a small carved figure of a leopard cub.

Those had been given to him with…affection. Without expecting anything in return. Just because he needed them.

The irony was—he didn't even have a name until recently when he chose one for himself.

Erebu.

Ere for short.

It meant "darkness" in ancient Akkadian. And it just so happened that Ere was the name of his alter ego, a split personality of which he was vaguely conscious, but who kept a separate life from him.

Then, about half a year ago, when he was forced to confront his past in all its horrific, ignoble glory, Ere became a part of him again. He was whole again.

Mostly.

Partly.

Sort of.

His whole life was on loan. His time was borrowed. He should have died a few times but was forcefully resurrected. He hadn't cared one way or the other whether he died or lived, but somebody did. Unfortunately, each time, that somebody was always evil at their core and revived him only for their own nefarious purposes.

Except for his most recent resurrection...

He shook his head determinedly as his hand began to tremble. He couldn't think on that.

All this was to say, as he stood behind the solid wood counter making specialty drinks for the town's most popular (and only) coffee and tea shop in the middle of bum-fuck nowhere Timbuktu (but not really, just an expression), clocking in his hours and collecting his minimum-wage paycheck at the end of each week, he felt a sense of accomplishment that sometimes evoked *feelings* that made it hard to swallow.

None of that sappy shit, he told himself sternly. *Keep it together. Fake it til you make it.*

Not that he had any idea what "making it" entailed. It wasn't like he'd ever had ambitions of his own.

"Hey, Binu," greeted his co-worker, the gorgeous punk-rock Barbie with blue hair, Mikayla Lane, before she disappeared through the "Employee Only" door to change into her uniform.

Her hair was purple a couple weeks ago, and green before that. He was mildly curious what the real color was. She was always changing it up, and it was never anything "boring."

Mike's red hair would be a fire-engine, neon red. Her blond would be platinum sprinkled with diamond dust. She looked like Amber Heard's twin sister, except taller and more buxom. And she had the gravelly, soulful voice of Diamante. She was sex on two, endlessly long legs, in other words.

Too bad he was asexual and couldn't fully appreciate the vision that was Mikayla Lane.

You sure about that?

What about those dreams at night, hmm?

But those dreams don't include tits and gams and a soft peachy ass, do they?

No, you like it a whole lot harder, a taunting voice whispered in his mind.

It was his own voice. The devil's voice.

"Stop that," he gritted beneath his breath.

"Huh?"

Mike came back just as he was talking to himself like a weirdo.

He turned his lips up stiffly at the corners and tried not to grimace at the feeling of his face cracking.

Goddamn Hydra and her goddamn heads. And claws. And teeth. And tail...

"Nothing," he said with as much nonchalance as he could muster on his fake, frozen face, the kind that probably resembled an actor with too many Botox injections and plastic surgery.

"Lovely day, isn't it?"

They both looked out the row of windows in front of the store, facing the sidewalks and the only double-wide street that ran through town. It was eight degrees outside (practically springtime temperature!), dark as night even though it was nine o'clock in the morning, and a bone-chilling icy mist was settling in.

"Good one, Binu," Mike said with a quirk of her luscious mouth, used to his unique brand of dry sarcasm by now.

"But you know, this place has grown on me. You've only been here, what, eight weeks? Give it time. This is my first winter here, actually, so I'm still getting used to the long nights and freezing temperatures. But that's what toasty fires are for, right? And big, hunky bears to hibernate with."

Given that she ended on a saucy wink, he knew she wasn't talking about the four-legged, furry sort of bears. She was referring to the native human (and non-human) males of the bipedal variety.

On second thought, the fur might still apply.

His eyes flitted helplessly toward the cheerful fire crackling in the shop's fireplace, then darted away again as if the sight burned his irises.

Fires and strange men. Those were things he needed to stay away from at all cost, his self-preserving sub-conscience warned him.

Something licked at the edges of his memory... something very, *very...*

HOT.

"Ha! Gotcha!" Mike crowed, startling him out of his disturbing thoughts.

Nothing fully formed, just blurry impressions. His funky imagination playing pranks on him, perhaps. Or...memories he'd forcibly repressed.

"You're thinking about someone turning up your internal heater, aren't you? I can see it on your face. You're blushing like crazy! It's a good look on you, handsome."

He took her compliment in stride.

He *was* handsome. His pretend form was, anyway.

His Binu persona looked like a GQ model—the lean, six-foot, branded turtle-neck, slacks, alligator shoes and glasses-wearing kind. It was a form he was comfortable in and put on often in the past. Girls tended to giggle at him and flirt. Guys tended to assume he was smart and loaded. Win-win.

Here in this coffee and tea shop, he dressed a whole lot more...casually (read: cheaply), since he was saving his pennies for a rainy day (but really, he just liked to see the digits go up every time he deposited his paycheck in his bank account). He got his clothes from online thrift shops. But he'd always had an impeccable sense of fashion, what looked good on whatever form he took. So, he always looked like a million bucks without even trying.

This knack came in particularly handy when the daytime customers stuffed fat tips into his cookie jar, which he was happy to share with Mike, who attracted her own considerable share of attention and admiration.

"I'm not blushing," he muttered, turning away to take another order and handing the fresh caramel cappuccino he just made to an awaiting customer.

"It's hot in here. Somebody should get that fire under control. It's shooting sparks everywhere."

"The only sparks getting shot are coming from your eyes, *guapo*," Mike tittered annoyingly at him.

"You must be thinking something extra naughty. I wish I could see your thoughts. Come on, what does she or he look like? You never let on your preferences. Give me a hint. I can keep a secret. It'll help me narrow the candidate pool for you at the club."

Being a barista was his day job, while being a bartender and occasional one-woman band was his night gig.

Yes, you read right—one-*woman* band.

Because at night, he took the form of a tall, voluptuous, flame-haired femme fatale named Erena, alongside Mike at the only bar in town, the *Night Owl*, which she co-owned with her best friend Yasmin.

Again, his disguise was premeditated. Bars were filled with men and women looking for a good time, a place to relax and shoot the bull. Get drunk and pick up tail.

Or so he'd heard.

He didn't participate in these activities himself, and if he ever did, it was because he was "on the job." For these scenes, a beautiful, sexy woman with a push-up bra and five-inch heels was going to get better tips than a professorial stuck-up suit.

"I'm shooting sparks from my eyes to smite you to ashes," he retorted with his best scowl. "I don't think naughty thoughts. I'm as pure as the driven snow."

She tilted her head in one of her thoughtful yet sassy poses. She had many of those.

"Where does that expression come from, I wonder? Driven snow? I mean, after you drive on snow, it goes from beautiful, pristine white powder to yucky gray and black slush. You'd think it should be 'pure as the undriven snow.'"

This was what he loved most about his job, even more than his big-boy paycheck—inane conversation with Mike and his other co-workers, sometimes a chatty, friendly customer, and the owner of the shop, Madison Peterson (AKA Maddie the Mad Hatter), Mike's other best friend.

It was so *normal*. So human.

He loved being human. Even if it was only pretend.

Their continuous chatting and teasing, and sometimes comfortable silences, put him at ease. Took him out of his own head. He lost himself in mundane, practiced activities. Taking orders, making drinks, swiping cards.

He loved this job. He loved this life.

Even though he was wearing a disguise, one of the countless humanoid forms he could shift into. Even though it was too good to be true, he soaked up every second.

So what if none of this might last? He'd learned by now to take his reprieve whenever he could get it. And life didn't get much better than this.

Absently, he rubbed the upper left side of his chest. Even though his heart beat within its cage, he felt hollow somehow. As if he was missing something vital.

Flames...you miss the flames...

"Hey Binu, aren't you heading out for the day? Your shift's been over for fifteen minutes. You'll be late picking up Benji from school if you don't hustle."

At Mike's reminder, he hopped to it, not bothering to change out of his uniform as he dashed out the door.

"Put on your damn coat, Binu!" Mike hollered after him. "You're gonna freeze within five seconds in that thing!"

He raised his hand and waved it at her without turning around, already breaking into a jog to make it to Benjamin's school on time. He bared his teeth in a joyful grin as the cold air whipped his uncovered face.

It was nice to have someone who cared about him, nagging at him to look after himself. Mike wasn't the only one, these days. He had so many...friendly acquaintances, he couldn't count them all on both hands. That had never happened to him before. Not in his whole existence.

He had a home to "go home" to. One he shared with people who welcomed his company. Inanna and Gabriel, Benjamin's parents. Inanna, who was his twin sister, it turned out, born of Tal-Telal and Ishtar, their parents.

His fucking parents!

He had parents...and they even wanted him around. He could scarcely believe his good fortune.

And then there was the most important person in his entire universe: Benjamin.

His beautiful, precocious, wonderful, sweet sunlight Benjamin.

Every morning, he woke up to Benjamin's boy-loud voice, happily chatting about whatever caught his fancy. His bubbly laughter and uninhibited guffaws accompanied by the softer tones of the adults speaking and chuckling along with him.

Every night, he got to tell the boy a bedtime story, after "Uncle Tal" told his, and before Benjamin's parents tucked him in. He got the same treatment everyone else did—a hug, a kiss, and the sweetest, most addictive words he'd ever heard—"Love you, Uncle Ere."

So, even though this routine happened every day, he never took it for granted. He couldn't wait to see Benjamin again.

Thankfully, the school was only five blocks away. And he didn't waste time putting on his jacket because he wasn't susceptible to human frailties. He could freeze, but it would take a lot longer than humans would, because of his accelerated healing abilities.

He was what Benjamin called a vampire-elf.

And he was also *more*.

What more, he'd rather not contemplate right now, since the mere whisper of those thoughts made his entire body quake uncontrollably.

He focused instead on putting one foot in front of the other, dodging ice patches on the sidewalk, as he ran toward the school.

How did the time fly by so fast? It seemed like just a few minutes ago that his alarm clock went off at six a.m. His life *Before* had always trickled along slowly, like drops of blood from a congealing wound. Now, there was never enough time. He wished he could bottle it up and save it. Every moment seemed so precious.

Turning a corner and dodging the occasional pedestrian as he jogged along, his grin spread wider as he thought about how Benjamin would greet him.

Usually, the boy was waiting in front of the school surrounded by other children, and sometimes a teacher or two. He was always chatting boisterously with someone, always in the middle of a passionate discussion.

His Benjamin knew no strangers. Everyone loved him, and he loved everyone. He could talk stone into melting. He could talk stars from the sky.

He was simply...*magical*.

Ere couldn't believe Inanna and Gabriel let *him* of all people have the privilege of picking Benjamin up from school. The trust they placed in him was mind-boggling, especially considering the fact that he used to be one of the Pure and Dark Ones' arch nemesis, Medusa's, foremost henchmen.

He was never the muscle, only the brain. But he'd done things...plotted things...

These plots had led to the destruction of the Pure Ones' home, the abduction and death of more than one of their highest ranks. He'd planted a spy and usurper in the Dark Ones' New England Hive as well. That traitor had been executed three years ago, by none other than Inanna and Gabriel.

He'd orchestrated Tal and Ishtar's abduction for a bloody, torturous reunion with Medusa, Ishtar's twin sister (who knew!). He himself had perpetrated the disguise that got the "Demon Warrior" Tal-Telal to let down his guard enough for their enemies to take him by surprise.

And all of this was only the tip of the iceberg. He'd done much, *much* more irredeemable things.

If he were Benjamin's parents, *he* wouldn't let an evil-doer like himself within a five-mile radius of the precious boy.

What were Inanna and Gabriel thinking! Dark Ones weren't supposed to be so gullible and trusting. Only Pure Ones suffered from those defects. But then, the two warriors possessed Pure souls, so perhaps that was the reason for their lapse in judgement. Ere certainly wasn't one to interfere with their parenting approach.

Even if he *was* Benjamin's sperm donor.

And, who was he to complain about their unfathomable trust in him, when it meant that he could have Benjamin all to himself for twenty minutes every day? Sometimes, he purposely dragged it out to as long as forty minutes, with a detour to the book shop, library, or to pick up some fresh-made bread and desserts at the bakery.

Ishtar, in her "Mama Bear" form, spent a lot of time at the bakery helping out and winning more business for the local shop owner with her delicious recipes. He and Benjamin would sample some of her desserts with a small cup of chocolate each while they chatted with the "old lady" before heading home.

Gods, but life was good!

If he wasn't careful, his grin would become so wide he was liable to split his face literally and freeze his lungs with a huge suck of below-freezing air. At that mental reminder, he pressed his lips together, only allowing the corners to curl.

He'd compared himself to Frankenstein's Monster before, at least where his irredeemable soul was concerned. How ironic that he now looked like the Monster in truth, a haphazard patchwork of skin, muscle and bones.

His true form was hideous. He witnessed it in the mirror every day. It reminded him of reality. That this slice of heaven he was living would not last. His "friends and family" couldn't see the real him.

He'd hoped before that he could show them, that he could learn to live in his own skin. And for a blink in time, he had shown them. Just as he'd shown himself the real face that he'd hidden away for so long, he himself couldn't even recall.

That hope had died a violent death along with the form he took in the battle with the Hydra. Perhaps he'd lost the ability to transform into the obsidian dragon forever.

He didn't know and he didn't want to try. Just thinking about it made him break out in a cold sweat and uncontrollable shaking.

Those memories were...*unpleasant*, to put it extremely mildly.

"Uncle Binu! You're here!"

Benjamin's booming little boy voice snapped him to attention.

Involuntarily, he grinned again and didn't care if he did split all of his scars. The happiness upon seeing his boy made him feel like he would burst if he didn't release some of the effervescent light that strained behind his chest bone, as if he had a tiny sun trapped inside him, impatient to get free.

"Sorry I'm late," he said, catching his breath, both from the brisk jog and the breathlessness he always felt around Benjamin. He took pains never to let the boy see his effect on him, however, lest Benjamin's head got too big.

How could *he* have created *that*? This walking, talking, beautiful miracle.

"No worries," Benjamin chirped. "I had company."

"Of course you did."

He always did.

"Come meet my new friend, Uncle Binu!" the boy said excitedly, tugging someone along behind him with one hand.

Ere was already nodding as Benjamin said this. The boy often introduced "new friends" to him. Even though this town was sparse in population, it seemed as if Benjamin had no shortage of new people to make friends with.

His eyes started with what the boy was holding in his hand.

He'd expected the small hand of another child or perhaps an adult hand, but what he saw was just one finger. An index finger, to be exact.

Not by itself, mind you, for it was certainly attached to a hand, not morbidly dangling by itself from a bloody stump. (Although, you never knew. Ere had seen far more gruesome sights).

But what he noticed immediately was that the finger was large enough to take up most of the room in Benjamin's grip. Which meant that it was attached to a *very large* hand.

"His name is Soren. Isn't that so cool? I've never met a person with this name before. I wonder where it comes from and what it means. I'm totally going to Google it when I get home..."

Ere only half listened as Benjamin did his thing, rattling off a string of tenuously connected thoughts, though they were always impeccably logical in the boy's own mind.

Mostly, he was still stuck on the size of that extremely manly hand. So, his eyes followed the finger to the rest of that very large hand, which was attached to a very thick, strong, manly wrist and muscular forearm, decorated by clearly defined, zig-zagging veins.

Wait.

Why was anyone wearing short enough sleeves to show tantalizing forearm skin in this weather?

Someone stupid, must be.

Nevertheless, Ere's Adam's apple bobbed as he swallowed. Suddenly, his mouth had gone completely dry.

What the devil was wrong with him? Perhaps the fear of seeing an ogre or troll attached to such a sizable limb? But no, *fear* was definitely not the emotion he was feeling right now.

But gods! That was the hottest forearm he'd ever seen in all his life!

It was forearm porn as far as he was concerned. Maybe he should write to PornHub when *he* got home and request that they add this kink to their suite of offerings. Must be an untapped market out there if looking at a stranger's half-naked limb could get an avowed asexual like him to perk up with reluctant, disorienting interest.

It would be a public service.

"...and he's visiting from a faraway place! Like one of those Scandinavian countries. More maybe Eastern Europe. He looks like a Viking. Doesn't he look like a Viking, Uncle Binu? Or maybe like a Viking deity, like Thor! Cuz he's too tall to be a mere mortal, right?..."

That forearm was certainly godly, Ere thought, absorbing snippets of what Benjamin was saying.

As if his eyeballs had a life of their own, they unblinkingly followed the lovely trail of extremely manly veins on the forearm to the rolled-up sleeves of a thin thermal T, to the clearly defined, anatomically perfect illustration of all the muscle groups of a man's upper arm, made somehow even more tantalizing by the fact that they were covered in a thin layer of wool and cotton.

Biceps, triceps, deltoid, oh my! Arm porn galore!

He was outright sweating by now. So, he skipped quickly over the broad, *endlessly* broad, shoulder to the long, corded neck, refusing the temptation of looking lower at the thick pectoral muscles in the periphery of his vision, and certainly nothing else below that.

(But, gracious, were those beaded nipples under that shirt? Hard like drill bits. From the cold, most likely. Certainly not the other thing that would make nipples pebble so deliciously...)

If he took in the man's face within the next hour, given how long this meandering perusal of his *arm* was taking, Ere would consider himself efficient.

But it wasn't entirely his fault. He had a long way to look up. *Way up.* The man was at least half a foot taller than him in his Binu form. In his real form, he would still have been an inch or two shorter. Next to Benjamin, the man looked like a colossus.

He forced his eyes to keep going.

A thick, golden beard with fiery highlights. It should have looked scruffy and unkempt, maybe wiry and rough, but instead, Ere thought it might feel soft, like sheep fleece. People had sheep here. Caribou and moose too, though those were wild. He wanted to test it for softness—the beard, that was, not the sheep fleece. He had the strangest desire to run his fingers through that thick, *manly* beard.

And he could already tell, without seeing or touching, that the hair hid an angular, unforgiving jaw. Probably unbreakable too, given how steely the guy's arm looked. Some overtly muscular men looked like boulders, with gym and steroid-enhanced bodies. But this guy's physique (what little Ere allowed himself to scrutinize) looked like it was wrought iron or reinforced tempered steel.

Yup. Totally unbreakable jaw.

Moving on.

"...he's friends with Maddie's husband, Tiger. Or, I think they know each other, because when Tiger came to pick Logan up for hockey practice, he stopped by to talk to Soren. Well, maybe they didn't exactly talk. They just kinda stared at each other all intense-like. But I think they were talking in their heads. You know, like some people could do..."

Here, Benjamin got all whispery, even though his version of sotto voce was as loud as another person's normal speaking voice.

On this point, Ere finally focused on the stranger's mouth, since a mouth was required to speak with. And Benjamin brought it up, so there was really nowhere else to look—

Except at those wide, full lips. Firm, yet soft looking.

Huh.

He unconsciously licked his own lips, caught himself doing it, and pressed them tightly together, determined to finish his perusal without any more outward reactions.

High, sharp, *perfect* cheekbones. Were there any cheekbones ever created on a man that was ever this perfect? The answer was a resounding: hell no! There never had been and never would be cheekbones this ridiculously perfect.

If he was the size of an ant, he'd cliff-dive off those cheekbones and hope to be caught upon those beautiful, full lips. If they weren't as soft as they looked and he broke upon impact, it would be a glorious, worthwhile sacrifice. Maybe he'd get lost in the beard instead. Maybe he'd root around in the thick, forest-like maze and never come out.

Distantly, a part of Ere pointed out that he was on the verge of losing his mind.

What the fuck was he doing waxing poetic about a strange man's face?! Even if it was all in his head, it was insane!

He was insane!

"...he hasn't eaten all day, can you believe it? He didn't say he was hungry, but I could hear his stomach rumbling from across the schoolyard! Do you think Mom and Dad will mind if I invited him home for dinner? I wonder what we're having. It's Thursday, so probably some kind of pasta. Do you like pasta, Soren?..."

But Ere wasn't done with his meticulous cataloguing of the stranger's features yet. There was more.

The nose was straight, high-bridged and a tad too long. But that only served to point like an arrow to those luscious lips.

As if anyone looking at this guy needed the reminder.

As if seeing that mouth all by itself wasn't enough to give an unsuspecting person heart palpitations.

His creator had to frame those to-die-for lips in the context of those dramatic cheekbones and unbreakable jaw and make observers linger even longer by leading them there with that arrow-like nose.

And then, Ere couldn't avoid it any longer.

He stared into the most startling eyes he'd ever seen, beneath dark golden brows that arched over them like spread eagle wings. Surrounded by the thickest, longest lashes. Two rows of them on both top and bottom.

There was a name for that. Distichiasis.

A genetic mutation that created double rows of eyelashes. He knew this because one of his favorite Golden Age of Hollywood actresses had this condition—the legendary beauty, Elizabeth Taylor.

Seeing this "mutation" on a man so...primally *male* was unexpected and jarring. But when Ere took in his whole face together, the luxurious lashes only added to his blatant masculinity, emphasized, bolded and underlined the intensity of the purely golden orbs they framed. As if two miniature suns blazed within his eye sockets.

Flames...he missed those flames...

Unbidden, the words whispered through his mind.

He shook his head slightly to clear it. Looked back at the stranger and hurriedly took in the rest—longish, wavy, golden and bronze hair hanging loose over his shoulders, a few strands covering his face, the left side of which seemed to be tattooed with elaborate symbols.

Ere wanted to have a closer look, but he purposely didn't let his gaze linger too long. Maybe the man didn't want his tattoos scrutinized. Maybe the long hair was to hide them. So, Ere focused on the hair instead.

The wild mane didn't look like it had ever seen a brush or a comb. But it was shiny and seemed clean despite that. He wanted to run his fingers through it even more than the beard. He wanted to feel it on his naked skin, not just his hands.

What the fuck *was wrong with him?!*

At last, he jolted back into full awareness of his surroundings, and most importantly, his *son*. And it hit him like a ton of bricks that Benjamin was going on about a *stranger*.

A big, over six and a half feet tall, muscular, lethal-looking stranger who could easily snap both their necks like dry twigs with his bare hands.

Those extra-large, veiny, long-fingered, strangely elegant hands...

Snap out of it, you dunce!

"Benjamin," he finally croaked through his bone-dry throat, "what did I tell you about talking to strangers?"

There. He sounded reasonably responsible and adult-like.

Inanna and Gabriel would be pleased. Surely, they would say the same had they been in his shoes right this moment.

Of course, they probably would have found their voice a lot sooner. They probably wouldn't have spent the last half hour ogling the stranger's hand, arm and face, nor daydreaming about cliff-diving off the unyielding ramparts of his cheekbones as an ant.

"But he's not a stranger, Uncle Binu," Benjamin argued.

Of course, he argued. Benjamin always had a ready response to every question.

"His name is Soren. He's a Viking warrior—"

"I thought he was a god? Maybe Thor?"

See, he was paying attention. He could multitask while committing every meticulous detail of a stranger's face to memory. He'd likely be able to pick out that hand and forearm out of any lineup based on the pattern of veins alone.

"Maybe," Benjamin allowed, his eyes rolling away to regard his heretofore silent companion in contemplation.

"If gods existed, he'd definitely be one, don't you think? But I'm pretty sure he's more like us."

"Like us?" Ere echoed, uncomprehending.

"Yes, like you and me," Benjamin clarified. Which didn't explain anything at all.

"Normal, you mean?" Ere tried to pin him down.

The boy chuckled like bubbling champagne until he could barely catch his breath.

"Uncle Binu, you are so funny! We're not 'normal.' We're *special*. And so is Soren."

"Hmm," Ere said noncommittally, while he narrowed his eyes at the stranger who had yet to contribute a single word to this rambling conversation.

And he also never took his unnerving gold eyes off of Ere's face. Not for one single second. If Ere had been scrutinizing him to the minutest detail, he'd stared hard enough to do the same.

Well, no matter. This wasn't Ere's true form anyway. This Soren could memorize all he wanted, but he'd be memorizing a shell, a ghost, a pretense.

Nevertheless, Ere felt stripped to his bones by the stranger's intense, *heated* stare. Not the other connotation of "heated," mind you, but the most straightforward meaning.

His stare literally gave Ere a burning sensation, as if his entire body was being roasted slowly over a bonfire.

Strangely, this was not an uncomfortable sort of roasting. Ere almost felt at ease.

Almost.

"So, can I bring him home, can I?" Benjamin whined, except his beseeching tone was not in the least abrasive as most children's wheedling might sound.

He looked and sounded absolutely adorable, with those big blue eyes, pouty lips, cold-pinkened cheeks and riotous blond curls.

Ere needed to put his foot down. That was the responsible adult thing to do, he was relatively certain.

"It's 'may I,' not 'can I,'" he stalled.

Benjamin wove his fingers together in a wish-making fist in front of his face and widened his eyes even more.

"Pleeeeasssseee, may I, Uncle Binu?"

"I don't think your parents would approve, Benjamin," he said in his sternest adulting tone.

"And I'm sure *Soren* has other matters to attend to. He is not a stray dog to—"

"Of course, he's not, Uncle Binu," Benjamin admonished. "Soren is a man!"

Yes indeed! Soren is a man with a capital M-A-N! Ere's internal voice shouted like an overzealous Dallas Cowboy cheerleader during pre-season tryouts.

What the fuckity fuck was wrong with him!

"Benjamin, I really think—" he started again, adding some sternness into his tone.

But he was interrupted by the late bell that released the after-school students who attended extra tutoring for advanced classes, shop or art or other crafts classes. The front doors of the school banged wide open and out poured a stampede of children of all shapes, ages and sizes.

He took Benjamin to the side to keep them from being trampled and waited for the herd to thin. As an afterthought, he realized that Benjamin was no longer holding onto the stranger's finger.

The man called Soren had disappeared as if he was never there.

Chapter Two

"Did you learn new things at school today, Benjamin?"

Ere always asked this question when he and his boy walked home together from school.

He hesitated to think of Benjamin as his "son" since he began living with the boy's true parents. It didn't seem right.

He would always love Benjamin as simply *his*, the only thing in this world that was his to protect. That he was exceptionally proud to claim. But he would never expect Benjamin to claim him back.

Being "Uncle Ere" was already more than he deserved.

He was genuinely curious about Benjamin's response, especially since he'd had little formal education himself, though his alter ego had once pretended to be an academic with several PhDs.

The fact was, he'd taught himself to read and write, as well as math, rudimentary science, and other disciplines, before he enjoyed a few years of real education when he took the role of the Crown Prince Cambyses of Persia during 6th Century B.C. The years of formal tutelage, with access to vast libraries, were but a blink of an eye across the span of five thousand years.

They were some of the best years of his existence.

He sometimes daydreamed that if he were "normal," he could make a profession out of historical research, much like his alter ego had. Perhaps he'd write stories on the side. He felt like he had a knack for it, since Benjamin enjoyed his storytelling immensely.

"I always learn new things!" the boy answered with a happy skip in his step, swinging their clasped hands between them as they walked down the sidewalk together.

"Miss Yasmin taught us Japanese origami in art class today. She's also my music teacher, and went on the same theme and showed us how to use the *koto*. Do you know what that is, Uncle Binu?"

He shook his head. He'd never had the opportunity to study Asian culture, and he was duly fascinated and impressed. That was all the encouragement Benjamin needed to launch into an enthusiastic explanation.

Other boys his age might eschew holding hands with anyone, especially in public, but Benjamin had no such reservations. He still proactively gave hugs and kisses with all his heart to everyone he loved (and he loved a great many people). You didn't ever have to wheedle affection from him; he gave it bountifully, eagerly and freely.

Ere observed that other children had different interactions than the ones Benjamin had with people around him. He'd always known the boy was special, of course, but seeing how other children behaved made the contrast even sharper.

For example, boys his age tended to be interested in more frivolous things. Their eyes were glued to screens whenever possible, and they participated in a lot more sports.

Benjamin, however, loved to read and daydream. If his eyes were glued to a screen, it was because he was researching a curiosity he had to the last possible footnote on the topic.

Another example—boys his age hated to talk to adults. Or, at least, they seemed aggrieved to be "nagged" by their caretakers with questions like, "What did you do at school today? What did you eat for lunch? Did you make any new friends? Did you finish your homework?"

But Benjamin enjoyed talking about everything. He flitted from topic to topic like an Energizer butterfly with dizzying speed. Ere rather suspected that he kept on talking in his dreams after he fell asleep.

In particular, Benjamin loved to talk to adults. He reveled in a good debate, and he could argue with convoluted, yet convincing logic on pretty much anything. The boy was a diabolical genius! Ere was constantly kept on his toes, astounded and perturbed in equal measure by the boy's brilliant intellect.

At a pause in Benjamin's excited monologue when he inhaled to take a breath, Ere hastily inserted another question, "Who's your best friend at school? Do you want to invite anyone home for a... what's the phrase? A playdate?"

Ere had heard other parents ask this question, so he thought it might be a parent-like thing to ask. Even though he was only an "uncle," he wanted to fulfill his role properly. He just didn't know where to start.

Now that he was formally a part of the family, not like when he was a "guest" at the Shield, he felt more self-conscious, and, ironically, less secure.

What if he screwed things up? What if they decided they didn't like him as part of the family and ejected him? What if...

"Everyone's my best friend!" Benjamin crowed. "And no one wants to come to our house because we don't have the latest video games. Auntie Aella and Sophie had a bunch at the Shield, but I got tired of playing the ones I had, so Mom and Dad gave the consoles away. I also don't have any more on my computer and iPad because I'd rather be reading. I like the feel of books, don't you? I like their smell too!"

Hmm. This conversation was not going as expected. Benjamin didn't provide the usual answers. Ere determinedly plodded on.

"Do you want to have playdates at your friends' houses?"

The boy rolled his eyes toward Ere to pierce him with those truth-seeking-missile blue orbs.

"I see my friends plenty at school, Uncle Binu. We have lots of fun at recess. I like to spend time with Mom, Dad, Uncle Tal, Auntie Ishtar, and *you*, when I'm out of school. It's the best of both worlds!"

"I just want to make sure that you're happy, Benjamin," he said. "Other boys—"

"I'm not like other boys," Benjamin pointed out. "I'm just me. And I *am* happy, Uncle Binu. I'm always happy! Well, most of the time anyway."

Ere's ears perked up like a bloodhound's at that.

"Most of the time? Not all of the time? Tell me, dearest boy, what would make you completely happy?"

At this, a worrisome sly glint entered the boy's gaze.

"I want *you* to be happy, Uncle Ere. What would make *you* happy?"

Ere blinked, nonplussed.

He called him Uncle Ere, not Binu. Benjamin was talking to the real him. Ere couldn't hide when he did that. It was unsettling as fuck that the boy could see his true form.

After a couple of seconds, he recovered with, "How could I possibly be less than happy when I have you as a companion, Benjamin?"

He wanted to smile flippantly, but he couldn't. All he could do was stare seriously into the boy's angelic eyes and tell the truth. Benjamin made him so very happy. Certainly happier than he'd ever been in his whole life.

"You didn't answer the question."

Ere was taken aback enough to pause in their stroll.

"I most certainly did."

"No, you didn't. You asked another question. By doing so, you're making me draw my own conclusions. You implied an answer but didn't give one directly. Ergo, you didn't answer the question."

The devil!

This was what Ere was talking about! This boy was ridiculously brilliant. Frighteningly so. It was almost impossible to win an argument with him. And he wasn't even ten years old!

"I am...h-happy, Benjamin," he forced himself to say. And this time, he tipped his lips up into the imitation of a smile.

"Of course I am," he said more firmly, and started walking again, swinging their still clasped hands between them.

"No, you're not," the boy said, looking at him so hard Ere thought he could see his accelerated heartbeat at this dogged inquisition.

"Pardon me, but you asked, and I answered. You can't tell me how I feel."

There, that sounded quite reasonable. Try arguing with that, ha!

"You're happier than you were before at the Shield," Benjamin allowed, his tone considering, "but that doesn't mean you're completely happy. I think you're missing something."

"What could I possibly be missing?" Ere chuckled rather awkwardly, a fake laugh even to his own ears.

"I have two great jobs that I enjoy. I have lots of friends. I live for free with people who feed me and are nice to me. I have my own room and my own bed, my own clothes and a bank account that is steadily growing. I get to spend time with a precocious, nosy, argumentative little boy for whom I have a strange affection. What could I possibly be missing?"

"Soren."

Ere stumbled hard enough to almost face-plant on the sidewalk.

Thankfully, he righted himself before he splattered onto the pavement and before he could drag Benjamin down with him.

"W-Wha—"

"I wonder how long he's visiting our town. I wonder where he's staying. I'm going to ask Mom and Dad whether he can come over for dinner one of these days. His belly really was rumbling! He looks like he can eat a lot. Mama Bear will be happy to feed him. She loves feeding people. What do you think of him, Uncle Ere?"

After that whirlwind of observations and ending question, Ere didn't know where to start. The transition from the previous topic to this "Soren" individual was jarringly abrupt. His head was spinning.

But this was Benjamin. He went on tangents like this all the time. One had to stay on one's tippy toes in the conversational rollercoaster of the boy's making.

"Uh...I..."

He couldn't think of a single thing to say. And he'd really rather not think of Soren.

Benjamin didn't usually have fixations on topics like this. Ere thought they were "done" with the stranger at the schoolyard. He had succeeded in tucking the meeting into the back corner of his consciousness.

Perhaps he'd bring out the memory to dissect and savor in the privacy of his own room at night, maybe revisit the experience in his dreams. But as he walked home with Benjamin, he focused completely on the boy and truly put the *impressive* Soren out of mind.

"He's awfully big, isn't he? Taller than the real you, too. Do you like tall people, Uncle Ere? You're the tallest of everyone who lives at the Shield. Does it bother you to be the tallest? Is that why you always pretend to be people who are shorter? But with Soren, you wouldn't have to pretend!"

"I…"

"I wonder if he's hairy all over cuz he has that big beard. I wonder if he has a hairy chest. Dad, Uncle Tal and you don't have hairy chests. Must be nice to cuddle up to a hairy chest, right? Like a big teddy bear."

"I really wouldn't know."

Since Ere had never had a teddy bear of any variety, stuffed or living.

"His hair looks like those pictures in science fiction of a sun with exploding volcanoes. You know—all molten gold and bright blond shot through with red sparks—"

"How poetic," Ere murmured faintly.

"—just like his eyes. I've never seen eyes like those. At least, not on people. They remind me of eagle eyes, except Soren's seem to shoot fire. Like he's got a superpower. Maybe they're phoenix eyes. Like in Japanese and Chinese anime."

There was Benjamin's fixation with the mythical bird again.

Dragons and phoenixes.

He'd been doing research on the subject since they'd inadvertently gone off on this tangent months ago during one of Ere's story-tellings.

"I've never seen a real phoenix. Are there real ones? Maybe he's one of us! Well, not including me, since I'm just a human boy. But maybe he's like Mom and Dad and Uncle Tal and Auntie Ishtar! Maybe he's like you, Uncle Ere! Wouldn't that be so cool!"

Ere made a noncommittal noise. The more Benjamin gushed about the mysterious Soren, the more uncomfortable (and hot) Ere felt.

Indeed, the man conjured an incredible burning sensation all over Ere's skin even in memory. Strangely, it wasn't uncomfortable. It was actually soothing. Made him feel like he was licked by warmth all over, like the heat of the sun was soaked into his always-too-cold flesh and bones.

Not the burned-to-a-crisp sort of sun, but the afternoon-catnap sort of sun. The nice, beachy, toasty sort of sun.

He wanted to bask in it and purr.

"Would you like to be his friend, Uncle Ere? I think Soren needs friends. I want to be his friend. Next time, I'm definitely inviting him home, since you want me to have a playdate."

"That's not—" Ere hastened to object.

But Benjamin shouted, "We're home!"

He burst inside the house just as Gabriel opened it, careening straight into his father's ready, outstretched arms like a cannon ball.

"Hi Dad!" Benjamin greeted while hugging the Dark warrior tightly with all of the unstinting fierceness in his little body.

"Is that my favorite ravioli I smell? And garlic butter mashed potatoes? And pecan pie! I bet there's pecan pie!"

Gabriel nodded a greeting to Ere as he entered more sedately behind Benjamin and closed the door, before answering his son.

"How do you know it's ravioli and not spaghetti or baked ziti or something else? We'll see if you're right at dinner. There's roasted eggplant too."

"Aww, but I don't like eggplant," Benjamin whined a little, finally sounding his age.

"And yet, you will still eat your serving," Gabriel said matter-of-factly while his son heaved a put-upon sigh.

"Come wash up and put away your things."

Father and son chatted easily as they walked together down the hall, their voices fading as they went.

Ere stared after them with a familiar, bittersweet pang in his chest.

It wasn't envy. It was...regret maybe.

He wished he was a better man. He wished he'd known Benjamin from the moment he'd been conceived. He wished he hadn't missed all those years that someone else got to love that boy, cradle him as a baby, smell his innocence and feel his soft, newborn skin.

Ere would never know. He'd never have any of those memories. He missed out on so many precious moments. A million priceless moments.

He knew he should be thankful for what he had now, and he was. He was thankful every day. But...

He regretted.

Dinner was filled with boisterous conversation and great food. With Mama Bear cooking most nights, it was food heaven in this household.

Ere still ate less than what others considered "normal," but he was eating a lot more than he used to.

He was still skin and bones though, as Benjamin often chided, being the only one who could see his true form. After what Lilith did to him, both the process of transforming him and the battle where she'd torn him to pieces (literally), he had a lot of rebuilding to do. It was a miracle he was even alive.

How could he have possibly survived that massacre?

His shaking hands told him he needed to stop thinking about it.

Maybe he was a ghost. Maybe this was all in his imagination—the home, the family, the jobs and friends. He knew it wouldn't last. He should just enjoy it while he could.

At least, Benjamin didn't bring up Soren over dinner, as Ere feared he would. He didn't know why the possible mention of the stranger put him on edge, but it did.

Just thinking about the encounter made him tense up all over. Made him break out in goosebumps and a feverish, full-bodied rash. Like someone was roasting him over a fire.

But admit it...you love those flames...

He shook his head to clear it.

Who in their right mind would love being burned? No one, that's who. He wasn't insane. He wasn't—

"*Binu*, are you all right?" Tal asked after dinner, as they stood together at the sink washing and drying dishes.

He'd called him *binu*, not the name of the form he took, but the ancient Akkadian word for "son." Ere could always tell the difference. Tal always called him "son." Always treated him as one, too.

Ere still couldn't believe that *the* legendary General of the Pure Ones, the one who freed them from millennia of oppression and slavery, was actually Ere'e *sire*! It boggled the mind.

He often studied Tal when he thought the other male couldn't tell. But, honestly, not a lot got by the blind, yet all-seeing General.

In his head, Ere couldn't yet bring himself to think of his hero as anything other than his full name—Tal-Telal, the Demon Warrior, or his title, the General. He couldn't think of the male as *father* or something even more intimate like *papa*. Even *sire* was an acknowledgement of a connection that Ere could still hardly believe was real.

Tal was a beautiful man. Ere didn't think so in the beginning (when he was obviously *stupid!*), because the General was covered in scars from millennia of horrific torture by Medusa (who was justifiably and finally beheaded by the warrior months ago).

But one only had to interact with Tal to see and feel his innate strength, conviction, goodness, protectiveness. And knowing what he went through, Ere appreciated that incredible power even more.

To have survived all that, to carry all of those scars, both on the outside and within forever, and to still be the leader and warrior that he was, the Mated Pure male who Nourished his female, the father who protected and loved his children...even a cuckoo like Ere... Tal was everything Ere thought a male should be.

He wished, oh how he wished! that he could be such a male as well.

But there was so much darkness inside him. He'd done so many terrible things. He wasn't fit to lick Tal's shoes. He was like the Gollum next to the resplendent magnificence of elves—Gabriel, Tal...

Soren.

"Where have your thoughts gone, *binu*?" the General's quiet query broke through his spiraling contemplation.

"It's nothing," he finally answered with as much nonchalance as he could muster.

"I'm just a little tired. A hot shower and a hot chocolate before bed should take care of it."

He could feel the warrior staring at him with those blind, turquoise eyes.

They used to be cloudy and opaque. Now, they were brilliant and bright once more, like gems, even though they were still blind. But that didn't prevent Tal from seeing in all the ways that mattered.

"Do you need Pure blood? You have not taken any since you arrived."

What he meant was, did Ere need *his* blood. For, Tal's blood was the Purest of all, given that Gabriel and Inanna were vampires, and Ishtar was half Pure, half Dark.

Ere didn't know why he'd always needed Pure blood to survive. It started after the first time he was "revived" by Medusa. He thought he only needed human blood and sometimes souls, like other vampires, but very quickly his Mistress and he realized that he needed more. If he didn't get a regular infusion of Pure blood, his own blood flowed black like tar, and his organs began to shut down.

Fuck. He really was a monster. Kept alive by feeding off others. He was despicable.

"I'm fine," he snapped, and immediately regretted it.

But the General didn't react in any way, simply continuing to look at him with care and concern.

"I'm fine," Ere said more softly. "I don't need Pure blood."

This was the truth, he realized.

He'd been prepared to lie, but once the words were out of his mouth, he was rather surprised that they were honest.

He hadn't needed Pure blood since he arrived on this family's doorstep eight weeks ago. This was the longest he'd gone without it. He hadn't experienced any symptoms yet from lack of it—the chills, the gnawing pain inside, the sluggish, black blood. His veins looked perfectly normal under his skin.

It was...strange. He hadn't noticed this change until just now when Tal reminded him.

But now that his mind was on the topic of feeding, he discovered that he was hungry for something else. The tips of his elongated fangs practically quivered for it.

Blood.

He wanted hot, sweet, spicy blood.

But only one unique flavor of it. He wanted *that* blood. None other would do.

And more. There was more…

Creamy, salty, tangy…

On his face, on his tongue, all over his skin, and deep inside…

His body clenched and pulsed with a hollow, overwhelming ache. Something was missing. Benjamin was right.

He needed it. He wanted it.

Ah, gods! Everything hurt without it.

"*Binu*—"

He felt strong hands grasp his upper arms to steady him as he gasped and staggered, inadvertently dropping one of the dishes he was drying onto the hardwood floor.

He didn't hear it shatter; his ears seemed filled with wool. He only saw it break into a dozen jagged pieces.

Like his face.

Like his body.

He was broken.

He was so fucking *broken*.

Someone's whimpering could be heard over the buzzing in his ears. He realized distantly that he was the one making that god-awful noise.

He was lifted like a baby into someone's arms. He was being carried through the house.

He should have felt humiliated, he knew, but he couldn't be bothered. He just tucked his wet face into the comfortingly smelling crook of Tal's neck and inhaled in ragged draws of breath like snorting cocaine. His…*father*'s scent finally calmed him enough to stop the confounded, helpless tears.

He became aware enough to protest, "I have to head to the bar. It's Thursday night. Mike—"

"Gabriel will call in for you. Between him and Inanna, one of them will cover your shift, do not worry."

"But—"

"Rest now, *binu*. Everything will be fine."

"I have a job," he muttered, but his eyes were already closed, his lids too heavy to lift again. His voice was fading with the sudden onset of exhaustion.

"I don't want to lose it…"

"Your jobs will be waiting for you tomorrow."

He heard Ishtar's voice from somewhere beside him.

"You're too good at them to lose them, baby."

Baby.

Ere had heard her call her Mate this endearment often, but it meant something different in that context. He'd never heard her use this term with him.

But now, he basked in the warmth of her tone. It was even better when accompanied by her fingers gently sweeping the hair away from his brow, her fingertips scraping lightly across his scalp.

Mothers did that, didn't they? Petted and stroked their children with affection and comfort?

He inhaled deeply on a shuddering sigh and felt his body finally relax.

The need within him hadn't subsided, but the pain had dulled to a throbbing ache. A little like hunger pangs. But he was so used to starving constantly over the course of his existence that he was confident he could ignore these pangs as well.

Even though his fangs quivered and seethed. Even though saliva pooled in his mouth, and his insides screamed with emptiness.

He would survive this too. Like he survived everything else...

Ere was naked and broken. Stripped to the bone.

His flesh was raw, pieces of it missing, he could tell, for he felt the air touch him differently, dig deeper where there should have been muscle to block it before.

Fuck, it sucked rotten eggs to have been eviscerated and torn apart by the Hydra. Remind him never to tangle with that evil bitch serpent again.

At least Benjamin was safe.

He'd made sure of it before the Hydra dragged him into the bowels of the lake to tear him limb from limb. And if that hadn't been enough, she'd fried him with hellfire, melted him with acid, and spewed poison all over him too.

Note to self: if he ever got lucky enough to pick the method of his ultimate demise, this would be at the bottom of his list.

Was he dead then? He ought to be, right?

But the dead shouldn't feel pain, should they? And he was in a fuck-ton shitload of **_PAIN_**.

He opened his eyes a sliver. (Ought he be thankful he still had lids to close?)

Everything was blurry. He couldn't tell where he was. Brown and black globs swam in his vision.

He was lying on something soft though. A couple of his skeletal fingers scraped the material beneath him. It felt like...

Feathers.

Silky but bristly on the edges. Lots and lots of them piled together. So soft...like floating on clouds...

He drifted into unconsciousness.

Later—he had no notion of how much later, time had ceased to matter—he was awoken by scalding heat. It felt like he was being blasted by flames in an inescapable furnace from all sides.

He panicked a little before realizing that he...liked the burning.

It hurt.

It fucking hurt!

But...he still liked it. He wanted it. It made him feel stronger. Made him feel alive.

He wanted to writhe and twist in the flames, not to escape them but to make sure they touched him everywhere. Healed him everywhere. For, he realized that the flames were regenerating the missing pieces of him, fusing together his tattered flesh, mending his broken bones.

But he couldn't move. He was paralyzed and weak. He could only let the scalding waves of heat embrace him, lick through him, penetrate him...

It felt devastating. Euphoric.

Terrifying. Blissful.

And then, he felt two large hands grasp his thighs and push them apart.

Wait.

What?!

No. Nononononononono...

He tried to clamp his legs together, but it was no use. No part of his body would obey him. All he'd managed to do up to this point was open and close his eyes. And scrape the tips of his fingers across a bed of feathers.

The hands kept parting him, inexorably spreading his legs wider.

Why?! Why, why, why!

There was only one reason he could think of. He'd played whore too many times not to know.

Please! Somebody stop it! He didn't want it! He couldn't take it!

Not on top of everything else. Wasn't he broken enough? Didn't he hurt enough!

He couldn't move, but he could feel his body shaking all over, as if he was having a seizure. His fear was so great, he was epileptic. His teeth chattered. His eyes rolled around in their sockets without seeing. His chest cavity quaked and rattled like a rusted cage. He couldn't draw enough air to breathe.

Just kill him already! He couldn't endure any more.

Please!

He felt the unmistakable stone hard thighs of a male between his own spread legs. Something scalding hot, iron hard, and silky soft brushed the tight bud of his entrance. One large hand splayed over his shuddering chest, pressing down, stilling him.

He wanted to fight the pressure. He thought it would make his breathing even harder.

But it didn't.

Strangely, the hand on his chest calmed him somewhat. His erratic breaths evened out, his hyperventilation subsiding into deep inhales and exhales.

But his mind was still petrified, horrified, terrorized, even as his body relaxed without his will to do so.

The fires around him burned just as hot, never abating. But the pain of regeneration was dulled to an echo of their previous sharpness.

The blunt, enormous hardness nudged again at his tightly closed bud, putting pressure there, but not penetrating. Just kept coming back with persistent, ever increasing pressure.

It didn't hurt like he thought it would. Nothing was getting rammed inside of him. And by the size of that thing, it would split him in half right down the middle.

Fucking gods! He wished he had tears to at least lubricate his dried-up eyeballs if he couldn't cry out his fear. He needed the release! But everything was dry as dust. Must be because of the flames that kept on roasting him.

And then, he felt something wet and satiny probe his hole. It licked and lapped all around the area, up and down the seam of his ass, flicking over and over, then pressing more broadly around his entrance.

That was the only wetness within the dry heat. He was stunned by the contrast, all of his attention focused on the place the soothing wetness touched him, making his hole clench reflexively, wanting it inside.

He wanted it on his cock and balls too, which he knew were hard and full with seed. His too-thin skin felt as if it would burst with the engorgement. He'd never in his whole existence been this hard before. Not even with extra doses of unguent to make him so.

*Did that mean he was...*turned on?

But...he didn't want this!

Did he?

The satiny wetness kept probing, licking, lapping. Without him realizing it, the sleek muscle slipped past the first tight ring of his entrance, delving into his channel with surprisingly little resistance.

Uhn.

He might have grunted. Did he still have a voice to make sounds?

He'd never felt this feeling before. No one had ever...

It...it felt...

His brain sputtered and stuttered, unable to comprehend the sensation, wrestling with the startling pleasure against the expectation of pain.

And it was *pleasure. It felt so, so,* good. *He felt a relief from an emptiness he never knew he had.*

But it wasn't nearly enough. Heaven and hell help him, but he wanted more.

His breathing got choppy again as he mentally begged for...something. He didn't know what. He just knew he needed it. Wanted it. He had to have it more than his next breath!

And then...and then...

The wetness was removed, though he tried desperately to clench his inner muscles around it to keep it from leaving him. In its place, the hard, hot, enormous pressure came back again.

This time, more insistent, more impatient.

He didn't care. He couldn't comprehend it. He feared the pain, but he wanted it to cleave him in two. He didn't care anymore!

The blunt, silky head was coated in a different kind of wetness. A slick, slippery, slightly viscous moisture. It persistently brushed the fluids over his already wet and loosened hole, making his bud clench and open reflexively every time he felt the pressure press across it, like a hungry little mouth.

A tight, hungry, greedy mouth for a big, fat, unforgivingly hard—

Just as his mind short-circuited on the last thought, the steady pressure broke through his first ring of resistance.

All of the breath whooshed out of his body as he instinctively exhaled and bore down, opening himself to the incredible heat and steel of the intrusion.

The never-ending, tunneling thrust that seemed to go on and on.

Where was that thing going anyway? Through his intestines and stomach and into his throat?

That's what it felt like. Like he was being penetrated everywhere. Filled up so full he couldn't speak if he tried. He even felt like it was in his mouth. On his tongue. He was gagging on it above and below, like a trussed-up hog on a spit.

Ah fuck!

It hurt. It hurt so bad!

And it hurt so good.

So, so good.

He wanted to hurt like this forever...

He was made to burn.

Chapter Three

"Mornin' handsome," Mike greeted when Ere hustled into *Drink of Me* two hours after his usual shift started.

He was shitty at this job thing, after all.

He'd only been a model employee for eight measly weeks before fucking everything up. Not only was he a no-show at the bar last night, but he also forgot to set his alarm for this morning (since he'd passed out before he could), and didn't wake up on time.

As it was, he'd thrown on the first clean thing he found—a gray turtleneck and black jeans—and ran out of the house without eating breakfast, without even saying goodbye to the family still sitting around the table, in the middle of their morning routine before Inanna and Gabriel took Benjamin to school.

"Good luck today, Uncle Ere!" the boy had shouted at his departing back as he rushed out of the door.

Yeah, he needed it.

He needed a double-shot expresso cappuccino even more than luck. Their strongest off-menu poison of choice.

Not that coffee did anything for an immortal like him. The foreign substances that affected humans didn't affect his Kind. Only organic compounds did, and only when combined with blood or vampire venom and other bodily fluids.

But he loved the taste of coffee. He loved the heat of it as it went down, and when it settled into his stomach, warming him from the inside out.

It made him feel more human.

After all these millennia, he still envied humans the most. Perhaps because the knowledge of death right around the corner made them live life more fully. Humans were so fragile and emotional. They were incredibly strong too. Just look at how far they'd come. Where gods once reigned supreme, humans were now the undisputed rulers of earth.

"A thousand apologies for my tardiness," he said to Mike, tying the uniform apron around his waist and pinning on his name badge. "It won't happen again."

"Pfft," she dismissed. "Happens all the time with me. I'm not a morning person, if you can't tell by now. At least, not the early bird, before-sunrise kind of morning person. Which is why I'm thrilled that you got that shift instead of me. Besides, hardly anybody comes in here before 7:30."

"That's why I like it," Ere said, murmuring his heartfelt thanks when Mike plopped the expresso in front of him in a hefty mug.

"It's so quiet here. I can spend hours just staring out the window at the snow or into the fire crackling in the hearth. It's peaceful. Like it's Christmas every day."

"But without the presents and decorations," Mike pointed out.

"Waking up alive and whole is a present in of itself, don't you think?"

She slid him a narrow-eyed look.

"You're a weird one, Binu."

"I hear that all the time," he murmured with a careless smile as he sipped his hot drink.

"Well, not to burst your bubble of peaceful solitude, but we did get one customer this early morning."

Ere straightened from his slouch over the counter and looked around the shop.

"Oh yeah? Looks like you got more than just one. It must be a full house right now."

Indeed, it was almost 8:30 a.m., their busiest time in the morning. Mike had already taken care of all of the seated customers, and was now multi-tasking efficiently with the walk-ins while Ere fired himself up with expresso.

"Yup. One customer who was waiting outside before I even opened up the shop. I confess I got here a half hour late because I wasn't expecting the shift—and don't start apologizing again," Mike put up a hand to stall Ere's contrition.

"It's not the end of the world. You cover for me all the time. Anyway, as I was saying, this guy was so silent and still outside the shop, over by the corner, that I didn't even notice him in the dark. Made me jump a foot high when he stepped forward and revealed himself. And you know I don't scare easily."

"Are you okay?" Ere asked, frowning with concern.

He wanted to kick his own ass for putting Mike in this position. She was a tough cookie, but she was still a defenseless human female. It was a small town and quite safe, but there were drifters who passed through.

Take that Soren guy, for example...

"I'm fine," she waved aside his worry.

"I would be better if the guy gave me the time of day," she huffed with chagrin.

"Eh?"

"The guy's totally H-O-T, okay?"

When Mike spelled it out in capital letters like that, Ere understood that she meant business.

"The stalker waiting for you in the dark corner outside?" He was confused.

"He's not a stalker," she muttered impatiently. "I never said he's a stalker. Just someone I've never seen before in town. He wouldn't even come inside the shop until I practically dragged him inside."

"Why would you do that?" Ere frowned. "You're all by yourself here. What if he was dangerous?"

"The only thing I'm in danger of near this guy is having my ovaries explode inside my body and not having packed a fresh change of panties in my purse."

"Why would you need..."

She smacked his shoulder and arrested the words coming out of his mouth.

"I swear you're like a Byzantine monk the way you're clueless about the ways of the world!"

"That's terribly specific," Ere noted. "Why Byzantine, not Buddhist? Is there a specific characteristic you noticed that qualifies me for one and not the other?"

"As I was *saying*," Mike drawled, rolling her eyes, used to these non-sequiturs her coworker often made.

"After the guy came in here, he just sat down in the back corner and ignored me. I even made him a hot chocolate and my special pumpkin-spice cappuccino on the house. Gave him two day-old but still flaky scones with butter and jam, also on the house. He never even looked my way."

"Is he blind?" Ere asked loyally. Because Mike was H-O-T herself. If he were a male with sexual appetites, he'd totally go for her.

"Thanks, honey," she cooed, now rubbing soothingly the same spot she smacked earlier.

"He looked hungry though. I checked on him a few minutes ago. All the food and drinks were gone, but he didn't order anything else. I asked him plenty of times—nothing better to do while waiting for more customers to roll in, but he never answered me. He barely even looked at me."

"That's just rude." Ere was affronted on her behalf.

"I just don't think I'm what he needs, and that man is definitely in need of something," she said with a soft and mildly cryptic look in her eyes.

"Well, next time, you leave him to me. It's not safe for a woman to—"

"Oh, he's still here, handsome."

"He is?"

Ere ringed up another customer and shifted to the machines laid out against the back wall to make their orders.

"Yup. Still sitting in the back corner staring out the window."

"But he's been here for, what, two hours already?"

"Sure has. There's no rule against it. I'm not about to kick him out. If nothing else, he's a damn pleasure to look at every time I walk by his table."

She got a strange glint in her eyes that Ere felt immediately suspicious of.

"Why don't you give it a try?"

"What do you mean?" he asked warily.

"Go take his order. See what he wants. Maybe he'll talk to you."

"I shall," Ere agreed.

He wanted to see this stranger and make sure he wasn't a threat. If he *was* a stalker, Ere would deal with it.

That's the beauty of being a shapeshifter. He could transform into any humanoid form, including someone extremely threatening, at least in looks. And because he also had the strength of an immortal, despite his skin-and-bones state, he was still many times stronger than humans. He'd take care of any threat to his friends. It was the least he could do to protect them.

"Try not to drool onto the linoleum when you see him," Mike smirked as Ere pulled up the bar to walk past the counter. "I just swept this place an hour ago."

Ha! Ere wanted to scoff.

Him drooling over anyone was an extremely unlikely occurrence. But he'd try to keep blood from being spilt, at least inside the shop, if he had to get physical with the stalker stranger who wouldn't leave.

He made his way toward the back corner that could only be seen partially from the front of the store, his strides brisk with determination.

Before he even arrived at the table, the words he'd formulated in his head to say were already spilling out of his mouth.

"Welcome to *Drink of Me*. May I take your—"

The words stuck in his throat and died a hasty death when the stranger turned away from the window to face him, spearing his feet into the floor with invisible stakes with those unforgettable gold eyes.

"*You*," Ere breathed.

The man called "Soren" merely stared at him, silent and brooding.

Well, Ere didn't know if he was in fact brooding, but he had a "Heathcliff" look about him, all stormy and dark, filled with oceans-worth of emotions and unspoken turmoil.

Ere wanted to smack himself.

The purple prose in his mind was annoying as hell! But he just couldn't seem to stop the melodramatic twists and turns of his fucked-up imagination.

"What are you doing here?"

He didn't actually expect an answer, since the man hadn't spoken a single word since their encounter yesterday. So he was knocked literally off his feet when the stranger said:

"Hungry."

That voice!

For the love of Loki's hairy balls, that voice!

It was fathoms deep, resonant, but smoky and husky at the same time, raspy and rough. Tinged with an erotic accent when he spoke.

(Yes, he meant erotic *and* exotic. Accents could be erotic, Ere was absolutely certain, because this guy's voice conjured all kinds of carnal cravings and sinful deeds).

Ere had staggered backwards against one of the wood beams that propped up the store's barn-style ceiling when the man uttered that single word. He wasn't drooling onto the linoleum, but he was in danger of melting into a disgusting puddle of liquified nerves.

"Uh..."

Articulation. He needed to articulate.

Right.

"What would you like to order? We have a large breakfast menu, but I can also have our cook whip you up something off—"

"You," the man rumbled like the god amongst mortals that he was.

Melting! Ere was melting!

With supreme effort, he mustered up the wherewithal to say, "I am unfortunately not on the menu. You will have to pick something else. I can always surprise you. What is your form of payment?"

The man studied him with those unblinking, piercing golden eyes, hypnotizing him with those obscenely thick and long lashes. He felt like an insect entangled in the Venus Flytrap of those lashes.

It wasn't fair! Why was he getting hot and bothered, on the verge of a heart attack, by a man like this?

Intimidating. Big. Tall.

Stern.

He looked strong enough to snap Ere in two with his bare hands, immortal or not. He made Ere afraid of him...but not in the usual sense of the word.

Wordlessly, the stranger reached into his pants' back pocket and retrieved a fistful of notes and loose coins. He put them on the table without ever taking his mesmerizing eyes off Ere.

It was a Herculean effort to drag his own eyes away, trapped by those lashes and glued to the twin suns as he was. But Ere finally looked down at the money spread out beside the extra-large manly hand laid flat on the table.

That was a big fucking hand.

Yet elegant, masculine perfection despite its size. With clearly delineated veins running across the back of it, sturdy knuckles and thick wrist.

Ere noticed the black script that seemed to be tattooed up and down the left arm and hand where the stranger's skin was revealed by the rolled-up sleeve. It was not a language he knew, which was surprising, because he knew a great *many* languages, given how long he'd lived and how he made an informal study of them.

"Hungry," the man grunted again, snapping Ere's attention back to the matter at hand.

He looked down at the money and squinted some more.

They were very colorful bills of a currency Ere wasn't immediately familiar with. They certainly didn't resemble Canadian or U.S. dollars, which was what was accepted in the store.

"Umm…"

The man pushed the money toward him with that massive hand. At the same time, a loud, thundering, prolonged rumble came from the vicinity of the man's stomach. He didn't have to repeat himself again for Ere to get the hint.

He was very *hungry*.

"All right," he said before he could think better of it. "I'll see what I can do. Be back soon."

But before he could take the money and go, his wrist was suddenly seized in an unyielding grip, though it didn't hurt him.

He swallowed his gasp of shock before it could reach his lips as he stared into those golden eyes again. The pinpoint pupils had dilated into round black disks, and Ere's skin where the man touched him felt scalded by flames.

Still, it didn't hurt. The heat of the stranger's touch was even soothing, radiating from his wrist up his arm and chest. It made him tingle all over, his nerves crackling just like the fire in the hearth.

"You have to let go for me to get your food," he whispered, his voice evaporated like smoke at the electrifying touch.

A silent staring match ensued. It could have been seconds, minutes or hours. Ere could stare into those eyes forever. He simply couldn't tear his gaze away.

"Come back."

Unbidden, those two, huskily uttered words cleaved Ere's heart in two.

It suddenly hurt to breathe. It hurt for his heart to beat.

His head felt split by lightning, and he was gripped by the desperate need to bawl like a man possessed.

He had to get away. He couldn't take this anymore. He tugged at his trapped wrist to no avail.

And then, just like that, the man let him go.

He stumbled in his haste to leave the stranger's confounding presence, all but running to the front of the store. He wanted to keep running, out of the shop and into the still-dark day.

What was happening? This was insane! Who the hell was this guy? Ere had never met him before in his life! In all his lives!

But he knew with absolute certainty even as he ran away that he'd be back.

He would always come back to those amber, sun-lit eyes.

*** *** *** ***

He watched the bane of his existence scramble away on colt-like legs.

Why did he insist on putting on the pretense? Taking different outer forms that belied the beauty within?

People called him "Binu" when he was at this human shop. They called him "Erena" when he worked at a club and bar at night. And that little boy who misinterpreted the warrior's name called him "Uncle Ere."

It didn't matter what he called himself or what others did, the warrior would know him anywhere, in any form.

He watched after "Ere" until he disappeared from view behind the front counter of the store. Nothing else held his attention, so he looked out the window again as the skies were just beginning to dawn, a slow kindling of flames behind wintry clouds.

The stark splendor of the landscape stretched around the town, nestled at the foot of towering mountains, close to a wide river that ran through them. It was a beautiful place, reminiscent of bygone times, hardly touched by human ingenuity and civilization. There was a wildness here that eased the warrior's soul.

He missed the ancient world. The relative simplicity of everything. Including the simpler beings that lived during that age. Beings without the heavy, complicated weight of souls.

He shouldn't have come here.

Occasionally, a human walked by the window from which he peered out. They always raised their head, no matter what they were doing or where they were going, to look at him. They would stumble or pause in their steps to stare, as if mesmerized by the sight of him.

He didn't like it.

He hated to be stared at, even though he tended to stare back. But not because he was interested. It was simply ingrained in him.

A King never looked away. It was a matter of asserting authority. Humans and other Immortals of old knew better than to look directly into his gaze. They were taught to keep their eyes cast submissively down.

But these modern humans were stupidly bold. They bowed at nothing, always curious, naively fearless. It both irritated and gladdened the warrior. He had no respect for those who cowered, after all.

Like the human boy with sunny curls who dared to hold his hand. Well, his finger, in any case, for his hand was much too big to fit in the youngling's tiny grasp.

Benjamin, he called himself. Benji, to his friends. Since the boy encouraged the warrior to call him Benji, he supposed he was considered to number amongst the friends.

He had merely been following Ere's scent when he stopped near the school to await the man's arrival. He had been tracking his prey for a few days since arriving in town. He'd missed him the day before, but he knew that Ere stuck to a schedule of sorts, always coming by the row of buildings where children gathered sometime after the sun started its descent from its highest point.

He'd stayed in the shadow of the building when he arrived, intending to be as inconspicuous as possible. But the boy had noticed him the moment he came outside.

Benji ran immediately up to him, introduced himself in a booming, eager voice, and grabbed his finger, dragging him along to the front of the schoolyard.

He was somewhat nonplussed that he'd let himself be led by such a tiny mite, but his feet simply followed where the boy went, as if they had a mind of their own. While they waited for "Uncle Ere" to arrive, the boy talked nonstop, roving from topic to topic with such dizzying speed that the warrior's head felt like it was spinning.

He only caught a few snippets of conversation, mostly focused on what the boy said about Ere. They lived together, it seemed. With a number of other people—the boy's aerie.

He also gave the boy his name without intending to. Somehow, it just slipped out when Benji asked. He seemed to have that confounding effect on people. Making them reveal more about themselves than they meant to.

But the boy had misunderstood. His name was not Soren.

What he had answered when asked was "Sorin," which meant "sun" in Romanian. That wasn't his original name either, but close enough.

Central Europe was where he'd spent the last few hundred years, away from the busiest parts of human civilization in the secluded, less-traversed mountains. Occasionally, he visited the towns to gather information, make connections. And because he'd been trapped in his half-Beast form, unable to fully transform into eagle, he couldn't avoid it.

He'd been searching for one very specific red-haired witch, as well as the warrior who'd left him for dead on top of the Fire Mountain untold millennia ago. Until he found them, just like the old witch had predicted when he'd still been the Eagle King, though she never specified the time and place, he'd been mostly dead.

The only thread of life he possessed at the time had been tattooed in the runes on the left side of his body and face. Without the spell's protection, the Fire Mountain would have swallowed him whole and destroyed him.

It did destroy him, in fact.

But he survived.

Only when the red-haired witch and her warrior king united to reignite the volcano they'd fought on top of many months ago was he reborn. But he was no longer the Eagle King.

He was something else entirely.

The composition of his face and body had not changed much in appearance, save the coloring, but everything else was fundamentally different.

Only one thing stayed the same. The memories he had before his defeat on top of the Fire Mountain against Prince Hulaal, as he was known then. Now, the earth Elemental called himself Ramses, the first-ever Dark King.

The warrior's memories were all he had of his original self. The only thing that kept him alive and sane. The only thing that helped him survive his rebirth.

Memories from a time before time. When gods of old still ruled the world. When he'd made a promise to the being that was the bane of his existence...and the true light of his reignited soul.

He was here to keep that promise, though he'd much rather be back in his mountains with no human civilization in sight. Alone and unencumbered.

He'd asked his bane to stay once before. He would not ask again. But he was a male of his word, so he would fulfill his promise and be gone.

If only his bane would let him.

As if his thoughts conjured the man, Ere returned with two large plates heaped with steaming food.

"Here we are. Scrambled eggs, hash browns, sausages, bacon and pancakes. I Googled the money you gave me. Romanian, huh? Don't see a lot of that type of currency around here. With the latest exchange rate, you gave me two hundred dollars, or thereabouts. Here's your change for one hundred. I also went ahead and calculated the rest of the change in U.S. dollars in case you need to spend more cash while you're here. The nearest travel exchange is at the train station on the other side of town, and it only opens on Tuesdays and Thursdays."

He took the money and stuffed it into his back pocket without speaking. Ere chattered enough for the both of them.

Besides, Beasts didn't speak human languages if they could help it. But since he'd been forced to live amongst humans for the last several millennia in a half-Beast form, he had to learn human speech in order to survive.

That didn't mean he liked speaking though. The sounds always felt foreign and strange striking his vocal cords and rolling off his tongue.

Instead, he simply nodded his thanks.

Ere nodded back, a slight smile curling his lips as if he was pleased.

His "bane" never changed. It didn't matter how many incarnations he'd had since Sorin first knew him.

He could be incredibly thoughtful, sensitive, playful and mischievous. He could be the worst prankster there ever existed, causing no end of trouble for Sorin, but he was never purely "bad." He'd been a child, wild and free, innocent to the ways of the world.

So fearless and bright and beautiful he took Sorin's breath away.

He still did.

But now, there was darkness too. Bottomless depths of it.

"I'll go get your beverages now. You seemed to like the hot chocolate Mike made, so I'll make you some more, and I'll also bring some orange juice and water."

Sorin snapped out his hand and grasped the male's wrist before he could walk away.

"Stay," he uttered in the language called English, and barely hid a grimace.

It wasn't his favorite human language. But then, he didn't like any of the human languages.

His bane seemed to like the way he spoke, however, for his face and neck flushed instantly red, the veins beneath his skin where Sorin touched him pulsing hot, sweet blood.

Sorin's fangs ached.

It had been so long since he properly fed. Not since months ago when they'd last been together...

At that reminder, something else throbbed with a different sort of ache. It hurt so badly, he unselfconsciously squeezed the hardness in his lap with his other hand to dull it, or at least distract himself from the burning insistence of it.

Ere's eyes followed the motion of his hand beneath the table, widening like a baby owl's at the flex of his fist.

"I-I-" he stuttered breathlessly as his saucer-round gaze locked on Sorin's hand.

Sorin didn't know why he was so fixated, given his lap was hidden from view by the table. But the more Ere stared, the harder and more painful he became.

Involuntarily, he squeezed himself again, flexing his wrist.

Ere's eyes practically bugged out of his head at that. He pulled wildly against Sorin's grasp, like an overly excited animal trying to escape its leash. It wasn't fear of being hurt that made him wild, though, or Sorin would have released him immediately.

No, it was a different kind of fear... fear, perhaps, of what he would do if he didn't get away.

Fear of his own desire.

"Be calm," Sorin commanded. "Stay."

"I just... I need..."

Slowly, carefully, Sorin reeled him in closer, pulling him inch by inch by the grip he had on Ere's wrist. Until his bane had no choice but to bend down close to his face, their mouths mere breaths apart from one another.

"You need *me*."

There.

He told Ere the truth.

If he were smart, he'd let Sorin finish what he started so they could both be on their way and never cross paths again. He could fulfill his promise and be done with it.

His heart gave a furious kick at that, bruising itself against its confining cage. He determinedly ignored it.

Ere stared directly into his eyes, boldly holding his gaze.

Lightning blue pierced molten gold. Even in this form, his eyes were his own. Perhaps he couldn't help it in this moment of truth. Perhaps he didn't even realize he'd revealed this real piece of himself.

They were *his* eyes.

The only eyes across time and space that Sorin had ever felt like drowning in. The only eyes that made him feel helpless and weak.

The only eyes to make him challenge Destiny.

"I don't need you," Ere whispered, his words so close Sorin could taste them.

"But you need a drink to wash down your food," he added, leaning away and straightening again, this fraught moment between them broken as if it never was.

"So release me now and let me get your beverages."

Chapter Four

Holy Mary Mother of God!

Ere wasn't by any means religious, and he certainly wasn't Christian. But there just didn't seem to be enough exclamations in the English language to express the range of his current sentiment. Like his heart was about to burst out of his chest, spout wings, and launch itself into the stratosphere.

That man!

What was it about that man that made him want to fall to his knees and beg like a supplicant? Maybe lick his toes while he was down there. Or lick something else altogether...

His hand!

The one under the table. The one popping veins on the back of it fisting, squeezing, torturing hot, steely, swollen, aching flesh through the cloth of his trousers...

Ere wished he was those lucky, blessed trousers. Better yet, Ere wished he was the underwear molded to that perfect, satiny skin. (He didn't doubt for a moment that the stranger's skin would be perfect and satiny because, case in point, forearm porn!)

Would he be golden all over? Would he be sprinkled with hair or completely bare?

Wait.

Did the man even *wear* underthings? What if he was commando?

Ere's imagination geared into hyper-drive, his synapses misfiring all over the place, making his face twitch like he had uncontrollable muscle spasms.

"You look like you need a drink, Binu. The alcoholic kind," Mike observed as he shuffled behind the counter in a zombie-like state to pour the beverages he'd promised to bring back to the corner table with its mysterious, obsession-inducing lone occupant.

"I don't drink," he murmured by rote, simply going through the motions on autopilot, his mind still stuck in the gutter.

Deep, *deep*, in the gutter.

This wasn't him! He never had these thoughts. He only had them for the purposes of seducing a target, carrying out a mission. He'd never had them for *himself*.

Did this mean that he was a sexual being after all? That he could be physically attracted to another person?

He let out a humorless laugh as he arranged the libation on a tray, getting ready to head back toward the corner table like a soldier going off to war.

"I sure can pick 'em," he muttered beneath his breath.

"Pick who?" Mike asked, catching his words, giving him "the eye" at his odd behavior.

"Men," he answered without thinking, just vomited the first thing that popped into his unfiltered brain.

"You mean our patron in the corner booth?"

Why bother denying it when the truth was written as plain as a neon sign all over his face?

He nodded glumly.

Mike whistled low, peering in that direction, though they couldn't see anything of the man in question except one forearm propped on the tabletop.

But as Ere knew extremely well, one vein-wrapped forearm was all it took.

"You sure can, pick 'em, that is," Mike agreed. "What are you going to do about it?"

"Nothing," Ere replied emphatically, if a bit dejectedly.

"Why not?"

Mike looked him up and down.

"You're hot, he's hot. You'll have hot surrogate babies together. All's well with the world."

"W-What?" he sputtered.

Surrogate babies? What was she talking about?!

"You know, you're both men, so passing on your genes will take some advanced planning. But anything is possible these days. So I'm sure you'll figure it out. You know you've found The One when your reproductive parts perk up with acute awareness and buzz with the need to...well, reproduce."

"You can't be serious," he said, aghast. "I don't even know him! He hasn't even told me his name! I don't want—"

"Are your gonads tingling?" she interrupted and looked pointedly at his crotch.

He couldn't help it. He looked down too.

And bizarre as it was, his balls did feel uncomfortably full, and his cock was bulging the front of his jeans like he was pitching a tent at a wilderness retreat.

"That-that's—"

"That's some impressive equipment you've got there, is what that is," Mike observed with a grunt and licked her lips reflexively.

"What are you packing in there? A bazooka?"

Ere whipped around so fast, the beverages sloshed over their glasses and almost flew entirely off the tray.

"Don't look at me! I have to fix this!"

He set the drinks haphazardly on the counter and stormed into the backroom, where he tried to manually rearrange his junk and talk it back down to flaccidity.

What the fuck was wrong with him? This wasn't *him*!

He didn't want sex. He'd never been attracted to another being in his entire existence!

Well...

He thunked his forehead onto the door of the room he'd locked himself in.

It wasn't entirely true. He had found certain people more attractive than others. But he always felt that it was more aesthetically speaking versus personally inclined.

He'd always hero-worshipped Dalair. He played the role of Prince Cambyses for many years during the Persian Empire, and Dalair had been his half-brother. Like Gabriel and Tal, Dalair was the epitome of everything good and strong in a male. Ere had admired and loved him. But it was like a brother.

Wasn't it?

He found certain men more handsome than others, and he judged certain women to be more beautiful than others. But he had never been *attracted* to any of them for himself. They could have been moving scenery for all he cared. A target at worst; art he could appreciate at best.

A gentle knock sounded on the wood beneath his forehead from the other side.

"Binu, are you okay in there? Do you want me to take the beverages to Mr. Corner Table Hottie?" Mike's muffled voice came through.

He didn't know how to deal with this. This attraction thing...*sexual* attraction thing...was completely throwing him for a loop. He was still hard and swollen and aching. And his hands were shaking like crazy. He couldn't go out there like this. Seeing "Soren" would make it so much worse. He had to get control of himself somehow.

"Would you please?" Ere whispered in a small voice.

There was a pause on the other side.

Then, Mike answered cheerfully, "Sure thing, honey. Don't worry. You take all the time you need. I'll take care of it."

And so, Ere hid cowardly in the supply closet, intermittently bashing his head against the door and muttering "fuck, fuck, fuck, fuck," for the next twenty minutes.

Until Mike came back and informed him that the Corner Table Hottie had left the shop.

Only then did Ere feel calm enough to reemerge. He couldn't meet Mike's gaze for the rest of his shift. To her credit, she didn't say anything about it.

This was when he knew: he'd made a true friend in Mikayla Lane.

*** *** *** ***

Almost three thousand miles away, Lilith seethed in a silent, pitch-black cavern, half of her serpent body submerged in a fresh-water pool, the top, human half, resting against one of the stone pillars of her new lair.

Though she had been the victor of the battle with the black dragon—her own creation turned against her no less—she had sustained quite a bit of damage as well.

At the very least, she'd eviscerated him. Literally. She'd torn him to pieces with her bare claws and teeth.

She took little satisfaction from this fact, however, since her ultimate prize had still eluded her, thanks to that troublesome monster of her own making.

Ah, the parallels.

Frankenstein's monster had turned against its creator as well. Why couldn't these confounded creatures simply *behave*?

She'd even lost her most effective General in the last battle. The Paladin.

Her attempts to command him while he worked for the other side had failed spectacularly. Not even the most tenuous of connections between her mind and his remained. Somehow, he'd found a way to revive his frozen soul. His will was his own again.

Which left Lilith with very little help. None of her other minions had the skills, intelligence and experience to match the Paladin. And none of them had the powers she'd concocted and coalesced within the Creature.

She'd made him into a fucking dragon!

She'd given him a Gift of immense magnitude. And he'd turned right around and tried to kill her with it, the ungrateful wretch!

She flicked the tip of one sharp claw against the screen propped on a stone table beside her, bringing up the image of the one remaining chess piece in her arsenal who wasn't a mere expendable foot soldier.

"What progress have you to report?" she demanded without preamble.

The tech master pushed his stylish glasses higher up the bridge of his nose and answered calmly, despite her ominous tone, "Nothing yet, Mistress. All we know is that the target is definitely not in New York City, or even in New York State. Our current hypothesis is that he's been taken westward, based on various physical and digital signatures we've triangulated. But that is our only lead. Exactly how far he's gone, we have yet to pinpoint.'

"I know I do not have to repeat myself: find him."

"Understood."

And she knew that he did.

He might be her only remaining "good help," but he was not irreplaceable. He might well be one of the foremost digital gurus in the world, ranked in the top ten at least, but there were still nine others. He knew she always had contingency plans.

She was not a patient woman. Not when it came to her "target."

"And the other? What progress on that front?"

"No evidence was found on top of Mount St. Helens after the unexpected eruption months back. Our team scoured the entire mountaintop even before the air completely cleared. All the satellite images caught was static. We can only assume that the Eagle King was destroyed in the blast. Nothing could have survived the volcanic explosion."

Lilith narrowed her eyes.

"I don't pay you to make assumptions or extrapolate. As you well know, we immortals are difficult to destroy, especially someone as powerful as the Eagle King."

"My team will certainly keep looking," he murmured dutifully.

"Don't attempt to placate me," she hissed, leaning in close to the screen to bare several rows of tightly packed sharp teeth at him, snapping her jaws.

"No, Mistress," he said more alertly, a gratifying amount of fear trembling in his tone. "I will personally look into it again. I'll leave no stone unturned."

"See that you do," she warned, sinking back against the column.

A split second later, her spiked tail whipped out and smashed through the screen, flinging it against the cavern wall thirty feet away to shatter into a thousand tiny bits.

Next time, it wouldn't simply be an image of the tech master she obliterated to smithereens. It would be the man himself if he didn't deliver on her expectations.

*** *** *** ***

You are welcome to a change of clothes while we launder the ones on you.

Sorin glanced briefly in the Tiger King's direction and gave a nod of thanks.

Animal Spirits of all kinds were meticulous about cleanliness. The serpents had their water. The cats had their tongues. And the birds of prey had their beaks and glands to ensure silky, flawless feathers. In their animal forms, whether they were Beast or Lesser Beast, they loved grooming themselves. It was a matter of pride and relaxation, like humans with their scented baths and hot showers.

But he hadn't had this minor luxury for many millennia, trapped as he'd been in his in-between form. Only recently, since his rebirth, could he take full Beast form.

The form itself, however, would take time to get used to.

He'd been an eagle before, the kind that no longer existed in the present age. His closest relative was the modern Philippine eagle, with a distinctive crown of feathers on its head like a lion's mane. His earliest predecessors had all possessed this extravagant head of feathers, just as their humanoid forms had wild, flowing hair that seemed to have a life of their own, like living flames.

They had been much larger than the eagle spirits now, their wing spans twice as wide as the eagles today even in giant form. Just as the Tiger King, Goya, was the largest predatory cat in his animal form amongst all of the giant cats. They were the only remnants of a bygone time.

Now... Sorin was still trying to reconcile his new form with who he used to be.

He was...

Different.

How long will you be staying in these lands? Goya asked him telepathically.

Though they were both in humanoid form, standing side by side on the edge of a plateau overlooking a large field outside of town where Beasts and Lesser Beasts honed their fighting skills, they still preferred to communicate without spoken words. They were both more animal than humanoid.

Goya explained earlier that he tended to spend more time on two legs these days because of his human Mate. He was also learning to speak human languages, starting with English.

Sorin, by contrast, took this form to track down his target and also because he wasn't ready to reveal his true animal form to anyone, much less strangers. He was a living myth, after all, the only one of his kind as far as he could tell.

He didn't know how he felt about that. Perhaps he was meant to be alone. Which was why he intended to go back to his solitude as soon as he fulfilled his promise.

Not long, he answered curtly.

But the Tiger King picked up on what he wasn't saying. That he would stay as long as it took to complete what he came here to do. And if he could help it, he would complete it as soon as possible.

He didn't want to be here. He didn't want to linger. But he'd do what he damn well pleased, and if someone had a problem with that, they could physically remove him themselves.

Have you found what or who you are looking for? Goya asked after several beats.

Aye, was his terse response.

The Tiger King practically bristled his authority in the tense silence between them.

Say it, Sorin bit out.

Every living creature in these territories belongs to me, Goya communicated slowly, clearly, letting each word sink in.

There was no mistaking his meaning: everyone here was under the Tiger King's protection. Sorin was being forewarned.

He gave a sharp nod, acknowledging Goya's ruling authority.

And then he turned fully to face the Tiger King.

What or who I am pursuing is mine, *no matter where or when.*

Again, Goya read him clearly. He respected the Tiger King's dominion, but his Claim on one particular target took precedence.

Goya narrowed his icy blue eyes.

Only Mates take precedence.

Sorin took one step closer, purposely invading the Tiger King's space. His shoulders tightened and the hairs on the nape of his neck bristled with aggression, while the tiger growled low and menacingly in his throat at Sorin's unspoken challenge.

MINE.

The impact of his Claim hit the Tiger King like a physical blow, knocking his head back with the resounding echo of the one, unequivocal word in their linked minds.

The edges of Goya's form shimmered pale blue, signaling that he was on the verge of transformation.

Sorin clenched his fists at his sides, stalling his own shift.

He didn't want to Challenge the Tiger King. He didn't want trouble. But he needed the other male to understand and accept his authority as well on this one thing.

He would not back down from it. He would not explain himself. And he would fight to the death to defend his Claim.

All of this he communicated through the intensity of his golden gaze, unblinkingly holding the Tiger King's stare. He might no longer be a king. He might have lost his metaphorical crown long ago, but he was a formidable male.

He bowed to no one.

As if the trainees on the field below sensed the explosive tension between the two dominant males, they stopped their mock battles to look up toward the plateau.

The few fraught seconds that followed stretched between the Tiger King and the once Eagle King in what seemed like endless hours, for all of their witnesses were holding their breath with apprehension and expectation.

Finally, Goya gave a slow blink, an unspoken acknowledgement of Sorin's Claim.

Muscle by muscle, he unlocked himself, forcing the amped up aggression out of his pores.

The Tiger King was not his enemy. He didn't want to fight him. But he wouldn't back down either if he had to defend what was his.

Tacitly, they both agreed to turn toward the field together as if nothing happened.

Goya tilted his chin to indicate that the fighters should continue their training. Immediately, the mock battles picked up again.

After a few more moments of not entirely comfortable silence, Sorin communicated, in the mental extension of an olive branch, *It is rare to see a tiger lead such a large contingent. I thought cats were mostly solitary, save lions.*

One does what one must.

It was Goya's turn to be curt, it seemed.

He'd allowed Sorin great lenience in overlooking his defiance and in acknowledging his Claim. But that was also consistent with a tiger's nature.

The largest and fiercest of all predatory cats were the least aggressive of all. They never initiated fights; they only defended. But when they did fight, they fought to kill. They gave no quarter.

And you? Goya asked in return. *It is rare to see an eagle without his aerie. You are a born leader. Your Kind comprised the Twin Goddesses' revered cavalry, in contrast to the rest of us land-bound foot soldiers. We could use a leader like—*

I am no longer Eagle, Sorin inserted abruptly. *And I have not been King for many millennia. I am here for only one thing. When it is done, I will be gone.*

Goya regarded him quietly for a long time. Finally, he gave one nod.

So be it.

With that, he walked away from the edge of the plateau, transformed mid-stride in less than a blink into a giant white Siberian tiger, and bounded down the rocky side of the mountain to the field below. He joined in the training and proceeded to show his young recruits how *real* Beasts fought.

Sorin remained on the plateau to observe the skirmishes until the sun had set below the horizon, and an inky black night enveloped the lands.

The training below reminded him so much of a lost time, a barely remembered way of life. When he'd been someone else. The second in command of the Goddesses' winged forces and his sire's heir.

When he'd first met, on a night much like this one, where every star could be clearly seen in the cloudless sky, the bane of his existence—

And the spark that ignited his immortal soul.

Untold millennia ago, Age of the Gods.

Bloody and weary, so much sweat and dirt streaking down his face he was barely recognizable, the eagle warrior tore off his helmet and threw it with the full force of his fury against the stone wall.

The loud clang in the otherwise eerie silence of the cavern would have made anyone jump two feet in the air with surprise, but his sire merely lifted a bushy auburn brow, unimpressed as ever by his display of temper.

We cannot keep going like this, *the warrior growled telepathically.*

He would never say so in front of his men, but here in the privacy of the eagle forces' royal tower, where he was alone with his father, he couldn't help but vent his frustration.

He was the Eagle King's Second-in-Command. He was the heir to the throne. He was famous, or infamous, depending on one's perspective, for always being impeccably controlled, disciplined.

Severe.

Even with his father, his words were always measured and considered.

But at his core, he was an Eagle Spirit. He was born with fire within him. There was only so much pressure he could keep simmering inside without an outlet.

The gods have turned on the Twins, sensing their weakness now that they have borne the punishment for the Transgression. They seem divided between themselves, further eroding the strength they once had together. We weren't made to fight the gods themselves. They are too strong, united in growing factions against the Twins. This is suicide.

And yet we are the Goddesses' soldiers, *the Eagle King said calmly, though his golden eyes glittered with his own temper.*

He felt the loss of their flock just as keenly, after all. The Goddesses might have created the Animal Spirits to fight their wars, but they did not live for their Masters.

The eagle warrior knew this. He knew his duty better than anyone else.

Eagle Spirits were the most organized and obedient amongst the Animal Spirits created by the Goddesses to fight on their behalf. By nature, they formed flocks, took up specific roles and responsibilities, gathered readily into formation in flight and in battle. In major campaigns, they were given command of all three realms, sky, land and sea, for they could fly everywhere, see everything from their superior vantage point and with their sharp eyes.

He knew that the Goddesses gave them life, and they could easily take the same lives away. But the gruesome wars they were fighting now, had been fighting for three centuries—this was torture.

In many ways, it was worse than nonexistence, if violence and death were all they knew.

With the Tiger King gone, and with his cub still too weak to assume leadership, the cats are struggling on land. The recent invasion of trolls, giants and shadow monsters has taken its toll. Their numbers have been cut by half.

As he spoke, the warrior shucked his armor and kicked it aside with disgust. It was riddled with holes anyway, despite having been "protected" by the Goddesses' magic. When fighting other gods, that magic wore off quickly. He bore too many wounds to count, but he was still better off than others—he was still alive to fight another day.

But at this rate, his days were clearly numbered.

The Snake King and his serpents are fighting the sea gods directly, churning up hurricanes and tsunamis so strong, we can no longer safely fly over water. And now that we are isolated on mountain tops, the other gods are picking off our aeries with targeted attacks. There's no escape. If something doesn't change, we will all perish before the next season.

Something will change, *his sire communicated, holding his furious stare.* We will receive aid soon. In fact, I have the Goddess's Gift now. As do the Tiger King's cub and the Snake King.

The warrior narrowed his eyes with suspicion. In the short couple of centuries since he'd come into existence, he had learned quickly to be wary of the Goddesses' "Gifts."

What is it?

Come, *his sire commanded simply. Then turned and walked deeper into the cavern without another word.*

The eagle warrior followed reluctantly.

The last Gift the Goddesses had given his flight had been magically blessed weapons and armor. Fat lot of good that had done. His men still died. He still bled and broke. All the Goddesses had done was give them false hope.

Here, *the Eagle King communicated, stopping before a bed of feathers in a hidden corner of the cavern, surrounded on almost all sides by a circular ring of large boulders.*

It was a nest.

Meticulously made. Rather like the nest that any male of their Kind created with their own feathers when they chose a Mate.

The warrior looked sharply to his sire.

You have decided to Mate again, father?

Of course not, *his sire scoffed, as if the notion was inconceivable.*

By the Goddesses' decree, the Eagle King had been given a "Dark One" as Mate. They said that the offspring of the union would be even stronger as a result. The warrior never knew his mother, since she died either giving birth to him or shortly thereafter.

His father never elaborated, and he never thought to ask. "Mating" was a perfunctory duty, just like everything else the Goddesses required of them. Their Kind tended to only Mate once and for life, however, so he took his father's reply at face value.

The nest is for you.

The warrior's head went back in shock as if his sire had suddenly struck him beneath the jaw.

Me? The Goddesses have already chosen a Mate for me?

He thought he still had a couple millennia at least before he had to tend to his own succession.

Not a Mate. A responsibility.

More like a bane, the warrior thought to himself.

And I'll need a nest for it?

Well, yes, *his sire said cryptically, stepping closer to the thick bed of feathers.*

How else will you hatch the egg?

The warrior couldn't help but wander closer as well. He peered down at the feathers like they were a bed of venomous snakes instead. And saw what he hadn't noticed from afar:

A pale blue egg the size of his closed fist.

Why not give it to one of the others? A Mated pair would make the most sense, *he sputtered mentally.*

What was he going to do with an egg? Who was going to command their flights? This was ridiculous!

No. It must be you, *his sire asserted indisputably.* The Goddesses want you to train the hatchling. Whatever lies inside must be raised and nurtured with the utmost care. For they are destined to be our Kind's greatest champion, just as the Gifts to the Land and Sea Animal Spirits will be theirs. And, of course, this champion will fight alongside us for the Goddesses against their foes.

I have no time for this, *the young warrior immediately balked.* I—

You will make time, *his father rumbled sternly, brooking no argument.* I have already redistributed your command. I will take a couple of squadrons myself.

But I am not a nester, *he continued to protest.* I am your best fighter. I need to...

You need to do your duty and hatch this egg. This is a direct order. Do not test me.

When his father took that tone, the eagle warrior knew there was no escape.

The Eagle King had ruled for millennia already. He was merely a hatchling by comparison. And he respected his sire too much to gainsay him.

How long will it take? *he asked, swallowing the growl of frustration churning through his throat.* What sort of creature is in there?

It will take as long as it takes, *his sire intoned unhelpfully.* And we will see what emerges when it does. The Goddesses said that we will know what to do once the egg hatches. So, do not think beyond the present task.

Which was apparently to hatch an egg. While his men were getting slaughtered in the Goddesses' wars.

And so, the young eagle warrior dutifully sat on the egg day and night in his eagle form, never straying long from the nest.

The sooner this was done, the sooner he could rejoin his men. He still didn't know why someone else couldn't do it just as well. One feathered ass was as warm as another.

He sat and he sat. Alternately cooing to the egg to encourage the creature inside to come out sooner, and cursing it for not hatching fast enough.

The egg grew steadily in size, which was the first surprising anomaly about it. To his knowledge, eggs didn't keep growing when they were already outside of a bird's body. Within a few turns of the sun, the egg became as big as his head in humanoid form. So, he transformed into the giant version of his eagle form and continued to sit on it fully with the right intensity of heat and pressure.

Until one day, as he dozed fitfully on the nest, dreaming of the last bloody battle he'd led his flight into, losing half of the flock, a quiet rustle and a tiny wiggle tickled him slowly to wakefulness.

And then, there was a louder crack, followed by another, the noises almost deafening in the absolute silence of the cavern.

The eagle warrior shifted off the egg and transformed into his bipedal form.

The cavern was too dark to see anything clearly, even with his acute vision. He carried the heavy object with its thick, fractured shell to the entrance of the cave, walking out onto the plateau on the tallest mountain peak above swirling clouds.

For a moment, the eagle warrior was mesmerized by the beauty of the inky black night, with only a few stars to decorate its robe. But because they were few, they seemed to shine even more brightly, beaming down at the Eagle Spirit and his package like heavenly guardians.

He could clearly make out the Constellation Byakko, the White Tiger of the West. Perhaps the spirit of the Tiger King himself was looking down upon them

SQUAWK!

The loud, obnoxious sound snapped the warrior's attention back to the egg in his arms.

A pair of large, round, sapphire blue eyes sparkled at him unblinkingly. That was what he noticed first.

He stared unblinkingly back, unable to move, involuntarily holding his breath.

The eyes were serpentine, like liquid pools they were so clear, with dilated black pupils in the middle. After an inordinate amount of staring, they blinked at him.

Or at least, it looked like they were blinking. But it was actually a semi-transparent membrane that shifted quickly over each eye. Like snakes, the creature had no eyelids.

Still breathless, the warrior took in the rest of the thing, bits of tough egg shell still sticking to its body.

It was the color of starlight, as if it had been born in this very sky, by the stars that were presently shining down upon them, instead of laboriously hatched beneath the eagle warrior's warm, feathered ass. Pale, shimmering scales coated its entire body, hard like armor, not unlike the scales of the giant Snake Spirits.

But aside from the serpent eyes and scales, it seemed to wear a crown of sharp, stone-hard thorns, including a spike on its snout, which was snuffling and quivering curiously, eagerly snorting in the eagle warrior's scent.

There were similar spikes all along its back, and it had a thorned tail like a giant lizard. The creature also had four legs, the two front ones smaller than the two large back legs, the proportions similar to a rabbit. Each leg ended in enormous, five-fingered claws.

Something shifted on the creature's back. A couple egg shells were hindering its movement.

The warrior gently removed the shells, careful not to make sudden movements to startle the beast, just as it opened its jaws in a wide yawn, revealing jagged rows of dagger-sharp teeth. Once all of the shells fell away, the creature stretched its back again, rolling its shoulders and rippling its scales.

And then, the things on its back began to unfold.

The warrior sucked in a sharp breath when he finally realized what he was looking at.

Wings.

Giant, featherless wings.

With curved claws at the joints. Covered in the same shimmering scales. Those wings were the most beautiful things he'd ever seen, though the rest of the creature could only be termed as ugly, a strange mix of different animals.

It chose that moment to dart out its long, curling tongue and swipe the wet, sloppy thing from the warrior's throat to chin, then mouth, nose and forehead.

Ugh. Disgusting!

And yet...oddly endearing.

The membranes shifted over its eyes again in that strange not-blink, and its over-large jaws curled in a serpentine smile.

It was kind of...sort of...possibly just the tiniest bit...

Adorable.

But then a strange rumble started somewhere in its belly, and before the eagle warrior could ask if it was hungry, a glowing ball traveled from its stomach through its throat and emerged unbidden from its slightly open mouth in a torrent of white-hot flames—

Directly in the eagle warrior's face.

Singeing his wild hair until it crackled and coating his face with a thick layer of soot.

He narrowed his eyes at the creature and scowled ferociously.

It hid its face behind its two front claws in a look of innocent contrition.

At least he wasn't burned to a crisp. He could only hope he was immune to the creature's fire.

For he knew instinctively, deep down in his very bones, that this accidental roasting was only the beginning...

Chapter Five

The *Night Owl* was booming, as usual, on a packed Friday night. Being the only action in town helped.

The locals filed in with a lighter bounce in their otherwise weary strides, for winter in these parts wasn't fun for anybody, even the strange sort who loved the freezing cold. The long nights and lack of sunshine didn't help. But at least when it was truly night, after work and before the weekend, folks felt free to party hearty with some beer chugging, loud laughing and dizzy-footed dancing.

Truly, the natives wouldn't know rhythm if it bit them in the ass.

They wouldn't know good music either. But thankfully, Ere, or rather, *Erena*, changed all that in the last few weeks by putting new songs in the karaoke machine, getting a better sound system for the place, and livening things up with his own performances.

The locals had a long way to go (read: when hell freezes over) before they'd adopt hip-hop, rap, and heavy metal though. It took some doing just to drag them into twenty-first century alternative rock and pop. You wouldn't believe how many closet Taylor Swift fans dwelled in these remote mountains.

Erena watched the usual awkward swaying and clunky hip shaking on the dance floor after the patrons had a few beers to loosen up. It was also open mic night, so she had off-key warbling to look forward to as well. And the night was just getting started at a little after 9 p.m.

Despite the expectation of nails-on-chalk torture ala upcoming performances, she absolutely loved her job.

"Hey beautiful," Mikayla caught her attention with a bump of hips, "Guy at the end of the bar is giving you the snake eye. You want me to tell him to chill out?"

Erena casually looked over one bare shoulder at the man in question and instinctively pulled the neckline of her blouse higher up on her bosom.

Not that she'd been flashing cleavage to begin with, but...She shuddered with delicate revulsion when the bloke made a show of sticking his tongue out and licking lasciviously all around his grimy-looking mouth.

"As opposed to giving me just the eye?" she quipped. "You had to add 'snake' as a modifier?"

"Don't you think it's appropriate?" Mike returned. "His eyes are a little crossed and the pupils look all wrong."

She leaned in closer to whisper, "Do you think he's a real snake?"

Mike knew about the Animal Spirits and other Immortal Kinds. After all, she and Yasmin moved here to start fresh, take on a new adventure, and also to help Maddie and Goya settle the territories. Make it a home for not only the unsuspecting locals, but also create a safe haven for Animal Spirits from far and wide.

Even so, she didn't know that Ere had the Gift of shapeshifting. She didn't even know he was an Immortal. As far as she was concerned, he truly was Benjamin's Uncle Ere, come to visit the family for a while. And since the boy was definitely human, she assumed he was too, though she knew he lived with Dark and Pure Ones.

She didn't know that he was both Binu and Erena, and that neither of these forms were his own.

Ere felt guilty about that. He vowed to tell her at some point...if he stuck around.

He was instinctively wary of revealing his Gift, given what happened with Ninsa, now Liv in her current incarnation. He'd lost his one and only friend when he showed her his true nature in the most horrific way.

He didn't want to risk losing Mike too. Real friends were so hard to come by. Especially for someone like him.

Most of all, he'd always wanted to be human. It was so...*normal.* Even if it was only pretense, he didn't want to give up the illusion just yet.

"Real Snake Spirits are infinitely more attractive. You know that, Mike," Erena chided. "Haven't you seen one in the flesh before? Isn't one of the Tiger King's seconds-in-command a Snake Spirit?"

Mike shrugged.

"He's okay, if you like the lean, malnourished looking ones—"

Erena snorted with disbelief. Maybe if you counted "malnourished" as being a perfectly proportioned, two-hundred-pound lethal warrior with eight-pack abs.

"—personally, I prefer the cats more," Mike elaborated. "I just *love* the way they purr. Especially when I stroke them just so between their—"

"Stop! TMI!" Erena protested, putting her hands over her ears.

Mike had a knack for talking dirty. When she, Yas and Maddie got together, those with a Y chromosome should be very, *very* scared.

The three of them always got up to no good, cackling like banshees, trading just as many purple jokes as purple eggplant emojis. Erena had no idea what that was all about, but between the three of them, vegetable emojis in general, and eggplants in particular, got an obscene amount of use.

Mike peeled her hands away from her innocent ears and smirked, "I was going to say *eyes*. Get your head out of the gutter, babe."

Yeah right.

If Erena's head was in the gutter, she didn't know where Mike's head would be. Somewhere with lots of loud, kinky orgies involving hairy, bearish men, probably.

Too bad there weren't any bear animal spirits, at least as far as Erena knew. Though Lilith's experiments might have yielded some manufactured ones. Erena knew of none that lived through the transformation process.

"Their rumbling purr when I pet them between the eyes right above their nose is so unbelievably sexy. I could listen to it all night long," Mike sighed.

"Pet a great many cats, have you?" Erena narrowed her eyes at her prolific flirt of a friend.

"Oh, indeed," Mike agreed unabashedly. "As many as I can get my hands on. But the growl...now there's a sound to die for. Those deep-throated, rumbling growls..."

She cast her eyes heavenward and made a show of fanning herself.

"I'm getting wet just thinking about it. My cli—"

"Customers, Mike!" Erena interrupted before she could further expound on the effect rumbling purrs had on her person.

"Don't let those potential tips go to waste!"

Mike was even more enterprising than she was flirtatious. She collected fat tips like nobody's business. A true professional.

The prospect of charming a customer out of more than they were planning to spend distracted her enough to saunter away, giving Erena a reprieve from all this exhausting girl talk. Mike wasn't nearly this forthcoming when Ere took Binu form.

Her friend's departure left her open for a sneak attack, however. Within seconds of Mike being gone from her side, Mr. Snake Eye got right in Erena's face.

"Well, ain't you a fine, purty thing. I could use some company tonight. My truck's right outside. Wanna come steam up the windows with me?"

Joy. She had a gentleman with superb manners and impeccable speech on her hands. One who referred to her as a "thing." How lovely.

She gave her best icy, close-lipped, fuck-off smile and said, "Alas, I will have to decline your thoughtful invitation, good sir. I already have an appointment tonight to have a root canal without anesthesia."

He scrunched up his already pug-like face at her and straightened to his full height.

Oh dear. He was rather large. Not so much tall as he was wide. And rather meaty, with arms bigger than most men's thighs.

"Eh? Whatcha talkin' fancy fer? Think yur too good for me or somethin'?"

He leaned further onto the counter and got his brick-wall upper body in her space, led by his out-thrust chin and a mouth full of onion breath.

Ye gods! Did he chew through a whole raw onion before coming over here? As far as Erena knew, none was on the menu at the bar. It smelled like something had died in his mouth and was now marinating in regurgitated onion juice.

"It's me, not you," she said gently, leaning back as far as the shelves behind her allowed, and struggled to breathe through her mouth. Except, then she'd essentially be inhaling his breath into her mouth, and the thought of that made her even more nauseous.

A customer was a customer, however. She didn't want to create a scene. She didn't want to add yet another mark in her "bad employee" book.

She could use her Immortal strength against him; she had no doubt who would be the victor if a skirmish ensued, her lack of fighting skills notwithstanding. But there were ignorant humans here. The locals didn't know about their Kind, and she really didn't want to be the upstart who broke the law of secrecy.

"Why don't I get you a drink on the house?" she offered instead in her most charming, placating tone.

Faster than she would have thought possible for someone lazy-eyed with alcohol-slurred speech, he shot out his hand and grabbed a fist full of the front of her blouse, tearing her neckline as he yanked her toward him.

Enough was enough!

Erena was about to get rough right back when, suddenly, the guy's hand was trapped in a much larger fist, forcing him to release her blouse with a pained squeak.

He was lifted three feet in the air and tossed unceremoniously against the nearest wall as if he weighed nothing at all. He crashed against the concrete with a loud thud and lay unconscious upon the ground in a crumpled heap.

The commotion caught Mike's eye, and she got two of the Animal Spirit bouncers to deal with the mess. She was about to come over to check on Erena when her eyes shifted to what, or rather who, was next to her friend. She smirked instead, turning away with a slow wink.

Which was when Erena finally faced her Knight in Shining Armor and realized who he was.

The stranger.

(But really, given how often she ran into him, did he qualify as a stranger anymore?)

You know him...You miss the flames...

That inner voice whispered through her mind again.

Instantly, her heart quadrupled its beat, and heat flooded her face.

"Y-you...I-I...W-what are you doing here?"

Shit! What was she saying? She was supposed to be Erena, not Binu. The stranger had only seen her as Binu.

He was a *stranger*.

"I mean, I've never seen you in these parts before. Are you new in town?"

She eked out a wobbly smile and tried to project the self-assured bravado that was part of Erena's persona.

"Thanks for the assist, by the way. Your order's on me. What can I get you?"

Inside, however, she was a quivering, nervous wreck. The golden-eyed god stared steadily at her, silent and brooding. She rather suspected that was his default expression. She Googled the name "Soren" earlier and it meant "severe." Seemed like a fitting moniker for the man.

"Umm..." she drew out the filler to, well, fill the yawning void of silence that stretched between them.

All this time (how long had it been? Minutes? Hours?), the stranger hadn't blinked and didn't look as if he would speak any time soon.

And then:

"You."

The one word seemed thrown down on the bar counter between them like a gauntlet. It was so heavy, she was tempted to look down to see if the sound of it alone cracked through the wood.

"Pardon?"

"Want. You."

If her heart sped any faster, she'd need a defibrillator.

"Sorry," she wheezed, her lungs not filling with enough oxygen to give her voice any strength, "I'm not on the menu."

Wait.

Didn't they have this conversation before? She was having déjà vu.

But she'd been Binu at the time. Was this guy some sort of cannibal? Did he go around everywhere ordering *people* for food and drink?

The stranger still hadn't blinked, but at Erena's response, his eyes lowered to her mouth, focused there for a few arresting seconds, then slowly lifted again to look back in her eyes, the sweep of his obscenely crowded, long lashes more pornographic to Erena than if Brock O'Hurn had stripped naked right there in front of her in the bar.

She was definitely having a heart attack!

Unlike Snake-Eye, this man reached slowly toward her, giving her ample opportunity to avoid his touch (which she stupidly did not!), gripped her wrist gently but securely, and brought her hand to his upper chest. Laid it with her fingers splayed right on his thick, stone-hard left pec.

Any remaining oxygen in her body whooshed out in a shaky exhale at the heat and strength of him, scalding, yet *oh so irresistible,* beneath the thin layer of his Henley, which molded to his muscles like loving hands.

Her hand. Which apparently developed a mind of its own and decided to claw its fingers into his chest like it wanted to attach itself to him forever.

"You. Want me."

Half-heartedly, she tugged at her wayward hand, and was surprised when he released her. She cradled the uncontrollably shaking limb in her other hand, then tucked both of them beneath her arms, holding herself together by sheer force of will.

"I don't know you," she said, suddenly angry at the way this stranger so easily unbalanced her.

Who did he think he was! They'd just met (that he knew of). And he used almost the exact same line on Erena as he did on Binu. He didn't even care that one was a man and the other was a woman! Did this guy go around hitting on everyone with those stupid terse lines?

Well, she wasn't desperate enough to fall for it. Or for him.

"I don't want you, pal," she practically snarled. "Go use your unoriginal caveman spiel on someone else. Excuse me. I have a performance to do."

It was still early for Erena's show, but she needed time to calm herself and focus. She couldn't think around him. She could barely breathe.

Determinedly, she turned away to head toward the bathroom to change.

"Sorin."

Involuntarily, she swiveled back to look at him at that.

"My name," he explained in that deep, smoky baritone. "You know me."

Wow. Three whole words strung together in a complete sentence. This was a record. But she refused to be impressed.

"I don't," she whispered.

Even as a voice inside her screamed *lie!*

"And I don't want to."

Liar, liar, pants on fire! was all she heard as she cowardly ran away from the confounding man called Sorin.

*** *** *** ***

The thirty or so minutes that Sorin waited for his bane to reappear felt like centuries. And given how long he'd existed, this was saying something.

He was not a patient male. Especially when it came to his bane.

But he would wait an eternity if that was what it took for *Ere* to come to him. He would not force the other man's hand. He didn't know what had happened to this child-like soul in the many millennia that they had been lost to each other, but he knew his bane had suffered.

Suffered greatly.

The way he'd recoiled from Sorin's touch when he tried to heal him. His ragged breaths full of fear that he couldn't hide in moments of weakness. The way he shattered into a million pieces beyond his physical brokenness...

Sorin had seen enough of the depravities of humanoids, both mortal and immortal, to guess at some of the evils his beautiful bane might have been forced to endure.

Animals weren't capable of such things. There was only physical need and dominance. Humanoids felt these emotions too, but their intentions were often more complex.

Including the drive to hurt another, to see the evidence of their pain. These intentions were what made one action instinctive, but a similar action cruel. And Sorin knew, without asking the question or hearing the answer, that Ere had suffered untold cruelty in his life.

He wanted to hunt down the monsters who had hurt his bane. Tear them limb from limb and smelt them to ashes with the fury of his flames. He wanted to fix Ere's brokenness from the inside out. Help him reclaim his true self.

But Ere had to come to him. And Sorin had to figure out how to...encourage him to do so.

Animals did not know the "art of seduction," as humanoids would say. They were primal, instinctual, and pure. They didn't know how to lie, how to be subtle and subversive. It went against the grain to even attempt such pretense.

But the direct approach wasn't working.

Sorin had made himself clear. He'd shown Ere that whatever his form, Sorin recognized him. Wanted him. Ere needed him to heal to the fullest. He was still riddled with scars, physically together but not whole. Sorin could complete the healing process and restore all of his powers.

But only if Ere let him.

He'd already rejected Sorin once, when he walked away before the healing was complete. He'd walked away despite Sorin's request for him to stay.

What they'd done together...the way they came together...it had changed Sorin.

Their joining had made an animal heart *feel*. And when Ere had chosen to leave him, it had *hurt*.

Absently, he rubbed his hand over his heart at the reminder. Even now, the organ that had never "felt" before, merely a muscle that pumped blood throughout his body, *hurt*.

He didn't like it. He wished he didn't feel it. But what had already happened could not be undone.

Presently, Erena glided gracefully onto stage in a demure, yet captivating dress. With her long, wavy, auburn hair, voluptuous proportions and flawless peach-toned complexion, she looked like an ancient goddess come down to earth.

The entire bar went still in awe and captivation, all attention focused on the center of the stage.

"Good evening," Erena said in her sultry voice, her words crisp and polished, with a melodious lilt.

People in these remote parts didn't talk like this. They certainly in their wildest dreams didn't look like this. But what they didn't realize was that the real person beneath this gorgeous disguise was even more beautiful, infinitely more enthralling.

No one saw what Sorin saw. Selfishly, he was glad of it.

If only Ere could see him for who he truly was as well. If only he would recognize Sorin's soul within this altered humanoid form.

"I would like to begin with an old song some of you might know. It is one of my favorites, you see. And recently, when I needed to be...heard, this song helped me hold onto hope that I would be. I hope you like it."

She settled into a chair with her bass guitar and pulled the microphone where she wanted it. It was a strange vision to see someone so ethereal and delicate looking holding such a "masculine" instrument. But because Sorin could see Ere's true form, he noticed only how right the instrument looked in Ere's strong, long-fingered hands as they started strumming the first few notes.

Where have all the good men gone. And where are all the gods?
Where's the streetwise Hercules to fight the rising odds?
Isn't there a white knight upon a fiery steed?
Late at night I toss and I turn. And I dream of what I need
I need a hero. I'm holding out for a hero 'til the end of the night
He's gotta be strong. And he's gotta be fast. And he's gotta be fresh from the fight
I need a hero. I'm holding out for a hero 'til the morning light
He's gotta be sure. And it's gotta be soon. And he's gotta be larger than life...
Somewhere after midnight. In my wildest fantasy
Somewhere just beyond my reach, there's someone reaching back for me
Racing on the thunder and rising with the heat

It's gonna take a Superman to sweep me off my feet...

Sorin's heart thundered like ancient drums as he listened to the haunting voice in that hypnotizing melody.

Those words...they reached inside him and clenched around his heart. He'd heard them before, echoing in his ears, filling his head until he could hear nothing else.

It was those words, this song, that called him to action from the remote mountain peaks of his self-imposed solitude. He'd only recently been reborn in a new form, remade and risen from the ashes of a fire mountain. He'd hardly known who he was, but he knew he had to answer this voice. This call.

He had to find the creature who so desperately needed him.

Up where the mountains meet the heavens above. Out where the lightning splits the sea
I could swear there is someone, somewhere, watching me
Through the wind, the chill, and the rain. And the storm, and the flood
I can feel his approach like a fire in my blood...

In that moment, as Erena launched into the refrain, her voice building in crescendo, she stared directly into Sorin's eyes.

Under the spotlight of centerstage, she probably couldn't see clearly into the audience. He was standing against the back wall, cloaked in shadows, dressed all in black, his arms folded across his chest.

Even so, he felt the force of her gaze the second their eyes met, clashed and held.

She was singing to him.

Did she know she was singing to him?

Did she know she was staring directly at the winged warrior who saved her? The male who pieced her back together in the forge of his flames? Who infused her with his own life force, with his body, blood and seed? Who strengthened her soul with his own, bound their fates irrevocably together...

Did she...did *he*—Ere—feel what Sorin now felt? Remember what he remembered?

96

Even though it happened thousands of lifetimes ago, it felt like yesterday.

This present time when his bane did not know him seemed unreal. His rediscovered memories...those were real.

It hurt him viscerally when Erena broke their gaze and looked away as she finished the song and started another.

Dismissed again.

Rejected again.

He clenched his jaw against the surge of pain in his chest, rubbed the left side impatiently to distract himself from the ache, and left his post against the back wall.

With two long strides, he walked out of the crowded bar and disappeared into the night.

Untold millennia ago, Age of the Gods.

Fresh off the battlefield, pumped with adrenaline and aggression, the eagle warrior sought out the nearest willing partner and dragged her back to his private cavern.

Female eagles were typically larger than their male counterparts in animal form, but he was one of the exceptions. His wings eclipsed hers as he poised over her, his claws holding her down. At the moment before their "cloacal kiss," they transformed into humanoid form by unspoken accord.

Eagles tended to mate for life, and the animal part of the warrior balked at copulating with a female who would not be his Mate. At the same time, he also had a Dark One base, and he was unique amongst the Eagle Spirits because of this.

The Dark side of him made him stronger, more deadly in battle, more aggressive. It also spurred a need inside him that wasn't common for other birds of prey—the need to fuck.

In eagle form, he felt the wrongness of the mating act down to the root of every feather. But in humanoid form, though other Animal Spirits took this form only to Claim human Mates, his guilt was somewhat assuaged, and his Dark side was more dominant.

The female was willing and ready beneath him, supporting herself on all fours, spreading her thighs to give him easy access.

He positioned himself behind her, over her, his much larger frame eclipsing hers fully.

Gods! He hadn't had this since he inherited the loathsome responsibility of watching and training the "bane." His cock and balls felt full to bursting. The pressure was unbearable. Now, he was a hair's breadth away from—

Whatcha doin'?

FUCK!

The bane found him.

He always did, the miserable overgrown lizard!

Following the eagle warrior wherever he went like an imprinted baby duck. Except he wasn't anywhere near as adorable, all lolling tongue, shark-like teeth and fiery breath.

Go away, he gritted out, holding the female in place with one commanding hand on her hip as she squawked with indignation at being caught by a witness.

I've never seen that big stick you have in your hand before. Is that a new sword? I suppose it's thick and hard and heavy enough to hurt if you struck someone on the head with it. But it doesn't look very sharp. Kinda soft at the tip actually. And why is it watering?

Shut. Up.

The female was getting antsy, shifting uneasily beneath him, the edges of her form shimmering to signal her imminent change. He needed to get this situation under control before he ended the night with even bluer balls than he had before.

Oh! It's attached to you, look at that! What does it do? Wait. Are you going to stick it inside her? But... it's too big! Don't hurt her, you big oaf! I won't let you!

The eagle warrior was knocked off balance without warning by a head butt to the chest. In the ensuing melee, the female decided she'd had enough, shifted into eagle form and raced out of the cavern, diving off the plateau with embarrassed haste.

Damn it! Get off me!

The overgrown lizard was unfortunately now three times as large as the warrior in humanoid form, and many more times as heavy. Having had enough of this shit, he transformed instantly into giant eagle form and knocked the creature off him with a sharp jab of his wing.

A struggle followed, where the eagle vented his broiling frustration and the creature batted him around in a playful game, delighting in making him growl with vengeful wrath whenever he could slobber the warrior with his giant pink tongue.

The more the eagle fought, the more the creature played. Everything was one big game to him, and he treated the eagle like his personal toy.

Finally, the eagle warrior disentangled himself and made his escape to the edge of the cliff. He dove off the ledge with the speed of a falling boulder, keeping his wings tucked close to his body to increase his velocity. He could hear the creature diving off to follow him.

Of course he did!

Why wouldn't the thing leave him alone? Why did it have to have wings so that the eagle warrior couldn't escape no matter how he tried?

In his giant form, the eagle warrior was still slightly larger than his bane, but the creature's wings were just as strong. Somehow, despite his unwieldly, serpent-like body, he was able to fly at incredible speeds, matching the eagle warrior easily.

Go away! *the eagle commanded again, though he had little hope that the creature would listen to him. He never did before, so why would he start now?*

Are you mad at me? *the bane communicated in a tentative voice.*

Would you care if I was?

The creature flew slightly ahead of him and was now doing circles around him, the damn show-off!

It would make me sad if you were mad at me, *the bane said in a sincere tone, all innocent big eyes shimmering blue like sunlit waves in the northern sea.*

The eagle warrior was immune to that look that had others eating out of the creature's hand, including his own sire. The rest of the aerie adored this ugly, scaly, thorned thing. The eagle warrior was the only one who didn't.

But you won't stop following me, *he pointed out.*

Because I want to be where you are all the time!

The creature flew around in loops, turning happily in the sky with a twirl of wings, expressing his ecstasy to be in the eagle warrior's company.

The eagle refused to be affected by this...charming display.

Then I don't care if you're sad.

Really? You don't care about me at all?

Not even the slightest.

Hmm...

Suddenly, a gust of wind shoved both of them off course, and the creature gave a startled yelp. One of his wings bent at an awkward angle, and he dropped from the sky with dizzying speed.

The eagle warrior's heart flew into his throat as he immediately dove after his bane.

Despite the thing's size, he was still mostly a baby. He was still learning the air currents. He could accidentally hurt himself fooling around mid-flight. The eagle warrior berated himself as he shot after the creature, trying to reach him in time before he really got hurt.

But the bane was falling too fast, tumbling head over tail to the rocky ground below, which rose up to meet them all too soon.

The eagle extended his head and stretched his wings to try to gain additional speed. He had to reach his bane! He couldn't let the creature get—

At the last possible moment, the creature turned and spread his wings, immediately stalling his downward momentum, a mere wing's length before he hit the ground.

The eagle only had half a second before he did the same. They both swooped back up into the sky, so close had they been to the ground that their claws scraped the rocks and scared unsuspecting small animals into hiding.

Woohoo! That was fun! *the damnable creature crowed.*

See! You do care about me! You were going to dash yourself on the rocks to save me!

Arrrgghhhh!

This was why the eagle warrior hated his bane!

He chased the laughing, spinning, flying snake around the clouds, promising retribution. But the creature merely laughed and played and teased and tumbled, unperturbed by the eagle's ire.

Finally, tired from the chase, the eagle settled onto a rocky ledge that shouldn't have been wide enough for two. And yet, somehow, the creature managed to land next to him and perch with easy balance despite the tight squeeze.

That was so much fun! We should do it again!

The eagle warrior whipped out a wing to knock the creature off his perch, but the bane anticipated the move, flapped his wings and coiled his tail to regain his balance without completely losing it.

That thorned tail sure came in handy, the eagle thought a smidgeon enviously. It was difficult to accept, as the master of the sky, that this strange creature might be even more at home in the clouds than him.

Admit it. This is much better than sticking your pole into the other bird. You feel better, right?

He would never admit it, but he did. The unbearable tension he felt after battle had entirely dissipated.

Next time, just come fly with me. I'll take care of you.

Now there was a novel idea. The bane taking care of him.

He decided not to comment. Perhaps if he ignored the creature, he would finally go away.

(Even though the eagle warrior didn't really want that.)

The other eagles call me Rai. But you never call me anything. How come?

Because then the creature wouldn't be…his. Everyone else called him by that name; it wasn't special any more.

They call you Sol. Can I call you Sol? Is it Sol or Soul?

No, was the eagle's only response. He let the creature guess which question he was answering.

Is it short for something else? Maybe…Solemnity? Since you're so humorless?

The eagle didn't deign to answer. He was not *humorless.*

Or…Solitude? Since you like to be alone so much?

And yet, the eagle was never alone these days. Not since the creature hatched from his egg. Well, even before that, in truth. Not since he was given responsibility for the egg.

Or, I know! Soldier. Since you're so good at soldiering.

If he didn't shut up soon, the eagle was going to shove him off the cliff.

How about Solicitous? Since you're ever so approachable and amiable and amenable?

Since when did the creature develop such a large vocabulary? The eagle didn't know how he learned all these things, but he seemed to soak up knowledge like a sea anemone. Confounded thing.

Or—

Bane.

What?

The creature turned toward him, eyes round, curiosity and happiness shining in his sapphire blue eyes at the fact that his favorite person was finally speaking to him.

You're an annoyance, a thorn in my side, a scourge. You're my bane. And that's what I'll call you, *the eagle said harshly, practically daring the creature to object.*

Instead of being offended, however, the unnatural thing beamed with jubilation.

I love it! A pet name just for me! I love being your Bane!

It's not a name, damn it, *the eagle tried to explain*, it's a descriptor. You're a blight on my—

But the creature was no longer listening, having launched himself off the rocky perch to tumble excitedly in the skies in a series of happy summersaults.

I'm Sol's Bane! His Bane! I'm Sol's, Sol's, Sol's! *he chanted in a sing-songy voice as he rolled in the air, dancing his strange serpent dance.*

That's not what I meant! *the eagle hastened to correct him.*

Why did the creature focus on the wrong part of the phrase? He was the most contrary, impossible thing!

But it was too late. The Claim had been made.

And the dragon would never let him forget it.

Chapter Six

Minutes after Erena finished her last song to a rousing round of applause from a very appreciative crowd, she changed into more casual clothes and dashed out of the bar.

Chasing after...

She stopped abruptly a few steps down the sidewalk, her breath puffing icily in the frigid night.

Where did he go?

She'd seen him leave three songs back, about twenty minutes ago. She'd already cut her performance short in her haste to go after him.

She *needed* to find him. She was desperate for it.

An involuntary whimper choked out of her throat, and she stuck her fist in her mouth, biting down on her knuckles, blocking any more helpless sounds.

What was wrong with her? She told him to go away. She'd stared straight into his soul when she sang, and then she purposely turned away, dismissing him.

He'd stood there against the back wall, tall and immeasurably strong. But he couldn't have been more vulnerable than if he'd been naked with his chest carved open, baring his bloody, beating heart to her.

His eyes...those glowing golden eyes. They'd burned with a knowledge and experience she didn't understand. But she felt the Bond between them nevertheless.

Unbreakable. Irrevocable. Infinite.

And she'd turned him away because she was afraid. She was a coward.

Who was he? Why was he here? What did he want with her? With Binu?

Why couldn't she get him out of her mind?!

She lurched into a brisk walk and made her way down the sidewalk by rote, her feet knowing where to take her even if her mind was whirling in a thousand different directions.

She was happy here, in these remote mountains, wasn't she?

She was well-liked; she had friends. And two jobs that kept her very busy, while also giving her the flexibility to spend time with Benjamin.

But then, why did she feel so hollow? Why was she certain this paradise of normal human life wouldn't last?

Lilith was still out there. Of course, there was that.

And as long as the Hydra lived, they would never be safe. The demoness wanted Benjamin. She wasn't going to rest until she had him. Erena couldn't let that happen. She had to protect her son.

But...

She was so broken. So weak now. She couldn't fight the Hydra again. She was too afraid. She hadn't taken dragon form since her resounding, horrific defeat.

She stumbled a step and raked a trembling hand down the side of her face. Despite the flawless skin any passerby would see, she felt the jagged lines of scars on her face.

His face. Ere's real face.

So broken...

He could barely protect himself, much less his loved ones. He was truly craven. Despicably weak. All he wished was for someone to protect him for a change. He was exhausted of being strong, holding it all together. Keeping all the millennia of accumulated pain bottled inside.

There was that awful whimper again.

He stopped and hid his face in both hands this time, not wanting anyone to see him fall apart, even though the streets were quiet, and there was no one around. He didn't even want the silent night to witness his breakdown. But he couldn't stop it.

One ragged sob escaped.

Then another.

And another.

Until he was bawling uncontrollably on the side of the deserted street, under the flickering light of an ancient lamp.

He'd tried to be his own hero his whole existence. He'd tried to save others too when he could. But in the end, he couldn't save himself. And he'd hurt so many through his terrible deeds.

He didn't deserve happiness. He didn't deserve to live. And he certainly didn't deserve a loving family and a son like Benjamin. He wished he was anyone but himself. He wished he could wear someone else's skin forever.

But he knew the truth. There was no hiding from it.

He knew the ugliness, darkness and brokenness inside. And now, his real face showed it with his countless scars.

He was a monster.

He hated himself.

Everything bad that had happened to him...he deserved it all.

"No."

With a gasp, he raised his face, undisguised, to look into the golden eyes he'd been chasing all this time.

His feet had taken him not to the home he shared with Benjamin, but to his ultimate destination—the man called Sorin.

Sun.

Sol.

Sun.

I miss the flames...the heat...the sun's embrace...Must fly higher to reach it. That golden, wondrous warmth and light...Why can't I ever reach it...

Someone else was in his head, whispering these thoughts, confusing his mind. But now that the thoughts were there, he couldn't shake them. He wanted to stare endlessly into those glowing golden eyes.

He wanted to *burn*.

He knew he must look a fright in his true form. His long black hair in tangles and knots down his shoulders and back. His face like a patchwork quilt, sewn haphazardly together. His mouth had not healed straight, the lips distorted with scars.

Only his eyes were the same.

His father's eyes, except a deeper shade of blue. He was ashamed of everything else about himself save his eyes.

As he stared into the perfect golden orbs of the most beautiful male he'd ever beheld, he felt the contrast between them down to his bones.

Sorin embodied strength, perfection, vitality. He was everything a proud, primal, warrior male should be. Just like Gabriel, Tal and Dalair.

Whereas Ere...

He was nothing.

Less than nothing.

A blubbering, frightened, weakling fool. Next to Sorin, he was Hell's lowest demon to Heaven's brightest angel.

It wasn't fair.

It wasn't fair!

Before he knew what he'd done, he struck the other male with his fists on his chest. Even as a part of him froze with shock at this unprovoked violence, he did it again. Pounded that stone-hard chest with his useless fists with all his might.

He promised!

He promised!

But he'd come too late.

Where was he all this time when Ere needed him? Where was he when he'd been an orphan boy? During the last battle of the Great War? When he'd been captured and recruited by Medusa to perpetrate terrible, horrible things?

Why was he here now?

It was too late!

Ere didn't understand where all these thoughts and emotions came from, but they flooded him all at once. He couldn't help himself.

He thrashed and fought and hit and kicked. Taking all of his fury and pain out on the male who stood still and solid before him.

Sorin didn't move to avoid the immortal-strength blows. He didn't stagger or step back as his body absorbed the beating. When an errant fist caught the side of his face and split his lip on his sharp canines, he merely turned to the side and spat out the blood.

The action, or perhaps the sight of his blood, made Ere abruptly stop, his arms dangling down his sides, hands numb and shaking from the beating they delivered. Chest heaving from the exertion and the violence of his emotions.

Sorin looked down at him (so strange to stand before a male who was actually taller than him in his true form, Ere reflected distantly). He hadn't defended himself and he hadn't struck back. He simply stood there and took it all.

Why didn't he say something?

What did he *want?!*

"You."

It was only the second word the other male uttered all this while.

Ere huffed a humorless laugh.

"You sure about that? Have you *seen* me? Take a good fucking look, man."

He snarled his lips to distort them further, flashing his elongated, gleaming fangs.

"I'm not that pretty boy Binu. And I'm not the sexy siren Erena. You wanna change your stupid fucking line before I take you up on the offer, mate?"

"Come with me."

Wow. Another coherent sentence. Three whole words.

If Ere had the presence of mind, if he hadn't been completely off his rocker, he might have made a scathing, sarcastic comment about Sorin's extensive vocabulary.

As it was, he felt all the fight bleed out of him, leaving him almost too weak to support his own weight.

As he listed to the side, Sorin reached out both hands to steady him by his arms. The heat of the other man's grip seeped through his clothes into flesh and bones.

Gods! He was so warm. Sorin made him so toasty warm.

He'd been cold all his existence. He needed to drink Pure blood to keep his own flowing. He kept fires blazing hotly, and all the lights turned on whenever he could in all of his dwellings, when he'd been his human alter ego.

It was never warm or bright enough. He was ice inside, consumed with darkness.

But Sorin's mere touch set him ablaze. The sudden heat on his icy skin stung. But it was a welcome pain.

After all, he was made to burn...

He wanted him.

Needed him.

He couldn't stand the emptiness. The aloneness. His own weakness.

Please, cruel sun god, fill him with light...

He came to wakefulness slowly, his body pulsing with soreness.

He tried to stretch his limbs, but found that he couldn't. Something hot and steely hard banded around his torso, pinning one of his arms. He was curled on his side, his long hair spread beneath him and down his body, shielding some of his nakedness.

He looked down at himself in the semi-darkness of the nest (and it was *a nest, for the bed of silken feathers he lay upon). What he could see of his body was more or less healed. No more torn flesh around protruding bones. No blood or bruises, only pale, pallid skin.*

There were faint blue lines, and some jagged scars where his top skin knitted together imperfectly, the wounds too severe to heal right even for someone like him. An Immortal who'd escaped more than his fair share of death.

And then, there was the shocking sight of his swollen, pulsing sex, arching straight up past his belly button, the tip ruddy with blood and dewy with moisture.

His brain stuttered.

He wasn't like that. He didn't feel sexual. He never got hard without "help." What could possibly have made him—

Something shifted behind him.

Inside him.

That was when he realized that the pulsing soreness that awoke him wasn't merely from his healing body. It was in his very core, stretched around an enormous, almost unbearably hard intrusion.

It throbbed with its own heartbeat within him; he could feel it. For his heart synchronized with that same beat, his blood flowed to that same rhythm. From his heart, through his arteries, to the rest of his body. To his own stone-hard sex, jutting demandingly against his belly.

For a moment, the realization that someone was inside him made his heart accelerate and thrash in panic.

He didn't want this! He didn't like sex!

He had to get away...but the mission must be done. He had to endure and keep up the pretense. Act like he enjoyed it. Loved it. Beg for it.

But... Wait.

Medusa was gone. Lilith was...not here. He wasn't on a mission. He wasn't ordered to do this.

Then, why—

The living furnace behind him shifted again, nudging deeper into him.

Holy fucking gods! How deep could that thing go? He was pretty sure he already felt it in his tonsils. He couldn't take any more.

And then, he did.

The furnace moved again in a voluptuous undulation and dug even deeper, forcing his anus to stretch to breaking point around an unbearably hard, thick root.

Oh fuck, it hurt.

He could feel himself tearing. Surely he was bleeding all over the place.

But his sensitive skin didn't break. His muscles didn't tear. He adjusted after a moment and automatically clamped down on the intrusion in convulsing shocks.

That...

That felt good.

This time, he did it on purpose, squeezing his core muscles around the silk-clad hardness inside him. And groaned helplessly at the unbelievable burst of pleasure in his dead and murdered ass.

Apparently, his ass was more alive than he thought. Alive enough to throb with pain and...

Wondrous, mind-boggling pleasure.

The deep, resonant groan behind him that vibrated from a stone-wall chest directly into his back, so that he felt the sound lick throughout his body, told him that the furnace liked it too.

How could something that hurt like hell feel so fucking good at the same time?

But if he was getting shafted (literally), then he was going to squeeze (also literally) every last drop of pleasure out of his tormentor.

He bore down and clenched his hole, pulsing his muscles around the monster cock inside him with vicious strength.

The owner of the instrument of torture hissed out what sounded like a garbled curse, pulled back and out of him a few inches, before shoving with brute force even deeper inside.

Uhn.

Good one. That taught him who was boss.

Not.

He shot his hips forward to release the fucking cannon a few inches, then shoved back against the male behind him with surprising strength of his own, grinding down at the root with a manipulative swivel and clenching his core muscles in rippling pulses around every hot steely inch inside.

The male growled long and low, shuddering uncontrollably behind him, caught in an unexpected crisis.

Scalding liquid heat flooded his insides, reaching every nook and cranny. He'd never been this full or felt this filled. He was overflowing with the male's hot cum. He could feel it leak out of him despite the airtight seal of his ass around the other man's sex.

At the same time, the creamy cum lubricated their joined flesh, making him move instinctively upon the heavy staff.

He had to move. He needed the friction. The numbing pleasure now far outweighed the stinging pain.

He began with small, tentative nudges that grew bolder into bucking squeezes and releases as he rode that massive, undying erection. His brain didn't register how he was able to do this. How he even knew to do this. His body had completely overruled his mind. He simply did what felt good.

So, so good.

Every pull and push against that hot, silken, juiced up rod inside him rubbed against something close to the entrance of his body that set his entire system off like fireworks.

He felt like he was flying. Soaring. He wanted to climb higher and higher.

Gods, nothing had ever felt this good!

What was this? He wanted to sob with desperation for the nirvana that seemed just out of reach, even as his body shook and shivered with the onset of his unraveling.

His free hand clawed at something to hold onto. If he was going to splinter apart, then he needed a lifeline. He needed—

One extra-large manly hand wrapped gently around his own near-to-bursting cock, which he'd completely forgotten up to this point.

He gasped at the heat and firmness of the touch. But the hand didn't squeeze or pump him up and down like he hoped. It simply held him as he writhed and wrung out his pleasure on that stupendous cock.

And then, a thumb swept gently across his sensitive cockhead, spreading his moisture around his glans.

That was all it took.

He exploded in a torrent of flames and incandescent sparks, shouting his release, spurting cum in hot gushes endlessly as he clenched convulsively around the hardness inside that felt so euphorically good. He felt it pulse and release as well, filling him anew, even as he emptied himself.

Ah gods! He wanted this feeling to last forever. He felt like he was soaring directly into the sun. He'd finally reached it...those dancing flames...

Just like the ones in the most beloved golden eyes.

*** *** *** ***

Somehow, Ere arrived at his front doorstep without any memory of getting here.

The last thing he recalled was blacking out on the street, his eyes rolling into the back of his head, and feeling strangely unconcerned because two strong hands were holding him up.

He'd instinctively trusted that Sorin would take care of him. And if the stranger he trusted turned out to be a serial-killer who liked to torture his victims, well, it was no better than Ere deserved. And nothing he hadn't suffered through before.

When he opened his eyes, he was standing here, in one piece, and Sorin was nowhere in sight.

Ere swallowed the hard knot of acute disappointment that Sorin hadn't taken him with him.

"Come with me" had apparently meant, "come with me to *your* home." Why he thought he'd be carried off to Sorin's lair for a night of endless orgy, he didn't know.

The man was a blatant tease, gods damn it!

First, the arm porn. Then, the come-hither smoldering looks. Showing up everywhere Ere went, putting temptation after temptation in his path. Using what limited words he had at his disposal to seduce Ere into a puddle of wanton goo, until he was ready to say yes to anything and everything if *Sorin would just fucking take him home!*

And just *fucking take him*, period!

Ere reflexively donned his Erena form when the front door opened to reveal Inanna.

"You're home early...Erena," she greeted, stepping back to let her inside.

"I'm tired," Erena murmured.

"You work too hard," Inanna said. "An eight-hour day-shift starting from 7 a.m., then a six-hour night shift from 6 p.m. It's too much. And you're looking way too thin."

"It's the form," Erena deflected automatically. "I can always make myself look plumper."

"You know that's not what I mean," the Dark warrior returned.

"Come on. Ishtar made chicken pot pie for dinner and chocolate fudge for dessert. We saved a couple big pieces for you."

"I'm not hungry," Erena said wearily.

"Humor me," Inanna insisted. "Keep me company while I have another slice of fudge. We haven't had much...sibling time. But..."

She looked away as if abashed and tucked a wavy golden lock behind her ear.

"I understand if you just want to rest. Or if you want to eat alone. I just wish you'd eat something before bed. Mama Bear's cooking will always make you feel better."

Erena didn't have the heart to say no.

She'd always had a close connection with Benjamin. She'd grown steadily closer to Tal and Ishtar too. But this sister, Ere's *twin* sister, she'd never spent time getting to know.

In a way, Inanna was like Sorin. Sorin was the male Ere could never be, and Inanna was the perfect child to their parents that Ere could never be either.

She was a fierce warrior with a loving heart. She'd led and won the final battle that ended the Great War, freeing all of the Pure Ones from Dark oppression. Tal had started it, and like father like daughter, she'd finished it. She'd been the Dark Queen Jade Cicada's right-hand woman. She was a devoted mother and Mate.

How could anyone compete with that?

"Okay," Erena heard herself say, even though she wanted to kick herself as soon as she said it.

"I'll have a few bites."

Inanna's bright blue eyes lit with happiness, the same eyes Ere had, that they'd both inherited from their father. At least there was one thing they shared in common.

"Wonderful! I'll heat up some pie for you."

She rushed into the large, open kitchen to do just that, while Erena followed behind more hesitantly, settling onto a stool at the counter.

"Where is everyone?" she asked, somewhat panicking that she might be stuck *alone* with this sister she didn't know and was rather in awe of.

"Benji is sleeping. Gabriel, Tal and Ishtar are visiting with the Tiger King. They should be back soon."

Erena wondered why Ishtar or Gabriel didn't stay home with Benji instead of Inanna. She and the General were the most experienced warriors amongst the four.

As if reading her expression, Inanna said, "I volunteered to stay this time, since I was hoping...well, I was hoping for just this actually, right here."

"You want to talk to me?" Erena asked, surprised.

"We never had time to get to know each other, have we? I realized I never created the opportunity."

"It's late..." Erena hedged, stalling. She wasn't sure she wanted a sisterly chat.

"Oh, you don't have to keep me company for long," Inanna immediately offered. "Maybe we can spend some time, just the two of us, on the weekend. You know, girl time."

Erena looked dubiously at her.

"Or guy time," Inanna rushed to add, "whichever you prefer. Benji says you have such an easy-going friendship with Mike at the coffee shop and bar that I thought..."

She trailed off as she laid a steaming plate of chicken pot pie in front of Erena with all the requisite silverware and napkin. She was making an effort, and Erena was being an ass.

Maybe she was a bad person, because she couldn't stop herself from blurting out churlishly, "Mike and I get along because she doesn't really know me. I can pretend to be whoever I want with her. You, on the other hand, know exactly who and what I am. You know the things I've done. I don't know why you want to get to know me. You already do."

Inanna propped her elbows on the counter and gave Erena all of her attention.

To distract herself from the laser blue beams of the warrior's penetrating gaze (and since Inanna's Gift was the ability to see through anything, the description was quite literal), Erena dug into her pot pie.

After watching her eat in silence for a while, Inanna said softly, "Yes, I know some of what you've done. I know you were Medusa's henchman. But I also know, having spoken with Sophia, about the heroic feat you performed at the last battle of the Great War—"

"I didn't do anything," she immediately refuted.

"You did. You took Ninti's place that day. You made yourself a target for the enemy soldiers while giving our outnumbered forces the hope they needed to fight with all their strength against impossible odds."

"I just pretended to be someone I'm not," Erena dismissed. "It's what I always do."

"You knew the risks," Inanna argued fervently, shaking her head. "You knew you could be captured, killed...or worse."

Yes, "worse" was exactly what happened.

Erena twisted her mouth and focused on swallowing the succulent, flavorful food that suddenly tasted like sawdust. "Worse" couldn't have happened to a more appropriate person.

"Well, I survived," she said flippantly. "All's well that ends well."

She was startled into dropping her fork with a clang when Inanna gripped her hand in a fierce hold.

"That's not true. I won't let you belittle what you've sacrificed so that the rest of us could be whole and free. While you lost so much of yourself. That was when Medusa got her claws in you, wasn't it? Tell me please, I want to know what happened."

She tried to pull away, but Inanna held her firm.

She gave a humorless huff and said, "How do you know I didn't *want* it? Maybe I'm just a bad egg and jumped at the first opportunity to flaunt my evil ways. After all, you're the golden child our father kept. I'm the one they th-threw away!"

Inanna's eyes widened with pain, her hold slacking.

"Ere..."

"They didn't even give me a name! I only chose Erebu because Ninti called me that. She said the sunset was her favorite time of the day. I've never been anyone's favorite anything..."

They were both silent for a long time after that outburst. Erena was starting to push away from the table when Inanna's words stopped her.

"You're Benji's favorite uncle," Inanna whispered.

"You're my favorite brother," she added with a tentative smile.

"I'm your only brother," Erena muttered, the burst of anger within her chest deflating.

"See, so special," Inanna said. "My *only* brother. Whom I didn't even know was so close back then. Sophia said you stayed with us for many years at the Pure rebels' base in the Silver Mountains."

"Sophia sure gets around running her mouth about my business," Erena grouched, settling back onto her stool and taking another bite with furious fervor, grinding her jaw as she chewed.

"She was only trying to help us get to know you," Inanna defended gently. "You're not exactly forthcoming even though you've lived here for the past two months. You're definitely no Chatty Cathy."

"Go you," Erena congratulated. "Ancient Akkadian warrior dishing modern slang."

"I'll never be as 'cool' as you, don't worry," Inanna teased. "You'll always be the coolest person in Benji's eyes."

That made Erena feel incredibly proud, so she took another big bite of food.

"I wish I knew who you were back then," Inanna said more seriously. "I wish I could have protected you."

"You liberated thousands of Pure Ones," Erena quipped around a mouthful of pie. "I think you've already overachieved."

There was another bout of awkward silence.

Geez, Erena thought, she could be a real ass. Maybe Inanna finally lost patience with her.

But she was wrong.

"Our parents didn't throw you away, you know," Inanna stated firmly, passionately, brooking no argument.

"You know them well enough by now to believe that, don't you? I don't know all the details, but at the very least it was an impossible time. There had been so many lies, so much pain. And Papa..."

Erena swallowed and hovered her fork over the fudge as a sharp stab of pain bloomed in her chest.

Yes, she knew just how horrifically Tal-Telal had suffered. Her own experiences paled in comparison. Made her ashamed to be such a whiner. Such a weakling.

"Everything he'd been through..." Inanna continued. "Knowing that you're here now, discovering you're alive...I really think it helped him heal. Truly and finally heal. Whatever happened in the past, you should never doubt that we all love you. We want to take care of you, now that we've finally found you, even if it's too little too late. But you have to give us a chance. And you have to give yourself a chance."

Erena dug her fork in for another bite, and was surprised to find that both the large piece of pot pie and the chocolate fudge were gone.

Huh. Guess the conversation worked up an appetite.

"Can we stop talking about such weighty topics? I just ate. You're going to give me indigestion," she complained.

Inanna reached out and squeezed her hand briefly before pushing off the counter to rummage through the cupboards.

"Shall I make some hot chocolate to help you wash the food down? How about the white kind, since you already had fudge?"

"You're very motherly for the Angel of Death," Erena said, referring to Inanna's role when she'd been part of the New England vampire hive.

"Well, I'm trying to be big-sisterly at the moment. How am I doing?"

Erena snorted.

"We don't know who came first, me or you. So I wouldn't be too boastful about that."

"Oh, I'm quite sure I came first," Inanna batted back. "I got all the good traits, after all, and left none for you."

Erena dropped her jaw, blinking like an owl at that KO shutdown.

"Too soon?" Inanna worried her lower lip. "I'm sorry, I was just—"

"You can't get all regretful after a flawless delivery like that!" Erena protested.

"Enjoy it, sister. You won't be getting many more of those in the future now that I've got your number."

Inanna smiled wide, delighted, and set about making hot chocolate for two.

Chapter Seven

"Yukon Territories, close to the Beaufort Sea in the north. On the edge of the Arctic National Wildlife Refuge."

"Are you certain?" the tech master asked by rote, even though he knew that his second wouldn't have given such specific coordinates if he hadn't double and triple checked the information.

"Yes. Shall I report it?"

"Not yet."

Though he couldn't come up with a plausible excuse why not yet. And since this conversation, as with all of the movements of the Mistress's minions, was recorded, he'd better think fast.

"Could be a ruse. We've gotten to the target before. His protectors would take all precautions. Likely they have our corollaries working their side too."

But even if they did, the tech master was the best. They wouldn't be able to hide from him no matter how many smoke screens they threw up. It was why the Mistress "hired" him, after all.

His second knew it too, because there was a silence laden with suspicion on the other line.

"Copy. I'll check again," came the cool reply.

He ended the communication, got up from his wall of screens, pulled on a beanie and sunglasses and headed out.

It was late afternoon on a Saturday in Sydney, Australia, where he was based, so quite a few people were out and about in the busiest shopping district.

He strode leisurely down Pitt Street with his hands in his pockets, whistling an idle tune. Trying to appear casual and harmless, like any other carefree, laid-back Aussie going about his weekend of relaxation.

Except for the fact that the scar on his upper right arm tingled, signaling that his contact was near. He had the same scar, after all.

It looked like an old small-pox vaccine shot that was supposed to have ceased being administered in the 1980s. A round collection of dots near the shoulder, typically the size of a dime.

But their scar, his and his contact's, were not created by the vaccine. Not the least because they were too young to have gotten it, though his contact was a few years older. It had a more distinctive shape if you looked closely enough.

It looked like a dandelion puff.

Which was why they called themselves the Dandelions. Those who knew what they were, anyway. There were tens of thousands more in the world who had no idea what the scar signified. No idea that they were all borne of Lilith's experiments over untold millennia.

They were the survivors. There were millions others who hadn't been so "lucky." Scattered across orphanages far and wide, many by the name of The Little Flower Orphanage in whichever local language based on the countries in which they were located.

They didn't know whether they came from mothers and fathers who still lived or merely from test tubes. Their sperm and egg donors most likely didn't know of their existence either.

Each survivor's scar was unique. It served as a sort of identifying tattoo to help Lilith and Medusa's researchers keep track of them. It also helped the Dandelions keep track of each other, though their creators did not know this. When adult Dandelions were physically close to one another, they could feel each other's presence, like the vibration of a tuning fork.

The tech master had had a plastic surgeon cover up his scar, then tattooed over it to hide it further. But beneath his skin, a subtle pulse remained. He could still feel the presence of a fellow Dandelion.

He sat down at one of the outside tables of a popular café and ordered a beverage, his keen eyes scanning the crowd behind reflective, dark lenses, while his lazy, slouchy pose in the chair belied the intensity of his concentration.

The man he was waiting for walked by him without the slightest acknowledgement. He sat two tables down at the same café and ordered a light repast.

The tech master pulled out his iPhone and plugged the buds into his ears, scrolling down a list of musical selections. As he started the playlist, he switched one of the ear pieces onto a different frequency while the other ear piece blasted some punk rock songs, loud enough to be heard by the waitress as she brought his extra tall mocha cappuccino.

"Great choice!" she shouted at him to be heard over the blast of his music, giving him the thumbs up.

Whether she meant his drink or his music, it wasn't clear, and he didn't care. He merely grinned back at her, making sure several other patrons saw the exchange, and gave her a flirtatious wink.

Meanwhile, in his other ear piece, he heard clearly, "What's new?"

"This song is flaming hot, mate!" he said loudly, banging his head along to the beat of the music.

"So, you've located the phoenix. He's on the move?"

"Right on! Let's party!" He switched to a grungy, techno dance mix.

"He's with the others? Hmm. What role could he have to play in all this? He's never even been on our radar before the Challenge with Ramses."

The tech master changed from a vertical head bang to a horizontal one, shaking his head like he was thoroughly immersed in the music.

"Keep this from the Hydra for as long as you can. We need to buy them more time. My gut tells me that the phoenix is there to help. He could be the key to defeating Lilith."

"Well, that song was pretty *impossible* to beat," the tech master muttered seemingly to himself, scrolling through his iPhone again.

"I know it's getting more and more difficult to evade her spies and probes. But we need more time. *They* need more time. We're working on an answer to the Hydra's next attack, whenever and wherever it should come. But our forces aren't strong enough yet. We need another dragon to fight the Hydra. Nothing else can defeat it. Destroy it once and for all."

The tech master finished the last of his drink and left a few bills on the table. He scanned the area casually and nodded at someone, winked and sauntered off.

Anyone watching his movements would have assumed that he had been looking at the cute waitress, who smiled and waved back as he walked away.

But the other Dandelion received his message loud and clear.

The tech master would do what he could to delay Lilith's discovery of the phoenix's existence and whereabouts. But it was a Herculean task, given how cunning and manipulative she was.

They didn't have much time before she launched the ultimate campaign to crush all who stood in her way.

*** *** *** ***

"I wanna go visit Tiger at the Peak."

Saturday was Ere's day off from work. Sunday was flexible, since Maddie covered at the café and Yas covered at the bar on weekends. He always let Benjamin choose what they would do for the few hours he devoted to the boy's amusement.

Last weekend was ice fishing at the lake. It took some doing for Ere to research how to go about an activity he'd never indulged in before. And if he had his druthers, he'd never indulge in again (he was not the outdoorsy, rough-it-in-nature type). But they managed to survive the excursion, though they came home empty-handed in terms of catches.

The weekend before that was easier, a matinee movie with popcorn and M&Ms. Ere loved movies, especially the animated kind. *Especially* when they involved dragons who were good guys.

The popular re-release they watched was *How To Train Your Dragon: The Hidden World*. Ere *very* especially enjoyed that one since Toothless got the girl. They mated and lived happily ever after by the end, with three little dragons in tow.

How many dragons in film actually "got some"? How many didn't die awful, horrendous deaths?

They always got captured and slayed at worst, flew off into an unknown sunset at best. Look at what happened to the nice dragons from the HBO series *Game of Thrones*. One of the three dragon children (the nicest one) got resurrected as an ice dragon for the harbinger of the end of human civilization—the Night King.

What kind of fate was that?

Unfair, that's what.

Shaking himself loose of unpleasant thoughts, he refocused on his boy and answered, "Of course. Whatever you like."

"Really? Whatever I want to do, and whoever I want to do it with?" Benjamin inveigled.

"Certainly," Ere said.

He didn't like the idea of sharing Benjamin's time with other people, but it seemed churlish and selfish to hog all the time with the little angel for just himself.

"Okay! Let's go! I want to see how Tiger trains his troops. I ran into Logan at lunch yesterday, and he mentioned that it's better than watching *Gladiator*!"

Ere narrowed his eyes.

"Since when do you watch R-rated movies? I am certain your parents wouldn't approve."

"I didn't watch it, silly," Benjamin dismissed. "I know I'm not allowed to. But Logan has, and he says watching Tiger and the Animal Spirits train is *way* more exciting."

"Hmm, I'm not sure Logan should be allowed to watch such violent movies either," Ere mused.

"Well, that's his problem," the boy lifted his shoulders in a shrug. "We can't control everything."

No truer words, and all that.

They put on their coats. Benjamin was bundled much more heavily than Ere and added ear muffs, a wooly scarf and mittens to the ensemble at Ere's insistence.

"Uncle Ere, will you do me a favor?" Benjamin asked.

"I will try," he said.

"Will you go as yourself today, not Binu or Erena or some other form?"

Ere stumbled off balance as he descended the last step from the wrap-around porch.

"I..."

"You can have my scarf to cover your face if you want, but honestly I don't think you need one. You look great just the way you are."

"Benjamin..." he stalled, swallowing thickly.

In moments like these he both loved and hated the boy.

Benjamin always saw more than anyone else. He was the most brilliant boy Ere had ever known. Perhaps the most brilliant person, period.

Which meant that he also knew how to manipulate others to get what he wanted. And he was manipulating Ere now.

He knew Ere would do anything to make him happy, despite the fact that Ere never expressed it in so many words. But it was clear to anyone who saw them together that the boy had him wrapped around his little finger.

But this...

Ere knew that Benjamin could see his real self, could see all of his hideous scars. The boy loved everyone, including the underserving, including monsters. So, his assessment of what looked "great" had to be taken with a grain of salt.

It wasn't that Ere was vain; he *wished* he was beautiful enough to justify vanity. It was simply that his disguises were his armor, his protection. A pretty shell with which to hide the ugliness and emptiness inside.

He couldn't let himself be so exposed. He simply couldn't.

"We don't have to talk to anyone," the boy cajoled, as if reading his mind. "We don't have to let anyone see us. You can wrap yourself in my scarf and borrow Dad's sunglasses. We can go back for them, if you want. With so many layers, no one can see your face anyway. We'll be incognito."

He finished the sentence with air quotes and crowed, "Ha! Always wanted to use that word!"

"I don't—"

"Please, Uncle Ere," Benjamin wheedled, breaking out the big guns—those gorgeous, sky blue, shimmering, limpid, puppy-dog eyes.

"*Pleeeesssee.* I just think you'll be more comfortable in your own skin."

No, he wouldn't.

"And if we run into anyone important, you can always switch to another form."

Well, there was that.

"It's mainly just you and me anyway. And I already see the real you."

There was that, too.

"Even with all the scars, I still think the real you look a thousand times better than fake yous."

"We may need to make you an eye appointment, Benjamin," Ere inserted.

"Soren sees the real you too, and he thinks you're beautiful."

Say what?!

Ere stumbled again as they walked toward the Peak, which was a good four miles away from the house. Normally, they would have asked Inanna or Gabriel to drive them to their destination, but the day was forecasted to be sunny, and the air was dry. The cold was bearable, and they both loved to walk.

But Ere suddenly felt the urge to sit down on the nearest dry patch of ground and collect himself. They hadn't even made it out of town yet and he was already out of breath.

"Wha-whatever do you mean? Explain yourself, Benjamin Larkin D'Angelo," he wheezed.

The boy groaned.

"Not you too, Uncle Ere. Parading out my full name. What did I say? Mom and Dad only use it when I'm in trouble."

"S-Soren. I mean, his name isn't Soren. It's Sorin with an i."

Ere shook his head when Benjamin opened his mouth to interject. He needed to keep the boy on topic before he dove down a tangential rabbit hole.

"What do you mean he sees the real me?"

What do you mean he thinks I'm beautiful?

"Well, when I got to be friends with him after school way back when—"

"You mean two days ago, on *Thursday*," Ere reminded him.

"Yes, *way* back when," Benjamin emphasized, completely missing the point. Or choosing his own interpretation.

"When I told him I'm waiting for my uncle to pick me up, he asked if I was waiting for the handsomest blue-eyed man in the world—"

"He did not! Benjamin, don't lie!"

Ere flushed crimson with acute embarrassment and anger.

He shouldn't get so riled because of the boy's words; he knew he shouldn't. Benjamin was only a boy. Boys exaggerated and made things up. In any other situation, he would have humored him and played along.

But... this was too important to Ere. The words felt like salt rubbed into fresh, bloody wounds. He just...he cared too much.

It mattered. It fucking mattered to him so much, and he hated that it did.

The boy blanched as his big eyes rounded even more, staring at Ere with a stricken expression.

"I'm not lying," he whispered. "I'm sorry I hurt you, Uncle Ere. Please don't be mad."

Ere started walking briskly again, shaking his head, clenching and unclenching his fists to steady his hands.

"I-I'm the one who should apologize, Benjamin. I do. I apologize. I don't know what came over me. Just...let's forget it and start over, shall we? I'll be myself today. I won't hide. Anyone who wants to take a good look at this Frankenstein's freak, they can have at it."

"But—"

Ere wrapped an arm around the boy's shoulder and split his face in a teeth-baring grin.

"Come on. We'll strategize the best way to spy on those warrior Beasts. What Kind is your favorite? Eagles, cats or snakes? Now me, I'm big fan of..."

Rattling off pros and cons for each type of Animal Spirit and engaging Benjamin in a heated, detailed discussion, Ere successfully distracted the boy from their first-ever row.

He was still afraid of being seen for what he was. But he knew, for his boy's sake, that he needed to start facing his fears.

How else was he going to protect Benjamin when the end finally came?

*** *** *** ***

Sorin watched the mock battles from his higher, hidden vantage point on one of the jagged ledges on the mountainside.

On the tallest peak of the mountain, tucked into a small cave beneath a flat stone overhang, was the temporary nest he'd made for himself over the past few days since his arrival in these parts. A couple of tenacious Labrador tea bushes shielded the cave's entrance, providing additional privacy and protection from the harsh winter elements, as well as a snack for Sorin.

He chewed a few leaves now as he watched.

Given it was the wrong season, they didn't taste great, more bitter than sweetly floral. But he made do.

While he had learned to interact with humanoids without raising too much suspicion and alarm, he naturally gravitated toward simple animal living. He'd take out-of-season edible plants over processed carbohydrates any day, every day.

It was a good thing he had something to gnaw on too. Because the training below was making him want to grind his teeth in frustration.

Half of the so-called warriors in the Tiger King's eclectic collection were Lesser Beasts—the weakened combination of animal spirits and other Kinds, whose preferred form was humanoid. Some of them weren't even...*natural*. There was something wrong with them.

Animal Spirits only existed in predatory cat, large birds of prey, and snake forms. But in the field below, there were grotesque-looking half-wolf, half-human creatures, one very large, very hairy man whose animal form had yet to be revealed, and other strange monstrosities that reminded Sorin of eons ago when gods ruled the world with their magic and fantastical beasts.

Except these creatures seemed *forced*, not created by the magic that existed in nature, in the universe, but by "science." The invention of humans.

The other half of the Tiger King's animals were Beasts, but most of them were untrained. They had the instinctive fierceness, but they weren't coordinated. They couldn't work together, and they weren't disciplined.

They let their animal instincts rule them, overly aggressive when their "fight" came in, but too quick to fall back when they felt the urge for "flight." This militia (and Sorin used the term generously) wouldn't stand a chance against a concerted attack by organized forces, be they human or Immortal Kind.

The attack *would* come. It was only a matter of time.

From the few exchanges he'd had with the Tiger King, he knew this to be true. They both felt it instinctively.

To Goya's credit, instead of choosing to run and scatter as animal spirits had done for many millennia since their numbers had dwindled from wars and hunts, he chose to stand his ground. He was preparing to defend his new home and the people within his territories.

This was especially surprising coming from a Tiger Spirit, whose very nature was solitary. But perhaps the Mating had changed him. Or perhaps Goya was simply one of a kind.

Nevertheless, the militia was still too weak. They were mostly large cats that dominated on land, but these mountains and plains were close to the sea and boasted several large rivers and lakes. They needed stronger water-bound warriors, but there were very few Snake Spirits.

Most of all, they were vulnerable to aerial attacks. If humans sent their drones and aircrafts to bomb these lands, there was nothing they could do. Fortunately, the likelihood was relatively small, given that those who knew about their existence were just as incentivized to keep it a secret as they were.

But Sorin would not rule out such an assault entirely, for he barely survived the one that led to his rebirth on Mount St. Helens. Somehow, the humans covered up that incident entirely. No doubt they could do the same if they were so inclined to invade these territories.

Regardless, the fact was that the Tiger King had no winged cavalry to either defend their position or to launch an aerial offensive if enemies were to invade from land and sea.

There were only a couple of birds in the group. One small, young falcon, nowhere near the stature of the eagles Sorin used to command. The other was an Andean condor. He was a large fucker, to be sure, but condors were scavengers by nature. They weren't nearly as aggressive as eagles. None of the raptors were.

Which was why only eagles could be kings of the sky, while different kinds of snakes could be kings of water domains, and occasionally a lion could lead a small pride where tigers weren't available or didn't want the responsibility. It was also why, when the three groups worked together in the war of the gods to battle foes in all domains, eagles always led the charge.

Humans didn't realize that their concept of archangels who fought back the devil and his demons was based on Eagle Spirits. Especially the later appearance of Lesser Beasts who could take the form of a winged man.

The Tiger King was right. They needed an aerial commander.

They needed Sorin.

He spat out his bitter tea leaves with enough force to make a small pebble leap from the ground in fright.

This was why he preferred solitude and seclusion. He didn't want to become embroiled in other people's battles. Other people's wars.

He'd had enough fighting to last to eternity. He'd paid his dues. Paid them dearly. He'd lost everything a male could possibly lose.

His men. His kingdom. His cause. His pride.

His life and identity. His very sanity.

Most of all, his *purpose*.

The spark for his soul. The soul he needed to *live*.

Without his bane at his side, he might as well have never been reborn...

Untold millennia ago, Age of the Gods.

Harpy battalion gaining fast behind us. Gargoyles dead ahead.

Sol soared higher, above the clouds, to expand his view of the aerial battle in full gory progress.

His Bane was leading the charge for the rest of the eagle formation as he always did in the decade since he'd come into his full size and powers—

Which he displayed now by opening his jaws to unleash a continuous torrent of pale blue flames at the army of gargoyles that blocked their path. Agonized shrieking ensued as several dozen enemy soldiers burned to ashes or plummeted from the sky from mortal wounds.

But several dozen still remained. And while the Bane recharged his powers, he brute forced his way into the enemy gods' defensive lines by colliding directly into their ranks, sharp teeth and claws leading the way.

Watch your rear! *Sol shouted through their mind link as he dove into the fray to tear a few gargoyles off of his Bane's tail.*

That's your job, *the Bane smirked.* Since you're always behind me.

With that, he swatted several gargoyles with one wing while bashing a few more with a mighty swing of his thorned tail, almost taking Sol's head off in the process.

Oops! Didn't see you there.

Little fucker.

(Except he wasn't so little any more, being thrice the size of Sorin in giant eagle form).

Like hell the Bane didn't know he was there. He always knew where Sol was. Their synchronization in battle was legendary. Sol was like an extension of the dragon's body and vice versa.

Sol didn't have time to berate him while he turned around to engage the harpies that had gained on them.

Gods and their monsters. The Twins weren't unique in their creative endeavors. As if command of rain, wind, thunder and lightning wasn't enough, they had to make flying uglies to fight the Eagle Beasts.

On the ground, the Cat Spirits fought giants and trolls with one eye, two eyes, hundreds of eyes. One head, two heads, many more heads. Same with limbs and other things. And in lakes, rivers and seas, Snake Spirits fought giant, man-eating squids, worms the size of whales and other bizarre monstrosities.

Fortunately, the Twins created Dragons of Sky, Earth and Sea to lead the Animal Spirits of their respective domains against the endless enemy onslaught. Unfortunately, with each battle they won, each new monster they eliminated, the other gods contrived to create even more—bigger, uglier, with stronger powers.

Sol had been born into the war of the gods. He'd never known peace in his life. And even though he didn't know any different and was exceptionally good at what he did—being the First General of the Eagle Spirits and their best warrior—he didn't live for battle as some of his brethren did.

He was tired. With every battle he grew wearier.

When would this end?

Was there an end?

Couldn't the gods just fight each other and leave their creatures out of this?

But he knew in the back of his mind why they didn't. He wasn't naïve.

With the powers gods had, a direct clash would likely end all civilization and life as they knew it. Perhaps everything would return to Darkness and Light. Nothingness and Chaos.

This was why he fought. He couldn't let that happen.

If it did, there would be no more Bane.

And though he complained fervently and consistently how he wished for peace and quiet without the Bane dogging his heels with every step, he couldn't imagine a world without the pesky dragon. Somehow, the overgrown, winged, ugly thing mattered to him.

Four harpies managed to attach themselves to his wings and tail with their sharp claws, tearing bloody streaks into him, effectively refocusing his attention on the battle at hand.

He lost one with a sudden dive and roll. Loosened another enough to crush it in his iron claws. But the last two tenaciously held on, tucking themselves out of reach and digging with long daggers into his flesh, beneath the tough protection of his feathery hide.

One of them steadily drew near his left eye. If it blinded an eye, he'd be useless. His soldiering days were done for.

He dove and spun, shot high, then low, trying to shake the harpies off, but it wasn't working. They only got closer to his vitals.

Suddenly, a blast of scalding heat engulfed him from behind. The harpies screamed shrilly in pain, all but blowing out his eardrums, before they disintegrated into dirty ash.

Sol, however, was merely a bit charred. Blackened but not burned. Though one of his tail feathers was still on fire.

Hmm. Might have overdone that one a bit, *the Bane of his existence murmured in his mind.*

He could feel the dragon behind him, practically panting on his ass.

Want me to blow that out for you? *the Bane asked solicitously.*

Fucker, *he muttered.*

Aww, I love you too, *the dragon cooed in return.*

He persisted in taking every insult Sol ever threw at him as an endearment. It was most infuriating.

Sol ignored him, making a sharp turn to head back into battle, but the Bane playfully caught his tail feathers between his dragon teeth and pulled him back.

The harpies and gargoyles have mostly scattered. Our eagles can take care of the rest. We won, Solemnity! Let's go celebrate!

Stop calling me that, *Sol growled out of habit, though he knew it was pointless.*

The Bane had been calling him ridiculous names for countless summers, after all. He'd never admit it out loud or mentally to anyone, but he rather enjoyed them.

Come on, Seriousness, let's clean off the gore in the waterfall.

Their hidden waterfall.

They found it recently when the Bane finally learned how to transform into humanoid form.

Verily, Sol didn't know he could until he dashed into a cavern one day to avoid the Bane while the dragon huffed and puffed in aggravation upon the rock facing on the other side because he was too big to come after Sol. Sol was laughing in triumph when there was a sudden white flash at the entrance of the cave that left a pale, tall man tangled in ankle-length white hair standing befuddled and dazed where there used to be a dragon lurking like a thwarted storm cloud outside.

Sol's first thought had been: he was the most beautiful creature he'd ever seen.

The Bane's first thoughts in his new form had been: Ha! Now there's nowhere you can run or hide that I can't catch you! Ready or not, here I come!

A clumsy chase ensued, where the Bane stumbled and fell over his own hair many times while he learned to use his bipedal form, and Sol had to resist helping him up every time he crashed that fragile human body into the hard, stone ground of the cavern. He was equally besieged by worry and laughter at the Bane's antics.

But he hadn't laughed at all when they found the waterfall within the cavern and bathed and swam and played in the pool. He'd been...

Confused. Disturbed. Amused.

And most of all—

Aroused.

Since then, they came to the waterfall often. It was their place. Their escape. As if submerging themselves under the falls and beneath the pool could wash away the stain of death just as cleanly as the blood and gore.

The Bane flew ahead of him with a mighty flap of those bat-like wings, taunting Sol with a wagging of his thorned tail to hurry and catch up. Sol grinned his eagle grin and flew faster, riding the dragon's tailwind.

As they approached the hidden opening of the mountainside, the dragon deftly shifted into man, landing gracefully onto the stone ledge as if he was walking out of a dream. Sol followed close behind, landing more forcefully and heavily behind him.

In this form, he was larger, taller and far more muscular than the Bane. For all the dragon made fun of him when he was three times as big in winged form, Sol traded insults right back in humanoid form.

What do you eat that you are still so thin as a twig? *he badgered now as he walked behind the Bane's pale figure.*

That hair of yours must be half your weight.

You love my hair, *the Bane quipped readily.* You love running your fingers through it, so it's a good use of body mass.

Sol harrumphed in denial, but it was true.

He loved the Bane's silky, moon-spun hair. Loved to feel it glide over his own skin. Dreamed about wrapping it around his fist and arm as he pulled back on it like the reins on a newly bridled Pegasus as he pounded into—

What are you thinking about? *the Bane chose that moment to look behind him, catching Sol in the middle of his torrid fantasy, making him stumble over nothing.*

Nothing, *he lied.*

Liar, *the Bane accused without heat, smiling angelically at him before turning back around.*

Sol cast his eyes heavenward to thank the gods for small favors.

One, the Bane's perfectly round, muscular rear end (the part of him besides his hair that got disproportionate weight, no doubt) was covered by the long, white skeins.

Sol had seen that naked ass. He knew how he reacted when he did. So it was probably a good thing said ass was covered right now.

Two, the Bane hadn't looked down when he turned around just then. If he did, he would have seen Sol's raging erection.

Not that the Bane hadn't seen it before. Sol was always amped up after battle. Since the day the Bane had interrupted his attempt to rut out the adrenaline high, he hadn't had another opportunity.

The Bane had made sure that every time, it was he who brought Sol down from the high. He would chase Sol through the skies, taunt and make Sol chase him back, mock fight him until he was so exhausted, he'd collapse the moment he landed on solid ground.

That didn't mean Sol's erection always deflated like the rest of him. But the sight of it never seemed to bother the Bane. It was as if he still thought of the thing as Sol's "sword," as if it was separate and independent from Sol himself. He didn't understand what it meant when the "sword" grew harder and thicker and even more erect whenever Sol looked upon him in humanoid form.

But today would be the day that the Bane finally learned.

Chapter Eight

It's leaking.

Sol was lying flat on his back on the bank of the pool, one arm tucked beneath his head, the other folded on his stomach.

He was clean, relaxed, and bone-tired. The only part of him that wasn't completely depleted was of course his stupid staff. It bobbed insistently against the tight drum of his stomach, the head swollen and aching.

And, yes, leaking his essence all over the place.

Ignore it.

He did. *He'd ignored the sexual part of himself for so long he barely recalled what release felt like.*

The Dark, aggressive side of his nature got its expression in battle. When he was peaceful like this, with his Bane, he let the animal spirit come through. He treated the Bane with the same unexpectant innocence and purity that the Bane used with him.

Well, he tried, anyway. And succeeded.

Most of the time.

But it's nodding at me, like it's trying to tell me something. And the little mouth is opening and closing like it's trying to speak.

Sol's entire body tensed into stone when the Bane dragged a fingertip from the root of his sex to the plump, needy tip.

He didn't move otherwise, however. This, too, he had trained himself to endure.

The Bane was always curious, and this wasn't the first time he'd touched Sol like this.

It was just that he didn't know what he was doing. His curiosity was always innocent, like a child with a toy. Thus, Sol had to forcibly tamp down more prurient urges. The Bane wouldn't understand.

Sol's poor beleaguered sexual organs didn't understand the torture either, dumb as they were, but Sol would cut them off himself before doing anything to wreck the Bane's innocence.

Or maybe it's hungry. Like a baby bird. It definitely wants something.

Sol heaved a put-upon sigh.

Maybe if he acted annoyed, the Bane would lose interest and flit to a different, less dangerous topic.

It's a part of my body, you know, *he grouched.* It's not a separate entity. Stop talking to it like it has a mind of its own.

But it's talking to *me, the Bane insisted.* And I think it's fascinating *because* it's a part of you.

Sol tried to turn to his side and end this ridiculous conversation more pointedly, but the Bane put two large hands on his hips and held him down with surprising strength.

Well, it shouldn't be surprising. The Bane was a sky dragon after all, whose animal form was thrice as big as Sol. His could obviously continue to harness that strength even in humanoid form. Sol was tempted to see who would be the victor if they wrestled in this form.

But right now, he let the Bane have his way. He remained flat on his back while the dragon held him by the hips. His eyes were closed, but he could feel his Bane's hot gaze upon his sex. It felt...different.

Something had changed.

I saw two lions mating yesterday, *the Bane suddenly blurted.*

Sol tried not to react. This thread of thought could go anywhere. The Bane's mind worked in mysterious ways.

You've seen animals mating before, *he pointed out nonchalantly.*

Yes, *the Bane agreed.* I never understood why males occasionally felt the need to stick their tool into a willing hole.

Because it felt good. But Sol wasn't going to enlighten him. He could learn that on his own, if and when the time ever came.

Looks messy.

Eh. Not in Sol's experience. You just stick it in, find release as fast as you can, then pull it out. Minimal fuss. Especially when you held the willing receiver still, which he never had any trouble doing.

But yesterday, after they came together in animal form, they changed into humanoid form and did it some more.

Hmm. That was unusual. Perhaps one or both of the participants had a Pure, Dark or human base form.

Over the years, the Twin Goddesses had mixed more Kinds together, trying to create stronger combinations. Their creations even mated naturally to produce even more mixed offspring.

Those "Lesser Beasts" as his Kind was starting to call them, preferred their humanoid forms. And in those forms, they did have a tendency to copulate more than necessary, not just for the sake of procreation and physical release.

They enjoyed it.

Sol didn't understand the draw himself, so he wasn't going to be helpful explaining it to the Bane if the dragon pursued that line of thought.

It looked kind of...nice.

How long did you watch? You shouldn't be spying on your comrades, *Sol admonished.*

They were doing it out there in the open field where anyone could see, *the Bane defended himself.*

I just wanted to see how this part worked.

Sol's muscles jumped when the Bane drew a finger lightly up and down his length again, this time rubbing his thumb around the painfully sensitive crown, slicking him with his own essence.

He manacled the Bane's wrist in an unyielding grip, holding his hand away from his throbbing, aching member.

The Dark side of him surged to the fore. His fangs punched through his upper gums with the intent to strike. The need and pressure inside him hurt so much it was almost unbearable.

Don't, *he warned through gritted teeth.*

But...but I want...

The Bane sputtered uncertainly.

He was never hesitant, always supremely confident and always a pain in Sol's ass.

The disappointment and confusion in the Bane's voice made Sol open his eyes finally and look at him.

Gods above! What a vision.

The Bane was kneeling between Sol's spread thighs, sitting on his heels. His ankle-length hair wrapped around his body like the finest silken robe. Even the gods could not wear better. The moonlight tresses glowed even in the darkness of the cave, as if they retained a light of their own, illuminating his pale, almost translucent skin.

His sapphire eyes shone brightly as well, like twin stars lighting the way. Right now, they were focused intently on Sol. There was a look of...something indefinable on the Bane's face.

Rapture. Longing. Exultation. Greed.

It was a painful combination. And it was so beautiful, Sol couldn't look away if he tried. He wanted desperately to ease that pain and turn it into pleasure. He wanted his Bane always to be happy.

What do you want? he asked quietly when the Bane didn't, couldn't, finish his thought.

The dragon swallowed, bobbing his throat, a hypnotically smooth undulation in his long, strong neck.

Sol's body burned hotter to witness it. His sex jerked and leaked some more.

Fucking hell! What was happening to him?

Instead of answering him directly, the Bane suddenly flicked those gemstone blue eyes to Sol's and asked, Have you ever mated before?

Sol answered truthfully, the only way he knew how, I've rutted before. I haven't taken a Mate. That would be...I am not ready.

But he was ready, a hidden part of himself whispered.

He staunchly ignored it.

I only remember you trying to rut once, the Bane frowned and scrunched up his face, as if the recall left a bitter taste in his mouth.

Have you rutted when I couldn't see?

To another male, this line of questioning might have sounded accusatory or overly invasive, but Sol never tried to hide anything from his Bane. He'd always given the dragon free reign over everything that was his, including his time, his energy and his person.

No. I haven't rutted since you...came along, he answered honestly.

Good, *the Bane said with a firm nod of his head.*

The expression on his face was rather fierce, as if he considered Sol his property and didn't like the idea of the warrior engaging in intimate physical activities with others.

*Sol didn't know how he felt about that. Everything he had he gave freely to the Bane, but...*this *kind of possessiveness over his person was new. It made his stomach tighten and his heart beat faster.*

They were venturing into uncharted territory.

Did you rut a lot before I came along?

No.

So how many then?

I don't make a habit of counting.

A hundred?

Sol rolled his eyes, so exasperated he loosened his grip on the Bane's wrist.

Fifty?

Sol sighed and closed his eyes again, hoping his silence would make the Bane stop this pointless interrogation.

What did it matter anyway? It was all in the past. Sol could barely recall. It had been over a century! Not since the Bane had become his responsibility.

And if he didn't instinctively know that the Bane would be hurt by his rutting, if only because he was giving his attention to someone else, he might have discreetly found some release over the years. But the Bane had always distracted him with his exuberant, child-like energy, and Sol's own instincts held him back.

Twenty? Would I be able to count them with both my fingers and toes? *the Bane persisted.*

I know how to count to twenty, *Sol muttered, frowning with annoyance.*

So? Count them for me. I want to know.

You're ridiculous.

But I want to know.

I don't remember.

Try.

Why does it matter! *Sol finally exploded, eyes open and blazing.*

The Bane was wearing his usual innocent, wide-eyed look. Except this time, there was a stubborn, determined gleam in his eyes.

He'd crossed his arms over his chest and was staring down at Sol like he wasn't budging from his spot until Sol enumerated all of the faceless, nameless birds he'd jabbed with his tool.

Fuck.

Less than twenty, more than ten, *Sol threw out, because he truly had no idea, it had been so long ago.*

The number was probably closer to ten, maybe even below double-digits, but whether it was one or one hundred, it simply didn't matter. None of that mattered.

Only the Bane mattered.

Immediately, the Bane deflated like the wind was knocked out of him, his entire face so crestfallen it was comical.

Except, Sol didn't feel like laughing.

Probably closer to ten, *he added.*

The Bane's lower lip started to protrude and quiver, his long, silky lashes fluttering down to shield his shimmering blue eyes.

Fuckity fuck!

Definitely less than ten, *Sol amended.*

The Bane sniffled once. Twice.

Sol knifed up into a sitting position and grasped the Bane on both upper arms, trying to hold the man together given how hard he seemed to be shivering.

Come on, dragon, *he coaxed.* It doesn't matter. It was just...it was a long time ago. I don't even remember. It was—

But I want to be the one you do that with! *the Bane wailed, throwing his head back and bawling like a lost little boy, big, grape-sized tears pouring from his eyes.*

I want to be the one to make you feel good! I don't want you to spend time with anyone but me! Touch anyone but me! And I don't want anyone to touch you but me!

Completely lost as to what to do, Sol awkwardly pulled the Bane into his arms and embraced him loosely at first, then more tightly.

They weren't ever physical like this. They only played and fought. This was...Sol didn't have the words to describe it.

Even though logically, he thought the Bane was being completely irrational. Emotionally, his heart hurt that his Bane was hurting. Even if the hurt was irrational, he wanted to do everything in his power to eradicate it. If he could go back in time and erase the few occasions when he let his Dark side have the lead, he would.

There's no one but you, *he soothed now, the words pouring out without conscious thought.*

No one matters but you. You are my entire world, you stupid dragon. You know that.

The Bane shuddered and hiccupped, his active bawling finally dying down, though the tears continued to run.

Promise.

What?

Promise I'm the only one. That I'll always be the only one.

Sol sighed.

I promise. You'll always be my Bane.

And if anything ever separates us, you'd wait for me. Promise.

I promise, *Sol replied obediently, smoothing his hands comfortingly down the Bane's back.*

And if one day...if I ever break, you'll put me back together and fix me. And you'll love me no matter what. Only me.

Sol's hands stilled. His heart and breaths slowed.

Something dark and oppressive weighed down on him. It felt like the heavy hand of Destiny.

Why would the Bane say such things? What had happened that he would need these promises?

As if they would *be separated. As if the Bane* would *break.*

Despite the natural heat of their bodies, Sol felt cold for the first time in his existence.

I promise, *he vowed.*

He'd say anything to ease his Bane. But he also meant every word.

He loved his Bane. Loved him in all ways.

This dragon was the spark for his soul. He wasn't alive without him.

Gradually, the Bane calmed, his tears drying. He stayed in Sol's embrace and sighed with contentment, nuzzling his face into Sol's throat, breathing in his scent in great, desperate gulps.

I want...

What, little dragon? What do you want?

I want you, Sol. My Sol. My *Soul*.

You have me. You always have and you always will.

I want more.

The Bane disengaged from Sol's embrace and slowly pushed him back to lie flat on the ground once more.

Sol's breath hitched in his throat when he saw the naked, scorching need in the Bane's far-from-innocent eyes. He was no longer a dragonling. He was fully grown.

And he wanted.

I want *this*.

Without preamble, the Bane took hold of Sol's heavy sex in one hand, his balls in the other. He squeezed both gently, but with unmistakable possession.

Then take them, *Sol rasped.* They're yours.

He slowly stacked both arms beneath his head and tensed his muscles one by one, reveling in the Bane's rapt, covetous attention on his body, practically salivating at the ripple of hard muscle beneath his taut, smooth skin.

I'm all yours.

*** *** *** ***

"He's here, Uncle Ere! Soren's here!"

Ere snapped his attention from the training field to the man emerging in long, brusque strides from the shadows of the mountain that cut into the valley.

Praise the gods, but the male could walk. His gait powerfully smooth, confidence and control etched in every step.

Dressed only in a thin, dark grey Henley and worn-looking pants that molded to his lower body almost indecently when he moved (oh happy day! No underwear!), the sight of the beautiful stranger made Ere's pulse race.

And made his heretofore dead and buried reproductive parts perk up and take notice as effectively as if the warrior had been entirely naked.

On that thought, saliva flooded his mouth, which had been hanging open since he caught sight of the mysterious man.

He shut his trap with an audible snap before the drool could dribble out and said, "It's Sorin with an 'i,' Benjamin. It means 'sun.'"

"Really?"

The boy's eyes immediately lit with curiosity.

"I'll Google it when I get home. But I still think Soren with an 'e' suits him too. It means 'severe.' Don't you think it fits? He's just so serious all the time. I don't think I've ever seen him smile."

"You've known him how long again?" Ere reminded him.

"Over eighty-six thousand seconds!" Benjamin immediately responded. "It's like *forever*!"

Ere rolled his eyes heavenward. Why did he ever think he could win an argument with the boy?

"And in all that time, he never once smiled," Benjamin said.

"You weren't with him in all that time."

Apparently, Ere couldn't resist a good argument. He wanted to win just once, damn it!

"Maybe he was dancing a jig in the coffee shop. Maybe he laughed so hard he got a belly ache at the bar. *I* spent more time with him than you, my boy. I know better."

Benjamin looked at him slyly.

"You like him a lot, don't you, Uncle Ere? You can't stop looking at him."

Ere sputtered, opening his mouth to object, even though for the life of him he couldn't tear his gaze away from the approaching goliath of a man.

"And I bet he was serious the whole entire time!" Benjamin crowed.

Come on, Solemnity! Catch me if you can...

The whisper of a distant echo flitted like a drunken moth through his mind.

Ere was distracted enough that he blinked rapidly, shaking his head, and didn't notice how close Sorin had gotten until the male's exotic scent and heat wrapped around him like embracing flames.

Could flames be *embracing*?

"Hi, Sorin with an 'i'!" Benjamin chirped eagerly. "What are you doing here? Do you know the Tiger King? Do you know about the animal spirits? But you must, if you're here, right? Are you one of them?"

As usual, the man was sparse with his words. As in, he simply didn't answer. Instead, he stared at Ere with those intense golden eyes.

Ere stared back, frowning, refusing to be the first to look away.

Let him stare all he liked. Ere knew how he looked.

Zig-zag scars crossed all over his face, distorting his features like a broken mirror. His long, dark hair probably resembled a rat's nest. (Not that he'd observed how rats nested before, but...)

He pulled back his shoulders and stood straighter, using every inch of his six and a half feet height. These were battle wounds. He had nothing to be ashamed of. Sorin wasn't to know that the jumbled mess on the outside now reflected the ugliness on the inside.

He drew in a deep breath and puffed up his skinny chest, trying his best to imitate a Magnificent Frigatebird (yes, that's actually what they're called) with its bright red, magnificent chest.

Until he remembered that the males only did this during the mating ritual.

Shit. He didn't want to send the wrong signal. He certainly wasn't looking for a mate!

As Ere struggled within himself, Sorin kept on staring, not saying a word.

He, by contrast, didn't have to puff up anything. He was plenty puffed up already.

Though "puff" was certainly not the right word for the slabs of stone heaped upon ropes of steel that he passed off as a flesh and blood body. His natural stance was military straight, imposing, unyielding. His shoulders wider than any Ere had ever seen, even on a man of his height.

Those long, tree-like legs led to a ridiculously well-developed backside, Ere could spy out the corner of his eye. The likes of which he had only seen on prized thoroughbred stallions. (Not that he ogled stallions as a rule. But after millennia of existence, well, one noticed things.)

All that was to say, Sorin did not need to puff, buff or polish anything. He was quite indisputably the most beautiful man in the world. In the universe.

At least, to Ere. Whose appreciation of beauty was vast and considered.

"Umm, so…This is my Uncle Ere, Sorin," Benjamin said between them, looking from one very tall male to the other even taller male.

"I know," the warrior deigned to grunt.

And Ere realized with a slight widening of eyes that he did.

Somehow, though he couldn't imagine how, Sorin *knew* him. Saw through his disguises and various forms.

Had he seen Ere's true self all this time? Scars and all?

"You—"

"Yes," Sorin cut in before he could ask the question or make the accusation.

"How…"

"I know," the confounded male repeated.

Then added, "But you do not."

Another whole sentence! If only Ere understood what he meant!

"See here—" he began.

But Sorin abruptly turned away, completely dismissing him.

He strode purposefully toward the mock battlefield as the Tiger King intercepted him midway. The two warriors exchanged some serious telepathic communication. Ere could only see them in profile, but both of their expressions and postures looked aggressive and argumentative.

Involuntarily, he felt a pinch of worry.

Sorin was no doubt a badass alpha who could handle himself, but he was confronting the fucking Tiger King, for fuck's sake!

Even if Benjamin's deductions were correct, that Sorin was one of them, an Immortal Kind, that there was Goya, the freaking Tiger King! Any normal person would at least show a modicum of respect.

As if Sorin heard his thoughts and was purposely being contrary, he displayed even more stupid male posturing by crossing his muscle-roped arms over his muscle-mounded chest.

Lordy.

146

Ere wiped his suddenly sweat-sheened brow.

How did it get so hot in below-freezing temperatures? Why were there so many muscles everywhere he looked? And on one male in particular?

"Don't worry, Uncle Ere," Benjamin soothed, misinterpreting Ere's discomfiture.

"They might look like they're arguing, but I can tell Tiger and Sorin will become the best of friends. They're really a lot alike. And Tiger's cool while Sorin's hot. So they balance each other out. You'll see."

Instead of putting him at ease, Ere's tension ratcheted up.

What did Benjamin mean they would become the best of friends? If anyone was going to be Sorin's best of anything, it was going to be h—

Ere cut off the thought before it could finish forming in his head.

Now where did that ridiculous notion come from?

"Hurrah! Look at those wings! Sorin's teaching the troops how to fend off an aerial attack!"

Ere snapped his gaze to the action.

Sorin. In the sky. Armed with a spear in one hand and a sword in the other.

Wings. Massive, gold, flame-tipped wings flapped from his back.

He looked like a mighty archangel of heaven as he unleashed the spear upon an unlucky trainee in the field below, then charged at another group with sword raised.

"I guess he's a Lesser Beast."

Ere barely heard Benjamin's boyish enthusiasm beside him, completely mesmerized by the sight he was witnessing.

But he had the wherewithal to answer, "Dear boy, I highly doubt that man is a 'lesser' anything."

No. Sorin was *more*.

He was always so much more.

"But I thought only Lesser Beasts can transform into a man with wings? Or other parts of their body into animal form, in addition to the whole body? Sorin has wings on his back. Look! He just transformed his feet into claws! That means he must be a Lesser Beast. Doesn't it?"

Ere frowned.

Sorin's winged man form was certainly magnificent and deadly as hell. But for some reason, he didn't think this was the warrior's ultimate form. And somehow, he was absolutely certain that Sorin wasn't a Lesser Beast.

"Wow," Benjamin continued to gush beside him, watching the mock battle display with rapt attention.

"I've never seen wings like his before. They're so wide! Much bigger than any of the other Lesser Eagles."

"Remember Rhys? He helped rescue me from Lilith. He's a Golden Eagle, I learned from Uncle Tal. His wings are maybe half the span of Sorin's. And his feathers! They look like they're made of metal, except they also look so soft at the same time. How is that possible? Metal is supposed to be hard."

Ere had no idea. His brain wasn't quite working at the moment. It was certainly too slow to keep up with the brilliant boy.

He could only watch unblinkingly as Sorin engaged half of the Tiger King's trainees all at once. Two raptor spirits in the sky. More than a half dozen cats on the ground. His golden feathers flashed brightly in streaks of sunlight, blinding some of his opponents. The flaming tips practically crackled with smoke.

Ere wondered if they actually burned upon touch. Perhaps that was why none of the other raptors drew close enough to find out. He seemed undefeatable in the air.

As if he knew his advantage too well and wanted to even the odds, he charged the cat spirits on the ground and stayed grounded, flapping his wings only for balance as he spun and kicked, lunged and slammed.

Oops, Ere thought. He'd assumed too soon.

The wings were not just for balance. On the ground, they were formidable weapons and shield as well.

When Sorin closed them around his person, they seemed impenetrable to claws, teeth, as well as sharp, man-made objects. When he extended them suddenly, they shoved unsuspecting opponents off their feet with the force of a thousand gales. When he swiped them sideways, Ere could practically hear the sizzle of burns, and he clearly saw the smoke.

The gorgeous flaming tips weren't just for show. They really were scorching flames!

A great white tiger's roar from one of the lower plateaus called a stop to the action.

And not a moment too soon. For the trainees were littered all over the field like the hapless victims of a tornado that just blew through, moaning and groaning their many wounds. Sorin had not gone easy.

"Maybe that's why Sorin is here," Benjamin said.

Ere had almost forgotten about his boy beside him. This was a shocking first, enough to make him pause.

"To help Tiger train our soldiers," Benjamin added.

"That would make sense," Ere murmured in agreement.

That made a lot more sense than his own fantastical imaginings—that Sorin was here for *him*.

Ha! Dream on.

"We could use all the help we can get," Benjamin said with a firm nod.

Ere finally focused on his boy.

"What do you mean?"

Benjamin turned those sky-blue eyes his way.

"Because Lily is coming to get me, silly. That's why I'm here, isn't it? To lure her into our trap?"

Ere couldn't hide his consternation.

"How...That's...You..."

Benjamin shrugged and looked back at the field, where the animal spirits were limping back to their various abodes, and the Tiger King was silently exchanging words with Sorin again. Goya in his giant Siberian tiger form. Sorin with his wings still half extended behind him.

"I don't know why she wants me, but she does. That's why Mom, Dad, Uncle Tal and Auntie Ishtar took me here, away from lots of people in the big city, away from the Shield. That's why Tiger has been recruiting more and more animal spirits. He's been training them here in the hidden valley for as long as I've been in town. Logan tells me all about it."

Benjamin looked up at Ere again.

"That's why you're here too, isn't it, Uncle Ere? You're trying to protect me too. And Sorin's here. Because you're here."

"I thought you said he was here to help train the animals," Ere inserted breathlessly.

The boy was a freaking savant! He knew things a nine-year-old should never know.

"He came here for you, Uncle Ere. But you keep ignoring him."

WHAT?

If these heart attacks he'd been experiencing were the boy's definition of "ignoring," Ere hated to think what "paying attention" would entail.

"So, I think he decided to help in other ways. I hope he stays even after his work is done though. I hope we can all be together forever."

Since when did he include the bird-man in their family circle? Ere's mind was a-boggle.

"Let's go say hi to Tiger before we head home," Benjamin shouted cheerfully, suddenly changing the topic, as he was wont to do, giving Ere mental whiplash.

"I'm getting really hungry. Oh! And let's invite Sorin to dinner! I already checked with Dad. He said I could."

"Since when?" Ere demanded, allowing himself to be dragged along by the hand as Benjamin tugged him toward the training field.

"Since the first day I met Sorin. I asked Dad that same night before bed. He told me that as long as you're okay, I could invite Sorin home. Say you're okay with it, Uncle Ere. Please! Pretty please?"

"I-I-" Ere stuttered, opening and closing his mouth like a useless, landed fish.

"He's *hungry*," the little fiend wheedled. "We have to feed him!"

And suddenly, Ere was standing right in front of the warrior again, whose golden eyes arrested his very breath with a single look.

"Okay," he wheezed, his own gaze trapped and captivated, unable to look away, caught in the Venus Flytrap of Sorin's lashes.

"Hurrah!" Benjamin rejoiced.

Hurrah, Ere's heart pounded.

And did a little celebratory somersault of its own.

Chapter Nine

The tension was thick enough to carve with a spoon.

Perhaps he shouldn't have come.

The boy would have gotten over the disappointment. His sunny disposition and endless optimism reminded Sorin so much of the Bane. It was uncanny.

And sometimes, it hurt to be reminded that his Bane was...gone.

The male sitting across the long, wooden table from him now—this *Ere*—he wasn't the same. Yet, somehow, he was even more beautiful and compelling than Sorin remembered. More fragile, but stronger too. More aloof, but also more touchable.

He was *real*.

The only reason Sorin was here, surrounded by strangers who regarded him with suspicion at best, hostility at worst, was because of Ere. When he had said "okay" to the boy's request for Sorin to come, Sorin saw the smallest gleam of pleasure in his eyes before he cast them down.

The same bright sapphire eyes. There were no other like his in the whole universe.

That small, spider-silk-thin string of pleasure that Ere revealed attached itself with the strength and tenacity of a reinforced steel cable to Sorin's heart and tugged. It tugged him all the way here, in fact, though he followed some distance away after the boy and his "uncle." Staying out of sight, but always near enough to protect them as they walked back home from the training field.

Perhaps he should have submerged himself in the lake before coming.

He likely reeked of battle, mock though it was and not as bloody as it could have been, given that he'd been holding himself back. But he hadn't thought too far ahead. He didn't realize what an invitation to dinner at the boy's house meant.

That he'd be meeting Ere's "people." And that four pairs of unacquainted, scrutinizing, sharp eyes would shine their bright, blinding, intense beams upon him.

He stiffened his shoulders and stared back, refusing to squirm in his delicate human chair like an ant being tortured under a magnifying glass in the direct light of a noonday sun.

"Benjamin tells me your name is Sorin with an 'i,'" the female called Inanna broke the fraught silence at the dinner table.

Sorin gave one curt nod.

He hadn't yet touched his food. The gigantic plate was heaped with two rare T-bone steaks, mashed potatoes, roasted sweet potatoes, and wild rice with a side bowl of local greens. It looked and smelled delicious.

One thing he'd come to appreciate about the years he was trapped in a Lesser Beast form, when he was forced to endure human civilization, was the food. He now preferred his meat to be cooked, though he still preferred raw seafood more. He liked his vegetables to be seasoned, and the various desserts humans made with fruit were his weakness. He couldn't get enough of them.

By the smells of the kitchen, dessert was definitely on the menu tonight. Something berry.

He was starving.

But he also knew enough about humanoid civilities to not shove his face in the plate the moment he sat down, and not come back up for air until he'd licked clean every surface. He was supposed to wait for the hosts to begin first. He had to take his cue from them.

They did not have a smooth introduction.

Sorin hadn't said anything since he arrived. He knew that humanoids might require physical contact when making a first acquaintance. The boy quite eagerly reached out to take Sorin's hand the first time they met in the schoolyard. He did the same when Sorin appeared on their doorstep a few minutes ago. But the adults did not extend hands to shake or arms to grasp. They certainly didn't do any of the "air kissing" Sorin had witnessed some humans did.

They'd simply nodded at him as Benjamin made the introductions, and he'd nodded back.

He didn't like to speak in human tongue. His grasp of Eastern European languages was better than his command of English. Probably because the tones were often more earthy and guttural. They came more naturally for his tongue and vocal cords.

Because his voice was so deep and raspy, his words were often no more than a rumble from his chest. But English required "enunciation." It felt like he was trying to tie his tongue into knots. Now he'd be forced to speak more than he was comfortable. He didn't like to expose weaknesses.

He glanced at Ere, whose eyes had not met his since his arrival, and hoped that he would not shame the man.

Meeting these people, eating in their company—this was important to Ere, he could tell. Thus, it was important to him too. He'd try to make a positive impression. If it killed him, he'd try.

"Where are you from?" Inanna asked on the heels of her opening comment.

"East," Sorin answered succinctly.

The female waited expectantly. When no other answer was forthcoming, she frowned a little.

Shit. Not a promising start.

"Let us eat before the food gets cold," an older-looking man, relative to the eternally youthful twenty-something Immortals around the table, at least, said in a calm, neutral tone.

Sorin immediately felt that he was the most reasonable amongst the group, the most likely to cut him some slack.

But he was also the most lethal of the group if he decided against Sorin. Despite his apparent blindness, the male was an experienced, formidable warrior.

"Benjamin, would you like to give daily thanks before we begin?"

"Yes, Uncle Tal!" the boy chirped happily, bouncing on his chair.

"I want to thank Daddy for letting me invite Sorin to dinner. I want to thank Uncle Ere for agreeing."

"I was worried you'd say no," he turned to Ere to whisper loudly.

Of course, everyone heard every word.

Ere ducked his head further, and Sorin noticed a faint flush creep up his pale neck.

The sight of it hardened him in an instant, for he imagined the spreading of that flush over other parts of Ere's body. Thankfully, the table hid his reaction.

But the boy wasn't done.

"I want to also thank Uncle Ere for showing us his real self. See, I told you everyone loves you!" Benjamin practically shouted.

Ere's face was now crimson and mottled, making his scars stand out.

Sorin fisted his hands on his knees beneath the table. He wanted to stop the boy from embarrassing his uncle. But at the same time, Ere needed to hear it. The words were nothing but truth.

"I know you're still Binu and Erena at your jobs, but I hope you'll be you at home," the boy continued.

"We love seeing the real you. Sorin thinks you're beautiful. He said so!"

"Benjamin," Ere hissed beneath his breath, obviously mortified. "Cease and desist!"

"True," Sorin put in.

All eyes flew to him, including the sapphire pair he'd been waiting to see.

He looked at no other but Ere.

Staring into those gemstone beams, he said slowly, making sure he enunciated each word and syllable:

"Most beau-ti-ful."

Jaws might have dropped around the table. Sorin didn't notice.

He only saw the way Ere's eyes widened. He saw a sparkle enter them that hadn't been there before, made even more brilliant by the wet shimmer that danced upon the deep blue pools.

It was Benjamin again who broke the ensuing silence.

"And thanks to Sorin for being here! I love making new friends. Thanks to Mama Bear for the delicious food. Amen."

The adults murmured their agreement and picked up their utensils as one, digging into the hearty meal.

For a few blessed minutes, Sorin ate in silence, focused on demolishing everything laid out before him. When he was ready for his second plate and bowl, he finally looked up from his food.

Ere was staring back at him.

He hadn't touched his own food at all, at which realization Sorin frowned. The man was thin enough as it was. He needed to eat. He needed nourishment.

At that thought, his still swollen sex jerked again, as if reminding him of its purpose—to fill and fulfill the male before him.

His Bane.

His lost, broken, beautiful dragon.

"What are you here in town for, Sorin?" Gabriel asked from the other end of the table.

Sorin did not take his eyes off Ere as he replied, "Mine."

Ere's face paled at the same time that it also flushed, a strange, riveting combination. He looked down at his plate and ate a bite of mashed potato.

No one at the table mistook his meaning.

Sorin felt the concern and confusion from Inanna and Gabriel. Fierce protectiveness from "Mama Bear," whose name was Ishtar, and who was also a Lesser leopard Beast. The same from Tal, but also something else. That male was difficult to read.

"Sorin is helping Tiger train the troops!" Benjamin volunteered. "Uncle Ere and I saw. It was awesome! Sorin has the biggest wings I've ever seen!"

The boy turned to him to ask, "What kind of eagle are you, anyway? I've never seen Eagle Spirits with wings like yours."

"Not eagle anymore."

Mama Bear got up and piled a new plate full of food with a fresh bowl of greens and set them in front of Sorin.

He nodded his thanks.

She gave him a hard look, then crinkled her eyes. The leopard approved of him.

That she was part Beast probably helped. He could communicate with her much more easily than the humanoids. And she could sense instinctively whether he was a threat or not.

"So you used to be an eagle? Just not anymore?"

The boy missed nothing.

"Aye."

"What kind of eagle?"

"No longer exist."

156

"So what are you now?"

Sorin didn't answer.

The adults at the table looked back and forth between him and the boy as if they were watching one of those human games. Perhaps the sport called "tennis."

It felt like an inquisition.

But they'd chosen the best possible interrogator. Sorin could barely stop himself from answering the boy's rapid-fire questions. He had a way about him that was simply irresistible.

"A vulture then?" Benjamin continued. "You're too big to be a falcon or a hawk. But the other vulture warrior behaved so differently..."

"No."

Silence descended upon the table again as everyone waited for him to expound.

He didn't. Simply digging into his food again.

They continued staring at him as he ate, and he let them.

In his world, eons ago when he'd been King, it was disrespectful to stare so openly at him like this. It challenged his authority, showed mistrust and perhaps dissention. He would never have tolerated this behavior. He would have put any perpetrator instantly in their place with a hard look or growl.

But he let Ere's people scrutinize and dissect him with their curious gazes. He knew that they only did so out of protectiveness for a member of their family.

It gladdened Sorin to see Ere so beloved, to know that when he finished what he came here to do, he would be leaving Ere in good hands, surrounded by people who cared about him.

Sorin set his utensils down and looked up across the table again.

Ere was actually eating this time, not looking back at him. His appetite seemed to have improved over the last little while. He was cleaning his plate rather efficiently.

Sorin approved.

He stared at Ere while the other man ate, a sense of contentment and satisfaction settling in his gut, along with the bountiful good food.

Yes. Ere would be in good hands. He didn't need Sorin after the last of the healing was done. He wasn't the Bane Sorin once knew. And Sorin wasn't his Sol. After he fulfilled his promise, Ere would be free.

And Sorin would finally let him go.

*** *** *** ***

"There's a blizzard brewing outside, and it's very late. I think your friend Sorin should stay for the night."

Ere started and almost dropped the dish he'd been washing as he stood next to Mama Bear who was helping him dry.

"He's not my friend, he's Benjamin's," he said reflexively. Defensively.

"I only met him on Thursday."

Never mind that Benjamin met him the same day, and Sorin was more his "age" than the boy's.

"And he's some sort of Beast. The feathered and winged kind. You know how hot they are."

He hesitated, belatedly realizing how that sounded.

"Hot tempered, that is," he clarified hastily. "He has plenty of internal heat to keep himself warm."

Ere grimaced as he heard himself talk. He sounded like a mean, whiny little boy, begrudging a guest the most basic of human comforts. Even if said guest wasn't human.

From Mama Bear's disapproving silent pause, she felt the same, though she didn't say so out loud.

"Nevertheless, I will extend the offer," she said instead, quite firmly.

Ere felt the chastisement all the same and ducked his head in shame.

"He could at least use the installations here to wash up," she added. "Beasts like to be clean, after all. Tal can give him some fresh clothes, though he might find them a tight fit. We'll see what we can find."

Ere grunted unintelligibly, biting his tongue to prevent from offering further comment.

The situation had been taken out of his hands. First, Benjamin invited the man. Then, his family slowly accepted the stranger. And now, he was sticking around like a long-lost relative.

All the while, no one seemed to notice or care that Ere's nerves were so on edge they felt like they'd been shredded by a thousand razors.

"Unfortunately, we don't have a guest room, and the couch in the living room is too small to fit Sorin's frame," Mama Bear continued in a deceptively mild tone.

"We will have to put him in your room, dear."

This time, Ere did drop the bowl he was washing with a clatter in the stainless steel sink. Thankfully, it didn't break.

"What?" he squeaked with dismay.

"But...but...I only have one bed!"

Mama Bear snorted a little to show that she thought Ere's reaction was overblown. She patted him comfortingly on the shoulder.

"It's an extra-large, especially designed California King. It's the only bed in the house that can fit people with yours and his height. And it's so big, five people could fit on it with plenty of space between them. You're a big boy, sweetheart. It's time you learned to share."

The "sweetheart" endearment helped to soften the edges of her implied criticism. He lived to hear such endearments from his family, especially Ishtar. And he knew she was only teasing with the last two comments, but he felt his face heat nevertheless with both acute embarrassment and shame again.

He sounded irrationally selfish, prudish and miserly. First, he begrudged a man shelter from a fucking snowstorm. Next, he complained about sharing comforts that didn't even belong to him.

This was Tal, Ishtar, Gabriel, Inanna and Benjamin's home. It wasn't his. He had no right to object to what they wanted to offer to someone they deemed worthy. Not when they offered their home to someone *un*worthy.

Him.

He picked up the sponge again and focused on the dishwashing, determined not to say another ungracious thing.

See, he didn't belong here, with this loving, giving, wonderfully *good* family. He was the perpetual raincloud that blotted out their sunshine.

"I like Sorin," Mama Bear murmured softly, in both a motherly as well as a star-struck girlish tone.

Ere could empathize. Who wouldn't like the man? Only Ere, apparently, and not even truly. He just resented the warrior for so easily disconcerting him whenever he was around. Hell, whenever thoughts of him popped into Ere's head. Which was much too often these days.

"He's very...*manly*."

He sure was, Ere agreed glumly in his own head, refusing to voice the sentiments out loud.

"The kind of man your father is."

His heart squeezed both happily and painfully at those words. *His father.*

He still couldn't believe that the greatest General across the Pure Ones' existence was *his* sire. He just wished he could be someone the General was proud to call his own. Instead, he'd been the Creature of his father's mortal enemy. He'd aided her in making Tal suffer untold misery.

"My very favorite kind of man," Mama Bear continued with a breathy sigh, "as you well know."

Who wouldn't adore that kind of man?

Strong. Loyal. True. Brave. Protective. Fierce.

"He's very handsome, isn't he?" she said offhandedly, glancing his way.

He mumbled in response, not confirming one way or the other.

"Goodness, but he's tall."

She was fanning herself. Why was she fanning herself?

"And such wide, strong shoulders. Must be because he needs them for his wings. Benjamin mentioned that his half-beast form is a spectacular sight to behold."

Ere grunted again, handing her another dish to dry. He had a few more and the silverware to go. He tried to hurry and finish so he could depart from this uncomfortable conversation.

"Those golden eyes..." Mama Bear trailed off with another sigh, putting a hand to her chest as if she couldn't quite catch her breath.

Honestly, it was a bit unseemly. She was a Mated female, after all. And Ere's *mother*, for fuck's sake. She shouldn't be all aflutter over another man.

"Is it just me or do those eyes veritably burn into you? But not in a bad way. They make a person feel so toasty warm."

It definitely wasn't just her, Ere thought begrudgingly. If only he was immune to the man.

"But of course, I can only guess, since the man doesn't look at anyone but you, dearest," she said innocently, casting him a look under her lashes.

"Uh..."

"Why, he didn't even glance at the rest of us at the table. He had only eyes for you, Erebu. He *likes* you."

"Um..." he searched for words to say, excuses to make, but he couldn't come up with anything when his mind was short-circuiting still on the memory of Sorin's magnificent eyes.

"Do you like him too?" she persisted as only a determined, nosy mother could persist.

"He thinks you're the most beautiful man, it's so romantic!"

"I wouldn't go that far—" he tried to take control of this runaway train.

"Do you think he is as well?"

"Of course," Ere blurted without thinking.

Then quickly backpedaled.

"Anyone would think so. I mean, just look at him. He's—"

"I don't think so," Ishtar said firmly. "Your father is the most beautiful man in the world to me. I love him more than the sun, the moon and the stars combined. But it's clear as day Sorin is the most beautiful man to you, dearest boy. What do you think that means, hmm?"

"I-I-"

Fuck! What was wrong with him?

He'd never stuttered so much in his entire existence!

What was it about this family that tied him in knots? What was it about them that he couldn't lie blithely like he always did. Every time he opened his mouth, unless it was truth that came out, the words stuck in his throat otherwise. He couldn't *not* be honest about what he thought and how he felt. No matter how he tried.

"It means you like him too. That's what it means," Mama Bear hammered home the point.

"Which is why I'm glad you invited him to stay the night."
What?!

He was coerced, manipulated, strongarmed into resentfully accepting that the bird-man was staying in his room. In his bed, no less! Since when was the invitation from him?

"And don't you dare sleep on the floor," she scolded, as if she could look directly through his skull into his thoughts.

He'd been planning on doing just that, so he colored with guilt.

"It's too cold. You're always cold. Sorin looks hot."

She giggled girlishly at that, making Ere grimace the way children grimaced the world over when their parent took questionable interest in their friends.

"Get it? He looks *hot*. I meant it for his Beastliness, but he definitely looks the other kind of hot as well. I am still learning modern American slang. It seems I can never grasp the concepts fast enough. I am sure 'hot' is already out of style."

Ere handed her the last of the silverware and resisted the urge to roll his eyes.

Honestly, mothers were *sooo* embarrassing.

"Go get a change of clothes, some towels and toiletries from Inanna, dear," she said, patting his back soothingly as if she knew how her teasing made him want to stick his head in the ground like an ostrich.

"Show your guest to the room you're sharing and be nice to him, Erebu," she ordered quite sternly.

"Sheathe your claws for one night."

"I don't have claws," he complained.

"You do. They're far sharper than mine, even if they're metaphorical. You have a tendency to strike first before anyone can take a swipe at you. Even if they weren't planning to. Words can hurt as much, if not more, than blades, my darling."

Ere felt his chest squeeze. He knew this to be true.

He immediately wondered whether any of his words had hurt Sorin. He had felt lower than dirt when he yelled at Benjamin earlier in the day.

As much as he tried to push Sorin away, he didn't want to hurt him. He couldn't bear it.

"That man likes you," Mama Bear said gently, but her tone brooked no argument.

"Take my word for it. Mothers know these things. Be kind to him. He's here for *you*."

For once, Ere didn't argue. Dutifully, he nodded, and left the kitchen to do as she bid him.

He had his own en-suite bathroom, so he heaped the items Inanna gave him into Sorin's arms, showed him the installations without meeting his eyes, and shut the door.

He himself couldn't stay in the house a moment longer. He needed air.

So, he let Ishtar and Tal know that he was going for a quick walk, just around the block.

It was already snowing heavily, but it was a soft, steady fall. The giant clumps of flakes descended upon his thinly clothed body like icy cotton balls. It was beautiful. Everything was glistening white under the pale streetlamps.

So pure. So innocent.

He wondered if he'd ever been this pure and innocent. Or if he'd been born with darkness and evil inside him from the very beginning.

Why had Medusa and Lilith chosen him to be their Creature? Their fucked-up experiment? Something must be inherently wrong with him.

He looked up at the black night and closed his eyes, letting the soft snow drift around him.

They felt like feathers, so light and airy. And for a moment, in his mind's eye, feathers were all he saw...

He awoke feeling more alert and stronger than he could remember feeling in a very long time.

The cave was dark but cozy. The nest he lay in toasty warm. Perhaps it was because a large furnace in the form of a man was lying against his side, radiating heat like his personal sun.

Even though his eyes adjusted to the darkness, the man's form was blurry. He could make out the overall shape and size, the approximate color of the man's hair—bright, light gold, shining like a beacon despite the lack of light in the cave. But he couldn't see clearly any distinguishing features.

The man was lying on his stomach, turned away from him, his arms folded underneath his face to serve as a pillow.

Hesitantly, he touched his hand to the man's incredibly broad back. And immediately jerked away as if scalded.

He was so hot. His skin like flames.

And yet, Ere wanted to touch him again. Couldn't help but reach out again.

When his fingers ghosted across the man's smooth, tawny skin a second time, he felt the same heat, but somehow, it didn't burn him. He even liked it. A strength he'd never felt before hummed through his veins when he made contact. His body simply came alive.

"Who are you?" he murmured to himself.

"How did you find me? How did you even know to look? You saved me and put me back together. You...you healed me with your own body."

He pulled away at that, remembering.

The man had come inside *him. It had hurt like a motherfucker. But then... it had felt good.*

Gods help him. It had felt so, bloody good.

The man had molded, reshaped and pieced him back together like he was Hephaestus at the forge, breathing life into something broken and inanimate. Funneling his own life force, his seed, his essence, into Ere.

Recreating him.

He'd given his blood as well.

Ere's fangs ached, practically quivering in his mouth.

The man had given him his blood. Let him penetrate and drink from every vein in his body.

Ah gods! He was starving still. He wanted so much more. He wanted to devour the male who'd protected and nurtured him. Preferably while the man was hard and pulsing inside him again, while he flooded Ere's body with Nourishing cream.

He grasped his head in his hands.

What was wrong with him? He never thought this way. Never felt these things. He never wanted anyone...that way.

Who was this man? And why did Ere crave him so desperately?

He had to get away. He didn't belong here. This wasn't him. Now that he was healed...

He glanced his fingers across his face and felt the edges of a multitude of jagged scars. Well, he was relatively healed. His current state was infinitely better than what his last memories had been—as tattered fish bait at the bottom of a lake.

It didn't matter. He was living on borrowed time anyway. He had a mission to accomplish. A son to protect.

Benjamin.

He must go to Benjamin. Lilith would be looking for the boy. She'd never stop until she found him. Until she caught him.

Ere had to destroy her once and for all.

Bolstered by that thought, he tried to get up from the nest, but a strong grip on his arm restrained him.

"Stay."

The man had turned toward him.

Ere wished he could see the stranger's face clearly, but the flames around them that seemed to rise from the feathers themselves, as well as the man's skin and hair, distorted his features. All he saw was bright, almost blinding, waving gold.

And the darker golden orbs of the man's eyes. Like twin suns. Blazing with an internal light.

"I can't," he answered, doing his best to look into the man's eyes.

But he couldn't maintain the gaze. It was too glaringly bright.

He looked away and added, "There are people who need me. I have to go."

The man was silent for so long, Ere was tempted to look at him again.

And then he said:

"I need you."

Ere's gaze shot involuntarily to his at that, and caught like a deer in headlights in those golden orbs.

He didn't understand it, but he felt almost compelled to say yes. He wanted desperately to stay. But he knew in his heart he must go.

As long as Lilith lived, his son would never be safe.

"I have to go," he repeated, fisting his hands.

"I-I love him. I have to go."

The man stared at him for endless moments. Stared into *him.*

Finally, he took away his touch, and Ere felt immediately bereft and cold.

"So be it," he rumbled, his voice deep and laden with something...like regret.

But the word was too weak to describe what Ere felt in his very bones at the stranger's words.

"I will take you."

And so, in much the same blur as when Ere had been taken here, to this strange nest, in this stranger's cave, the man took him where he wanted to go. He must have been unconscious most of the time, for he couldn't recall the flight, couldn't remember anything he saw.

But the vision of those gigantic, golden, flame-tipped wings stayed with him.

Even after the man was gone, having left him in a strange town in the middle of strange mountains, he continued to dream of those beautiful wings.

And then he blotted it all out. Just like he buried the memories of his horrific demise at the claws of the Hydra.

He had work to do, after all. He was running out of time to enjoy a pocket of "normality" before he must face his demons again.

Once and for all.

Chapter Ten

Lilith marveled at the profound silence around her. Inside her.

Now that Medusa was obliterated from this universe, her Dark soul never to be reborn, Lilith felt the tiniest pang of...something...at the absence of her monster.

She was utterly alone once more.

No matter. She didn't need companionship. She didn't need anyone but herself.

Even though, once upon a time, the thought of not having her *partner* would never in a million years have crossed her mind.

The operative word was "partner," however. Someone equal to her in every way. Medusa, by contrast, was simply her monster.

Lesser.

The Dark Princess possessed all the necessary ingredients for Lilith's venom to take root. She was proud, strong, confident and shrewd. With Lilith's "encouragement" and supplements in the form of poison and magic, that pride turned into a god-complex. Her strength turned into cruelty and sadism. Her confidence warped into a disregard for others. And her intelligence was used to advance greed, vengeance and world domination.

What was that human saying? *The Devil cannot tempt those who are not predisposed to sin.*

Well, if there wasn't such a saying, there ought to be. For it was only truth.

It had been interesting, enlightening, and, in a sense, fulfilling, to observe how one monster she meticulously created could, in turn, create her own little monsters too.

The tortured General.

The poisoned twin.

The beautiful Creature.

Chaos, fear, hopelessness, and destruction were so easy to spread when you didn't have to do everything yourself.

Too bad Tal-Telal and his Mate escaped Medusa's clutches. Even executed her in the end, despite their Pure do-gooder ways.

But Lilith's greatest disappointment was the Creature. Not the least because he was partly hers as well. She'd cultivated the darkness inside him like the most attentive gardener with the ficklest plant. She'd seen it bloom in all its bloody, thorny glory within him.

And then, she made him into a fucking dragon.

How dare he turn on her, his creator. His *god*.

*Oh, sister...*a faint whisper blew through the cavern like tendrils of wind.

Lilith stilled, holding her breath. Listening.

I never wanted this for you. It was never supposed to be this way.

Lilith bared her serpent teeth in a gruesome smile.

What way is that, dearest twin? What did you think was going to happen when Mother Darkness and Father Light stuffed my ashes into the shell of a fox spirit to learn my "lesson" the hard way?

*If only you learned...*the faint voice lamented. *If only you grew...*

The way you did? Lilith snarled derisively. *A goddess growing a soul like cancer in humans. Pathetic.*

Love is the strongest power of all, my darling. Not our magic, not the gods and all their creations.

We shall see, Lilith hissed. *Watch and learn, my Pure, miserable half.*

Absolute silence descended once more, leaving Lilith alone with her thoughts.

Unbidden, they wandered to a time during her endless toils as a despicable parasite among immortals when she was not entirely alone. *He* had managed to break through the walls she'd erected around herself, the icy reserve in which she submerged herself.

The one brilliant light in her endless darkness.

But even he, or the promise of him, disappointed her.

One could argue it hadn't been his fault, being captured and enslaved by the Dark Queen Ashlu, his beloved family held hostage to guarantee his acquiescence. It was no excuse in Lilith's view of things. He let another female own him, fuck him, ruin that Pure, radiant light.

Lilith snarled in memory, hatred and vengeance filling her to overflowing. She would never forgive or forget.

She raised one of her many tentacles in her current form and rotated it this way and that before her serpent-eyed scrutiny.

The limb moved like seaweed waving in currents. And then, it shifted like water itself, becoming more and more amorphous. Finally, it dissipated slowly into a formless cloud, just like the rest of her.

At last.

She'd harnessed another power. The Hydra was the Gift that kept on giving.

Lilith's demonic, delighted laughter echoed through the cavern where the body of a giant squid used to be.

*** *** *** ***

Ere didn't know what he expected when he came inside from the cold and entered his room, but it certainly wasn't the sight that greeted him—

Sorin lying naked on his stomach upon his bed, his arms beneath his head, his face turned toward the center.

Two things happened all at once.

All of the saliva in Ere's mouth dried up like the Sahara, and all of the blood in his body rushed immediately south, leaving him swaying dizzily on his feet. He had to brace one hand on the door frame to hold himself upright. Because...

Holy Mary, Mother of God!

Was he dreaming?

He must be dreaming.

There was no sight in all of creation across the history of time that compared to the vision before him now. He didn't know where to look, his eyeballs ping-ponging like pellets in a pinball machine. There was so much to see!

The bed was huge, as Mama Bear rightly pointed out, but so was the man. Five people would definitely not fit in there with him; he took up almost all of the space.

(Well, only one person *needed* to fit in there with him, and that one person was most certainly going to be Ere).

170

His body on autopilot, he closed and locked the door softly behind him without in any way distracting even one iota of attention from the male focused in his sights like a target in the crosshairs of a Ruger Precision Rifle.

When Mama Bear coerced him into inviting Sorin to stay the night, in his wildest fantasies he couldn't have foreseen this particular turn of events.

He thought he'd come back to find Sorin brooding in a corner—he was so good at that silent staring and glaring thing. Maybe he'd choose to sleep on the floor, if he slept at all. Ere rather wondered whether he did. He seemed like the sort of male who would keep at least one eye open while he rested.

Ere had planned to trudge inside, mutter a few words if he absolutely had to (though he hadn't expected Sorin to be talkative based on his experience with the man thus far), flop onto the bed fully clothed, squeeze himself on the edge of one side and pretend to sleep.

He didn't expect to *actually* sleep. That was out of the question when Sorin was in bed with him. Or even in the same room, house, or honestly, even in the same town.

Come to think of it, Ere had suffered insomnia since Thursday night, the day he met the stranger. And when he did sleep, he dreamed about Sorin. Which really wasn't much better than thinking about him while awake.

His unconscious mind was rather...wild. At least as far as Sorin was concerned.

Perhaps Ere's healthy imagination never conjured a naked Sorin laid out upon his bed like a visual feast because Ere himself would never have done such a thing. He eschewed nudity if he could help it. And if he had to be unclothed, in the shower for instance, he tried not to look too hard, and he tried not to touch his own skin. He always used an intermediary like a nice thick sponge. The more material between him and his own body the better.

Even after he realized that his real self wasn't terribly hideous (that was *before* he got riddled with Frankenstein scars), he didn't like to acknowledge the flesh.

It wasn't that he was a prude. With a past like his, one couldn't possibly maintain any vestige of modesty. It was that he disgusted himself. And couldn't imagine why anyone else would ever want to see or touch him if he didn't even want to see or touch himself. He was like the shiny, red, perfect apple in *Snow White and the Seven Dwarfs*, filled with poison and rotten worms inside.

But he certainly wanted to see and touch Sorin.

Lordy, did he ever!

That man was made for seeing and touching. All that broad expanse of flawless, smooth, golden skin. All those hills and valleys, bulges and hollows. Defined, steely muscles that went on and on for days *and* nights. Longish wavy hair that shone a burnished gold even in the darkness of Ere's room, with only a few stray beams of moonlight to illuminate him.

If Ere looked and acted like Sorin, beautiful beyond belief, confident and animalistically *male*, he'd probably strut around everywhere naked. It would be a gift to all Kinds to look upon him and be awed.

Now, mind you, Ere wouldn't be standing here ogling the warrior if he didn't appear to be thoroughly insensate to the world around him.

Unconscious. Passed out.

It was a damn good thing he happened to be lying on his stomach instead of his back. Because Ere didn't think he could handle the full monty without a proper heart attack.

Although...maybe after he looked his fill of the backside, he could ever so gently roll the colossus over to take a peek of the front. Something to look forward to.

He wanted to rub his hands together with covetous glee. This must be his belated Christmas present. He never got one in his whole existence. Nor a birthday present either (since he didn't know the exact date of his birth, to be fair).

But *this*—this beautiful, magnificent specimen of primal maleness displayed so unstintingly on Ere's bed, for Ere's personal viewing pleasure—well, he might start believing in Santa Claus after all.

Wait.

He paused mid step, foot half raised in his tiptoeing journey across the few feet of distance from the door to the bed, like the Grinch whole stole Christmas.

What if Sorin wasn't totally, dead-to-the-world asleep? What if he was a light sleeper? What if he opened his eyes at any moment and caught Ere red-handed (so to speak) in the act of nefarious peeping?

The fear of getting caught dampened his enthusiasm like a wet blanket.

Staying a few feet away from the Holy Grail of temptation, he whispered, "Psst. Bird man. Are you awake?"

Okay, that was a low blow. He grimaced as the words left his mouth.

Sorin was obviously far more than "bird man." Ere didn't know why he felt it necessary to talk down to the male, to discourage his attention rather than invite it. He wanted to believe that it wasn't due to an overdeveloped self-protective mechanism. Reject before being rejected.

But he'd be lying to himself.

"S-Sorin…" he said louder, in an almost normal voice, "if you don't wake up now to defend yourself against some serious X-rated eye-fucking, don't cry to me later that you weren't forewarned."

Nothing.

Just deep, even, hypnotic breathing.

And endless, golden gorgeousness.

Ere resumed his tiptoeing across the room, pausing every so often to assess potential dangers of discovery like a weasel in the henhouse. (Truly, he needed to work on his mental metaphors. None of them painted him in a positive light).

He descended onto the bed in a slow, smooth slide, hands first, followed by chest, stomach and lower body. Rather like a baby Harp Seal (minus the adorableness) sliding onto a sheet of ice.

Fortunately, the bed was one of those Westin Heavenly beds, with perfect weight distribution so that one occupant would not be disturbed by the movements of other occupants. And with not a single creaky spring in the mattress, since it was made of memory foam. Also fortunately, Tal and Ishtar weren't stingy about sheets. The bed was covered in thick, high-quality satin. The better to facilitate Ere's sneaky slide.

Once he lay fully on the bed, he turned just as smoothly and surreptitiously so that he was facing Sorin on his side, his head propped on one hand while the other was free to...wander and explore.

He hesitated to start with a touch though, because what if Sorin had hypersensitive skin and awoke not by sound but by the slightest touch? No, the better strategy would be to look his fill, commit every hair and line to memory, *then* venture into tactile territory.

A ray of moonbeam filtered through the semi-transparent window shade to bathe Sorin's face in pale, bluish-white light.

Wow.

Ere's breath caught in his throat while his heart sped up with giddy eagerness.

Sorin with his eyes open, those intense golden orbs probing like hot irons into everything he stared at, was intimidating at best, fucking terrifying at worst. Looking into those eyes was like looking directly into the sun. In other words, not advised if you didn't want your irises burned.

The aura of god-like strength, warrior badassery, and ultimate leadership of every Kind made plebians like Ere want to prostrate himself at Sorin's feet and kiss his toes in worship. Which was probably one of the reasons why he tended to give Sorin a hard time. He was just a contrary, against-the-grain kind of guy.

But Sorin with his eyes closed was another story.

The stern lines in between his eyebrows and around his mouth were almost invisible. Despite the full, manly beard, and thanks to those feathery lashes, he looked...accessible. Touchable.

Thoroughly fuckable.

The conscious man was definitely *not* fuckable.

Well, theoretically he was. And anyone who looked upon him would immediately make use of their imagination to that effect. But Ere doubted he'd ever be the one who got fucked. He was most definitely the sort who did all the fucking.

Because, come on! The man screamed control and dominance. He'd never let anyone near his tender bits.

While Ere was on the subject of tender, he noticed that the wavy, silky-soft looking golden tresses that fell over the warrior's face added a subtle veil of vulnerability. And his full, wide mouth did the rest.

Ere involuntarily licked his own lips and parted them.

In all of his existence, in so many millennia, he couldn't recall if he'd ever been properly kissed.

The best memory he had was of Ninsa taking him by surprise with a quick peck when they had been children lifetimes ago.

While married to Sophia's previous incarnation, Kira, they'd never kissed the way lovers did. Not even on their wedding night. They'd been best friends, and save the act of consummation, they'd been completely platonic friends.

Finally, there was Olivia, Benjamin's mother. There had been no kissing on that fateful night either.

To this day, Ere didn't know why Olivia, why that night, or even why *him*. The whole ordeal had been a murky blur.

One moment he'd been sitting with his Pure blood source (who turned out to be Lilith in a Pure One skin!) in the private section of a dance club surveying the peasants bumping and grinding mindlessly on the floor below. And the next he'd homed in on a human woman in white, practically humped her right then and there, and dragged her to his lair to do the nasty a few minutes after the encounter.

Maybe it had been a full moon that night. Maybe the stars aligned just so. Maybe Olivia was doused in a potent pheromone that only affected Ere, and to an uncontrollable, mindless degree.

That was the only night across his long existence that he hadn't needed "help" to get an erection. He'd been hard all night. He'd fucked her until they were both raw and sore.

She'd had the presence of mind to ask him to put on a condom the first time. She'd brought one with her. But after they came together rather explosively, she couldn't be bothered to protect herself.

She *wanted* his seed. Begged for it. Wanted to feel it fill her to overflowing.

And he'd *needed* her.

He couldn't get enough of emptying himself into her willing, soft body. He needed her blood too, even more than her flesh. He'd taken it. Almost to the point of draining her. He'd started taking her soul as well, too lost in the primitive drive to merge himself with another, to consume her the way she consumed him.

To not feel alone, for once in his miserable existence.

But when the sun came up, all of the urgency and need he felt the night before evaporated as if it never was. As if he never felt any of it.

He'd scrambled off the bed, roughly yanked on his pants, forgoing the shirt and shoes, in his haste to make a mad dash out of his basement abode. He never went back there for fear she'd be waiting. He never wanted to see her again.

It had been a terrible mistake. He didn't know what came over him. He spent the rest of that morning retching out his empty stomach in the shower of one of his other hidey holes. And after that, he kept sporadic tabs on her just to make sure they never had occasion to run into each other.

It was a wise decision to forsake the apartment he took her to that night, because she left messages with various people there in the hopes of finding him and seeing him again.

Including a note that she was expecting his child.

Ere never believed her. Pregnancies among Immortal Kinds were a minor miracle. Most often, it only ever happened when the partners were Eternal or Blooded Mates. "Catching" his sperm was like catching a disease from him. In other words, it should have been impossible. Or very nearly so.

Somehow, Olivia caught "it."

Ere was finally faced with the undeniable, physical proof when he laid eyes on Benjamin for the first time in Dark Dreams, Mama Bear's all-things shop.

He simply *knew*. This boy was his flesh and blood.

Benjamin was the best of him.

The very best of everything.

The mistake he'd made had been his disservice to Olivia. He knew from the few tabs he kept on her that she'd never been happy while alive. Perhaps the fragment of her soul that he took that night led to her unhappiness. Perhaps he ruined her just like he ruined everything else he touched. She was yet another sin he had to atone for, in the never-ending pile of sins weighing down his immortal soul.

But one thing was certain: Benjamin was not a mistake.

He was Destiny, love, goodness and joy coalesced into one living, breathing being. He was Ere's to protect.

He couldn't fail. No matter what, he couldn't fail his boy.

The end would come with Lilith. He accepted it. He didn't have much time. Certainly no time to delve into his present obsession with kissing. He didn't deserve it. But...

He wanted it.

Wanted it with *Sorin*.

So badly it physically hurt.

He'd never kissed anyone for pleasure. Or even pain. None of the "targets" he'd whored himself to on Medusa's command had required it. Not on their lips, in any case. On other parts of their body, certainly. But it seemed that the touching of mouth upon mouth was universally recognized as *personal*. More intimate than fucking.

As he looked upon Sorin's face, relaxed and almost boyish in slumber, he was possessed by the craziest, awfulest, most irresistible *need* to kiss him.

Ere wet his lips again and inched his own face a little closer, until only a hair's breadth separated them.

He hadn't even realized that his hand was hovering shakily above Sorin's hair. He wanted so badly to touch those golden waves, wrap the silky locks around his fingers. He wanted to smooth his thumb over Sorin's soaring brows, like the spread of eagle wings. He wanted to feel whether the double-rows of lashes were soft like feathers or rough like bristles.

Ah gods. This man!

What *was* it about him? What was it about *him*?

He was beautiful, true. But Ere had seen countless beautiful people. The rub was that Sorin was the *most* beautiful to Ere. He couldn't even be objective about it.

Ere had never wanted anything so badly before. He'd never even *thought* about sex in anticipatory terms, and now he couldn't stop. His mind was deep, *deep*, permanently buried in the gutter where Sorin was concerned.

And then, just as his fingers grazed a few wayward strands of that silky gold—

Sorin opened his eyes.

*** *** *** ***

Sorin knew exactly the moment Ere would try to bolt.

The male's eyes went round with surprise as soon as their gazes clashed. A deep flush flooded his face in an instantaneous conflagration of embarrassment and...guilt. The sort that children wore when they were caught doing something they shouldn't.

But before Ere could snatch back the hand that was hovering over Sorin's hair, Sorin grasped his wrist in a lightning-fast move, trapping his target gently but firmly.

Immediately, the other man's eyes dilated with a strange combination of excitement and fear, desire warring with apprehension.

Sorin knew he had to do the right thing.

This was it.

The moment that would bring them closer or push them farther apart.

From the time Ere came to him to mutter a reluctant invitation to stay the night, he'd tried to gain the man's attention, connect their gazes, find a few moments for private conversation.

Not that Sorin would ever be an eloquent conversationalist, and certainly not when he had to speak in human tongues, but he and his Bane had never had issues communicating. They'd been so in tune with each other.

Their telepathic link went far beyond the typical animal spirit connection. Even beyond Mated bonds in many ways. If only he could get Ere alone, truly hold his attention for more than a couple of minutes, Sorin felt almost certain he could reestablish some semblance of that long-ago bond.

Though they were no longer the same individuals, a part of him would always recognize his Bane.

But Ere had diligently avoided all eye contact, never mind physical touch. He'd avoided even the slightest brush of their clothed bodies, always going out of his way to give Sorin a wide berth. And then, he'd disappeared entirely for hours.

Sorin had been tempted to go in search of him. It had been a hard battle waged within himself to be patient and wait, to let Ere come to him.

This was Ere's room, after all. He had to return. This was his family and his home, Sorin kept telling himself. With all the time he had on his hands as he waited, he thought of how he could break through Ere's reserve.

Despite everything that had transpired between them, from his hearing Ere's call for help, finding and retrieving him, literally piecing him back together and healing him with Sorin's own body from the inside out—to now—repeatedly putting himself in front of Ere, reminding him of his need for Sorin, reminding him that his healing wasn't yet complete, reminding him of the ghost of their bond...

Ere refused to accept him. Refused to let him closer.

Sorin could only accede that the bond they'd shared lifetimes ago was gone. Ere was a different person now. They both were.

But whatever remnant that remained of his ties to this man insisted that Sorin fulfill his promise: If he ever broke, Sorin would do everything in his power to fix him. Heal him. Bring him back to life.

That was all he was here for, Sorin told himself sternly. That was all he would allow himself to hope for—Ere's complete revitalization.

But the man had to let him in. Sorin could not give if he refused to take.

So, he got himself clean with the typical thoroughness of an animal spirit. And laid himself out on the bed in the most nonthreatening way he could think of.

It went against every dominant particle that made him who he was to lie on his stomach, naked and exposed, eyes closed, vulnerable to attack. He'd never let anyone close enough to see him this way. Only his Bane.

As an Eagle Spirit, or any of his avian Kind, the back and shoulders were the most vulnerable parts of their body, for in either animal or humanoid form, it was the base for their wings. Any damage to those areas could cripple him forever, take away his reason for existing—the ability to take to the skies. A raptor who was grounded would rather die than continue a flightless existence.

But he gave Ere his back. He gave the man his trust. This man who was little more than a stranger now. But who still held the most important part of his soul—the spark of life.

He'd known exactly when Ere returned. When he entered the house and came into the room.

He'd felt Ere's burgeoning desire as the man gazed upon Sorin's nakedness as if it was his own. In the most basic way, they were still linked. Even though both of their forms were different, they were still physically drawn to each other. In some ways, even more than before.

He put all of his faith now in that tenuous connection, that simmering, alternately fragile, yet voracious desire. Hoping it was enough to persuade Ere to choose him.

So, before Ere could pull upon the wrist that Sorin had trapped, he brought the hand to the side of his face, laying Ere's cool fingers lightly upon his hot skin.

Yours.

He pushed the thought to the skittish, owl-eyed male and prayed to every merciful god he could think of that he was heard.

He was.

Ere's eyes widened even further, though it seemed impossible, and Sorin saw comprehension darken his irises.

The other man darted his gaze to his hand upon Sorin's skin as if the appendage was not his own. He wiggled the fingers slightly, brushing away a strand of hair from the corner of Sorin's mouth, and his eyebrows lifted in surprise as he realized that, yes, indeed, the hand was attached to him, and he was actually touching Sorin.

Yours, Sorin repeated in his mind.

Whatever you want. Take it.

And then, to make his demonstration of trust complete, he closed his eyes once more and put his own hands back beneath his head, showing without words that he was letting Ere have free rein over his body.

Minutes ticked by, during which total silence Ere didn't move at all, his hand still, his breath held.

And then he said, "You're more talkative telepathically."

A pause.

"I like it."

Another pause.

"Not that I disliked the one to three word grunting approach to communication. It rather suits you. Gives a whole new meaning to succinct. They should put your picture in the dictionary next to the word 'terse.' My picture would be next to its antonym, without a doubt. But do go on. Tell me more. Now that I can hear you in my head, I'm all aquiver for your scintillating colloquy."

Sorin almost smiled.

This Ere sounded like his Bane. The dragon loved to drive him mad with endless mental contortions and convolutions. Sorin could sense that Ere talked more when he was nervous or uncertain. His words were his weapon and his armor. But he'd had too much experience with the Bane to fall for his baiting.

He had nothing else important to say at the moment. He simply waited for Ere to work through his nerves and make the next move.

"Hmm. Nothing to add?" Ere said after waiting a few beats.

He seemed uncomfortable with silence. This was like the Bane as well. He needed to fill every space with chatter. Only when the Bane was alone with Sorin, at their private waterfall or sitting together on a secluded peak, was the dragon content to be still and silent, even in his mind.

Especially in that brilliant, whirring, lightning-quick mind.

Sorin focused on keeping his breaths even and deep as he waited for Ere to take the initiative.

To come to him. Accept him.

His heart clenched with a sudden, stabbing pain at everything they'd lost to be here now. Virtual strangers. Neither of them fully alive. His lashes fluttered and a muscle in his jaw ticked beneath his beard.

It hurt to be so alone. Cut off and isolated from the world.

But Sorin had never needed a crowd. He'd never wanted to be King. He just needed and wanted one other who was entirely his.

His Bane.

As if he sensed that Sorin was in pain, Ere's hand gently stroked his cheek, a mere ghost of a touch that tickled.

And comforted too.

Sorin resisted leaning into his touch. It took all of his willpower to do so, but he controlled himself. He remained absolutely still, breathing deeply, eyes closed, as if he'd fallen asleep.

"I remember you..."

The soft murmur was barely audible.

At first, Sorin thought he heard wrong. Could he possibly mean...?

"You saved me," Ere continued.

Ah. So he was only remembering what happened months ago, not eons ago.

Nevertheless, it was a beginning. Sorin knew that the likelihood was highest that Ere never recalled his past life as the Bane. If only Sorin himself could forget as well.

It physically *hurt* to recall everything he'd lost.

The hand grew bolder, the strokes upon Sorin's face more assured as a thumb coasted across his eyebrow, over his eyelid and lashes. As fingers touched his nose and cheek, glancing through his mustache and beard, skirting shyly around his lips, but always coming back, each brush longer and more confident than the last.

"Thank you for saving me," Ere said quietly.

"I'm sorry for being...inhospitable. Ungracious. Churlish. Oh, very well, I'm sorry for being an unmitigated ass. I'm grateful to be alive. Really."

Sorin's brow itched to frown.

There was something Ere wasn't saying. He was grateful to be alive, but not happy. And he was grateful to be alive, but not for himself. Somehow, Sorin knew this to be true.

As if sensing his doubt, Ere added, "Look at what I'd be missing if I were dead."

At that, he glided his thumb adventurously over Sorin's lips, then more intimately along the seam.

Sorin parted his lips to give the curious wanderer better access, but otherwise maintained his somnolent pose.

The fingers paused, hesitating. But they didn't venture further. Instead, his hand lifted away from Sorin's face entirely.

Had Ere used up all of his courage then? Was this as far as he would go tonight?

And then, Sorin felt the lightest of tentative touches upon his back, directly between his shoulder blades.

"This back," Ere whispered. "It's so broad and strong. Like it could carry the weight of the world. Or perhaps it already has."

He'd tried, Sorin thought. He'd failed.

In the end, it was the Bane who won the Goddesses' war, though there were no real victors, only loss. It was the Bane who sacrificed himself to save Sorin.

The hand smoothed over his shoulders, stroked its way across his trapezius muscles to his deltoids and down the deep groove of his spine.

Gods! His touch.

It had been an eternity since Sorin was touched like this. No one but the Bane had ever touched him this way.

He shivered uncontrollably, his muscles tensing no matter how he tried to relax.

He was so hard and hot, he must be burning a hole through the mattress. His sex throbbed viciously, the tortured head leaking his essence, drenching the sheets beneath him. Lying on his stomach added even more pressure. But he welcomed the pain. It helped him focus.

He was here for Ere. Whatever pleasure or release that would come of this, it would be Ere's to take.

He remembered the acute fear and agony in the other male's eyes when he'd done what he had to do to heal him. He knew that there'd been pleasure too, but Ere had not been a full participant. He'd been helpless in Sorin's care. Their coupling, such as it was, had been torture and ecstasy in equal measure.

Sorin didn't know what Ere had been through; he knew very little about this incarnation of his Bane. But he knew trauma when he saw it. The ugly, violent, soul-deep kind. He would never add to it. Even though he knew without a doubt, on the most primitive, basic level, that Ere wanted him, the male had to take what he wanted with both hands.

He had to *choose* Sorin.

The hand grew ever bolder, as if its owner's confidence grew in proportion to the length of Sorin's stillness and silence.

The tips of curious fingers glossed over the end of Sorin's spine, delved into the shallow dimples on either side, then hesitated for a few fraught seconds—

Before they skimmed between the tight muscular globes of his ass.

He couldn't prevent the rough exhale that pushed out of him.

This was...

He'd never...

Even his mind stuttered on what Ere's meandering touches were leading to.

When he'd made himself vulnerable, when he'd given Ere his trust, he hadn't thought about any other implications for the position in which he'd exposed himself.

He and his Bane had never gone that far. They'd touched and taken each other with their hands and mouths, but never *there*. Not because they didn't want to, but because they never had the chance. Their time together was over before it truly started. Yet every moment was carved indelibly into Sorin's soul.

And when Sorin had come inside Ere, this broken male who had to be put back together, it had been necessary for the healing process. Sorin had barely noticed his own pleasure; he'd focused so completely on reviving the broken dragon.

Did Ere want that from him?

Do that to him?

Yes, those taunting fingers said, as they came back over and over to his ass, the touches growing firmer, bolder, delving deeper in places that no one had ever touched him before.

Ere had grown uncharacteristically quiet as he explored, but his ragged breathing was loud in the silent room. Sorin thought he could hear the other man's heart pound. Or perhaps it was his own.

He didn't doubt that if he let Ere have all of him, it would hurt like a fucker. But it was no more than what he'd already done to Ere. And Sorin wasn't afraid of pain. He wasn't expecting pleasure either, even though he knew Ere had felt it with him after the initial pain.

He was focused only on what Ere would feel, what Ere wanted. Needed. It was a gift—the act of ultimate trust of granting someone entry into your body. Knowing that they could hurt you more than just physically.

This man had the power to shred his heart and soul.

Sorin made his choice.

The next time those fingers stroked from the top of his ass cheeks to the sensitive strip of his perineum and the base of his scrotum, he opened his thighs slightly wider in wordless invitation.

Ere's sharp inhale made both of them freeze.

For long, paralyzed moments, Sorin waited.

And waited.

And then, with breath held, he felt Ere's thumb press firmly from the root of him, over his taint, into the tight seam between his glutes, to rub slowly, intentionally, over his entrance, setting every nerve in his body on fire.

Especially *there*.

But before he could brace himself for more, Ere took away his touch completely.

Sorin was so bereft and bewildered, he forgot his pretense and opened his eyes, immediately seeking out Ere's gaze with his own. Showing all of his unguarded need, his desire, stripped of pride.

He was not a King. Not a warrior. Not a savior. Nor anyone's Champion.

He was only a male in this moment.

And he *needed*.

"I need you too," his other half finally answered.

Chapter Eleven

For once, Ere held Sorin's gaze unflinchingly as he whispered the words.

The moment he uttered them, he knew them to be true. Truer than anything he'd ever voiced or even thought.

They were true on a soul-deep level. He was born with these words engraved into the fiber of his being: Here exists Erebu (whatever his name is), who needs Sorin (whoever he turns out to be).

It didn't matter. None of it mattered. What they called themselves. Where they'd been. What they'd done.

He didn't "know" this male laid out in all his truthful, naked glory before him. But he *knew* this male on a level that defied logic, time, and experience.

Ere considered one of his faults to be self-centeredness. And cowardice. And pessimism. And... Oh very well, he had more faults than a reasonable person would wish to enumerate, especially in present circumstances. When he really ought to focus on the miraculous opportunity at hand.

The point was—

For tonight, he was alive.

He wanted to *live*.

He wanted to be fearless.

He wanted to *know* another person, *this man*, with nothing but skin and breath between them.

He wanted to burn in ecstasy.

He wanted, he wanted, he wanted...

Staring into those mesmerizing golden eyes, looking directly into Sorin's soul, seeing his pain, his need...need for *Ere*, no one else...he felt like the most powerful person in the world. He felt as if he could conquer entire armies, pluck the stars from the sky. He could do anything.

He wanted *this*, more than anything he'd ever dreamed to want in the whole of his existence.

Where to start? he wondered.

But then, he realized it didn't matter. It wasn't the where that was important. It was simply that he *start*.

"I want to touch you," he said in a surprisingly steady voice, though he felt as if his heart would pound out of his chest at any moment and his lungs would collapse from the strain of his forgetfulness to breathe.

Sorin didn't even blink. He didn't close his eyes again either, like Ere surreptitiously hoped. (It would be so much easier if the intimidating male could just read Ere's mind and do exactly what he wanted without being asked, and let Ere do whatever he wanted without scrutiny and judgement).

Then do it, the warrior rumbled in his mind. His telepathic voice as deep and gravelly as his speaking voice, except more resonant, making Ere feel it vibrate throughout his body as if Sorin had struck his internal gong.

Alrighty then.

"Turn over."

Wow. A demand, followed by an order.

With any other male of Sorin's stature and presence, Ere would have prepared himself to be pummeled into mince pie for making such assertions.

But Sorin simply did exactly as Ere bid.

Well, there was nothing simple about the slow, smooth, make-his-balls-blue rolling motion the male executed as he turned from his stomach to his back, rippling every muscle in his torso, back and buttocks in the process. And making Ere's Sahara-dry mouth overflow suddenly with saliva.

He licked his lips to stop the leakage and didn't even care that he looked like a starving hyena before a freshly hunted buffalo. Brought down, but still alive. The blood and meat hot and succulent.

Okay, that was rather gruesome.

Ere blinked to clear his blood-crazed madness and focused on the fresh meat—er—delectable feast of beautiful, warrior male.

The rear view had been exceptional. Incomparable. But the front...

Dearest, merciful, heavenly gods!

(As a nihilistic soul, this was really saying something about his frame of mind at the moment).

He wanted to leap upon the man and do his best championship bareback bronco riding imitation.

Didn't matter that he'd never been "in the saddle." Not without "help." He was absolutely ready and willing to figure it out as he went along. He was determined to make the professional team after this night.

But only with this particular bronc.

As if Sorin sensed the frenzied direction of his thoughts, he said, *Take off your clothes first.*

For once, Ere didn't hesitate.

He stripped out of his sweater, undershirt, jeans, socks and underwear in record time. He didn't allow himself to feel self-conscious as he straddled Sorin's hips as soon as he was done, grabbed his bearded jaw with both hands and dove in for his first *real* kiss—

And almost konked himself out as he bashed his nose into the other male's.

"Motherfucker!"

He reeled back and covered the front of his face with one hand. His eyes watered uncontrollably.

Was he bleeding? He had to be bleeding. He threw his head back to stem a potential flood and gasped through his mouth at the freakishly intense pain that rippled across his face.

There was a snort.

He thought he might have misheard.

Then, another snort.

No, he wasn't imagining it.

Tentatively, he slanted his eyes downward while trying to keep his nose tilted toward the ceiling.

Yet another snort.

Followed by a trembling so severe Ere felt like he was sitting directly on top of a category six earthquake.

And that's when he saw it—

Sorin's smile.

More than a smile. A breathtaking, all-out, teeth-baring grin. He was laughing silently, his whole body shaking. His eyes squeezed into golden crescents, glittering with mirthful tears.

"Careful," Ere was distantly shocked that he had the wherewithal to whisper in awe.

"You might shake loose a spleen if you don't let that laugh out. You only have the one spleen. I hear it's one of those noncritical but irreplaceable body parts. Rather like me. Annoying but one of a kind."

That only made Sorin laugh harder, the guffaws finally tumbling from his throat, rumbling deeply through his chest, quiet but heartfelt, making Ere practically melt into a puddle of adoring goo.

"Oh, Solemnity," Ere breathed, "you've finally learned to smile."

He'd only meant to tease, but to Ere's confusion and dismay, Sorin's smile disappeared.

In its place was a naked, heart-rendering pain. A pain so visceral, Ere felt it grow claws, reach into his own chest, and shred his own heart into bloody bits.

He was about to flounder an apology, not knowing exactly what it was he'd be apologizing for, but he just felt he needed to offer it abjectly.

But Sorin surged his torso and hips off the bed in a move so smooth and fast, Ere didn't even realize he'd been flipped onto his back until the colossus of a warrior male trapped him solidly beneath him, skin upon hot, naked, glorious skin.

All the breath whooshed out of him at once, leaving him wide-eyed and panting, his hands clapping upon Sorin's massive biceps reflexively, his legs bending at the knees to bracket Sorin's hips as the male unapologetically ground their erections together in a heart-stopping undulation.

Say it again.

What?

Ere had no idea what he wanted. His brain cells had completely given up the ghost the moment their naughty bits came into contact.

For the love of Loki's hairy balls! Nothing had ever felt this *gooooood!*

That small friction totally changed Ere's perspective on life. Because hallelujah! He finally understood what all the to-do about sex was about!

He tried to squirm beneath Sorin to have that eyes-rolling-in-the-back-of-the-head sensation again, but the male was too heavy, too solid. He wouldn't budge an inch, and Ere had no hopes of budging him without his assistance.

Not unless he used his dragon strength. Which, A, wasn't by any means a guarantee to work with the man, and B, Ere wasn't really sure he wanted to.

Shockingly, he *liked* being overpowered. He *liked* melting into a puddle of goo underneath Sorin's deliciously hard, primally male body.

Say it.

"Uh..."

What was it he'd said? It had been just a second ago, and Ere couldn't for the life of him recall.

"Y-you've finally learned—"

Not that.

Sorin pressed further into him, giving him even more of his weight, more of his hardness and strength.

Was this supposed to be punishment? Well, good gods! At this rate, Ere would stutter all night just so Sorin could sink him all the way through the mattress.

But no. Ere frowned with concentration. There was definitely something better than just being flattened into pattycake by the male's muscled magnificence.

Friction. That's what he needed. Mustn't forget that. He taxed his on-strike brain cells and finally came up with:

"Solemnity."

Before the word was fully out of his mouth, Sorin's own covered his, swallowing the last syllable.

It wasn't a tentative kiss. There was nothing tentative about the male, Ere quickly realized. He wanted; he took. Ere suspected he only ever asked for permission with *him*. And that made all the difference in the world.

It was an open-mouthed, hot, voluptuous, tongue-filled invasion. And holy gods, how he loved it!

His fingers dug into the stone-hard biceps he was still gripping like a lifeline until they hurt. He instinctively wrapped his legs around the male's hips and crossed them over the taut, perfect globes of his ass, desperately trying to pull him closer.

Their erections ground against one another, and they were so close, with not a single molecule of air between them that Ere could swear he felt Sorin's heartbeat pulse in his sex, syncing in time with the same throbbing ache in Ere's own. They were both leaking pre-cum like broken faucets, slicking their skin, satin upon satin, steel against steel.

Sorin's kiss began as a desperate assault, his bold tongue driving into Ere's mouth. Plundering. Staking. Taking.

Ere desperately sucked on him in return, wanting to keep him inside, savoring every taste, wanting to bite him and devour him, his need was so great.

And then, the male suddenly pulled his head back.

Perhaps, like Ere, he simply needed to gulp in oxygen. But at the moment, Ere didn't think he cared if he died of suffocation if this was how he went.

His first *real* kiss!

And he was fucking awesome at it!

Sorin's body didn't lie. Couldn't lie. He was hard enough to pound coal into diamond.

Ere felt it. Reveled in it. His surge of confidence in making this unbelievably beautiful man this turned on completely trumped his fear for once. He'd worry about where Sorin would stow that thick, satin-encased steel pipe later. Right now, he was doing the mental Pachanga in celebration.

"Come back," he invited.

More like begged. Moving his hands to either side of Sorin's face to bring his lips closer.

The male lowered his face once more, but resisted the last centimeter. He stared down into Ere's eyes with unbridled desire mixed with...something else.

There's that sweet, aching pain again. That phantom clutch around Ere's heart, squeezing it like a squeaky toy, making his insides burst with small explosions of tenderness, confusion and profound loss.

His eyes watered. His lips quivered. He bobbed his Adam's apple repeatedly.

What was *wrong* with him? Why did Sorin look at him like that?

My Bane.

Ere didn't understand.

"Yes. I know I'm a nuisance. I'm contrary and difficult. I'll work on being better tomorrow, okay? Just...come back..." he wheedled.

Sorin's body shook against his as if the male was splintering apart. Ere could feel the pain inside him as if it was his own. It literally took his breath away.

Why? Why was he hurting so?

My Bane, the warrior repeated, his voice breaking even in its telepathic transmission.

Before Ere could ask him what he meant, what he could do to comfort him, Sorin's mouth closed over his again.

This time gently. Reverently.

His soft lips trembled, and his breath shook. He sipped at Ere's mouth like a man dying of thirst, but didn't trust that the life-giving water he drank was real, that it wouldn't disappear like a mirage in a desert wasteland.

As if he'd been dying in that wasteland for a taste of Ere's lips. As if he would simply perish if he ever lost them again.

Lost *him* again.

On and on the kiss went, full of nibbles and tender bites, deep, slow penetration and licking that fired up every one of Ere's nerve endings and turned them into exposed live wires.

He tried to take control of the situation. Tried to hold Sorin's face still, with his hands clawed into the hair at the back of the male's head, so that he could plunder right back, do some aggressive claiming of his own. But Sorin was always slightly ahead of him, leading so effortlessly, that Ere could only follow.

It was all he could do to keep up. To suck on Sorin's tongue when it came inside and drink from Sorin's lips when he retreated. He could only silently beg and desperately cling to the male who was driving him insane with lust, with need, so raw and overwhelming he felt like crying.

As it was, he might have made some shameful begging noises, like a starving mut whining for the smallest scraps. His body couldn't take much more of this. He needed—

Sorin suddenly took his heavenly mouth away and began trailing wet, sucking kisses all over Ere's patchwork face, over his brows, eyelids, cheeks, jaw...and every one of his ugly scars.

"No..." he moaned. "Come back. I want..."

But Sorin ignored him, cutting off his needy whimper with a bruising, possessive kiss to Ere's throat.

That would definitely leave a mark. At least until morning, even with his immortal healing powers.

He growled at Sorin's aggression, sensing that the ante had just been raised.

Sorin growled right back, a warning, dominant rumble from the back of his throat, as he moved to Ere's chest and scraped the edges of his fangs across the suddenly too-tight skin.

Ere gasped at the stinging pain and felt a thin line of blood well to the surface.

It was going to be like that, was it? Well, two could play that game.

Apparently, Sorin was an animal spirit with a Dark One base. Lovely fangs included. Ere let his own fangs punch through his upper gums and fill his mouth with saliva. He hissed like a cobra warning its prey and undulated his upper body to try to dislodge Sorin so that he could go on the offensive.

But Sorin wasn't having it. While Ere didn't use his dragon strength in this form, Sorin was far stronger. He kept Ere pinned down by his greater mass and weight and kept him exactly where he wanted.

He lapped in rough licks at the beads of blood that oozed out of the shallow cut he made, using his vampire saliva to keep the wound from healing too fast, instead of closing it.

"You've never fed from anyone like this," Ere rasped, somehow knowing his words to be true, though he had no idea where the thought came from.

No.

"Even though you're a Dark One."

I am animal first.

"But you must have…needs. Cravings. H-How—"

Ere stuttered when Sorin finally lapped the cut closed to suck gently on his nipple, torturing the hard bud with greedy little flicks and soft, gentle licks.

"How have you survived?" he finally got out. "How have you lived?"

Ere was both Dark and Pure, and neither. But even with that half vampire side of him, he needed blood on a regular basis. Specifically, Pure blood.

Not recently, it was true. Not since Sorin revived him. But he'd needed regular infusions of blood throughout his long existence.

I haven't.

Ere frowned. That didn't make any sense.

What did he mean? He hadn't survived? Hadn't lived? But he was here now. Was he—

Stop thinking. Only feel.

To hammer home his point, quite literally, Sorin flexed his hips and ground the entire length of his hard, heavy sex, from root to hot, satiny tip, along Ere's equally eager and ready member, making every coherent thought in Ere's head scatter like billiard balls on the break.

"Uhn," he groaned low, reduced to the intelligence of amoeba at the onslaught of indescribably *goooood* physical sensations.

And then, completely without his permission and out of his control, his overextended dumb fuck of an organ blurted a premature spurt.

No, no, no! It's too soon, he thought in utter mortification. Nothing even happened yet!

Well, plenty had in terms of *his* pleasure, more than all of his countless, meaningless encounters strung together across many millennia. But the benchmark, admittedly, was super low.

Even so, Sorin hadn't gotten off yet, or anywhere near it. What abject failure of a lover was he that he couldn't even get his partner off?

It wasn't rocket science. He'd done it an obscenely large number of times with his targets. He couldn't come like a randy boy pulling his whistle for the very first time *now*! Not when it truly mattered!

Except, his body had a mind of its own.

The initial spurt had apparently unlocked eons of blockage, collapsed the whole dam, so to speak. And suddenly, he was ejaculating in great globs of thick cream onto his stomach, Sorin's torso, all over both their groins.

And it just went on. And on. And on!

His body shook as if it was caught in a seizure, so hard his teeth rattled, his heart thundered, his lungs billowed with the violence of his release.

"O-o-oh, f-fuck. S-sorry," he stuttered through the humiliating ordeal, turning his head into the mattress and catching the loosened sheet between his teeth, as if mangling the fabric into gnawed up strips would help his run-away-train of a body throw on the emergency brakes.

The irony was that he didn't feel pleasure in proportion to the intensity of the release. It felt good, certainly, but it was releasing-pressure sort of good. Kind of painful too, honestly. Like his cock and balls were cramping at the same time. In fact, that's exactly what was happening. Could reproductive parts get Charley horses?

If Sorin laughed at him now, he would just die.

He wanted the bed to turn into a miniature black hole and suck him into an alternate universe so he could disappear and pretend this never happened. And he'd only come back through the portal when his new and improved alternate self was a bonified sex god.

Sorin didn't laugh. He moved down Ere's body, easing his weight off the top half, and held Ere firmly by the hips. Slowly, thoroughly, he licked at Ere's semen-splattered stomach, bathed his still-shuddering, stupid, hyper-sensitive cock with meticulous care.

Ere hissed with pained pleasure when Sorin's mouth closed over the leaking crown, when his big hand held Ere's undying erection in a firm, calloused grip as his tongue probed the oozing slit.

Squeezing, sucking, eating his cum. Milking him with perfect pressure until Ere's pump dried up at last, though it never lost its stiffness entirely, as if waiting for the right moment to spring a second life.

Down boy, he told the overzealous idiot. But said idiot wasn't receiving messages.

He was already sore and sated. At least physically. Even though, emotionally and spiritually, he still wanted *more*. Good thing his witless penis ignored him, because it twitched happily, wanting more too, not appreciating its limits in the least.

Sorin meandered back up his body and kissed him again. His mustache and beard, soft as they were, started to rub Ere's face raw, but Ere didn't care.

Voraciously, he opened his mouth in welcome and thrust his tongue into Sorin's wet warmth, groaning with renewed passion when he tasted himself, when Sorin purposely pushed a dollop of his own cream into his mouth and made him swallow.

Good?

Ere flushed so hard his skin was probably the color of lobster by now.

To be honest, he wasn't a huge fan of his own spunk. It was a little bitter, salty, kind of glue-like. At the same time, when he was fed from Sorin's tongue, it was the most erotic act he'd ever been party to, and somehow, mixed with the taste of Sorin's mouth, he couldn't get enough. He just wanted the kiss to go on forever.

And he was stiff as a skiff again.

His one-hour orgasm (exaggeration, of course... but only barely) so thoroughly discombobulated him that he didn't even notice Sorin's hand settling between his splayed thighs, working between their bodies. Those long, thick fingers gently gathered his essence (there was a helluva lot of it) and rubbed along his taint. Gathered and rubbed. Gathered and rubbed.

With each pass, the fingers sank deeper, circling the tightly shut entrance to his body, pressing his own cream over the sensitive pucker, lubricating it. All the while, Sorin kept kissing him, feeding him that nubile hot tongue, making him shudder and gasp, so turned on he couldn't stand it.

Oh gods! How he wanted this man!

And then, before he even knew what had happened, a finger slipped past his first ring of muscle, making him lose his breath and freeze.

Sorin didn't pull out. Instead, he slowly but surely burrowed the digit further inside, making Ere burn despite the lubrication, despite his care.

"Hurts," Ere whispered into Sorin's mouth, sharing his breath, borrowing his strength.

Should I stop?

He started to nod, as an uncontrollable shiver racked him.

But then, he shook his head.

"I don't care," he said defiantly. "It...It feels good too."

His breath caught as Sorin curled his finger and rubbed.

"There. Right there."

Ere's whole body began shaking, his hips gyrating, humping Sorin's hand shamelessly.

"Please...p-please...."

Tell me what you want. Say it.

"M-more...inside...*fuuuuuck*...want to feel you inside..."

Sorin added a second finger, and that hurt a lot more than the first. The remnants of his cum wasn't providing enough lubrication.

Not that Ere had ever been fucked with care before. When he was used, they enjoyed his pain. He'd never had lubrication. No one had gone slow. Or if they had, it was only after they'd ripped him open and wanted to prolong the agony.

A choked sound escaped him, and he shut his eyes tightly against it. Which was stupid. Closing eyes didn't block out sound.

Why did he have to remember the ugliness? Why did he have to ruin things?

Keep your eyes open. Look at me.

Helplessly, Ere shook his head.

Do it, dragon. Look at me.

It was the "dragon" that did it. The word somehow imbued Ere with dragon-like strength and courage.

He snapped his eyes open and stared into those brilliant golden orbs.

Sorin's eyes.

Gods! They were so beautiful. Fully dilated, enormous black pupils ringed with blazing gold. Like a solar eclipse.

"Beautiful," he couldn't help but whisper.

He was hypnotized by their intensity, the windows into this warrior's soul. The pain below became a distant throb. This *thing* between them, this inexplicable connection—it was all he focused on.

Trust me. Give yourself.

"Okay," he breathed, unblinking.

If it hurts, know that I am the one giving you this pain.

Strangely, the thought of that made Ere feel better already. Could he really *enjoy* pain if Sorin was the one who brought it to him?

The mind-boggling answer was *yes*.

Your *choice,* the warrior said, keeping their gazes fused.

Your *pain.* Your *pleasure. Tell me to stop; I will.*

"Don't stop," Ere immediately uttered.

Sorin added a third finger.

Oh, fuckity fuck!

Ere writhed helplessly, impaled upon Sorin's thick fingers, trying to escape the burn. But with every minute movement, Sorin's hand rubbed against that secret gland inside, so swollen now it felt like it had quadrupled in size.

Say it. What you want. Demand it.

Ere's eyes blazed sapphire blue, clashing with Sorin's gold like two titans going head-to-head in the final galactic battle, with the fate of the universe in the balance.

"Fuck me," he growled, baring his sharp, gleaming fangs.

"Hurt me. The pain and the pleasure. As long as it's you, I want it all."

Sorin held his eyes a few moments longer, penetrating him down to his very soul, a murky, swampy abyss though it was.

But Ere felt like the intense golden rays of Sorin's eyes shone a fiery light upon the darkness within him, burning away his past, his nightmares, like the sun renewing each day.

No matter how terrible, horrible, how bloody and despicable, you could always count on the day to end. The sun would always rise again.

At last, Sorin broke their gaze, and slowly shifted lower, flexing his hand within Ere, curling his fingers just so.

Ere kept his eyes wide open, biting down hard on his lower lip, drawing blood.

He could focus on nothing else but the pain and the pleasure building in equal measure within him, stoked by Sorin's hand.

And now, by Sorin's hot, wet mouth and probing tongue. The vampire venom in his saliva numbed some of the burn, but the pulsing, voracious, unbearable ache remained.

Ere's breath grew shallower as all of the blood in his body seemed to pool in his groin, throbbing in time with his heartbeat, produced by the organ that had apparently relocated to his ass. The tantalizing wetness of Sorin's patient laps around his entrance made him clench reflexively around the fingers inside him.

They were unbelievably thick. He was unbelievably stretched. But still, he wanted *more*. He wanted to be branded and owned.

This man.

Only by this warrior male.

"Now," he commanded, his voice frayed but strong.

"Take me now."

Slowly, the fingers left him, leaving his opening loosened and bereft. But before his muscles could remotely adjust, Sorin thrust inside him to the hilt in one powerful surge.

Motherfucking gods!

Ere arched almost entirely off the bed, eyes and mouth open on a silent scream. He cursed mentally in every language he knew, and in made up gibberish too.

That fucking hurt!

"D-did you grow a fucking canon when I wasn't looking? Fudge nuggets and Barbara Streisand! Peanut butter jelly and horseradish sauce! Did you split me in two right down the middle? Pretty sure I'll have a tattoo in the shape of your cockhead in my fucking larynx!"

Sorin paid him no mind, merely settling that big, steely body on top of his, anchoring them both with his solid weight.

Your voice seems to work just fine, the male rumbled in his mind, serious as ever, though Ere thought he felt the smile on his lips when Sorin took his mouth again in a coaxing, soothing kiss.

Pity I can't gag you with my cannon cock.

Did he just...?

"Did you just make a joke, Solemnity?" Ere gasped. "Armageddon must be right around the corner. The world is ending. Hell has fro—"

His words died a sudden death when Sorin began to move.

How could something that hurt so much upon entry feel so unbelievably good once it was inside?

His hands clawed into Sorin's back on their own accord. His mouth devoured Sorin's tongue, mimicking the shameless wanton way his ass clenched around and sucked down Sorin's sex. Pulling him ever deeper.

Deeper.

Wanting to merge their bodies into one. Desperate to swallow him whole.

Feel me, that gravelly voice commanded in his head.

Oh yeah, Ere felt him all right. He'd feel him for the rest of eternity.

Needing to make his own mark, needing to *take,* he broke their kiss and latched onto Sorin's corded throat. Sucking hard. Bruising skin.

The male arched his neck to give Ere better access, knowing exactly what he wanted.

Do it.

Ere struck in an instant, punching his fangs into Sorin's jugular vein, gorging on the hot, sweet ambrosia that rushed into his mouth.

Sorin's blood.

It was heaven. He tasted just like heaven.

It didn't matter that he was Dark or animal. Since he brought Ere back to life, Ere only wanted him. Needed him. He didn't even know he'd been waiting all this time. Perhaps longer than he knew.

It felt like he'd waited forever.

And now he was finally, *finally*, where he was always meant to be.

Chapter Twelve

Sorin shuddered in rippling quakes from head to toe as Ere pulled the life force from his body.

His blood fed steadily into Ere's mouth, the dagger-like fangs in his throat burning like swords fresh from the forge. Ere's venom sizzled through his veins, demanding, conquering, staking his claim. It didn't numb the fierceness of his possession, like he could have intended, as vampire venom often did.

No, he wanted Sorin to feel every fiery tingle, every scorpion sting. Just as Ere himself welcomed and reveled in Sorin's possession of him—the pain, the pleasure, every nuance and note.

The voracious suction would leave him black and blue, even in the morning. His long hair would hide the marks before they faded, but Sorin didn't want to hide them. He'd proudly display this male's possession of him to the world.

Below, Ere's ass wrung his cock in rhythmic pulses, convulsing with bruising strength. His legs wrapped tightly around Sorin's hips. His hands clawed bloody streaks across Sorin's back, trying to pull him closer. Deeper. Trying to make him come undone.

He flexed his buttocks and nudged within that unbelievably tight heat by incremental degrees. But the friction of even the smallest movement was enough to make the male beneath him lose control.

"Fuck, fuck, fuck!" Ere pulled haphazardly out of his throat to groan, biting blindly down onto his shoulder.

Sorin barely noticed the stinging pain in his throat and shoulder. Not when his cock was getting squeezed in a satiny vice so hard, he saw stars flash before his eyes. He ground his teeth to bite back a guttural pain-pleasure groan.

"Please..." Ere tossed his head feverishly upon the bed, his eyes shut tightly, his face scrunched in intense concentration, jaw locked.

His entire body clenched around Sorin's, every limb, every muscle. Especially the hot, tight, satiny channel that sheathed the most intimate part of him. Sucking on him, milking him desperately.

"I need..."

Sorin held back by sheer force of will.

All these millennia of reining in his Dark side had pressurized that will into the indestructible strength of diamonds. His body obeyed him in all things. He had perfect control.

Tell me.

Ere clawed new bloody streaks down his arms, his neck and chest, reduced to growling like a savage animal, his need was so great.

Sorin's heavy muscles jumped at the small wounds, thin trails of blood slicking his hot skin, sizzling as they almost immediately evaporated. The flames within him raged into an inferno, spreading like wildfire throughout.

He could feel the pressure building. If he wasn't careful, he'd torch the whole house down around them.

He should have had the foresight to make a simple nest upon the bed. At least scatter a thin layer of feathers on the sheets to protect them. But he hadn't anticipated how the night would evolve. He hadn't expected *this.*

He'd wanted it. Dreamed of it. Yearned and longed for it.

But he'd never taken Ere's desire for granted. And in the end, what the dragon wanted was all that mattered.

"You," Ere gritted out in a ragged, tortured voice that both of them barely recognized. It was deep and primal, broken with emotion, but steely with resolve.

"I need *you.* Come. I need to feel it. Your seed inside me. Flooding me. I want you to fill me so good I'll be leaking your cum for days. And then I want you to fill me some more. So I'll never stop overflowing. So I—"

Sorin slammed his mouth onto the dragon's to shut him up.

Fucking gods!

This man!

He pumped his hips powerfully, once, twice, making Ere hiss into his mouth and bite his bottom lip at the hard pounding.

And that was all it took.

Millennia of controlling his body was all for naught. It belonged to the dragon now. What Ere wanted, Ere got.

With the only remaining fragment of intelligent thought left in his mind, Sorin materialized and unfurled his wings and wrapped them tightly around both of them—a moment before his flames engulfed them.

As his body broke apart in cataclysmic release, pouring his life force into the dragon. Remaking him. Healing him from the inside out.

Sorin maintained the seal of their lips throughout his undoing, catching every one of Ere's whimpers and groans, as he absorbed everything Sorin gave him, his body clutching greedily for more.

Always *more*.

And Sorin knew that he was forever lost to this male. This man who was his Bane, yet also not. This man who was equal light and darkness. Joy and pain. An infinite myriad of experiences and emotions.

He enthralled Sorin, body, heart and soul.

Before, when Sorin had tried to heal him, it had been pure instinct. From the moment he answered the dragon's faraway call, his instincts had overruled all conscious thought.

But now, with their mouths fused, the way Ere held him, fully aware and involved...his words...gods! his fucking words!

Sorin felt healed too. He'd never known what he'd been missing until he had it at last within his embrace.

He would never let this dragon go.

Endlessly, he poured himself into Ere, until, just as the greedy dragon demanded, Ere was overflowing with his essence, rivulets of his cream leaking down their thighs, slicking their bodies.

The protective cocoon of his wings prevented the inferno he'd started from spreading beyond the two of them, locked together tightly as one flaming nucleus, no telling where he ended and Ere began. The bed would likely not survive their mating, but at least the house would.

Not that Sorin gave a fuck. He was too busy filling and fulfilling his male to the letter of his commandment.

His cream slicked Ere's vise-tight channel enough that he could move without hurting the male. And so he did.

Ere's mouth opened in a silent wail of ecstasy when Sorin began to thrust in earnest.

Look at me. Keep your eyes open.

See me.

Their gazes fused as Ere did as he ordered. He could see the male's undiluted pleasure as he moved within his body, stroking him deep and hard and slow. Plowing his swollen bundle of nerves inside with every pass. Making him clutch desperately at every hot, steely inch of his thickness.

Now look down.

He gathered Ere's noodle-limp body into a half-sitting position, supporting all of the male's weight in one arm while bracing both of them with the other, his wings wrapped tightly around them like a chrysalis. He kept his eyes on Ere's face as Ere obediently looked down at where they were joined.

Slowly, painstakingly, Sorin pulled all the way out, until the engorged, ruddy head of him pulsed against Ere's entrance, his slit convulsing and leaking cream like an open mouth, the thick veins around his column distended as if angry.

Ere whimpered and moaned at the loss of him, his stretched hole gaping with emptiness, quivering and clenching, hungry to devour him again.

"D-don't," the male pleaded. "Come back. I need…"

Sorin undulated his hips and thrust the head of him inside the starving hole, stretching Ere anew.

The dragon's breath hitched and he bit his lip at the painfully pleasurable intrusion, his eyes involuntarily starting to close.

Don't look away.

Sorin pulled completely out again as if to punish him.

Ere clawed at his chest and growled.

And he surged back inside, but only letting Ere have half of his length, before pulling all the way out again.

"Stop torturing me!" the dragon railed. "I can't stand it! I'm begging! *Please*…please, please, please…don't leave me…"

Look, he commanded a final time, before plunging inside, this time to the hilt.

And he began to move in earnest, his cream creating the silkiest friction as he plundered. He rose up slightly on his knees and braced Ere off the bed so that he could gain the leverage and distance he needed—to piston into the male.

Deeper, faster, harder.

Over and over and over.

Until Ere couldn't bear it any more, his eyes squeezing tightly shut despite his best efforts to keep them open, his face contorting in a beautiful pain—

As he shattered piece by piece in Sorin's arms, within the protective cocoon of Sorin's wings. As an explosion of ecstasy blew him apart, his sex erupting hot waves of milky cum between them without the slightest touch, just on the pressure alone of Sorin's cock inside him.

Sorin roared his own release at the indescribable completion and euphoria on Ere's face. This was what he was made for—to fulfill and protect this dragon.

His Bane.

His Erebu.

His beautiful curse.

His wicked salvation.

*** *** *** ***

The tech master sent his encrypted message and finished covering up his tracks.

Since his contact with a fellow Dandelion, he knew he was being followed and watched. Despite every precaution, Lilith was likely on to him. His cover was compromised.

Head down, shoulders hunched reflexively against potential threat, he quickened his strides.

The private plane was waiting for him in the abandoned airfield. He could hear the distant sound of its engine. If he could just get airborne...

He had an escape plan. Actually, he had many. When a man worked for the she-devil, he couldn't take enough precautions.

His plan would take him to the Pure Ones in New York City, where the head of the Dandelions resided. A special human among the Immortals, right there within their Shield.

Three of the Elite would meet him at his secret landing location. They weren't taking any chances with his protection, sending half of their best warriors to bring him in.

The engine of the plane grew louder as his rapid footsteps took him closer. He was practically running now. He could feel an unknown presence bearing down on him, the danger was so palpable, its invisible hands closed around his throat to choke the air from his lungs.

He was so close. He was almost there.

Look! He could see the plane!

The engine cranked up, as if it saw him too. He'd programmed the autopilot to recognize him visually.

He broke into a flat-out sprint, his lungs bellowing as he ran.

He wasn't like some of the other Dandelions. He didn't excel in physical activities. His Gifts were all cerebral. It was why he was the best positioned to take down Lilith's empire from the technology side. Everything was digital these days. Her resources were mostly locked in virtual vaults. And the tech master had just made 99.9% of it disappear.

Oh God! Only a few more steps.

But even as he stumbled toward the plane, he knew he was already dead.

"Going somewhere?"

The demonic voice resonated behind him, all around him. It was in his head, he knew. He didn't bother to stop to look.

He kept going, but his feet began to drag.

The plane was so close. So close!

"I am disappointed in you," the voice hissed and chided. "Haven't I paid you well? Haven't you obtained every material possession you've ever wanted?"

He didn't bother to answer. None of those things mattered to him. They never had.

All he'd ever wished for was a family of his own. A mother and father. Siblings if he was lucky.

A *normal* life.

But he wasn't normal. None of the Dandelions were. They were aberrations created in her labs. Or pushed out of convenient wombs and discarded like so much trash. The ones she deemed "promising" were taken away to experiment further on. The ones that took longer to show Gifts were sometimes fortunate to be forgotten.

A lot of them simply died of unknown causes and never developed into adulthood. They were "unnatural," after all.

Abominations.

The small two-seater plane's side door automatically slid open as he approached. He practically leapt for it, throwing himself physically into the belly of his getaway ride.

Tsk. Tsk. The voice was a thunderous echo now, resounding within his pressurized brain.

You cannot run or hide from a god, stupid human. And now, you will learn what it is to truly burn.

An unholy silvery blast hit the plane and split it right down the middle, engulfing the entire thing in a vortex of hellfire.

The tech master opened his mouth in a soundless scream.

The pain was unreal. Every particle of his physical being individually eviscerated one by one.

With his last conscious thought, he prayed that his allies received his message. It could be the key to destroying the Hydra. It might be their only chance.

But he would never know...

As all evidence of the plane and the tech master disappeared into dust and sparks as if they never were.

*** *** *** ***

"Why is Sorin carrying the mattress outside?"

Ere absolutely loved Benjamin's curious mind. The boy's brilliance knew no bounds. But sometimes, he asked the most inconvenient questions.

This was one of those times.

"Eh..."

"And why is the mattress charred black? Did you set the bed on fire, Uncle Ere?"

Why, yes, indeed he did! In more ways than one.

He scrounged his orgasm-numbed brain for a reasonable explanation.

"It's all Sorin's fault," was the best he could come up with.

Five pairs of eyes turned on him as the entire family stood in a horizontal line watching Sorin heap the ruined mattress onto the side of the street for Monday trash pickup.

Ere watched too, unable to help himself from admiring the contours of Sorin's flexing back, shoulder and arm muscles, clearly delineated through his thin thermal. The sleeves were rolled up to his elbows, showing off those porn-worthy forearms. And his ass.

Gods, that ass!

Clenching, perfect globes of steel that bullets would probably bounce off of. And that tight seam between the cheeks. Ere wanted to pry them apart with his hands and lick—

"You're really red, Uncle Ere," Benjamin observed further.

"Are you still burning from the fire that cooked the bed? The whole house is so hot, it feels like summer in NYC without air conditioning. Look! All the snow from the blizzard melted around our house, but everything else is still buried."

"Er..."

Ere could no longer form intelligible words. He was simply thankful his family kept their gazes above the neck.

Below his waist, he'd grown a third limb, and there was nowhere to hide.

Fortunately, his jeans prevented the stupid thing from jutting straight out from his groin. Unfortunately, the zipper and button were creaking with protest trying to hold his mammoth erection behind their walls and imprinting themselves painfully into his rigid flesh even through layers of cloth.

Sorin came back to the house but didn't enter, standing just shy of the threshold. Though a whole firing squad of Ere's family stood before him, staring unnervingly, he only had eyes for Ere.

Immediately, he took in Ere's fever-flushed face and the action below his waist.

Ere stared back, and watched in fascination as Sorin's body reacted reflexively to his own arousal.

First, one thick pec jumped, then the other. Then, his obscenely well-developed biceps flexed, and every one of his eight-pack abs turned to corrugated steel, like one of those superheroes in the movies whose body transformed into hard armor before a duel. Except, Sorin remained tantalizingly flesh and blood.

Hot, sweet blood that Ere could practically taste on his needy, addicted tongue.

A throat cleared somewhere beside him. Ere couldn't take his eyes off of Sorin to see who it was.

"Breakfast, anyone?"

He had to get out of here. He wanted to be alone with Sorin. They couldn't risk setting the house on fire again.

So, Ere finally gathered enough wits to say, "Thank you, but no. Sorin and I will get some brunch at *Drink of Me*. I might not be back til much later. We have...uh...some things to do."

He was already walking out of the house toward the golden-eyed warrior before he finished speaking.

Without a single look in his family's direction, he tossed behind his back, "Terribly sorry about the bed. I've already ordered a new one with expedited shipping. It should be here in a few days. Until then, I'm staying with Sorin. Toodaloo!"

Ere didn't hear what his family had to say to that.

He simply started walking briskly down the sidewalk, stomping his boots through three-feet-deep snow. But he knew that Sorin followed, however silently. Ere could feel the heat of the other male behind him.

He was only wearing a turtleneck sweater, jeans and a relatively light goose down jacket, but he was comfortably warm. Didn't feel the cold at all. Besides, the sun was out, however pallid it was behind some gray clouds. It still radiated warmth and brightness that glistened off the serene, snow-covered landscape.

It was beautiful. And Ere felt completely charitable with the world.

Might have something to do with being shagged into loopy bliss half the night, then falling asleep in his lover's embrace while the male still throbbed deliciously within his cum-slicked channel.

All. Night. Long.

Gods!

Ere was glad they trudged in silence along the deserted streets. Their telepathic connection was silent as well. Then again, Sorin wasn't a male of many words. If Ere didn't draw him into conversation, he wasn't likely to initiate one.

Which, under the present circumstances, suited Ere just fine. His thoughts and feelings were a complete mess. His body, on the other hand, knew exactly what it wanted. And it wanted *more* right *now*.

In the most basic ways, his mind and heart wanted more too. Every part of him trusted that Sorin would make him feel so unbelievably good. Protected and safe.

And yet, a tiny part of him held back. He didn't really know this man, even if he *knew* him on a fundamental level. He didn't know what their...coupling meant. Only that they both needed it.

Badly. Desperately.

But what did it change?

Sorin was still mostly a stranger, and Ere was still going to die fighting Lilith. He'd already made up his mind about it.

That wasn't to say that he wanted to die; he didn't.

He really didn't.

He would have fought to live for his son, for his family, if nothing else. Even if he didn't deserve to live.

But now, he wanted to live for Sorin too. Last night had been the best night of Ere's entire existence, hands down. No comparison. It transcended anything and everything he'd ever experienced before. Even when he'd been happiest with Benjamin.

His connection with Sorin was different. It made his deadened soul sputter back to life. It gave him *hope*. It made him *happy*.

But.

He was still fighting Lilith. He was still determined to end her once and for all. And he was realistic enough to know that the odds of survival going against the Hydra were slim to none. More like none. At best, he'd take her down with him. And even that wasn't guaranteed with the combined forces of the Tiger King's militia.

She'd come soon. Ere knew it in his bones. They might have a few days more at best to prepare for her attack.

A few more days, and nights, with Sorin.

He stumbled a little as his heart lurched.

Sorin paused behind him but didn't rush forth to steady him.

Ere really liked that about the male. He didn't treat Ere as if he was someone broken and fragile. He seemed to know exactly how far to push him, how much he could handle. As evidenced by how Sorin healed him in the beginning, and also last night.

It had been different last night.

It wasn't just about healing. That wasn't even on Ere's mind, and he didn't think Sorin did what he did to heal him. That Ere felt more whole and stronger than ever this morning *because* of last night was merely a bonus.

Sorin had taken him exactly the way he needed and wanted to be taken. And he'd let Ere claim him back, however he wanted.

Ere's face felt hot enough to fry an egg as his mind ran through all the scenarios of how he wanted to *take* Sorin. How he wanted him *now*.

He'd been too exhausted and blissed out to do even a fraction of what he wanted to do to the beautiful warrior, but they had all day. And maybe tomorrow. And if they were lucky, the day after that.

Oh, the possibilities!

Ere's stomach chose that moment to gurgle loudly.

It's a miracle! He was actually *hungry*. For food! Like a normal person.

All that fucking had worked up an appetite in the best possible way. Ere was eager to devour his brunch so he could work up a different kind of appetite in short order. He didn't dare look behind him for fear the sight of the male he'd marked as his would reduce him into a lust-crazed maniac right here on the snow-covered streets.

Thankfully, they arrived at the café, and it was open. The sidewalk and streets around it cleared of snow.

He hesitated briefly at the door.

He'd be entering the shop in his own skin for the first time. For a moment, he wanted to don his Binu disguise out of habit and comfort.

Sorin's quiet heat behind him made him square his shoulders, however. He had to try to be himself. If a beautiful, strong, warrior male like Sorin wanted him, there must be *something* right with him.

Taking a deep breath, he pulled the door open with a jingle and walked inside, Sorin following close behind.

Mike and the other owner, Maddie, were on duty this late morning. Despite the blizzard the night before, the place seemed to be as busy as usual.

People in these parts seldom let a small thing like a snow storm prevent them from going about their days. It came with the territory. And the fact that *Drink of Me* had the best brunch menu helped with their motivation to get out of the house.

Ere avoided looking at the front counter as he took Sorin to the corner back booth the male had chosen before. He also ducked his head a little so his long hair would shield most of his scarred face from view. There were a couple of kids about, and he didn't want to scare them unnecessarily.

They sat down with Sorin facing the front of the shop, while Ere presented his back. He unfolded the menu and put it in front of his face, pretending to study it with great concentration, even though, of course, he knew the items on there like the back of his hand.

Sorin simply looked at him, silent as ever. Ere could feel the male's intense golden stare penetrating him layer by layer.

"What can I get you, handsome," Mike said over his shoulder.

They hadn't even sat for two minutes, that was how good the service was here.

"Oh, it's you again," she addressed Sorin. "Are you looking for Binu? He's not on shift today. But listen, we have a great brunch menu, including Maddie's signature Spanish Tortillas. So you should at least get fed while you're here."

And that was when Mike saw Ere sitting with hunched shoulders in the seat opposite Sorin, trying to make himself as small as possible.

She came closer so she stood at the table's edge between them to get a better look at him.

"Sorry, didn't realize he had company for a second. What can I get you two?"

Was it just Ere, or did she sound peeved? Did his scars disgust her like he feared?

"Um…" he began, his voice higher pitched than usual. He cleared his throat and tried again, still hiding his face in the menu.

"We'll get two orders of the blueberry waffles with jam, butter and fruit on the side. Two of the Spanish Tortillas, double the meat, double the cheese, everything in it. With a side of sausages, bacon and half the ham. On second thought, just bring the entire thing. Oh, and two chocolate chip muffins if you still have those."

Mama Bear made the pastries for the café, and they went fast.

"Sure. And to drink?"

Crap, she sounded downright curt and surly now. Was his real form that off-putting?

Maybe he was being oversensitive. After all, Mike didn't say anything untoward.

But it was in her tone. She flirted and chatted like nobody's business. With new clientele, she always stuck around longer to get to know them and make them feel welcome. But with Ere, it seemed like she couldn't wait to leave his table.

"Hot cocoa, coffee and water for both of us. Maybe in that order."

"You going to let him do all the talking, stud?" she addressed Sorin, not confirming Ere's order.

Yup. She definitely sounded surly.

And accusative.

Was it Ere's imagination or did she put extra emphasis on the word "stud"?

"He knows my wants," Sorin replied, not taking his eyes off Ere.

Wow. A whole, four-worded sentence. This was a record. Ere was impressed.

"Well, aren't you the lucky one," Mike practically gritted out between her teeth. "First Binu, then Erena, and now this…whoever this is. You sure get around for being in town all of three days. Wonder who you'll bring in tomorrow. Better yet, don't come in at all."

Wait. What?

It occurred to Ere that Mike was upset about Sorin…playing the field?

214

Was she miffed on behalf of Binu? Or maybe Erena? Miffed that Sorin was out with Ere, who was *both* Binu and Erena?

Oh dear. He had to stop this. Sorin didn't deserve her misdirected umbrage.

He stood up to go after her as she left their table with a huffy spin.

"Wait," he called out. "May I speak with you...Mike?"

She didn't turn around to acknowledge him.

But she did say, stomping her way to the front of the shop, "I don't know what to tell you, stranger. That man you're sitting with is a no-good two-timer. Three-timer. Hell, maybe more. I've personally seen him make the moves on my friends. And now he's here with you. *With* you. Clear as day, the way he can't even look away from you."

"But—"

"Word of advice. He may look like he's totally into you with those eyes and that stare of his, but he does the same damn thing to everyone else. Well, except me."

She sniffed, sounding disgruntled that Sorin didn't take undue interest in her, while also blaming him for taking too much interest in others.

"You're not special. I'm sorry for being a bitch not knowing you from Adam, but my friend likes him. Both my friends, I think. I don't want Binu to get hurt seeing him here with someone else. No offense."

"Mike—"

"Gotta put these orders in. Nothing personal, but I don't socialize with the 'other man.'"

The other...

Oh, for the love of Loki's hairy balls!

There was nothing for it. Ere followed her past the front counter, even though non-employees weren't allowed.

"Hey," Maddie said from a few feet away, trying to get his attention, ostensibly to tell him he couldn't follow Mike past the counter.

He grasped Mike's elbow, dragged her into the private back room and looked the door behind them.

"What—" she started to exclaim, her brows furrowed, her body tensing for a fight.

Ere explained in the most expedient way he knew how. He shifted into Binu form right in front of her.

"Hi, Mike," he said in Binu's voice.

To her credit, she didn't scream. But her eyes did round to saucers and her jaw promptly dropped.

"And...hi again, Mike," he said in Erena's voice as he transformed into the female disguise.

Impossibly, her eyes widened some more, the whites startlingly bright in the dim room.

"What's going on in there?" Maddie shouted from the other side of the door, pounding on it.

"Are you okay, Mike?"

"Tell her you're fine, I have to talk to you," Ere whispered quickly. "Just a few minutes. I'll explain everything."

"Uh...yeah, fine, Mads," Mike said haltingly, her eyes trained on Ere like he was a figment of her imagination and might poof into smoke if she looked away.

"Just catching up with an old friend. Everything's cool."

"Are you sure? Why is the door locked?"

Ere changed back into his real form and pleaded some more with his eyes for Mike to understand.

"I'll be out soon. Just need a little privacy for this conversation. Don't worry about it, Mads."

Mike narrowed her eyes, and Ere got scared.

This didn't bode well for him. An angry Mike was a volatile Mike. Fists might be swinging in his direction soon.

"You have exactly two minutes. Either way, I'm warning you now to expect a beatdown. You're either an imposter or you've been deceiving me for months. Prepare yourself for at least a bloody nose. Now get talking."

Ere sighed internally with relief. He wasn't looking forward to the bloody nose, but the truth would finally come out.

It was time he owned up to who he was.

Chapter Thirteen

It took so long for Ere to come back to the corner booth that Sorin was of a mind to go after him. Instead, he kept vigil, staring a hole through the door that Ere had shut behind him, though it was barely visible from where Sorin sat.

Finally, the door opened again, and out walked the waitress with her head held high, a look of satisfaction on her face.

Sorin narrowed his eyes in a frown.

The woman had disrespected Sorin quite overtly, but he shrugged it off. He'd long since inured himself of human reactions. His height, bearing and overall *presence* always made those around him uncomfortable, especially if they were the weakest of all Kinds—mortals. He simply ignored them as a rule.

But this woman also disrespected Ere, and *that* Sorin took note of.

He was well aware that the man could take care of himself, but he had...vulnerabilities. He'd withstood untold physical pain, Sorin knew, having found his wrecked body at the bottom of a lake. That Ere survived attested to his courage, determination, sheer stubbornness and innate strength.

But his sense of self was fragile.

In this aspect, he was completely opposite of Sorin's Bane. The Bane always knew where he stood with everyone around him, especially Sorin. He possessed a brash kind of self-confidence and absolute certainty in his beliefs.

For example, the Bane believed that he would become the mightiest of all dragons, land, sea and air, and set about achieving it. He did.

He believed that the raptors would follow his lead when he charged ahead of them into battle. They did.

He believed that even though he was a strange-looking lizard with wings, many times the size of a typical Eagle Spirit, he fit in with the rest of them. He believed that they were his family, his friends, comrades for whom he would die, and who would die for him in return. They were.

He believed, even before it was true, or more accurately, before Sorin realized it was true, that Sorin loved him above all else, "forever and ever" (as the Bane was fond of saying). Sorin did.

Gods! Did he ever love his Bane.

But Ere...he had none of that confidence and self-possession.

Even though his family clearly loved him, Ere himself did not count on it. He only seemed to rely on himself. And even then, Sorin sensed that he did not judge himself highly, despite all evidence to the contrary.

A couple minutes later, Ere finally emerged from the room.

One nostril was stuffed with what looked like a shredded paper napkin, his cheek shiny red from an obvious collision with someone's fist. But strangely enough, he was smiling, as if he enjoyed the bloody nose immensely.

He sauntered over and plopped himself down on the seat across from Sorin again. Casually, he plucked the tissue out of his nose and wadded it into another napkin.

His nose probably stopped bleeding as soon as it started, given his immortal healing powers. That he had to stuff anything to stem the flow in the first place said a lot about the power of the woman server's punch.

"Well, now that that's out of the way, I find I am hungry enough to eat a whole cow! Mike should be over soon with the first of our orders. Can't wait to dig in."

Sorin assessed his eagerness and *happiness* with the same intensity with which he always gazed upon Ere.

He wanted to know everything about the man. What made him tick. What caused different emotions to flitter across his face. Most of all, he wanted to know what made Ere happy.

He'd given the male pleasure last night. Fed Ere's body with his own. Healed him the only way he knew how, by joining their bodies and souls, funneling his life force into the still broken male.

He'd witnessed the beautiful agony of ecstasy on Ere's face as he found release after shuddering release. But that wasn't the same as joy and happiness.

Ere might be hungry for food, but Sorin was hungry for knowledge of *him*.

And he was also hungry for food.

Soon, the female came back with the first platters of their repast. She glared at Ere and ignored Sorin this time. Ere grinned beatifically back at her and even winked, practically beaming his effervescent joy.

Fuck, he was beautiful.

Sorin's body burned to possess him, his sex pulsing hot and hard in the confines of his trousers. But more than that, he wanted to soak in Ere's happiness. He was his Bane in that moment.

Sorin's heart twisted and ached with profound loss—that his Bane was sitting right in front of him, that same, yet vastly different, beautiful soul. But he didn't know Sorin at all.

Those memories...a hundred, thousand, million memories that bound them together as one...Ere didn't have them. He didn't understand. And because of that, Sorin felt his Bane's absence all the more keenly. As if he'd died all over again, and there was nothing Sorin could do.

After the server walked away, an energetic bounce in her step and a sassy sway in her hips, Ere began devouring everything on his plate with hearty forkfuls.

"That's Mike, by the way," he said in between gigantic bites. "She's my best friend here. The best! She might have appeared bitchy just now, but I deserved it. We're good though. Phew! She packs a solid punch for a human. So proud of her!"

He looked up and saw that Sorin hadn't touched his food.

"What's wrong? You don't like what I ordered? We can get something else if you want. I have the entire menu memorized. But I can also ask for off-menu specials. What's your fancy?"

Sorin used the excuse of focusing on his food to lower his eyes from Ere's sparkling sapphire gaze.

He didn't reply as he methodically worked through his own platter.

His heart hurt so badly he couldn't breathe. His chest felt filled with acid, his throat convulsing to swallow food that must have been delicious but went down like rocks.

Ere wasn't his Bane.

Ere didn't know him.

A scuffle with "Mike" made him happy. His family, and in particular the boy called Benjamin, made him happy. His body needed what Sorin gave him to heal, but that was all. He didn't *need* Sorin.

Not the way Sorin needed him.

But it wasn't even really Ere, was it? It was an echo of the Bane's soul in Ere.

Ere was his own person. Someone who wasn't Sorin's Bane. Not really. But somehow...against all odds...against his own judgement, yet *again*, Sorin Fell.

And it fucking *hurt*.

He steeled himself and clenched his jaw as he chewed and swallowed the food he didn't taste.

He would keep his promise to his Bane. He would fix the broken Ere if it was the last thing he did. No matter what it took from him.

Even if it broke him in return.

Ere didn't find his silence strange, for which Sorin was grateful. The dragon ate and prattled on, more cheerfully talkative than Sorin had ever seen him. He reminded Sorin of the boy Benjamin in this moment. Pure, unburdened, open joy.

When they were done, it was Ere who had the presence of mind to pay this time, whipping a plastic card out of his back pocket and jogging to the front of the shop before Sorin even noticed.

"Shall we?" Ere said when he came back to the table, standing at the edge, not sitting back down.

"What?" Sorin responded, his voice gravelly deep.

Ere hesitated slightly.

"Um...I mean, shall we leave? Together?"

He shifted from one foot to the other and hooked a long strand of hair behind his ear.

"I told Benjamin's family I would stay with you for a while. I thought...well, I guess I should have asked first. It's just, I thought..."

Sorin didn't like his hesitation. He wanted Ere to have no doubt of him.

"Yes," he confirmed. "With me."

Ere's expression visibly relaxed, then scrunched up again.

"You do have a place of your own, right? Preferably not in the mountainous wilderness?"

He should have checked in advance, Sorin thought. But this was just like the Bane—taking the leap first, looking where he leaped second.

"Have nest," he grunted, getting up from the booth and walking with long strides out of the shop.

Ere blanched a little beside him, his own long legs easily keeping pace.

"Nest, you say?" he squeaked. "Like, made of sticks and feathers and bird...goo...on mountain peaks? Or gods forbid, in a t-tree?"

"In cave," Sorin expounded helpfully.

"Oh," the dragon said, a note of disappointment in his voice.

"So, not a deluxe suite of rooms at the Grand Hyatt then."

Sorin didn't know what that was, so he didn't bother to respond.

He headed toward the edge of town. It was only two blocks away, given that the town center itself was only eight blocks in total. The base of the tallest mountain in the range was another three miles from there.

The early afternoon sun was strong enough that last night's snow had melted, then hardened in the freezing temperatures, making it easier to stomp through, as the streets and sidewalks were still buried in the stuff. Sorin's borrowed boots crunched through the snow, packing it tighter, Ere's lighter steps crunching right beside him.

He was content to be silent, but Ere was not.

After a few minutes, the dragon began his questions.

"So...I always wondered...how did you hear my call, find me, and...save me?"

"Soul."

"Sol? Is that a name?" Ere misunderstood. "Like Solomon or...Oh, I know! Solemnity! Is that your nickname, by any chance? Along with Silence, Severity, Sternness, Solitude, Somber, Strictness..."

He grinned at his own wit, while Sorin's heart squeezed painfully.

"Hey, how about this one—Stiffness."

He snickered with good humor.

"I should call you Your Splendiferous Stiffness. Your Stiffened Magnificence. Your Majestic Stiffy Stoney Staf—"

"*Your* soul," Sorin rasped, torn between anguish and laughter.

This was his Bane! Even when he accepted that the Bane was gone, Ere unknowingly, flippantly brought him back.

"Mine?" Ere echoed, the teasing sparkle still glinting in his eyes.

"Are you mine? My Solemnity, my Sol?"

Gods! His heart and soul felt torn in two.

Sorin didn't trust himself to speak out loud any more.

It is your soul that brought me to you, he explained as clearly as he could.

I used to know that soul. I used to know a different version of you, dragon.

Ere was so surprised, he stopped walking.

"Truly? But...how is that possible? I thought I've always been, well, *me*. I don't remember another life before the ancient Akkadian Empire, when I was born."

He started walking again and faced forward, looking away from Sorin, the humor dying by slow degrees from his expression.

Sorin immediately wished it back, even if he was the butt of Ere's jokes. Even if his heart twisted with old, yet blindingly fresh, pain.

"I've lived enough lives as it is," Ere murmured, more to himself than to Sorin. "I'm just too cowardly or stubborn or contrary to die, I guess."

I knew you before that time, Sorin communicated, leaving no room for doubt.

You were a dragon then as well. The first-ever sky dragon created by the Twin Goddesses.

Ere smiled a bitter smile, keeping his gaze on the distant horizon ahead.

"Really? Lucky me. Was I as magnificent then as I am now? Pity I can't recall."

His voice dripped with sarcasm, but Sorin ignored it.

You were the most powerful of all dragons, land, sea and air, he said seriously. *Blindingly bright. Pure. Good. Full of hope and joy. Beautiful.*

Ere looked down and kicked at a loose stone at his feet. They had passed the town's outer edge by now, the only two people walking in the stark landscape of the tundra. Not that the town's streets had been packed before, but now, there was no one for miles. Not even small animals, for the blizzard had chased them into their hiding places and burrows.

But Sorin didn't feel alone. With Ere at his side, he had everything he ever needed in the world.

"Guess you're disappointed in the new me, huh?" the male muttered. "Maybe you should have left me at the bottom of the lake."

Don't be stupid.

Ere's head snapped up, and his startled blue eyes met Sorin's fiery gaze.

Did I feel *disappointed last night when I was inside you? Did I* sound *disappointed when I released my Nourishment into you?*

Ere's cheeks flushed immediately with a wash of dark pink, and he looked down again.

How many times did you make me come? Do you still feel my seed inside you? Is it leaking out of your hole even now?

"O-Okay," Ere uttered breathlessly. "I take your point."

His stride faltered, and he adjusted the growing bulge in his pants, squeezing hard before cupping himself between the legs, putting pressure *there*.

Sorin didn't think Ere was conscious of what he was doing, the action was so reflexive. He knew, could *feel* vicariously, that Ere's channel pulsed with soreness and emptiness at his words. At the reminder of how it felt to be filled to bursting. To be slicked with hot cream and throb with ecstasy.

Determinedly, he turned his mind away from more primitive, prurient thoughts. He had to make Ere understand. He deserved to know about the Bane.

He was a Gift from the Goddesses to their loyal Animal Spirit armies, to help us win the Goddesses' wars, Sorin began.

He could feel Ere's eyes upon him again.

Good. The dragon was listening.

I did not perceive him as any kind of Gift when my sire bade me to look after him. It was my sole responsibility to hatch him, and I resented it.

I could have been leading my flights of raptors. I could have won countless battles. I wanted to do anything but stay in the dark, secret corner of the royal cavern, sitting all day and night on top of a fucking egg.

"You *hatched* him?"

Sorin didn't have to look at him to know that his eyes must be round like a baby owl's.

Ere looked him up and down, his expression conveying extreme doubt.

I was in Eagle form, Sorin explained, understanding that Ere was imagining his current humanoid form perched on top of an egg.

"You can turn into a full-fledged eagle? Goodness, the things I begin to learn about you. I don't know you at all."

No, Ere didn't know him. In so many ways, this male didn't know him.

Sorin decided to ignore the question, steering them back to the original topic.

Dragons are born from eggs.

"Well, I wasn't hatched," Ere said. "I was created. By means I'd rather not ever think about again, much less discuss."

Human magic, or rather, science, did not exist those many millennia ago. Only the gods possessed the power of creation. And the first dragons were hatched from eggs.

"You know, you just answered the age-old chicken and egg conundrum."

Sorin flicked a glance his way, frowning slightly at the non-sequitur.

Ere met his eyes briefly.

"You know, what came first. The chicken or the egg? You just said that the Goddesses created the dragon eggs. So I guess the egg came first."

Sorin shrugged, and Ere sighed.

"Do continue," he waved in Sorin's direction.

"You sat on an egg all day and night, and hatched a baby dragon. I just bet it was the cutest thing in the world. You fell in love at first sight."

It was the ugliest thing I ever saw.

Ere sniffed, taking offense on behalf of the dragon he'd never met.

But it grew on me.

"Does 'it' have a name?" Ere asked testily.

Rai. Everyone called him Rai.

"What did you call him?"

Trust Ere to always pick up on what Sorin didn't say. He hesitated, knowing that the brilliant man would immediately put two and two together.

But the truth must come out. It always did.

Sorin inhaled and exhaled deeply, as if a heavy weight had finally been lifted.

After all these millennia alone, most of it half-dead, he could share his soul-deep loss with someone who might understand. Who might even care. None other than the reincarnation of Sorin's dragon.

Bane. I called him My Bane.

*** *** *** ***

Ere realized the futility and madness of being jealous over a dead dragon. And by the sounds of it, dead for many millennia. But there it was.

He was jealous.

Furiously, colossally, ridiculously jealous.

It didn't matter that the dragon and he supposedly shared the same soul, reincarnated in this current shell. He didn't know his previous self, Sorin did. He didn't have the same body. Sorin knew that body. Perhaps in the same ways that Sorin knew Ere's body last night.

After all, the male had called him "his Bane."

Silly Ere had been secretly delighted that Sorin seemed to have given him a nickname, however unflattering. Only to realize now that the warrior had seen someone else in his mind while he fucked Ere into euphoric oblivion.

He gritted his teeth and clenched his fists.

Strangely, he didn't feel hurt. He only felt crazy *mad*!

Possessive, territorial, wrathful, and mad, mad, mad!

He didn't have the wherewithal to analyze why he felt this way. He just went with the flow.

If there was one thing he'd accepted over the course of meeting Sorin, it was that nothing made sense with the male. The instant, explosive, sexual attraction. The undiluted, inexplicable *need* and *longing* Ere felt for him.

And the strange, seething resentment that he could never fully possess Sorin; he didn't *know* the male. Something always refused to click into place. And Ere felt like he was running on a treadmill (he hated the damned things, what was the point?), always chasing the vision of Sorin in front of him, but never able to reach him.

He snuck a narrow-eyed glance toward the warrior and saw that Sorin seemed lost in thought, unaware of his attention. He took this opportunity to absorb the full, staggering impact of Sorin's beauty in profile, with the afternoon sun bathing his face in striking gold and intriguing shadows.

This man was *his*.

Ere had Claimed him last night. He didn't want to share any part of Sorin, not even with a ghost of a memory.

But it seemed that the memory of "the Bane" was more than just a ghost for the warrior. Ere didn't really want to learn more, even though he supposed others might be curious about their past lives. He wasn't.

What was the point of knowing how he used to live when he didn't plan on living much longer? Not that he wanted to die, but he was pragmatic and realistic at the end of the day, and he didn't expect to survive round two with the Hydra. It would already be a miracle if he managed to take the demoness down with him.

Nevertheless, as long as he was still on this earth, Sorin was *his*.

Because of that, Ere wanted desperately to know everything about him. Even if it meant confronting this long-dead version of himself.

"So, tell me all about this special Bane of yours, this ugly little dragonling you hatched with your well-cushioned feathered derriere. Did he follow you around like an imprinted duck?"

Yes, was all Sorin said in their mind link.

Ere waited a few beats for him to expound, but the male was suddenly reticent, his expression a mix of longing and sorrow.

It hurt to look upon him.

Ere fixed his gaze straight ahead as well, as they matched their long-legged strides.

"And?" he prodded gently, quietly, the initial burst of envy subsiding in the face of Sorin's pain.

"Please tell me. I want to know."

For long moments, Sorin didn't speak, not out loud certainly, and not even mentally. But then, he slowly began. And his thoughts in Ere's mind were so vivid, the emotions so strong, Ere felt like he'd been transported back in time, standing right beside Sorin, living what he lived.

Sorin described the Age of the Gods, the rise of the Twin Goddesses, the advent of the first animal spirits, Dark and Pure Ones, Elementals.

The animals came first. They were the gods' foot soldiers, created to live and die by the Goddesses' whim. Then, an animal fell in love, the first-ever Tiger King, Goya's sire. But the Pure Goddess didn't return his feelings, didn't even know how.

The Tiger King died for his love, and the Universal Balance was shaken as a result. Other gods banded against the Twins, pressing their advantage while the Goddesses were weakened from their punishment.

War ensued. Many wars, over countless years.

The animal spirits couldn't win against gods, not even with the Twins' powers supporting them. So, the Twins began to experiment, creating other nascent beings in their own image—the Pure and Dark Ones.

They bred the earliest immortal humanoids with chosen animal spirits to make them stronger. Sorin, who used to be called Sol, was one such hybrid. An eagle spirit with a Dark base. More powerful, more aggressive, driven by bloodlust and...other lust.

"Wait," Ere interjected, unable to hold himself back no matter how hard he tried.

Oh, very well, he didn't try that hard. He had to know.

"Just how many people have you slaked your lust with? Ballpark?"

He couldn't be sure, but Sorin might have rolled his eyes.

Irrelevant.

"But I want to know," Ere persisted. "On behalf of the Bane, we'd like to know."

Sorin released a put-upon sigh.

Tough. Ere wasn't going to let this go until he got answers. He folded his arms across his chest and speared the other male with a determined glare.

I keep my promises.

"Which means what exactly?"

There has been no one since the Bane.

Seriously? But...that was what, *thousands* of years ago now? Ere blinked incomprehensibly.

"You...haven't had sex for—help me with the math, I might be short a couple of millennia—but safe to say between five and ten thousand years? And you have a Dark One base?"

Sorin's jaw clenched so hard, Ere feared he'd break it.

I was half dead for most of it.

"What do you m—"

If you stop interrupting, I will explain, Sorin growled in his mind.

Ere bit back his questions and nodded for Sorin to continue.

Even with the mix of animals and Pure, Dark Ones, their armies weren't strong enough. The other gods were winning. With their actions, the Twins had isolated themselves from everyone else. And because they had always been the most powerful, this was the perfect opportunity for the lesser gods to eliminate competition.

So, the Twins imbued all of the ingredients from their creatures, with the magic of Elements from themselves, into one being—a dragon.

One each for the sky, land and sea. The sky dragon was the most powerful, probably because the raptors were the most organized and deadly of the Twins' animal spirit armies, which the sky dragon would now lead.

And lead them he did.

At first, Sorin and his sire trained the dragonling in the ways of war. Taught him how to harness his strength, size and power even as they learned to adapt themselves, for no one had seen a creature like this before.

The way a raptor fought was not the way a dragon would fight. Aside from physiological differences, a dragon could breathe fire and other deadly things, like poison, acid, debilitating smoke.

Sorin and his Bane trained together, learned and fought together. Always. They coordinated their flights as one, knowing at all times where the other was, how to leverage each other's strengths as if one was an extension of the other. Both mind and body.

After the Bane grew to his full size and became experienced in battle, the dragons and animal spirits began to turn the tide of the war in favor of the Twins. They could finally see a ray of hope to end all the pointless suffering.

But the Goddesses betrayed them.

They didn't care to put an end to the countless deaths. If their creatures died in the war, they would simply make new ones. Everyone was dispensable, even though their creations felt, thought, lived and loved.

The Bane must have discovered the Goddesses' plot somehow, Sorin did not know. He only recalled the desperation with which the Bane loved him toward the end. As if he might disappear at any moment. As if they would lose each other forever.

When the time came, Sorin saw the arcs of Destiny too late.

The Goddesses had sent their land, sea and sky forces into one final galactic battle against their enemies. It was impossible odds. Countless animal spirits would perish, perhaps even all.

He didn't know what the Bane planned, but he knew that the dragon would *do something*. He was determined to stay close to the Bane to protect him.

But when the time came, it was the other way around. Sorin was caught in an ambush that tore through his entire aerie.

The very sky felt like it was going to crumble and crash on top of the world. Filled with fire, smoke, falling debris. Lightning streaked. Thunder boomed. The lands howled with rage, mountains fissured, volcanoes erupted. The sea churned in furious vortexes, tidal waves crashed upon each other, killing even the sea-bound creatures in crushing whirlpools.

When Sorin sustained one too many critical wounds, fixed in the sights of two mighty gods, the Bane suddenly came between them, absorbing the force of the gods' thunderbolt, wind funnel and fireball all at once.

Sorin had watched, paralyzed by pain and shock, as the dragon filled with blinding light, before unleashing it all in concentrated force upon his target.

But it wasn't at the other gods that he directed the power. It was at the Dark Goddess whose back had been turned to dispatch another godly foe.

Before Sorin knew what was happening, all three dragons turned upon the gods en masse, including the Twins. And where they led, the animal spirits followed.

"Well..." Ere sputtered, "t-that must have taken diamond-grade balls to do."

It did, Sorin agreed.

The Bane spoke to me with his last strength in our minds. He knew what the Goddesses planned. He knew that winning their war would mean the decimation of all of our Kinds. They didn't care.

So, he made a plan with the other dragons. He wanted to take all of the gods down, including the most powerful of them all. Whether or not the dragons would be successful, the outcome would be the same: we were all likely to perish. There was nothing to lose.

But there was the smallest hope that there would be something to gain. Our freedom from the Goddesses' will. For those who survived, we could finally stop fighting, and learn to start living.

Loving.

Sorin stopped walking and stood still with every muscle clenched, eyes on the horizon.

Ere stopped as well, mesmerized by the sight of him. The myriad of emotions carved into the lines of his face.

He did it for me.

The warrior shuddered on a ragged breath, forcibly controlled his shivering and hardened his expression with determination.

The Bane had dealt the Dark Goddess a mortal blow. It weakened her enough that the other gods and animal spirits quickly tore her apart particle by particle. The Pure Goddess would have been next, but she did something none of us expected.

Goya, the new Tiger King, still untried in his rule, was struggling against an onslaught of gods and their monsters. They had him cornered. He was too wounded to counter.

Instead of flying to the aid of her Twin while the Dark Goddess still stood a chance, the Pure Goddess chose to defend the Tiger Beast instead. The blast of power she used to push back his enemies on land drained all of her strength, leaving her vulnerable to other gods' attacks.

They tore her apart too, just as the surviving beasts and the dragons tore the rest of the gods apart.

In the end, there were no more gods. Barely any animal spirits remained. Their fragments, their magic, showered upon the creatures of land, air and sea. Over time, they gave rise to Immortals—Dark and Pure Ones, Elementals and Beasts. With the final act of the Pure Goddess, the gods' dying magic transformed into the sparks of souls, seeds that bore fruit in the form of mortal kinds.

"What happened to the dragons?" Ere whispered.

"Gone."

Ere jerked at the startling word spoken out loud in Sorin's deep, pain-roughened voice.

"What happened to you?"

Slowly, Sorin turned to face him. Turned those intense beams of golden light directly at him, setting him afire where he stood.

It was a hellish fire, not the same flames as the ones Ere loved.

It was agony and loss. Pain and despair. Death and loneliness. And unfathomable grief.

It brought Ere's heart and soul to their knees.
"Gone."

Chapter Fourteen

They reached the end of the dirt path that led to the foot of the tallest mountain, where Sorin's nest was located. In a cavern he discovered on the north side just beneath the peak.

His story wasn't finished, but he was done telling it. At least for now.

Ere looked like he wanted to ask more questions, but Sorin stayed him with a penetrating look.

The other male visibly shrank back from whatever he saw on Sorin's face, knowing when to bite his tongue for a change.

We must go up, he said, focusing on the matter at hand and shutting off the mental corridor for strolling down memory lane.

Ere looked up, way up. Craning his head so far back, he almost tipped over.

"How? It's too steep to just hike up there. Unless we want to take the long way and freeze our rocks off in the process. We don't have equipment. And even if we did, I'm not much of a climber. I'd probably plummet to my death a quarter of the way up by slipping on a pebble. I—"

Transform. You're a dragon, Sorin reminded him.

Ere's looked at him sharply, a ripple of fear and apprehension distorting the patchwork features of his face.

"I can't," he whispered. "I...I can't."

Then, hold on.

Ere had only time to draw in a surprised breath and reflexively clutch Sorin's shoulders as he wound both arms around Ere's torso and lifted them off the ground with one mighty leap. He materialized and unfurled his wings, flapped once, twice, gaining velocity and height, beating harder to take their combined weight.

It wasn't easy to become airborne directly from the ground with not even a whisper of wind to lift him. Never mind trying to fly two males at once. Only the most seasoned raptors could do it on the first try.

But Sorin was different. Ere would soon see exactly how different.

"Your wings," Ere breathed, uncurling one of his hands from the death grip he had on Sorin's shoulder to stroke the softer, inner feathers he could reach.

Making Sorin quake with pleasure at his unthinking touch. It felt as if Ere was stroking his cock directly, light grazes that set his blood aflame.

"They're so beautiful. I've never seen anything like them before. Are the border feathers really on fire, or is that just my imagination? Is this how you almost burned down the house?"

Sorin didn't answer. He couldn't just now.

His body was burning at the dragon's closeness. It would take some expert aerial gymnastics to take him mid-flight, but he could do it. He could hold onto the male with one arm, use his other hand to rip off his trousers and free Sorin's aching member. It would be so easy to wrap one long leg around his hip and thrust inside that silken, fisting heat.

He'd beat his wings to mimic the act of thrusting on a solid surface. He'd drive into the male over and over again with the force of hurricane gales. He'd drench Ere's insides with his scalding cream, easing the way for *more*.

So much more.

He might lose sense of direction and plummet them to their deaths. He'd only done this once before in eagle form with another raptor, so it wasn't the same. In his humanoid form, the Mating meant more than simple release.

No, that wasn't precisely true. It only meant more with *him*.
This male.

His form and incarnation didn't matter. It was his heart and soul Sorin craved.

For the rest of the flight, Ere didn't speak, merely tucking his face into the crook of Sorin's neck. It felt as if the male was drugging himself on Sorin's scent, the way he inhaled longer and more deeply than his softer exhales.

Sorin's hardness throbbed impatiently, leaking his essence through the front of his trousers. The altitude and freezing air should have made the wet spot incredibly uncomfortable, but his natural body heat burned away any frigidness. In fact, he warmed them both despite the unforgiving environs. If Ere shivered, it wasn't from the cold.

Finally, he crested over the edge of the cavern's entrance, hidden by the Labrador tea bushes. He set Ere down and steadied the male with one hand while he wobbled on his feet. With his other hand, Sorin parted the bushes to reveal his nest.

"Come."

He gestured for Ere to follow him inside.

"I sure did. Don't need the invitation." He thought the male muttered beneath his breath.

Sorin frowned with incomprehension. Until a dark stain in the front of Ere's pants drew his gaze.

Ah. So, he wasn't the only one reeling from the effects of their proximity.

His sex pulsed and leaked some more, aching so badly that he squeezed himself hard in one fist, trying to control the need.

Ere's sapphire eyes fixated on his hand. He swallowed in one, long, convulsive gulp.

If you want this, say it.

Sorin moved his hand lower to cup his heavy scrotum through the fabric, giving Ere an unobstructed view of his rampant erection. The outline thick, long and obscene.

"Um..."

With a strange gargled sound, Ere tore his gaze away, darting his eyes around the cavern, lighting immediately upon the thickly feathered nest, which took up most of the space.

"I like what you've done with the place," he said with a whistle.

"So homey."

Perhaps the male was being sarcastic. Sorin sometimes couldn't tell. It was his default state, but occasionally, he meant the things he said.

A slight shiver passed through Ere's body, and he unconsciously huddled in on himself, cold now that he was no longer in Sorin's arms.

Sorin immediately noticed. But instead of pulling the male into his embrace again, as tempting as that was, he wanted to give Ere space and distance.

If the male wanted him, he must come to him. Sorin would not force his hand, nor even instigate his desire. He'd already given too much of himself to the male. He couldn't afford to give more, no matter how much Sorin wanted to, not if Ere didn't give back.

He set his gaze upon four small piles of dry wood arranged around the nest, and ignited them one by one visually, letting Ere see the flames dancing in his eyes, revealing this small power to the male.

"Neat trick," the dragon said, the awe in his voice belying his nonchalant expression.

You can do it too. Perhaps not with your eyes alone, but with gesture or breath. Try it.

"Uh...no," Ere said firmly. "I don't know what you think I can do, but setting things on fire with a look or a flick of my hand has never been my Gift. Hell, I barely figured out how to breathe fire in dragon form, almost too late, in the last battle with the Hydra."

You can do many things you've never done before if you concentrate your thoughts and harness your power. I will help you find your Gifts. I will help you defeat the Hydra.

Ere visibly perked up at that, straightening from his habitual slouch.

"Truly? Can you do that? I-I haven't taken dragon form since...well, you know. You saw. I don't know how any more. I don't even know how I did it to begin with. It just happened. One moment I was trapped in a tightly sealed sarcophagus in my current form, and the next Dalair—he's another friend of mine, more like a brother, except we're not related—broke me out. And suddenly, I was transforming. I have no idea how to do it again. What if I'm too broken? What if—"

He suddenly cut himself off and tightened his lips, as if he hadn't meant to reveal so much. He hunched his shoulders again and looked away from Sorin.

But Sorin wouldn't let him go back into hiding.

I will teach you. This is why you came with me, is it not? So that I may help you.

Ere's cheeks flushed suddenly. He didn't look at Sorin, keeping his gaze on one of the small, intensely bright and toe-curlingly hot bonfires.

"Actually, I came with you so we could fuck each other into next Sunday without the threat of burning the whole town to the ground," he muttered.

Then, he slid a nervous glance at Sorin.

"Hope you don't mind."

Fuck.

Sorin's entire body quaked with barely checked lust. His fangs elongated until they dripped with saliva in his mouth, while his cock grew incredibly harder, jerking and leaking pre-cum in desperate need.

It was all he could do not to rip his clothes to shreds as he doffed them with efficiency, while Ere stared at him with unabashed hunger.

Naked, he stepped into the nest, the diameter longer than the largest human bed, even the one he'd slept in with Ere. He knelt on his shins and faced the dragon, one hand holding his jutting staff like an offering, the other pulling his scrotum down to stall his release.

He was already so fucking close. His pre-cum so copious, it slicked his entire column, making it glisten with dewy wetness in the firelight.

"Do it," he rasped, his voice like sandpaper scraping through his throat.

Come take what you want.

*** *** *** ***

Ere wasn't going to wait for a better invitation.

He'd waited long and patiently enough as it was. He should get the Nobel Prize in Physiology for his forbearance, for he'd been hard since they left the house this morning. Hell, his erection hadn't waned since last night when he found Sorin on his stomach spreadeagle and naked on the bed!

Surely, it was a miracle of science his body hadn't already erupted in flames. Or erupted in something else.

Ere set his mouth in a determined line. He wasn't going to be a dropped yogurt. A preamy creamy. A blunderspunk. Not even if it killed him.

He was going to drive Sorin crazy first if it was the last thing he did. He'd obliterate all memories of "the Bane" from the warrior's mind, with sex so hot, lava from the earth's core would freeze in contrast.

He divested himself of clothing with all due haste, and he wasn't even embarrassed by it. He was beyond embarrassment at this point. The Holy Grail of mighty cock-hood stood proudly before him, heavy, long, and thick, from a tight nest of golden curls.

Ere couldn't wait to discover all the places the male had hair. Immortals didn't usually have hair besides on their heads. But the most ancient ones sometimes did.

At the sight of that tantalizing fleece, Ere's mouth watered. He clambered gracelessly onto the feathered nest, almost fell on his face, but righted himself without incident and promptly lowered to his belly until he was eye-level with Sorin's groin.

Without preamble, he stuffed his face full of the male's crotch, snorting up his intoxicating scent like a human cocaine addict. Ere had seen the sort in his clubs. He'd pitied the humans their debilitating drugs. It made them weak, ripe for all kinds of extortion and bribery.

But now he understood. Finally, he comprehended what it was to be *addicted*.

He was making a cake of himself and he didn't care! He wanted this man so badly, he was already frantic that it would never be enough. No matter what they did together, he would never get enough.

"Easy."

Sorin's extra-large, extra-manly hand curved gently around the back of his skull, more comforting than controlling.

Ere heard himself whimper as his tongue darted out to taste the glistening essence coating the male's most private skin. Salt and sweetness. Oh gods! He tasted and smelled so good.

Ere had never wanted to do this to another person in his whole existence. It had always seemed so...unsanitary, for one. Too intimate for another.

The targets he fucked and, more often than not, got fucked by, just shoved themselves in his face, used any and every hole he had in the most expedient, careless way. He'd hated it. The choking, the watery eyes, the disgusting taste, the gooey, slimy consistency, and the atrocious smell.

But everything was different with Sorin. He wanted to lick every inch of the male's body. Learn every bulge and hollow, every edge and curve. He wanted to merge with his strength, physically, spiritually become one. He wanted to burrow beneath the warrior's skin and never leave.

He was so strong. So safe. So protective. Ere wanted it all.

He wanted *in*.

As he panted and lapped sloppily around the base of Sorin's cock and balls, sucking on his sensitive skin, wrapping one hand over Sorin's and squeezing his cock demandingly, he insinuated his other hand between the male's spread thighs, beneath his stones, to press and rub across his swollen taint and tightly puckered star.

Wanting *in*.

"No."

Sorin let him have a few passes, but then shackled his wrist in a firm grip, twisting his arm behind his back and forcing him up to meet the warrior's flame-filled gaze.

You want to fuck me, earn the right.

"B-But...last night..." Ere sputtered, his new-found, lust-fueled confidence flagging a bit at Sorin's commanding, unyielding tone.

That was then. This is now. When you're dragon enough to submit me, you can fuck me any way you like. Not a moment before.

Whoomph, went Ere's body, every cell exploding in a simultaneous conflagration of volcanic desire.

Holy gods, that was hot! He practically nutted one right there! Preamy creamy or not!

Game on! he thought, and just barely resisted pumping his fists in a rush of adrenaline.

240

"Permission to suck your cock like a Hoover, sir," he said like a good little soldier, staring up into the warrior's golden orbs, his arm still twisted awkwardly behind his back.

One of Sorin's thick pecs twitched a little, and the corner of his mouth might have curled. But the beginning of a smile was gone before it could fully form. His expression was control and discipline incarnate. Implacable. Bulletproof.

Sexy as all fuck.

"Proceed," that deep, husky voice rumbled.

As soon as Sorin released his arm, Ere got to work.

He wrapped both hands around the male's staff, and Sorin let him, taking his own hand away. Ere licked his lips lasciviously, eyeing his prize like a starving man. He experimented by flattening his tongue at the base of the long, hot, vein-wrapped column and slowly, meticulously dragged it up, leaving a trail of saliva behind, filled with his vampire venom.

A Dark One's venom carried the intentions of its master, used most often to subdue prey. In this case, Ere's intention was to make his saliva feel like a thousand tiny hands stroking against every cell of Sorin's skin, sending a continuous buzzing sensation through his epidermis wherever they touched.

The male gasped in shock, his glittering eyes widening.

Neat trick, eh? Made that one up on the fly. In fact, he was making everything up. He'd never wanted to please anyone as much as he wanted to please this male. More than wanted.

Needed.

Ere smiled smugly as he kept on licking up the satiny column of flesh, his tongue happily riding over the ridges of distended veins. Until finally, *finally*! he arrived at the juicy crown. Here, he closed his lips greedily over the fat head, sucking on the sensitive glans, tonguing the weepy slit.

Sorin hissed, the hand he still had at the back of Ere's head tightening in his hair.

Yes! He liked it.

Ere was going by instinct and desire alone. He did what he wanted to do, but also adjusted as he went along to give Sorin the most pleasure. He stared unblinkingly up at the male, watching for the smallest reaction. He listened to the sound of his breathing, felt every quiver and tensing of muscle beneath his hands. And smelled the deepening aroma of the warrior's mating musk.

Gods! He smelled and tasted like heaven. Better than ambrosia. Better than *life*.

Ere didn't have much finesse, sucking and slurping, kissing and licking, around the male's throbbing cockhead, while his hands squeezed the rest of the column in tandem to the friction of his mouth. Slowly, methodically milking Sorin's sex.

The thin stream of pre-cum wasn't enough. Sweet like nectar. Merely an appetizer. Ere wanted the main course. He hungered for the thick, tangy cream.

The hand at the back of his head fisted a hunk of hair and tugged.

Suck me harder, the warrior demanded. *Take me deeper.*

Ere wanted to respond, but didn't want to remove his mouth from Sorin's stupendous erection. Pity he hadn't figured out how to communicate telepathically with the male. There was so much he wanted to say as he played. Like—

I'll suck you and swallow you however I damn well please. You told me to take what I want, and I'm taking it.

I'm taking you.

I want to make you come so hard and so long, your cream will overflow my mouth and throat, leak down my chin and chest, my stomach and groin, so I'm slick with your seed. So I can jack off with it coating my skin, and paint you all over with my cum.

That's the plan, man. Don't rush an artiste *at work.*

Sorin's chest depressed on a shuddering exhale as his pupils blew so wide there was barely a ring of gold around them.

Ere looked up at him in surprise, his lips lax for a moment around the warrior's cannon cock.

You heard me just now?

Sorin tightened his grip on Ere's hair and flexed his hips, pushing a couple of inches down his throat in response.

You want me to come, make me. Where is this "Hoover" you spoke of?

Ere's eyebrows lifted at the challenge before they slammed back down.

Oh, game fucking on!

He sucked on Sorin's engorged cockhead with strong pulls that hollowed out his cheeks. With every draw, he took the male deeper, ever deeper into this throat.

But holy shit, he was big. Maybe even bigger than Ere. And as his friend and once-upon-a-time wife, Sophia, pointed out, Ere's member was plenty intimidating as it was. No wonder sex with Sorin had felt like he was being split in two.

And yet, even as he recalled the pain, he immediately also remembered the burning pleasure. So much unbelievable, volcanic pleasure. That perfect pressure. Ere had never felt so alive as when Sorin was inside him.

This wasn't the same, taking Sorin in his mouth, but it was just as good. Well, almost. The best part was Sorin's taste and smell, so many ways to drive him wild.

He sucked the male as deep as he could, opening his throat wide and stretching his lips to breaking point. But it wasn't enough. Sorin was only halfway inside and he was already at the limit.

Ere tried to compensate by stacking his hands on the rest of the length that didn't fit. Squeezing and twisting in time with the pulls of his mouth, the swallows of his throat.

Open for me, dragon. I intend to make your throat so sore you won't be able to speak on the morrow.

Absurdly, his words inflamed Ere's passion to unseemly heights. So much so that his own cock convulsed dangerously, on the knife's edge of climax. By sheer dint of will, he held himself back.

He wouldn't release until after Sorin did. He wouldn't!

Sorin made good on his threat as he started to move. At first undulating his hips gently, only nudging against the back of Ere's throat. Then steadily picking up speed and depth.

Fuck that. Ere wanted him to lose control. His eyes blazed with blue fire as he stared up at the male.

He used one hand to cup Sorin's scrotum firmly, kneading the heavy balls in his tight clutch, while his other hand continued the clenching, milking motion along the male's tortured stalk, and his mouth worked the plump cockhead relentlessly.

Sorin's lips pulled back to bare his teeth in a feral snarl. He kept their gazes fused, a colossal battle of wills waging between them. His buttocks clenched as he snapped his hips, thrusting his big cock deeper and harder into Ere's throat.

Thanks to plenty of practice, though not by any choice of his own, Ere's gag reflex disappeared when he wanted it to. He would surely lose his voice for a while after this, and his throat would chafe with rawness. He didn't care. He wanted this male to lose control, to lose his *mind*, and it was happening right before his eyes.

So fucking beautiful.

As Sorin stared unblinkingly into his eyes, Ere could see what he felt as if those feelings were his own. The force of his seed surging through his stalk was only contained by the immeasurable strength of his will. Every muscle cramped and hurt from the tension of his iron-clad control. His balls were full to bursting, veritably throbbing in Ere's hand. His blood sizzled through his veins, burning through him like wildfire.

Especially *there*.

Pulsing in his sex with a life of its own, calling for Ere to drink it. To penetrate him where it would hurt the most, but also where it would give him the fiercest pleasure.

The next time Sorin pulled back slightly to thrust deep again, Ere held him tight in his hand and mouth, preventing the movement—a split second before he sank his fangs into Sorin's dorsal vein, right beneath the head of his cock.

The warrior threw back his head and roared.

His body quaked uncontrollably, every vein and tendon on display, every muscle turned to steel. As he poured his life force in scalding gushes into Ere's mouth, overflowing his lips, leaking down his chin just like Ere wanted.

Endlessly he came. Endlessly, Ere milked him. With his hands, his lips, drinking his blood and seed in equal measure, reveling in the sheer intensity of his pleasure-pain.

Ere found his own release a moment later. Just like that. No touch, no stimulation. Solely by witnessing Sorin's unraveling.

True to his promise, he came so hard he splattered gravity-defying white globs of cream all over Sorin's thighs and groin, his own stomach and chest, as Sorin's seed and blood overflowed his lips, leaking down his torso to mingle with his own cum.

With one hand, he continued to milk Sorin's stalk, while he used the other to gather their juices together, rubbing it into Sorin's groin, beneath his scrotum along his taint, two fingers teasing the warrior's tightly shut hole, dipping shallowly inside as it quivered with Sorin's contractions like a tiny mouth.

When the warrior's release finally began to ebb, his cock jerking with aftershocks and small bursts of cream in Ere's greedy, insatiable mouth, he moved his hands to grasp onto Sorin's perfect ass, kneading the hard globes like a cat. He was purring loudly like one too, probably a trait he inherited from his mother's side.

Sorin tipped his head down again to look into his eyes, the animal spirit's own gaze sparkling with immense satisfaction.

Is this what you wanted? To make me come undone?

Ere sucked harder on the painfully sensitive crown in answer, making the warrior hiss as his undying erection pulsed more cream onto Ere's awaiting tongue.

Yes. Always.

He arched an eyebrow and let go of Sorin's sex with a wet, smacking pop.

"And now I want you to make me come again. That was just the pre-show."

Sorin reached for Ere's neglected, yet (over)eager cock, but Ere intercepted his hand.

"No touching. Just fucking. If you even sneeze in my prick's direction I'll probably blow. Make me come with your monster cock inside me."

At his bold words, said monster cock jerked with anticipation, more than ready for round two.

You're sore, the male reminded him, his expression a mix of concern and possessive pride.

"I like it," Ere said, speaking a truth he never thought he'd utter in this context.

"I like feeling you with every step I take. I want to be fucked hard and deep. Make me scream your name."

He turned around and got on all fours, presenting Sorin with his naked ass.

But the male didn't grab him by the hips and pound into him as he expected. He didn't do anything at all.

Confused, Ere looked back behind his shoulder. Weren't they doing this? Didn't Sorin tell him to take what he wanted? He couldn't have been more explicit.

The male's desire remained rampant, as demonstrated by the eighth Wonder of the World that was his magnificent manhood. But he was gazing at Ere with an unreadable expression.

Just when Ere opened his mouth to urge things along, Sorin got into position behind him, taking hold of a hip with one hand while gathering the cream from his wet cock with his other hand to rub around and into Ere's hole.

Ere dropped his head and hissed, taking slow, deep breaths to relax his body and open up. Despite the incredible burning of his sore backdoor, still unrecovered from last night's exertions.

I will hurt you.

"Don't care," he growled through clenched teeth.

"Need you. It feels good after you're inside. I want it. Please... just, do it fast. Rip the Band-aid off—"

Without warning, Sorin pushed inside with one mighty thrust.

"Oh fuck oh fuck oh fuck oh fuuuuuuuccccckkkkk!"

Okay, never going to use the rip-off-Band-aid analogy again!

He was going to carry giant bottles of lube with him from now on no matter where he went. How did normal people *do* this sort of thing? And he actually asked—

The giant steel rod in his ass began to pulse subtly. He could feel the burst of hot, thick cream coating his insides, soothing the indescribable burn.

Yes! The best natural lubricant there was! He'd be sure to prep himself with it more thoroughly before penetration next time.

Then, Sorin began to move. And all coherent thought flew out of Ere's mind.

Ah gods! That spot...

He hit that spot with every push and pull (hard to miss when he took up the entire inside of Ere's ass). Until every square centimeter inside Ere felt like his prostate stretched and tied around itself. He didn't have a body, mind or soul any more. He was only a receptacle of pleasure.

Undiluted, raw, screaming *pleasure*.

Soon, he was shaking uncontrollably, splintering apart. And true to his claim, he shouted Sorin's name until the cavern echoed with his cries.

Sorin held him together with both big hands on his hips now, moving steadily inside in a rolling, smooth, slick motion that gave all the pleasure to Ere, but minimized the friction on his own sex.

The heavy musk of their combined arousal filled the air. Despite the freezing temperatures, Ere felt as if they were cocooned in a fog of steam. He didn't feel cold at all. Not with Sorin's body bracketing his, his maleness inside him, torching every cell into a blazing inferno.

He started to push back, wanting to absorb more of Sorin. Always more. He couldn't get enough.

He rocked into the male in counterpoint to Sorin's thrusts. The wet sounds of his channel sucking greedily on Sorin's cock filled the cavern, mixed with their gusting breaths, low groans and guttural growls. The bonfires crackled. The wind outside whistled.

And Ere was lost to the symphony of their mating dance. It was the most erotic, gorgeous music he'd ever heard.

He'd been orgasming without ejaculation for some time now. Ever since Sorin began to move inside him. His body couldn't handle any more of this; he needed physical release. He was desperate for it.

He looked behind his shoulder and bit his lip, his eyes pleading with Sorin wordlessly.

The warrior didn't make him beg this time. He let go of one hip to reach down and take hold of Ere's dryly sputtering cock by the base in a firm, controlled grip, avoiding the ultra-sensitive head.

Come for me, dragon, he commanded in their linked minds.

And Ere came again on a broken sob.

Unbelievable pleasure and relief flooding every broken piece of him. His seed gushing in continuous creamy ribbons, coating the feathers beneath him, leaking down the column of his sex and over Sorin's hand that held him. There was so much of it. He felt like he was making up for lost time. Years' worth. Hell, *millennia's* worth.

He hardly noticed when Sorin's chest covered his back, when the male's forehead fell to his shoulder. When he penetrated Ere's neck with his Dark One fangs and drank. Ere was too lost to his own euphoria. He knew and felt nothing else.

Not Sorin's wings enfolding them both. Not the flames that blazed around them.

He was the fire himself. It was inside him. Everything burned. And nothing hurt. He could feel himself healing. The skin of his face pulled tight, and the raised scars itched. He felt only the most incredible, mind-blowing pleasure. It was all he knew.

Until Sorin came too, erupting inside him in a hot, milky flood, a long, low growl tearing through his throat, muffled by Ere's shoulder as he continued to drink with deep, burning pulls.

Ere sighed at last. His body beyond replete. Bonelessly, he crumpled into the nest on his stomach.

Sorin moved the hand at his hip to wind an arm around his torso, somehow maneuvering them both onto their sides without breaking their connection.

Ere pushed his ass as snugly as he could into Sorin's groin, taking the male as deep as possible and holding him there. With Sorin's body surrounding his, his arm around his middle, giant wings cocooning them both, one hand still holding his half-hard sex, and the warrior's own undying erection covetously sheathed within him, Ere sighed deeply and fell into contented slumber.

Never knowing that the male who gave him everything he needed and wanted did not rest.

Never seeing the heartache and anguish on Sorin's face as he pressed a feather-light kiss that carried all of his emotions, all of his love, into Ere's hair.

Chapter Fifteen

When Ere awoke, it was well into the night.

He had no concept of time, and he didn't care. Why measure it at all when he knew it would end? Might as well enjoy the last hours and days, savor every moment and stretch them into infinity.

All he noticed was that Sorin was no longer beside him.

Inside him.

His body had already recovered from the rigors of their joining, this time much faster than before. Maybe he was getting used to it.

Or maybe he simply craved the sweet pain only Sorin could give him. He craved it so much it was no longer pain. He was addicted to the mind-bending burn.

His well-used channel clenched around emptiness, throbbed with need. He missed the warrior with a savage hunger.

Stiffly, he pulled on his haphazardly discarded clothes. The fires were still blazing around the nest, illuminating the cave. It must be sub-zero outside, but he didn't feel it. Somehow, Sorin's lair retained his heat.

He inhaled deeply and exhaled on a sigh. The cavern also retained Sorin's scent, his drugging, addictive male musk. Smoky, wild, and forbidden.

Ere's stomach chose that moment to growl loudly, protesting the fact that it must be way past dinner time, and apart from the hearty brunch they shared at the café, he hadn't eaten anything else.

Well, if one discounted gorging on cream and blood.

Mmm...he licked his still-swollen lips in memory, as his dick perked up in a weary but eager salute.

With nothing better to do, he picked at the top layer of feathers he'd slept upon, casually exploring.

The nest was intricately constructed. He could see twigs and branches sticking out along the perimeter like a protective barb-wired fence. But somehow, the center of the nest had the perfect support, not unlike a Westin Heavenly bed, Ere's favorite sleeping accommodation. Except it was even better, for the feathers made him feel like he was truly floating in a golden, flaming cloud...

Hmm. He frowned and picked up a feather to look more closely.

The bottom of the long feather looked normal enough, if outrageously pretty, glinting orange, yellow and red in the firelight as if it was encrusted with precious jewels. Down toward the calamus, tufts of the softest down fluttered and curled. Toward the middle, the barbs began to wave and weave.

There was no other way to describe it. It was like a dessert mirage, the veins losing substance as they spread further to the tip. Until finally, at the end of the feather, the vane crackled like real flames, shifting with the air.

Ere enclosed the tip of the feather in his hand, seeing if it would burn. It didn't. He only felt the most delicious heat lick his skin.

He stroked the feather under his chin, testing the feel of that. More heat, the flames caressing his face and throat like loving hands. He brushed it down the middle of his chest, to his groin, leaving a sizzling trail of sensations, like tiny bursts of electricity that woke up all of his nerve endings. Even those he never knew he had.

He dragged it over his half-hard cock, and it hardened painfully to full arousal beneath his trousers, straining the fabric as if it wanted to pound its way out of the confines like a battering ram.

Ere's eyes snapped open when he realized that they'd closed of their own volition minutes ago. He'd been so lost to the pleasure. Just one fucking feather.

No wonder he had no hope of resisting the man himself.

At that thought, he made his way to the entrance of the cave, still holding the feather like a candle to guide him, even though his vampire vision worked best at night. He didn't want to release it. He felt closer to Sorin when he held something of the male's in his hand.

When he pushed aside the shrubbery that shielded the mouth of the cave and poked his head out into the freezing night, he found the object of his newly acquired obsession standing at the edge of the steep ravine, his back turned towards Ere.

Quietly, he padded on bare feet to stand beside the warrior. The moment he was within arm's length of Sorin, he no longer felt any cold. The male was his very own sun, and he was doomed forever to be the cold, worshiping moon that orbited jealously around him.

Ere frowned as something snapped in his fractured mind. *Moon*. Moonstone.

Something to do with pale, opalescent, shimmering scales...

"Hungry?"

Sorin's brusque query in his ridiculously sexy, gravelly voice distracted Ere from the disorienting images in his head.

"Starving," he admitted. "What's for dinner? Shall we fly into town and grab some grub? *Drink of Me* has a knockout dinner menu. Comfort food, Maddie calls it. She sets the menu every week, and the Chef's Recommendation is always one of her own recipes."

"We?"

Sorin turned slightly but not fully toward him, so that Ere could see him arch a questioning eyebrow.

"Well, okay. If you want to be specific—*you* can fly *us* into town to grab some grub. I don't have those gigantic extravagant wings, after all."

"You do."

Ere frowned, not liking where this was going.

"I don't. I haven't been able to transform into dragon since...you know exactly since when. And it's not like a black dragon flying into town is the best idea ever, even if we have the cover of night."

You haven't tried. You are not born dragon, not like my B—not like Rai.

Ere heard the stumble and didn't like it. He was so unfathomably jealous of his former self.

Like me, in this current form, you were made into what you are. Human science made you. Ancient magic made me. You are not fully Beast. You can transform into in-between states, including materializing wings as a man.

I don't want to.

Ere folded his arms and scowled.

Why was Sorin pushing him right now? He was hungry. They could start the whole training-to-kill-the-Hydra thing tomorrow, couldn't they? On a full stomach. Maybe after some more shagging and rest. With Sorin's miraculous cock inside him.

We do not have time. You cannot delay. The Hydra will come soon. We must be prepared.

"I'm talking a couple hours to have *dinner*," Ere groused. "I'm not pushing Destiny to next year."

If only he could!

Destiny waits for no one.

Ere rolled his eyes.

"Oh, for fuck's sak—aaaaaaaagggghhhhh!"

His words morphed into an unmanful screech when Sorin wound one arm around his back and hurled both of them off the ravine into the black abyss.

And then he let go.

He fucking let Ere go!

Ere was going to *kill* him!

Gut him! Push his balls through a cheese grater!

What the fuckity fuck!

He flailed and clawed. But what the hell was he scrambling for? There was nothing but air! Nothing but empty, insubstantial *air*!

And so freezing, he felt every drop of sweat and tears that formed from the sting of the wind turn immediately to icicles. His eyelashes were caked with them. He could barely keep them slitted open to see.

Not that there was anything to look at. There was nothing around him but endless night. No clouds, no stars. He no longer knew which way was up or down.

Gods! He was going to plummet to a (slightly) early demise.

How far up were they? He hadn't paid attention. How many more minutes did he have? Seconds? Unless there were jutting cliffs he'd bounce off of first, breaking half his bones before plummeting further?

Oh goody. Something to look forward to.

On the bright side, he was likely to die on impact. It would no doubt hurt before his consciousness was wiped out, but it would be over in an instant. He hoped.

On the not so bright side, he wouldn't live to fight the good fight. He'd leave the protection of Benjamin to others. Capable though they were, how could they possibly beat the Hydra?

At this thought, Ere scrambled and flailed again.

Gods damn Sorin to Tartarus and back!

Why did he have to push so soon? Literally?!

Ere wasn't ready. He wasn't going to miraculously spout wings. He couldn't transform into a dragon.

He wasn't ready!

As his limbs froze with numbness in the unforgiving cold, the feather he'd forgotten he still clutched wiggled free of his unfeeling grip, its vane catching the wind to lift it away.

No!

Ere's almost entirely frozen shut eyes cracked wider at the sight of his prize floating up and away, taunting him with its tendrils of flames.

He clawed thin air again, trying to doggy-paddle toward the feather. In vain, of course. This wasn't water. He was treading *air*. There was nothing to tread at all!

But that was his goddamn feather!

He hated Sorin with the strength of a thousand suns right now, but there was no reason an innocent feather had to suffer Ere's wrath by extension.

He *loved* that feather. It was *his!*

The jagged ground below was becoming more visible the farther he fell.

He didn't notice. All he could see was a brief flicker and spark from the feather's flames. Maybe it was his imagination. He was probably too far away now to see anything. But he could swear it was there, floating carelessly through the night sky, taunting him to chase it, catch it, possess it again.

The ground grew ever closer, seconds away from impact.

Ere didn't look down, all of his attention focused on the goal he could no longer see. He gritted his teeth and squeezed his eyes shut, fisting his hands and locking all of his muscles.

He imagined himself spouting giant black, bat-like wings, the same kind of wings that he had as a dragon. He imagined flapping those wings in great, gusting, gravity-reversing heaves, not only stopping his freefall but shooting him like a rocket back up into the sky after the lost feather.

Higher and higher he soared, but he couldn't see where he was going. It was too dark. Panic gripped his heart at the thought that he'd truly lost it. His only link to Sorin (the great big bully, whom he hated with every fiber of his being!).

He couldn't lose the feather.

A sob choked out of his ice-sealed lips. He needed that fucking feather!

Suddenly, a cannonball of flame knocked into him, throwing him off course. The fire subsumed him, burning away the icy cold, unfreezing his limbs, his face.

He finally opened his eyes and looked directly into Sorin's flame-filled golden orbs, his fiery wings encapsulating them both in a concentration of orange and yellow light that cut through the night like a shooting star.

Ere's first reaction was weeping elation. But before he could shed any unmanly tears, the blackest rage took precedence.

He pushed Sorin with all his might, punching the heels of both hands into the male's chest.

They burst apart with a sonic boom. Sorin tumbled head over heels through the sky before digging into solid earth like a crashing meteor a hundred yards away. The ground beneath him cratered and cracked from the epicenter of his collision. He landed hard on one knee and one fist, his flapping wings preventing mortal impact.

Ere landed more cleanly on his feet. He didn't pause to think how that was possible, too focused on taking down his nemesis.

He shot across the barren ground like a bullet, rushing at Sorin, who strangely (stupidly) stood still, as if waiting for him to come.

He collided with the warrior male like a wrecking ball, knocking them both into the ground so hard, they scraped through stone and dirt like a bulldozer.

"You made me lose my feather, you-you *bully*! I hate you!"

Ere punctuated this award-winning speech with a right hook to Sorin's jaw, snapping the male's head to the side, bloodying his mouth. He sat astride the warrior's middle as Sorin lay flat on the ground. His back was likely scraped raw from the force of Ere's collision, but Ere blocked out every twinge of concern. The meanie didn't deserve it.

(Okay, that sounded just a tad too puerile even for him).

Instead of retaliating like Ere expected, Sorin simply lay still beneath him, turning his head to face him again.

He was smiling, bloody lip and all.

A real, teeth-baring, breathtaking smile.

Ere was stunned into stillness and silence, spellbound by such a rare, glorious vision.

But you found your wings, Sorin said quietly in their linked mind.

Eh? What was he talking ab—

And then Ere noticed the flapping, fluttering appendages attached to his back and shoulders.

He slowly, cautiously turned his head to look behind him, slightly afraid of what he'd find.

The giant bat-like wings he'd only imagined in his mind extended around him like an ugly black cape. The arching bones that spread the leathery membrane like a ship's sail looked strong as steel. Sharp, curving thorns punctuated the points and connections.

Ere heaved an aggravated sigh.

"Brilliant. Your half-form is a fucking archangel, and I get to be a flying rodent. That's poetic justice for you."

*** *** *** ***

At the bottom of the mountain, the Tiger King had built a large compound for the animal spirits under his protection, especially those that felt more comfortable in the wild than human civilization.

There, they quickly showered in the communal stalls, borrowed a change of clothes and shoes for Ere, since he'd been flung off the mountain peak barefoot, and headed back out to town for victuals.

The compound had a large mess hall of sorts that served both raw and cooked food. But Sorin sensed Ere's discomfort amongst the animal spirits who were strangers to him, and understood that the café he worked at was more than just a place to eat; it was an extension of home.

He made Ere fly himself into town, however, if the male wanted to go. It was an opportunity to practice using his new half-form.

Ere didn't argue. He simply materialized his wings, and as they both leapt into the air and took off, he purposely extended the wing closest to Sorin with a snap, knocking Sorin suddenly to the side mid-flight. Then, he flapped those giant black wings mightily, gained speed and quickly pulled out ahead, leaving Sorin in his proverbial dust.

Message received. Ere was "mad at" him.

The dragon had been petulant and uncharacteristically quiet since they wordlessly agreed to head into town. Sorin didn't mind. There was a child-like quality to Ere that reminded him of the Bane. In so many ways, despite his experiences, Ere retained an indefinable, indefatigable innocence.

His soul was pure. Perhaps not purely *good*, but it was the effort that mattered. He *cared*. He tried. He was the bravest man Sorin had ever met.

Ere was a natural in flight. Maybe it was muscle memory, or rather, memories retained by his reincarnated soul.

He adjusted to the wind currents, the contours and weight of his half-form, instinctively, never faltering for a moment. Just like the Bane, he seemed even more at ease in the skies than Sorin ever was, and that was saying something.

He stuck the landing flawlessly when they found a darkened, deserted corner of town to transform back into humanoid form. Sorin landed some twenty feet behind him, following his long-legged lead.

"Oh, hey, Ere!" the woman named Mike called out as she rushed around with platters of food in both arms.

"Grab your usual booth. You're in luck, it's free right now. I just cleaned it. We're real busy here tonight, so come up to the counter when you're ready to order. You might have to serve yourselves, no offense."

"No problem, Mike," Ere said easily, his face lighting up for the first time in the past hour.

"Do you need me to help out? Sorry I was MIA today. Inanna let you know, right? I'm taking a few days off. Sorin and I..."

He trailed off with a cough, clearing his throat.

Mike darted her keen eyes from Ere to Sorin, not missing a thing.

"Yeah, Inanna mentioned you guys were...busy."

She waggled her brows, and Ere flushed crimson.

Sorin could only see part of Ere's profile as the man was turned mostly away from him, still ignoring him. But he felt the increased heat of Ere's body. His own immediately responded, throbbing with possessive heat and effervescing his mating musk in the space between them, his animal Bond trying to pull Ere closer into his orbit.

Whether by accident or in response to the call of his body, Ere stepped slightly closer to him, before he seemed to recall himself and jolted forward again.

"Don't worry about it, hun," Mike said as she spun away with her trays. "Maddie, Mama Bear and I have it under control. Go make yourselves at home."

"Ishtar is here?" Ere perked up again.

"She's the main chef today. We put her to work in the kitchen. I'll let her know you're here with your man."

"He's not—" Ere began to protest, but Mike already walked away.

Sorin's hands involuntarily clenched into fists at the words Ere cut off.

He's not my man.

No. He supposed he wasn't.

He was just the male Ere let fuck him to assuage his newly discovered carnal needs and to accelerate the last of his healing.

Sorin's chest felt flooded with acid, the way his insides shriveled and died.

This wasn't his Bane, he had to keep reminding himself. He shouldn't expect anything in return. He was here to fulfill a promise—to make this present incarnation of his dragon whole again. To make him strong enough to fight his own battles.

Nothing more.

The animal in him rebelled at this thought. He knew in the root of his soul that he'd found his spirit Mate. His Eternal Mate. There could be no other for him.

Not then. Not now. Not ever.

Unlike Pure Ones, where a pair had to choose each other to cement their Bond, and unlike Dark Ones, who could Mate without love, he was an animal first. He was born an eagle. He Mated for life. His love was unconditional and eternal.

Even if the Mate he'd chosen didn't reciprocate.

They made their way to the back corner of the café and settled into their booth, each taking their usual favored seats.

They were both silent for many moments, with Ere pretending to look at the menu he'd told Sorin before that he knew like the back of his hand.

Finally, the male said reluctantly, "What are you in the mood for? I think I smelled lamb and venison. That's a special treat. The typical fare is beef and chicken."

"You choose," Sorin answered.

Ere folded his arms across his chest and looked to the side, anywhere but at Sorin. He was obviously still holding a grudge.

Sorin let him stew. Never taking his eyes off Ere's face to gage his emotions.

He was pleased to see that the jagged patchwork of scars marring the male's otherwise hauntingly beautiful visage had receded to faint lines. Sorin wondered if he knew how rapidly he was healing. Soon, if they continued to...come together as they had been, Ere would be good as new.

Ere grumbled something under his breath that Sorin wasn't able to decipher.

Say again, dragon.

Ere huffed a breath of sheer annoyance.

"I wanted that feather," he said, still not looking at Sorin. Still angry.

Sorin didn't know what feather Ere was talking about. He hadn't noticed.

I have many feathers.

"I wanted *that* one," Ere pouted stubbornly.

Irrationally, to Sorin's thinking.

But the Bane often behaved the same. He would get fixated on something and dig his heels in.

Like the way he had to win every argument and wouldn't stop until he had the last word. The way he was ridiculously possessive of Sorin, jealous of anyone who spent time with him. And he made no bones about it. He always stuck to Sorin's side like a shadow and practically growled and hissed at others whenever they came near Sorin.

When Sorin couldn't take it anymore one day when they'd still been merely comrades in arms, he asked the Bane why he behaved this way.

Because dragons love treasure. We hoard it and never share. And you're my greatest treasure, Solemnity. You're mine, mine, mine!

Only MINE!

Sorin's heart hurt with a stabbing, twisting pain at the memory. Unable to help himself, he cast his eyes down to hide it.

"I'm going to put in our orders," Ere said as he got up from the table, still not looking at Sorin, still mad about the lost feather and stewing in whatever else grudge he was holding.

"I'll wait until they're done and bring it all in one go. Be back in ten to fifteen. Mike should be coming by to get our drinks. I want hot chocolate."

Sorin watched him go without answering. Ere didn't linger for it, probably used to his sparseness with words by now.

He didn't know what was so special about the feather Ere lost. He didn't know if it was a long tail feather, or wing feather, or one of the smaller ones closer to the body. There were dozens of variations in color, size and substance.

He reached under his shirt and transformed part of his chest on his left side into animal form so that he could pluck one particular feather, the one whose calamus's tip contained the blood from his beating heart. It would not grow back. Unlike all of his other feathers in animal form.

His heart would always be wounded from this moment on.

He breathed deeply through the stabbing pain and shifted back into human flesh, his left pec bleeding through his shirt before a thin layer of epidermis healed over the wound. The hole in his heart wouldn't heal, but at least it was not visible externally.

Only Sorin knew.

He plucked loose a few strands of his long hair and began to weave. It was a simple thing. Despite the size of his hands, all raptor spirits had nimble fingers. They made intricate nests, after all. And the half-breed Lesser Beasts usually built homes for their mates with their own hands. It was a skill their mostly human descendants never lost.

Mike came and went with their drinks. Soon, Ere returned with platters of food balanced on each shoulder.

"All right. I got us venison steaks and lamb chops. Lots of sides, including wild rice and greens. Birds like that sort of thing, right? Ishtar will come by later with dessert. It's a surprise."

He seemed to be in a much better mood than before, Sorin noticed. He was smiling again. And chattering. The brief time he spent with his friends and family in the front of the shop must have helped.

They ate mostly in silence. Well, Sorin was silent, which was not unusual. Ere was more talkative, relating random observations and some of the things he discussed with his friends. The feather grudge seemingly forgotten.

Sorin was loathe to remind Ere of it. But it didn't make sense to hold onto something that no longer belonged to him. He wanted to give it to its rightful owner before they were interrupted by Mike or Ishtar or anyone else.

"Here."

He reached across the table and deposited the item in his fist beside Ere's almost empty plate.

Ere stopped mid-chew and looked down, his eyes sq
first, then widening with pleasure, the blue-green orbs sp;
gems.

He rubbed his hands on his thighs, then wiped them on the
napkin for good measure, before picking up Sorin's gift with the
utmost care and reverence.

"It's...it's..."

"A feather," Sorin brusquely supplied.

Ere sent a glare his way.

"I know it's a feather," the male ground out, scowling with
annoyance.

Then, he looked back at it, and all of the frustration instantly
disappeared from his face. It's as if he couldn't stay mad when
gazing upon his prize.

"It's the most beautiful feather I've ever seen!"

He let the hair-spun chain that looked like finely-woven gold
threads dangle delicately from his hand, the feather hanging off the
end as he stared cross-eyed at it like he was hypnotized.

"It looks so soft, and it is, but it's also not," he murmured,
caressing the downy barbs and vane with his other hand.

I strengthened it with my fire, Sorin told him. *It will never lose
its form.*

"An indestructible feather," Ere breathed. "What a wonderful
oxymoron."

And then he noticed the bright red blood held within the
calamus.

"What's this? It looks like liquid rubies. So sparkly."

Sorin didn't reply, letting Ere come to his own conclusions.

The male spent a few more minutes admiring the chain and
feather, then clutched it covetously to his chest.

"Is this for me? Do I get to keep it?"

Sorin grunted. Wasn't that obvious?

To his slight horror and concern, Ere's eyes welled with tears.

"Thank you," he whispered.

"I love it."

Sorin gave one brief nod and glanced away, clenching his jaw.

How easily it would have been to mishear the words as *I love
you.*

But he didn't mishear. He wasn't the kind of male to delude himself.

Ere put it around his neck, fanning his hair out over it, and tucked it beneath his shirt.

"You're forgiven."

Sorin looked back at him, his expression implacable once more.

"Just for that, I'll work extra hard on my training tomorrow. I won't let you down," Ere vowed, pure happiness giving his entire person a vibrant glow.

It's yourself you shouldn't let down, Sorin said. *And the ones you seek to protect. You owe me nothing.*

"So…. You're just putting up with me out of the kindness of your heart?" Ere needled.

His eyes darkened suddenly.

"Or is it for the memory of 'the Bane'?"

Sorin didn't reply.

Animals did not lie. But he also didn't want to reveal the truth. He felt painfully, nakedly vulnerable as it was.

Ere was about to say something else when an elderly, plump female arrived at their table with two plates of desserts. One piled with some sort of cake and cream, the other with a fruit-filled pie.

"Here you are, gentlemen," the motherly matron said. "On the house."

She pinched Ere briefly on the cheek, making the male grin and grimace at the same time.

"Eat up, my boy. We need to put more meat on that boney frame."

"I will, Mama Bear," Ere said obediently.

The woman looked to Sorin, her eyes assessing before they softened.

Be patient with him, she communicated in his mind, startling him, though he didn't show it outwardly.

He's worth it. He's priceless, my beautiful Erebu.

I know, Sorin answered, and saw in the light that shone within the female's eyes that she understood he did.

"All right, I'll let you boys dig in. I'll be here all next week to help out, so come back any time you're hungry, hear?"

"Yes, Mama," Ere agreed dutifully, making the old woman's face wrinkle with a beaming smile at his words.

When she left them, Ere turned back to Sorin to share, "That was Ishtar in Mama Bear form. I don't think she can take different humanoid forms like I can. I've only seen her in animal form, this one and her natural Dark One form."

Sorin nodded. He sensed Ishtar's spirit in the matronly figure. This explanation did not surprise him.

For a few more blessedly quiet minutes, they devoured their desserts.

And then Ere broke the silence, as he was wont to do.

"Will you tell me the rest of your story?" he asked suddenly, drawing Sorin's full attention.

"What do you mean everybody was 'gone'? Including you. What happened after the war of the gods?"

Chapter Sixteen

Ere resisted the urge to take the feather out of his shirt to examine in depth under a bright light. Which was not provided by the comforting ambience of the diner.

He'd only had a few seconds, no more than half a minute really, to look at it without appearing strange and neurotic. More than he already was, anyway.

It was a small feather, one of those that birds had closer to their bodies, not from the wing or tail. It was fluffy at the end, unconscionably silky to his touch, and stiff at the tip, the veins of the vane hard but malleable, like real gold dipped in living flames.

It was no bigger than a half dollar, though those coins had long gone out of mint. But skinnier. It fit perfectly within the notch of his sternum, just before the rise of his pecs (what little muscle there was, unlike Sorin's thick slabs of satin covered stone).

The feather's ruby tip made it endlessly fascinating to Ere. Even more so than the flaming vane.

None of the feathers in the nest looked like it. Not that he'd had time to examine every single one, but the glint of red would have caught his avariciously keen eyes, he felt. None of them had the crimson liquid swirling just at the end of the calamus, trapped there like a drop of blood.

Ere's heart kicked at the thought.

Was it blood? It was such a bright red, it didn't look like blood. But rather a sparkling ink that Ere would have loved to collect for his hand-written letters.

He felt the feather fill his entire body with the most delicious heat, even though it only touched the smallest inch of skin. He wanted to touch it. Hold it. Pet it. Stroke it.

My Precious... he wanted to hiss like the Gollum from *The Lord of the Rings*.

He barely felt the intricate woven chain around his neck it was so fine. He was relatively certain it was made of Sorin's hair. The strands glinted like flames in the light, far surpassing the beauty of precious metals and gems.

He couldn't resist reaching up to finger the chain along his clavicle. It was by far the best gift he'd ever received.

Not that he had all that many. There was the comb that Tal made that Mama Bear had given him when she still thought he was Binu. There was the leopard kitty he (stole) convinced Mama Bear to let him have when he'd been snooping in her and Tal's chamber at the Shield.

That was it really. That was all he had.

And Benjamin.

Benjamin eked out this particular treasure for the top spot by a hair.

But honestly, they weren't comparable. One was a living, breathing being who was, in the end, his own person, not anyone else's. And one was an inanimate object that belonged solely to Ere.

How he loved, loved, *loved* this fantabulous feather!

For a while, Sorin didn't speak. He was silent for so long, Ere almost forgot the question he asked. The warrior was a master of brooding, manful solemnity. He was gazing out the window at the quiet night.

Ere wondered what he was thinking. Though they could now communicate both ways through their mind link, he couldn't sense the male's emotions, couldn't anticipate the direction of his thoughts.

Ere prided himself on his ability to read people. It was how he proved his usefulness to Medusa and survived her ire for thousands of years, after all. But Sorin was a complete enigma to him. Locked up tighter than the Sphinx.

Thus far, he knew three things about the warrior: one, he broke the mold for Alpha with a capital A; two, he was incomprehensibly attached to a dragon he dubbed with the unfortunate nickname of Bane (and Ere benefited from this connection by extension); and three, they had ridiculous sexual chemistry between them.

Ere and Sorin, that was.

Ere would rather not think of Sorin and the Bane together. He really didn't want to think of Sorin and *anyone* together.

But that wasn't his call to make. Sorin had lived long before him, and would likely continue to exist long after he was gone.

Selfishly, he hoped the male would always remember him as the best fuck he ever had. He was looking forward to cementing his place in the Hall of Fame of Sorin's flings over the next however many days before Armageddon came in the form of the ugliest dragon in creation.

He continued to sneak surreptitious glances at the magnificent profile of the golden god while Sorin stared out the window of the café.

At least those intense flame-filled eyes weren't trained upon him so he wouldn't see Ere compulsively finger the chain and feather beneath his shirt. He couldn't seem to help himself. He *needed* to reassure himself every second that it was still there.

Finally, when Sorin began to speak in their linked minds, Ere dropped his hand with a guilty start.

The warrior didn't seem to notice, for his gaze continued to be trained on the barren winter landscape outside.

There weren't many animal spirits left at the end of the gods' war. Not the originals, in any case.

Those who survived scattered to the four corners of the earth. There were no more aeries. No more colonies of predatory cats. And the serpents were even more solitary, disappearing deep beneath the seas.

The gods' sparks showered upon all living beings, imbuing some of them with more magic than others. Dark and Pure Ones, who were fashioned after the Twin Goddesses, were the most populous Immortals. But even they were few and far between. Animal Spirits numbered even fewer, and Elementals were the rarest of all.

Over time, Dark Ones rose to power, their very nature dominating and savage.

"But not you," Ere inserted. "You're not like that."

Sorin glanced at him briefly with those unnerving gold eyes.

You do not know me.

Ere swallowed, feeling chastised. How was he ever supposed to know the male if he didn't give Ere some clues!

But then he stuck out his chin and repeated with conviction, "You're *not* like that. You said so yourself. You're an animal first. Eagle warriors protect. They don't conquer and subjugate."

Sorin stared at him unblinkingly. Rather intimidatingly.

Ere refused to look away. He might not have known the male for long, but he knew this much. Sorin was the noblest Beast he'd ever met.

Well, all Beasts had an innate nobility and purity of spirit. But Sorin was special. If it was worth anything, Ere would stake his life on it.

Sorin turned back to the window, ostensibly dismissing his protest.

Without the gods and other Immortals to keep them in check, Dark Ones abused their power. You must know of the Blood Moon Queen, Gaia, who hunted Elementals and Animal Spirits almost to extinction, for these Immortals were the only ones strong enough to challenge her. She made Pure Ones into Blood Slaves, and ignored the cowering humans for the most part. They were too weak in those times to matter.

"Not anymore," Ere muttered.

No. Not anymore, Sorin agreed.

Now, humans rule the world. But millennia ago, Dark Ones reigned supreme. Queen Gaia was succeeded by her daughter, the most infamous Dark Queen of all—Ashlu Da-ni-gal.

"The bitch," Ere contributed.

Sorin grunted.

Ere would take that as agreement.

A few decades into her rule, she heralded a tournament for Dark Ones far and wide. The queen was taking a Consort.

Sorin paused and drew a deep breath.

I applied.

"You did what?!" Ere burst out.

Sorin still didn't look at him, keeping his gaze focused toward the window.

I'd spent millennia mostly alone. Wandering from civilization to civilization, wilderness to wilderness. Life as an eagle was simple. You hunted. You ate. You shat. You slept.

"Lovely imagery. Do go on."

All I had to do was avoid the Dark Queen's guards. And when I could, I saved as many of my Kind as possible from the annual hunts.

"You spent *thousands* of years alone?" Ere whispered. "But that's...that's awful."

I promised.

Ere sat up straighter at that.

"Promised who? The Bane? He *made* you spend eternity alone?"

Ere was beginning to hate the selfish dragon with a vengeance. It was the pot calling the kettle black, but nevertheless.

Sorin shrugged, as if it didn't matter what he'd endured.

Even if I hadn't promised, I didn't want a Mate. I rarely encountered a Raptor Spirit, and I have no love of humans. Like I said, it was easier to be an animal. Easier to be alone.

My soul had long since left my body behind.

Ere rubbed his chest as his heart kicked again, this time like a maddened mule. He couldn't bear it.

His own existence had been less than ideal (a gross understatement). But at least he'd had moments of reprieve. When he'd been an orphan and had a friend, before it all went to hell. When he found the Pure Ones' compound in the Silver Mountains. When he had almost a decade of true friendship and even love with Dalair and Kira...

How could anyone exist for so long without a comforting word or touch? It hurt to imagine it, never mind live it.

I applied to Queen Ashlu's tourney because I had a thought to end the Dark Ones' reign. Because of my Dark One base, I was eligible. If I became her Consort, I had access to and control over her.

"From what I heard and read, no one controlled Queen Ashlu," Ere put in. "She was as cunning as she was ruthless. After all, she spawned Medusa, my former Mistress of Evil."

I'll rephrase. As her Consort, I would have the perfect opportunity to kill her.

"Oh," Ere gulped, and waved weakly in Sorin's direction. "Sounds like a perilous plan."

A foolhardy mission, Ere didn't add. He knew the ending. Queen Ashlu ruled for three thousand years. She obviously wasn't assassinated. This didn't bode well for Sorin.

It didn't matter. I was already dead, the warrior said, as if reading Ere's mind.

Again, Ere's heart thrashed like a berserker gerbil in his chest, bloodying itself against its cage.

What I didn't count on was a formidable adversary that met me at the end. The Gray Witch warned me of this.

"Wait. There's a Gray Witch? I feel like I'm in an episode of *Game of Thrones*."

I needed a Dark noble's identity to enter the tournament. I needed armor and other fripperies. A trader told me to seek the Gray Witch with the coins I had. She gave me what I needed, as well as these words:

"A queen becomes Queen
A slave becomes Mate
A King falls in flames
A winner loses in games
A queen gives way
A Mate displaced
A Champion reborn
A King transformed.
A stone heart in fire
A soul dances higher
When True Love reveals
And old wounds heal."

"Spooky," Ere said. "And somehow you remembered them after all this time. Must have made an impression."

I didn't understand, nor did I care, for the words' meaning. But when I was leaving, she touched my left arm. Immediately, the left side of my body felt as if it was thrown into the broiling lava of the Fire Mountain. The burn was like nothing I'd ever endured.

It left these.

Sorin rolled up his sleeve to reveal intricate lines on his forearm and the back of his hand, like tattoos of ancient runes, now barely visible beneath the fine golden hairs on his skin. He arched his neck to the side and gestured to the left side of his throat and face. The tattoos were almost invisible, but as Ere stared transfixed at them, they seemed to glow, as if they had a life of their own.

How had he forgotten them? Too distracted by the drool-worthy forearm porn, and other, even more tantalizing attributes, he surmised.

She told me that the engravings would protect me when the time came. They would keep me alive until I found the one I'm searching for.

But it would cost most of what remained of my soul. She said I would be transformed one day, when the time was right. Reborn into another form. And only then will I find that which I lost.

She should have just spelled it out plainly that I was to die that day.

Sorin said all of this matter-of-factly, without even a hint of emotion, while Ere flinched and squirmed in his seat, no more flippant commentary to throw out. He didn't want to hear the rest of the story, but he had to know.

I did die that day, when my opponent bested me on top of the Fire Mountain.

He was an Earth Elemental, stronger than any I'd ever encountered before. I made the mistake of taking him to the mountain to reason with him, away from the prying eyes and ears of the Dark Queen's court. I thought I had the advantage on that peak, attacking from the skies while he was grounded below.

I was wrong.

"But...you're here now," Ere whispered.

He wanted to learn about how Sorin survived, not how he perished. He wanted to get to the "good" part. He needed it.

My memories of the millennia since are indistinct. At some point, I must have trekked down the mountain. I must have existed in some form or fashion. But I was not entirely aware of myself. I was not a thinking, feeling being.

One day, I learned through the sentinels of a vampire hive that there was a Dark King over New England. The first-ever Dark King in the history of Immortal Kinds.

I don't know what made me think of the warrior who defeated me that day on the Fire Mountain. Except that only a Consort of the Dark Queen could become King. That was my logic. What little I had of it. What little remained of my mind.

Ere winced.

It sounded like Sorin was describing a mindless, emotionless zombie. The living dead. He hated that the male ever suffered such a state. Like the brightest flame turned to gray, dirty ash.

I put myself in a position where our paths would cross. We dueled. But the Challenge was interrupted by a Red Witch.

"I'm sensing a pattern."

On instinct alone, I flew off with her to the nearest Fire Mountain. Some part of me must have sought to recreate the events of the past. Perhaps she could remake me with her magic. Perhaps she would fail and I could finally cease to exist.

Oh gods, Ere thought, as he swallowed the lump in his throat.

How unbearable must Sorin's existence have been to think this way? He wanted desperately to…to…it was stupid, but he wanted to wrap his arms around the male's lean waist, lay his head on that chiseled chest and never let go.

I got my wish.

I died truly that night. The form you see now rose from the ashes. I am not the same as I was. The eagle warrior known as Sol is…

Gone.

*** *** *** ***

The text message from an unknown caller ID came while he was sleeping. There was no time signature when he swiped his phone in the morning to check it. All it said was:

"You're it."

And then, in a blink, the words disappeared.

He scrolled up and down the screen, backed out and checked his other apps. Nothing. As if the words were never there.

But he knew they had been. He'd read them, and now he couldn't unread them.

He was "it." He was the new tech master.

The position came with a ridiculous amount of material wealth. He could retire in two years, and he was only in his twenties.

Of course, this supposed that he was still alive in two years. Which, if the tenure of his predecessor was any indication, longevity in this role—in any role within the Mistress's organization that wasn't a lowly ignorant minion—was questionable.

He surveyed the old tech master's work room, a high-security steel box filled with gadgets and screens, one last time. For the past few hours he'd tried to retrieve any useful information, download any files that hadn't been stored on the Cloud.

Nothing.

Every piece of intel the tech master had amassed, every digital signature or footprint, was wiped entirely clean. No traceability.

Just like the missing man himself.

He had no illusions that the old tech master was sitting on a sunny beach in the Caribbean sipping mimosas, surrounded by playgirls, living the good life. If that were the case, this tech room would still be operational. Months of his own work, anything tangentially related to what the tech master had been working on, wouldn't have been suddenly wiped out of the system thirty-six hours ago.

He'd spent that time trying to retrace his steps and recover what he could. He got zilch. The tech master was good. One of the best in the world. He himself didn't rank in the top ten.

Which was why he was surprised to read the text this morning.

Surely the Mistress had other, better, candidates on her backup list. His scope thus far had been extremely narrow. Mainly focused on locating a few people, including a nine-year-old boy. The tech master, on the other hand, controlled all of the Mistress's digital empire. There were a million things going on at any moment, and nothing remained from his tenure in the role.

He didn't know where to start. At this rate, he might be "fired" before he truly began.

A red dot flashed on the corner of one of the giant, wall-mounted screens before it suddenly lit up with two words:

"Find them."

Immediately, the words disappeared and the screen went dark again.

The new tech master understood now why he was chosen as the successor.

He also comprehended that if he didn't deliver on this first request from his Mistress, it would also be the last he received.

*** *** *** ***

They'd been silent, both verbally and telepathically, since departing the café for Sorin's nest. They were silent now, too, in the cozy cavern of Sorin's temporary home.

Sorin knew why he didn't speak. Aside from his usual taciturn nature, he was too raw from revisiting the past to share anything more. He felt utterly, painfully alone in his memories, his experience. Even though Ere was right here with him, not two feet away.

He hadn't told the male the whole truth, only parts of it. He hadn't lied; Beasts couldn't lie. It was against their very nature.

But then, Sorin was no longer the Beast that he'd been born. He was something else altogether.

The fact was, he might not have recalled much of what happened after his defeat by the Earth Elemental on top of the Fire Mountain when he was Sol, but he remembered how it *felt*. He'd been an in-between creature. Mindless. Soulless.

He didn't know what he did or how he lived. But he remembered the endless agony of loss—the moment when the Bane disappeared from the world. He wanted to disappear too. He was trapped here on earth in a half-dead form. Not a man, not an animal. He couldn't shift to full eagle form.

Death would have been a solace, but it had been denied him.

Presently, he doffed his clothes as Ere removed his own. By tacit agreement, they stepped into the nest together, lying down side by side.

For the first time, Sorin didn't track the other male's every move with his eyes. He kept them lowered or averted.

It would be interpreted as a sign of weakness. A sign of submission in any other male. But he simply couldn't look at Ere. This man who did not know him. This soul who did not recognize Sorin's the way he recognized his.

It hurt too much. He couldn't bear it.

And if it made him craven to hide from the pain, then he would own his cowardice.

Tomorrow...

Tomorrow he would don his impenetrable, unfeeling armor. He would train the dragon, heal him, make him strong enough to leave Sorin. Whether to die in valiant battle with the Hydra or to live this new life he'd made for himself.

But tonight…

Sorin closed his eyes.

Tonight, he prayed for a brief reprieve. No more questions. No more words.

The faintest touch upon his collar bone made his chest muscles jump.

He kept his eyes shut.

Please…

Not this night. If the dragon wanted use of his body…ah gods! It would destroy him.

Ere shifted closer. He could feel the male's coolness in stark contrast to his own heat. Whenever the dragon was near, he had the irresistible urge to bring him closer, wrap him fully in his embrace.

He didn't do so now. His body wanted it. He was already hard and aching. It was what he was made for—to fill and please this man. But the pain in his heart paralyzed him.

Hesitant fingers grazed his shoulder, dancing lightly down his biceps, the crook of his elbow, to his forearm, leaving a trail of sparks upon his skin.

He deepened his breathing to control his senses, holding still, muscles tensing in both dread and anticipation.

Fingertips tickled lightly over his skin, tracing patterns to his hand. There, they grew bolder, the touch firmer, as they drew over the back.

At first, Sorin thought he was following the path of his veins, but then he realized that Ere was tracing the runes tattooed into his skin. He felt the fire burn beneath his epidermis, and he knew without seeing that the symbols must be glowing. All along the left side of him, his skin must be lit up with streaks of bright gold.

And then he felt it—a gentle kiss upon the back of his hand.

Another.

And another.

Pressed onto each of his knuckles, into his palm.

Ere's soft lips traced back up his arm, the same way his fingers had traced down. Up his forearm, the tender inside of his elbow, up his biceps to his shoulder and collar bone. Those closed lips bussed his throat, the side of his neck, his jaw and cheek, and finally his temple and along his hairline where the tattoos ended.

The male scooted ever closer until his cool, sleek body was fitted perfectly against Sorin's, skin to skin. Their almost equal heights allowed their body parts to align exactly. Chest against chest, stomach against stomach, groins pressed together, cocks pulsing against each other.

Ere was hard too, the silky slide of his staff against Sorin's making him shudder and leak with want.

But Sorin didn't move. Didn't thrust his hips like his body demanded. He kept his eyes closed and his hands to himself.

Though no words were exchanged between them, he knew, he *felt*, that this wasn't about fucking. It wasn't about lust, though the desire that always blazed between them enfolded them now.

It was something else.

Ere pulled one of Sorin's arms around his back to rest over his waist so that Sorin was holding him snugly. He smoothed his hand along Sorin's shoulder over and over in a repetitive motion, and Sorin knew instinctively what he wanted. He unfurled his wings and wrapped them tight around the both of them.

Ere sighed and pressed a soft kiss upon Sorin's mouth. He laid one hand upon Sorin's chest, right over his heart, and tucked his face into the crook of Sorin's neck, breathing him in.

Below, he held both of their cocks loosely in his other hand, his long fingers not long enough to encircle them completely. His thumb grazed Sorin's weeping head to spread the sap over the sensitive glans, making Sorin shiver with an internal orgasm, though there was no external release. He did the same to his own cock and shivered as well, pressing his body even closer into Sorin, his breath damp and ragged against Sorin's throat.

He did this leisurely over and over, as if he was sleeping-walking, or sleep-touching. As if he was dreaming and didn't know what he did.

Methodically, he spread their moisture over both their pulsing cockheads, until their essence blended indelibly together, and they shuddered continuously with an undemanding, relaxing pleasure, inwardly focused, a flood of warmth that reached every crevice within.

All the while, he pressed soft, sporadic kisses to Sorin's throat and jaw and mouth, gentle grazes, like a kitten nuzzling.

Sorin tightened his arm around Ere's back and reached up his other hand to spread into the male's thick, wavy, silky hair, cradling the side of his head.

Slowly, he opened his eyes a sliver, peering into Ere's face through the dense thicket of his lashes.

The dragon gazed steadily, slumberously back at him, his eyes a deep sapphire blue, shining with...something new.

Something that made Sorin's heart skip a beat beneath Ere's hand still pressed on top of it. Holding it.

Slowly, the dragon smiled.

A small, fragile smile that Sorin had never seen him wear before.

The hurt within Sorin's heart began to dull to an aching throb. He closed his eyes again and exhaled deeply.

And then, at last, he slept.

Unplagued by memories or dreams. Only knowing the comfort of the other male's body against him, one hand over Sorin's heart, the other still holding the most private, intimate part of him, his thumb slowly caressing, their breaths fused as one.

For the first time since his past life, when he was another man, with a different dragon, Sorin was no longer alone.

Chapter Seventeen

Ere awoke to stillness and cold. Once again, he was alone.

One of these days he was going to chain Sorin to his side, maybe bind their waists together with the male inside him locked up tight.

He shivered pleasantly at that mental image, and his lips quirked with glee.

Suddenly, he wasn't so cold any more. But that only lasted so long when one lived in a cave on top of a snow-capped mountain in the middle of winter.

Hastily, he pulled on his clothes and borrowed shoes, hugged his arms around himself to fight off the icy chill, and exited the nest.

For a moment, he forgot the bone-cutting temperatures as he stared at the scene before him.

Thick clouds blanketed the skies like ghostly snowbanks drifting in the air. He could barely see the ground he stood on. Dreamy mists swirled around him, rolling over distant mountain peaks that seemed to undulate around his own like the curved body of an Eastern dragon.

It was beautiful and stark. It took his breath away.

He imagined that this landscape appeared much the same tens of thousands of years ago, during the Age of the Gods. There was no human civilization in sight for miles and miles. Only majestic mountains, jagged cliffs, gray-blue skies and wave-like clouds.

Did Sorin have the same view when he was an eagle warrior? Had his aerie lived in mountains like these?

It made Ere feel closer to him to imagine so. He wished he knew Sorin when he was Sol. He wanted to know everything about the male.

He stepped closer to the edge of the ravine, or where he supposed the edge to be, for the mists that swirled as high as his knees completely camouflaged the ground. His heart beat faster, from both fear and excitement.

He shouldn't fear, he knew. He'd materialized those black, bat-like wings twice before already. If he stepped off the ledge, he wouldn't plummet to his death.

But it was all so new. He didn't feel...completely natural.

He'd never taken this half-form until Sorin showed him how. Well, not so much showed him as forced him to discover it himself by hurling them both off the mountain. He was still getting used to it.

A flicker of gold drew his eye to one of the larger mounds of clouds in the distance.

He stared arrested as sparks of orange flame played hide and seek amidst the white, rolling mist. The sparks scattered high, then low, then they disappeared entirely, making Ere hold his breath. Only to emerge some distance away, just the tip of a wing, a lick of fiery tongue.

Without conscious thought, his wings unfurled and lifted his feet off the ground. Their mighty flaps dispersed the mist around him, but more clouds wound around his body like caressing hands, enfolding him within their airy embrace.

He chased after the flickering flames through the thick haze, sometimes gaining speed to track it, sometimes pausing to regain his bearings.

He didn't know how far he flew or where he was. Everything was hidden by the thick, impenetrable mist. He was so focused on his quarry that he no longer noticed the cold. And, too, the tiny feather beneath his sweater pulsed with radiant heat, making him crave more of the same. More of the man.

Sorin.

The flames picked up speed, leading Ere on a hell of a chase. He flew faster and faster, the wind whistling around him, the flap of his wings like thunderclaps in the total serenity of his surroundings.

His heart thudded like an ancient drum in his chest, filling him with anticipation and adrenaline. He wouldn't lose that flame. He would find it. Grasp it. Keep it.

But first, he had to reach it.

His lungs billowed; his breath gusted with exertion as he increased speed.

The fucking, flaming archangel was doing it on purpose, he was certain. Making Ere chase him halfway around the world. He must have flown thirty or forty miles already. He hadn't even had breakfast. His wings were tiring, his body too heavy. This form wasn't...natural. At the very least it wasn't aerodynamic.

He began to slow despite his best efforts.

Stupid bird, he thought. Didn't Sorin know he wasn't built for this? He wasn't what anyone would mistake for an athlete, much less a winged-warrior. He didn't *do* long distances.

And he was *hungry*, damn it.

The café in the village must be an hour away by flight now, and at the rate he was going, maybe more. He'd have to land soon. His wings were aching. He feared they might fold like a rusted, old umbrella.

Just then, the flames began to double back, drawing closer at the speed of a rocket it seemed.

Ere opened his wings at full sail, letting the wind fill them so that he hovered in the air, coming to an abrupt stop.

He wasn't imagining it. The flaming missile was coming straight at him, no hint of slowing down.

He couldn't see well for the clouds. He couldn't see Sorin's face or body. All he glimpsed were gigantic, flaming wings, bright bursts of red, orange, gold and yellow. They were different from Sorin's wings. Bigger. Broader. Completely engulfed in flames, rather than just at the long-feathered tips.

It occurred to Ere that the thing coming at him might not be Sorin. His heart stuttered with apprehension.

What had he been following all this time? What sort of creature could this be?

But...his instincts didn't ring with alarm. Whatever it was, however his heart thundered, he wasn't afraid.

He *wanted* it to come to him.

At last, a golden crown appeared. On top of a bird-like face. It wasn't an eagle, that was for fucking sure. It wasn't like anything Ere had ever seen before.

Gigantic wings spread wide, slowing its approach until it seemed to float in the sky like the flames that engulfed it. Revealing a proud, mighty chest covered with a metallic-looking armor of feathers. Two three-pronged claws tucked close to its body. And an extravagant, peacock-like tail that trailed like dragon fire. The whole being was made of flames, cutting through the mists and sky like a fiery sun.

It was the most beautiful creature Ere had ever beheld. And a long-forgotten part of him Awakened at the sight of it.

The creature opened its bird-like beak and let out a piercing, echoing screech.

Ere's entire body immediately felt like it burst into flames. His face exploded with heat. Involuntarily, he opened his own mouth to answer the creature's call—

And let out a thunderous roar that shook the mountaintops that surrounded them.

The fire bird's intelligent, familiar, golden eyes pierced into him unblinkingly. Suddenly, it dove. Like a flaming arrow, it shot downward, its torch-like tail tantalizing Ere to follow.

He did. He didn't know how he was able to move so fast. He wasn't aware of himself or the landscape around them. He was focused only on the beautiful creature shooting like a rocket toward the ground below.

He had to catch it. That was his only thought.

It was his.

Like the feather that embedded into his chest like a flaming gem, as much a part of him as his own beating heart.

That magical, fantastical creature was *his*.

He finally knew what it was: a phoenix.

And he was its Mate—

A gigantic, fire-breathing, obsidian dragon.

*** *** *** ***

He was bigger than Sorin would ever have guessed.

The broken creature he found at the bottom of a lake and pieced back together didn't look like this. That pitiful thing no longer existed.

This was something else.

The most magnificent dragon Sorin had ever seen. Beyond anything he could even imagine.

It was the exact opposite of the Bane, was Sorin's first thought.

Where the Bane was shimmering moonlight that belied his steely strength, this obsidian dragon was all darkness, danger and indomitable will.

Where the Bane was full of light, his maw ever ready to curl in a teasing grin, this dragon's massive jaws seemed permanently carved in a devilish sneer.

The Bane had been no runt, more than thrice the size of Sorin's old giant eagle form. Their earth dragon comrade tens of millennia ago had been larger. But even he hadn't been as big as the fucker coming after Sorin like a target-locked meteor.

Sorin's phoenix form was likely as big as the Bane had been. Much larger than any raptor Beast, in other words. But the black dragon was even bigger, despite that Sorin's humanoid form was larger. Their half-forms were about the same; Sorin had wider wing span, Ere had greater wing mass.

But this dragon took the cake.

It made Sorin feel almost fragile and small by comparison, which was something he had never, and never imagined he would ever feel.

The dragon knew it too. Because his sneer grew into a toothy grin as he increased speed and chased Sorin through the skies.

Remember what you said, Ere's dragon voice, deep and resounding, echoed in Sorin's ears.

He didn't reply. He knew exactly what Ere was referring to.

If I'm dragon enough to submit you...

Sorin's heart pounded with both exhilaration and a tingle of anticipatory fear. The thrilling kind. The best kind.

Fuck that.

He wasn't some milkmaid fleeing from a leering lord. The dragon might be bigger, but Sorin was mightier. He was a warrior. And it was time he taught this overgrown lizard something new.

He reversed course just as they almost reached ground level, shooting right back into the sky, disappearing through the clouds, as he let his flames turn to smoke.

Come on, dragon, he taunted in the foggy haze as Ere shot back up as well, growling with frustration at losing him.

Let's play.

*** *** *** ***

"Ere, honey, are you all right?"

Ere shoveled his food as efficiently as possible with shaking hands. His muscles were Jell-o after this morning's...rigorous exercise.

But not the kind of exercise he most preferred when it came to the male sitting next to him.

"Peachy keen," he mumbled around a mouthful of eggs and ham. "Never better."

Mama Bear looked at him doubtfully. So did everyone else around the dining table back at Tal and Ishtar's house.

He and Sorin had decided to get themselves fed and get Ere a change of clothes back in town. He had a hankering for Mama Bear's cooking, so he decided to canoodle his mother into feeding them, which she did readily and happily in her elderly female form, cheeks rosy, smile wide.

Ere didn't know why she liked to shift into this form around people who knew what her true form was—a tall, lithe, long-haired Dark One. "More beautiful than Arwen from *The Lord of the Rings*," as Benjamin would say.

He suspected she did so because she was used to it when she lived by herself keeping a shop called Dark Dreams in New York City. And also because she was his and Inanna's mother. Benjamin's grandmother. Perhaps she thought it more natural to take a grandmotherly form, even though the boy could see everyone's real selves within the disguise.

Ere didn't complain. He loved hugging Mama Bear. Her plump, matronly figure felt just like her namesake should.

"You like having two black eyes, a broken nose and bruises covering every patch of skin I can see along the neckline of your sweater?" Inanna queried with a raised brow, arms folded across her chest.

She didn't look at Ere while she spoke. Instead, she was shooting daggers at Sorin, who sat across the table from her, next to Ere. Rightly assuming that the damage was done by the golden, taciturn, muscle-bound warrior.

"Oh indeed," Ere chirped agreeably, smiling as he chewed. Then wincing when the split in his lip cracked wider.

"I might wear my battle scars on my face, but Sorin here didn't get off light. His booboos are hidden underneath the clothes. Aren't they, sugarplum?"

Sorin's scowl at the name-calling was knocked off kilter when Ere purposely elbowed him in his tender ribs. He grunted in pain but didn't retaliate.

Ere grinned wider. The male was on his best behavior in front of Ere's family. He wouldn't hit Ere back like he deserved.

Ha! Payback was a bitch, and Ere never played by the rules.

"Your scars are lighter beneath the bruises though, Uncle Ere," Benjamin said. "Honestly, I can barely see them under all the colors."

"Well, that's something to celebrate, isn't it?" Ere winked one blacked eye, still slightly swollen.

In a few hours, his Immortal healing abilities would fade away the surface wounds. The small bandage on the bridge of his nose should help it heal straight. It had been broken countless times before. But he had smart bones. They didn't need help to set right. The butterfly bandage was merely for show. Because Benjamin insisted on making him wear it. And who was he to deny his doting boy?

"Where's the General?" Ere asked the table at large.

Tal was the only family member not present. Ere felt a pang of disappointment that he'd missed his father.

"At the training grounds with the Tiger King's beasts," Inanna answered. "We're all going after breakfast to join them. We've been kicking the mock battles up a notch."

"A joint contingent from the Shield and the Cove are arriving this afternoon," Gabriel added. "We have much to prepare. Our enemies will act soon."

"Who's coming?" Ere asked, spearing a hunk of sausage from Sorin's plate.

The male ignored him, as if Ere ate off his plate and stole his food all the time. Mama Bear silently put two more sausages in front of Sorin and smiled at him when he thanked her with a small nod.

"Hope they sent the best of the best."

"Cloud and Valerius. Eli, Rhys, Maximus and Ariel," Gabriel revealed.

Ere whistled low.

"Big guns."

"The Dark King himself may also come," Inanna said. "But it is not yet certain."

The brief pause in Sorin's chewing was the only reaction he had. Methodically, his jaw started working again as he focused on demolishing the last of his food.

"And Dalair," Inanna said this softly. "The Paladin will also be here."

Now, it was Ere's turn to pause. He set his fork and knife down on the table.

"Huh. I'm surprised Sophia would let him."

"He's his own warrior," Inanna admonished. "Besides, Jade said that Sophia is the one who urged him to join us. I believe the exact words were, 'Little Cam is going to need his big brother to look after him. Nobody bullies our Erebu and gets away with it.'"

Ere inhaled and exhaled deeply to disguise his shuddering breaths.

Trust Sophia to know exactly how to reduce him to womanish tears. He sniffed, trying desperately to still his quivering lips.

"Will you join us in training?" Gabriel asked, likely an attempt to distract him from the near breakdown of gratitude and relief.

"No."

It was Sorin who finally spoke, his word final.

"We train alone."

"Yeah," Ere agreed, trying to smooth over the abruptness of Sorin's speech. "We have our own thing going. It's not really a... a team sport."

Benjamin nodded emphatically at them from across the table. From the way he wiggled in his seat, he was obviously swinging his legs jauntily with excitement.

"I know, Uncle Ere!" the boy boomed loudly in his one-volume voice.

"The dragon and the phoenix are a special pair. Training by yourselves makes total sense."

All eyes turned to the angelic, cherubic face.

Benjamin blinked with innocence, looked back at the gaping adults and shrugged.

"What did I say?"

*** *** *** ***

By evening, Sorin and Ere were weary and bruised to the bone.

The dragon was a fast learner, not surprisingly. He only took Sorin's hits once, never making the same mistake twice. That being said, with the Hydra, with their enemies, one fatal hit was all it took. They wouldn't hold back like Sorin did, with the intention of teaching Ere a lesson rather than kill him dead.

Dragon fire was the first thing to come back to Ere. He learned quickly how to shape it, harness it, make it shoot in a concentrated stream like a flaming spear, versus spread in a broad wildfire blaze. He learned how to use nature to his advantage, how to leverage the wind to disperse or fan the flames. How to induce avalanches and obliterate boulders with a fiery missile.

Dragon smoke was a new trick he added to his arsenal. He learned how to breathe it around him and use the clouds to hide his form, blending invisibly within them. He added the burn of the flames to the smoke as well, using it like a weapon, singeing everything the black tendrils touched.

He was a natural at flying, so all Sorin had to do to hone that skill was lead Ere on a wild chase. In his phoenix form, he was slightly faster, but Ere learned how to catch his orange flames with his own blue blaze, using it like a lasso to draw Sorin in.

Whenever their flames touched and tangled, rashes of sparks lit up the skies like a lightning storm. They circled each other in winding loops, creating blue and orange disks of light that illuminated the landscape below like the Aurora Borealis.

And when they came together like the clash of titans, Sorin taught the dragon to grapple and fight with his claws, his massive jaws, those tightly packed rows of razor-sharp teeth, as well as his magic.

Physically, Ere's dragon was bigger, broader, despite being sleek and lean. He also had the upper hand of having four claws instead of Sorin's two. His long, muscular tail had scaly spikes, including deadly thorns on the tip. But Sorin was seasoned at fighting in the sky, using his flaming wings and tail to their utmost advantage.

Ere would catch him. They'd tangle. But Sorin always found a way to get free, leaving the dragon gasping and grunting with new wounds in his wake. At the rate that Ere was learning and adapting, he would be Sorin's match in no time. Plus, he had a huge incentive—

If he submitted Sorin…

A full-bodied shudder shook through the warrior as he accompanied Ere down the mountain to the Tiger King's enclave.

They cleaned themselves in the communal shower, Ere standing under the blast of water right next to Sorin in the same stall. No one else was around. They all gathered with the visitors in the Great Hall for supper after a grueling day of training.

He felt the dragon's keen, covetous eyes on his body, his own blatant arousal bobbing against his stomach despite his best efforts to control his lust.

The adrenaline pressurized from hours of mock battle demanded release. But it wasn't just that. He didn't delude himself. He wanted the dragon with a vengeance.

Always.

"How about treating me to an appetizer before we head in to dinner with the esteemed guests from the Shield and Cove?" Ere asked with sly innocence, his sapphire gaze focused on Sorin's weeping cock.

"No."

"Don't I deserve a small reward for doing so well today? I've never trained this hard in my whole existence. Besides, you'll love it just as much as me," the dragon wheedled.

"Those blue balls of yours must hurt like a fucker."

They did.

His scrotum felt as if it would explode from the pressure inside at any moment, but Sorin didn't comment. He ignored his aching cock and stones as he efficiently soaped up his torso, neck and arms.

Ere's gaze never left his groin. The male barely paid attention to his own ablutions, haphazardly wiping a tattered sponge over his bruise-mottled skin. He licked his full lips at the sight of Sorin's stone-hard, throbbing sex, his own bobbing eagerly with vicarious need.

"I can wash your back," Ere said huskily, mindless desire deepening his voice. "You can wash mine too. Pleeeease...a little back scrubbing never hurt anybody."

Sorin looked into the dragon's fully dilated black eyes, the ring of blue barely visible, and decided to give him something to look forward to.

He learned quickly as well. He learned that nothing motivated Ere quite like the prospect of fucking him. Or getting fucked by him in return. Now that the male was comfortable with him and with his own appetites, he wanted Sorin all the time.

He could smell the dragon's need in his smoky musk, hear it in his panting breaths. He could swear he even heard it in Ere's heartbeat.

Ba-bump. Ba-bump. Ba-bump.

Want you. Want you. Want you.

Ba-bump. Ba-bump. Ba-bump.

Fuck me. Fuck me. Fuck me.

He speared the dragon with a look and crooked his finger.

"Come here."

Ere was immediately upon him like an eager puppy before the second word finished forming on his lips.

Wash my back. See that you get every crevice clean.

"Yes sir," Ere obeyed eagerly.

Sorin tried to hand him the sponge he used, but Ere ignored it. He dropped his own as well. He simply soaped up his hands, rubbed them together with glee, and went to work on Sorin's broad shoulders and back, digging his fingers into aching muscles. Making Sorin tip his head forward with a groan of pleasured pain.

He braced his hands on the stone wall before him and spread his legs.

Ere's magical hands touched him everywhere he could reach, roved the front of his torso as well, squeezing his pecs, pinching his nipples, scratching over the corrugated steel of his abs, to take him in hand possessively. Slicking the soap over his pulsing shaft in a tight, clenching grip. Kneading his full sacs knowingly, while pulling them down to stall his building release.

That's not my back you're washing, Sorin communicated gruffly. Even his telepathic voice was frayed with sexual frustration and anticipation.

"Oh, sorry, you mean here?"

Ere's tone was full of innocence, but Sorin wasn't fooled.

The hand that palmed his stones left to flutter curious fingers beneath them, rubbing along his perineum to insert between his ass cheeks, spreading them, a bold thumb leading the way.

The dragon zeroed in on his tightly shut hole, rubbed and probed, dipping the tips of his fingers inside as he involuntarily clenched and unclenched his ass against the persistent, relentless, roving touch. But they never ventured past the first ring of muscle.

Ere was waiting for his permission. They had a deal.

Though at the moment, Sorin barely remembered what it was as pleasure spiked in breath-stealing bursts.

The dragon pressed his forehead between Sorin's shoulder blades as if he could no longer support his own weight. His heated breaths huffed against Sorin's back, growing more agitated by the moment.

Sorin could feel him shaking. His dragon wanted him badly. His hard, thick, steel pipe of a cock nudging restlessly along the seam of Sorin's ass while he fingered him around the entrance to his body.

"You're so tight. So closed off," Ere rasped against his water-slicked skin, his other hand continuing to milk Sorin's cock, squeezing pearly dew from the plump head.

"Tell me no one has taken you this way. Tell me this is all for me."

Tell me you're MINE.

Sorin's own body shook at the greedy, heady words.

He wanted Ere to possess him as no one ever had. But now was not the time.

When it happened between them, Sorin would lose the last piece of his heart and soul to this confounding, contrary, courageous dragon. He wasn't ready to let go.

Not yet.

"Enough."

He couldn't take any more. He was a hair's breadth away from shooting his load. And he knew that when he did, when his body opened helplessly during climax, Ere would push into him, their deal bedamned. With his fingers or his cock, it didn't matter.

The dragon had yet to earn the right.

With a sudden twist, he reversed their positions against the wall, forcing Ere back until he pressed against the slick stone, Sorin crowding him with his massive body, front to front.

He didn't touch the dragon with his hands, keeping them braced on the wall beside Ere's head. But he pressed his hot length against Ere's and ground their sex together with slow, powerful undulations.

Silk against silk. Steel against steel.

The exquisite friction of their cocks made Ere's eyes roll back inside his head in mindless pleasure.

"Look at me," Sorin commanded, making the dragon snap his eyes open once more, fusing their gazes.

"This what you want?"

He slowed the rolling of his hips to slide the entire length of his erection along the dragon's from root to tip in one smooth glide.

Ere gasped and moaned, his eyelids involuntarily lowering.

"N-not quite," he stuttered.

"More. I want *more*."

Sorin bent his knees slightly and angled his cock lower, the fat head probing insistently along the seam of Ere's ass, splitting the round, muscular flesh open, seeking that hungry mouth that quivered and clenched to suck Sorin in.

"Fucking gods!" Ere growled, writhing helplessly against him, jerking his hips to ride Sorin's cockhead, trying in vain to swallow him inside.

He clutched at Sorin's back, clawing desperate streaks across his skin.

"Stop torturing me! I need this...I need you..."

Sorin stared unblinkingly into the other male's face, seeing every contortion of ecstasy in his expression, every blazing vein of desire in his glowing blue irises, burning around disks of pure, passionate black.

He was about to lose it just on this alone. The way the dragon reacted to Sorin's body was indescribable. So damn easy to set aflame.

He rocked against Ere's hole, letting the tip thrust inside but not quite. Letting Ere feel the incredible pressure but not the burn he craved. Not the stretch and splitting pain that harkened the euphoric pleasure to follow.

"Kiss me then, if you're not going to fuck me," the dragon begged without even a shred of pride.

"Just enough to tide me over. Something to dream about later tonight, you fucking tease."

This last he growled as his eyes blazed fiery blue, his fangs gleaming white, razor sharp and dripping with desire.

The dragon Beast was going to come out if Sorin didn't stop. It didn't matter that they were inside. Ere would transform and blow through stone walls if he had to. He might be playful, but he was all sleek power and stubborn will. There was only so much taunting he'd tolerate before he went after what he wanted full force.

And he wanted Sorin.

He stilled against Ere just as their cocks shuddered with internal release, his own pulsing against Ere's hole, the dragon's throbbing against his stomach, squeezed tightly between their bodies.

He pressed into the male as closely as he could, immobilizing him against the wall. Softly, he brushed his mouth over Ere's panting, open one, thrusting his tongue inside just once in a slow, deep lick.

Before the male could suck on him to prevent his retreat, he backed out again, licking Ere's lust-swollen lips and playfully nipping with his teeth.

And then, he pulled entirely away. Separating their bodies until nothing touched.

Ere looked at him, stunned and stoned, gasping for breath.

He wrapped one broad hand around his tortured sex and squeezed in a tight, clenching motion, gathering a dollop of cream at the pulsing tip.

Casually, he wiped his essence-coated fingers across Ere's open mouth. The male automatically darted out his tongue to lick Sorin's hand, then swiped all around his lips to collect every drop.

There's your reward, Sorin rumbled in the dragon's mind, making his pupils blow obscenely wide.

Train harder tomorrow, you'll get more.

And with that, he turned heel and walked away.

The other male's desperate, needy groan and inventive curse echoed through the communal stalls behind him.

Chapter Eighteen

Dalair was here.

Ere should have cared more.

He didn't.

He was too distracted by something else. Some*one* else. And not in a good way.

His top lip curled in a barely-contained snarl on one side as he glared daggers at the eagle-boy seated next to Sorin in the Great Hall.

"Our contact behind enemy lines is no longer viable," Cloud was saying, though Ere barely paid attention.

All of his focus was on the way auburn-haired eagle-boy leaned closer to Sorin, flashing flirtatious dimples in a come-hither smile.

Ere stabbed at the potatoes on his plate with murderous intent, scraping his fork on the dish with the screech of nails upon chalkboard.

The Tiger King sitting at the end of the long table squinted in pain at the obnoxious sound. If he were in animal form, his ears would be flattened with annoyance.

"But he left behind a virus that piggybacks onto any signal that indicates our enemies are homing in on our location. We don't have much time. They already know where we are. Where the boy is. They could attack as soon as tomorrow."

Would that be tomorrow morning or night? Ere wondered.

Because the hours made a difference. A lot could happen in an hour, never mind twenty-four of them. He could finally pin Sorin down, for instance. He could finally earn his just reward. He'd only gotten a small taste earlier. He wanted more.

So much *more.*

Despite scarfing down three T-bone steaks, loads of potatoes and rice, and a couple of lamb chops, Ere was still hungry. He was *starving,* in fact.

But not for food.

"Do you think Lilith will bring human weapons and machines to launch a full-scale attack? Or will she use more stealth?" Maximus asked.

"Either way, we must be prepared for the worst. How do we protect the human town? She will not spare any who is caught in the crossfire."

Ere's glare turned sharper, hotter, when Sorin dipped his head closer to the eagle-boy's.

They were obviously communicating telepathically, as animal spirits could amongst their own. Ere wondered whether they shared a more unique bond as two raptors. Even though Sorin was no longer an eagle, he was still the baddest fucking bird of prey on the planet.

Ere hated eagle-boy with a vengeance.

As if his thoughts brought the man's head up, the eagle-boy named Rhys raised his pretty yellow eyes and joined the discussion.

Not the same kind of flaming gold that Sorin had. There were no eyes in the world to match Sorin's.

"Sorin says we should lure Lilith and her minions into the mountains toward the north and west. There is a ring of jagged peaks that surround a barren valley. Only rocks and earth. No water. She is strongest near or in water, right? And she is an earth dragon. She cannot fly. Grounding her on dry land would be our best approach. Best done far away from the human village."

Sorin says?

Ere sneered.

Why didn't Sorin speak to him instead? Why did he share his very logical plots with a stranger eagle-boy? He could communicate telepathically with Ere too. Why didn't he use Ere as his interpreter instead?

"A solid plan," Dalair agreed from Ere's right side.

The man he loved like a brother, and maybe, once upon a time, crushed on with puppy love, was finally sitting right next to him. Sensible, healthy, whole. Sophia sent him. He was here to fight alongside Ere in the final battle.

Ere should have been more excited, elated or ecstatic. A warm kind of joy did fill his chest at Dalair's solid, comforting presence next to him. But...

All he wanted to do was leap across the table and wring the eagle-boy's neck.

"We need proper bait to lure her into the trap, however," the Paladin said.

"She will not make herself vulnerable to attack that way. My bet is that she will use the humans as collateral to distract us. This town is in the middle of nowhere with a sparse population. She will take the chance that she can always cover up its obliteration. But at this point, so close to her end game, I doubt she cares whether she exposes Immortal Kinds to humans. It may even be her desire."

What is her end game? the Tiger King asked the table at large.

Or perhaps only other animal spirits could hear him in their minds.

Ere could, in any case. So he decided to provide his perspective.

"She wants to become a god," he said with nonchalance that belied the seriousness of his claim.

"She is already the strongest dragon in the history of creation. Her base form comes from millennia of snake venom injections. She has Dark and Pure blood flowing through her from both Medusa and her previous shell, Wan'er. She herself was a fox spirit, so checkmark on the animal part. Medusa was a telekinetic, which means she must have some of the Element earth—"

"Yes," Cloud said. "Given that Ramses is the most powerful Earth Elemental that ever existed, and he was her sire."

Ere blinked at him in stunned silence.

He'd suspected something like this before, but was never able to prove it. He wondered whether his dead Mistress knew about Ramses, and vice versa.

The Dark King had not come to the party. Yet. No one knew for sure whether he would.

"Just so," Ere continued smoothly. "And when I held Clara and her girl child captive—"

The shadow warrior Eli bared his fangs in a threatening growl at Ere. If looks could kill, he'd be blown to smithereens right now.

"Sorry," he apologized hastily with a clearing of his throat. "Water under the bridge and all that."

"Go on, *binu*," Tal said, though he was half turned towards the shadow warrior warily, as if preparing to fend off an attack upon his long-lost son.

"Well, I...collected some of their genetic material," Ere said weakly.

Eli's growl deepened, his light green eyes turning ominously black.

"Um...it was only a tiny pinch. They were barely aware."

"Better skip to the so-what, dragon," Ariel muttered beside Maximus.

Ere moved on with alacrity.

"All that is to say, Medusa-slash-Lilith also possessed the Element fire."

Here, he rushed his words before Eli could swoop like the specter of death on top of him and tear him to shreds with his bare hands. The warrior was extremely proficient at that. Ere had witnessed Eli's battle prowess many times before.

"They have the Element water from the Serpent King and his Mate. And Medusa chose you as her Consort for the Element air," he said to Eli.

The warrior's gaze unfocused as if lost for a moment in unpleasant memory. He hadn't suffered like Tal did at Medusa's hands. No one could possibly compare. But he'd suffered nevertheless.

"They also acquired the venom from the Serpent King," Cloud inserted. "We arrived too late to save him."

"They have the blood from the Tiger King's beating heart," Dalair added, nodding to Goya, whose brows lowered menacingly.

Ere wasn't the only one present who had bad deeds to answer for. Dalair had executed his share of missions while under Medusa's control for two years. Including destroying Goya's home in Siberia, along with most of his clan.

"All Lilith is missing to become a god is the last remaining ingredient—the flame-tipped feather from the Eagle King," Cloud concluded.

Ere's eyes immediately went to Sorin.

The male looked back at him stoically, giving nothing away.

"But not just any feather," Cloud continued. "She must possess the one feather that cuts into his heart. It will contain his blood in the calamus. She needs that blood and the flame from the vane to seal her powers, combining all of the ingredients."

Ere's hand strayed to his chest involuntarily, feeling the tiny feather on its silky chain beneath his sweater.

Sorin tracked his movement but didn't change his expression. If anything, his face became even more unreadable.

"The Eagle King is gone," Rhys inserted. "Ramses fought him on top of Mount St. Helens. He made the volcano erupt, burying everything under rocks, lava and ash. When I went up there to find him and Eveline, there was no one else."

He looked to Sorin as if for confirmation.

Sorin didn't look back, simply holding Ere's gaze.

"It's true," Ere whispered. "The Eagle King is gone."

Goya looked between them with narrowed eyes, but didn't communicate anything telepathically. Cloud also pierced them with his eerie ice-blue gaze, considering.

"Then perhaps we won't have to worry about fighting a god. Just a giant fucking Hydra," Valerius grunted.

"How do we destroy it when the heads regenerate?" Inanna asked. "How do we even get close enough to do damage?"

"Oh, that can always be arranged," Ere said, drawing all eyes to him once more.

"You just have to be prepared to die in the process."

He shoved away from the table before anyone else could speak.

"You need a kamikaze idiot to get her in a bind. Good thing you have a volunteer. Me."

A round of murmurs and mutters swarmed the table, several people trying to speak at once.

The only person who didn't open his mouth was Sorin, who steadily held Ere's gaze with his intense golden eyes.

"I'll let you all map out the details," Ere said with an exaggerated yawn.

"Gotta head off to bed now to get my beauty sleep. I suppose we'll need to use Benjamin as bait in this trap."

He looked to the boy who'd been idly swinging his feet at the end of the table next to Tal. Listening avidly to everything the adults had to say (curses notwithstanding). His big blue eyes were keen with intelligence and a maturity beyond his years.

Hell, beyond even Ere's years.

"Are you ready, little man?"

"Ready as I'll ever be!" the brave little soldier chirped.

"Good," he said, his voice growing husky.

"It will all be over soon. I won't let the bad guys get you, my boy. I promise."

"I believe you, Uncle Ere. I know you'll kick Hydra butt!"

He gave a brief nod and forced himself to turn and walk away.

But before he made it to the tall double doors of the Great Hall, a hand grasped hold of his arm.

He almost smiled as he turned, thinking that Sorin was coming with him. Instead, he stared into Dalair's silvery gray eyes.

"A word," the Paladin said.

Ere swallowed back a pang of disappointment.

He looked beyond the warrior to Sorin sitting with Rhys at the table, two heads close together again as if in an intimate conversation.

The warrior didn't look at Ere. He hadn't spoken to him at all tonight. Neither verbally nor telepathically.

Would he still come back up to their nest?

Well, it was Sorin's nest, technically. But Ere was definitely commandeering it for tonight and any other remaining nights he had on this earth. So if Sorin wanted to bring some floozy eagle-boy to their cave, he could think again.

"Of course, brother mine," he answered Dalair, forcing his attention to the man before him.

"Lead the way."

*** *** *** ***

Sorin's hands tightened into fists upon his thighs beneath the table when he witnessed the warrior called Dalair follow Ere out of the Great Hall.

The man dared to touch what was his. Sorin wanted to rip his head off just for that.

But then he remembered that Ere wasn't his.

Not truly.

Ere needed him to heal. Needed him for strength and training to defeat the Hydra. That was all.

How easily he forgot.

Conversation flowed around him. Most of the Pure and Dark warriors continued to plan, preparing for the best welcome for the Hydra's forces.

The young eagle next to him continued to flirt and charm, throwing dimpled smiles his way, touching him lightly on the shoulder and arm whenever there was the opportunity.

He recalled the eagle vaguely. He'd met the man before somewhere. Perhaps even in his animal form. Most likely he'd met him when he was half-dead. After all, he'd been the Eagle King that Challenged Ramses to the death on top of Mount St. Helens.

The man named Rhys served as one of the Chosen guards of the Dark King. He used to be part of Goya's clan, one of the few surviving members. All this, Sorin gathered as he listened to the eagle talk with half an ear.

Now that the focus of his attention had left the table, he directed his thoughts inward, shutting out the external world.

His body was primed for sex. Adrenaline still buzzing through his system like wildfire. He was still aroused, his undying erection aching, his balls throbbing from the prelude in the shower stalls.

In a different life, before the Bane came into his responsibility, he might have taken the young eagle up on his unvoiced yet blatant offer. He might even take him in humanoid form, for the man possessed a pleasing, lithely muscular figure. He would take Sorin's cock like a pro.

But that version of Sorin existed eons ago. If he ever really existed at all.

In this form, this life, he didn't recall anyone before the Bane. And, now, there would be no one after Ere.

If the dragon went to his death battling the Hydra, Sorin would not survive him. He had Sorin's feather, after all.

He had Sorin's heart.

*** *** *** ***

"So."

"So."

After these eloquent opening salvos, Dalair and Ere descended into companionable silence.

They sat on top of the rock overhang that overlooked the training field below. It was where the Tiger King often came to observe the proceedings, growling orders to his beasts. From this vantage point, Ere felt like they were floating halfway in the sky, disconnected from the world around them. Neither grounded on earth, nor soaring through the night.

It was peaceful up here, engulfed in silence and darkness, with only the faint twinkling of stars behind wispy clouds.

"Sophia would have come," Dalair said in his low, quiet voice, "but we feared that Lilith would use her powers against us."

"Understood," Ere responded. "Wouldn't want to trigger the end of the world by accident."

"Or on purpose."

"That too."

"She worries for you," the man who used to be his brother said of the woman who used to be his wife.

Though it had all been pretend, the years he spent with Dalair and Sophia were some of the best years of his life.

"Nothing to worry about," Ere reassured. "I know what I'm doing."

"Do you?" came the doubtful query.

"I'm a fucking dragon," he boasted with a toothy grin. "I can do anything."

"I remember. I couldn't believe my eyes when you exploded out of the sarcophagus. I've never seen anything like you. You were..."

"Magnificent," Ere supplied.

"Gorgeous. Splendiferous. Awe-inspir—"

"One big-ass, ugly, scaly motherfucker," Dalair said with finality.

Ere sniffed.

"Don't make fun of my ass. I can't help it if it's big. All hereditary, you know. Check Tal's out. His is bigger."

"The way you fought the Hydra..."

He could feel Dalair's gaze on him.

"You *were* magnificent, Erebu. Brave and strong."

"But not strong enough," Ere muttered.

Dalair shook his head.

"You saved all of us. Most of all, you saved your son."

Ere whirled on him.

"Sophia told you about that, did she?"

"*You* told me."

He narrowed his eyes.

"When did I ever—"

"In your letters. Remember? I read them all."

He looked away again, feeling abashed.

"Oh."

They were quiet for a while after that.

Ere wondered what Sorin was doing. And it had better not be the eagle-boy.

He wondered whether Sorin would be awake or asleep in their nest when he got back. He'd definitely be naked. The man didn't have a shred of modesty.

And why should he?

He was so beautiful he made Ere's teeth hurt from grinding them to keep from groaning every time he beheld the warrior.

But Ere wanted to be the only one to see him thus. All that smooth, golden skin over steely mounds of muscle. He had a bit of body hair, light sprinkles on his arms and legs, slightly more on his chest. The hairs glinted a burnished gold in the firelight, like the most coveted treasure a dragon could hoard.

Best of all, Sorin had a thin line of hair that bisected his middle, splitting his abs and arrowing below his navel to fan out into a soft, tantalizing fleece around his groin. Ere's favorite treasure trail.

He smelled utterly delicious there. Ere should know, having buried his face in the man's lap more than a few times by now.

He wondered whether Sorin's beautiful cock would be full or sleeping. He wasn't sure he'd ever seen the male's sex relaxed before. He'd always been hard and pulsing when Ere was near.

Ah gods! He was starving for Sorin's cream. The honeyed dew of his pre-cum wasn't enough. Ere wanted the whole shebang. He wanted to feast upon the endless buffet that was the warrior's glorious body.

"You've changed, brother."

Ere started at Dalair's voice. He'd forgotten that the male was still there, so lost in his own, rather X-rated thoughts.

"How so?"

"I've never seen you so confident and in charge of yourself before," Dalair said. "You look like a man who knows what he wants and isn't afraid to go after it."

"And I wasn't such a man before?"

Ere didn't know why he bothered asking. He knew very well he had never been such a man. He'd pretended to be on many occasions, but he'd never truly been secure in himself.

Dalair shook his head, looking out into the night sky.

"There were some things in which you were unmovable in your conviction. You refused to fight when battle training was part of our upbringing. You only learned to defend, never to attack. You protected my mother while I was gone. Because of you, she never again suffered abuse, not even by the King's hand."

"I sound rather heroic, eh? If somewhat wimpy."

Dalair went on, ostensibly ignoring his contributions to this walk down memory lane.

"It was the other things you weren't sure of. Like whether you were attracted to men or women."

"Oh that. I've got that figured out now."

Dalair slid him a silvery look.

"Yes. I am well aware."

Ere might have blushed. He blamed it on the feather he wore, making him hot even in these sub-zero environs.

"I've never seen you so fixated on anything or anyone before," Dalair observed.

"Except you," Ere ventured.

"Never me, brother," Dalair sighed, leaning back to lay his head on his folded arms, one leg balanced over the other's knee.

Ere did the same, mimicking his pose. This reminded him of how he whiled away his youth with Dalair on top of their hill just outside of Persepolis city.

He missed those times. He missed his brother.

"Why are you so certain?" he asked.

They'd never talked like this before. Never talked about what they...felt for one another. They weren't brothers for real. Even the real Crown Prince Cambyses of Persia was only half related to Dalair by blood. But Ere had never been that boy. He'd always been an imposter.

He felt Dalair shrug beside him.

"You might have been attracted to me at one point, just out of curiosity. But you were never in love with me. We loved each other as brothers. You loved Kira as a sister when she came to us. Sophia told me."

"Y-you...loved me?" Ere whispered, afraid he'd heard wrong. Afraid he'd just made a thorough ass of himself.

Dalair turned his head to face him.

"Yes. We loved you," he replied gravely.

"We hurt you. We betrayed you. And don't forget that you betrayed us too. But know that, even then, even when I hated you, I loved you still. You'll always be my brother."

"Ditto," was all Ere could eke out in his thin, breathless voice.

Dalair turned away again, a smile spreading across his lips.

"You got your revenge though."

Ere turned back to face the sky as well.

"I sure did. Many times over," he gloated.

"The stabbing at Medusa's lair was a nice touch," Dalair said casually. "Did it feel good to push me to the edge of death?"

"Absolutely," Ere readily agreed. "Nothing like sinking a sharp blade into yielding flesh and pulling it out with a spray of blood. I felt like I was on the set of *Spartacus* or *300*. Next time, I might doff my shirt and paint my abs to add to the drama. Maybe film myself on an iPhone and send it in to HBO producers as an audition reel."

"But you didn't kill me."

Ere sighed.

"No. I'm not terribly good at killing."

"Are you ready for the Hydra?" Dalair asked in all seriousness.

"As ready as I'll ever be," Ere replied with as much gravity as he could.

"You won't be alone," the Paladin said.

"We'll do this together. Don't get it in your head to do something stupidly heroic."

"Too late for that," Ere returned. "This is *my* son whose life is on the line. If Lilith captures Benjamin, it will be a fate worse than death. I know. I've lived it."

"You don't have to sacrifice—"

"You forget I've fought the Hydra before," Ere cut in. "None of you tangled with her as long as I have. None of you got dragged to the bottom of a watery grave. Torn apart piece by piece, until fish bait in a pool of piranhas had more substance than my skeletal frame."

Dalair flinched.

Ere pushed relentlessly on.

"I know what it will take to defeat her. And I *will* defeat her. I just don't expect to come out alive on the other side."

He shrugged.

"Not a biggie. Nobody else has to die."

Dalair inhaled a breath to argue.

Ere cut him off.

"Did you know that my previous incarnation—my first incarnation—managed to kill gods?"

The other male turned to look at him again.

"I was one of the first dragons. A real badass. A real *pain* in the ass. A bane..."

"How did you do it?" Dalair asked.

Ere frowned in concentration.

"I don't remember. I don't have those memories...yet. I wish I did."

So I could know Sorin as the Bane once knew him, he thought to himself.

He'd hoard those memories like the treasures they were. Sorin loved his Bane, Ere was certain. Maybe if he remembered, he would experience the way Sorin loved *him*.

"He died too, my previous self," Ere murmured.

"I don't think your sacrifice is a prerequisite for defeating the Hydra," Dalair said gruffly. "You must focus on winning. Surviving. *Living.* You have a lot to live for, brother. Family and friends who love you. A son who needs you—"

"He doesn't even know who I really am."

"Then live to tell him about it."

"He deserves the parents he has. Inanna and Gabriel are the best."

"He deserves to have you too."

"But I might never deserve him," Ere whispered.

"You never will if you don't try," Dalair argued rather heatedly.

Ere was silent for a while, simply staring up at the stars and clouds.

And then he said, "I don't deserve him either."

Dalair didn't ask who "him" was.

"Don't you think you should let Sorin decide for himself?"

Ere couldn't look at his "brother." Not even when the darkness hid the embarrassed flush on his face.

"Is it so obvious?"

"Blatantly."

Ere sighed.

"I want him so bad," he admitted miserably.

"Tell him."

"I'll be dead soon. What's the point?"

"Shut up before I throw you over the ravine. All the more reason to tell someone you love them if you might not have another chance, don't you think?"

"If you throw me over, I'll just hover with my wings. Ha!"

"Ere..." Dalair said with clear exasperation.

"Hey, wanna take a ride on the wild side?" Ere sat up suddenly, hoping to distract Dalair with the excitement in his voice.

Dalair looked at him in question.

"Come on," Ere urged, grasping his hand to pull him to his feet.

He ushered Dalair to the edge of the stone ledge. They must be several stories above the field below. An accidental fall might not kill an Immortal, but it would hurt like hell.

He looked at the brother of his heart and smiled his biggest, brightest smile.

"Take a leap of faith with me."

Dalair searched his face with those silvery, warm eyes. He nodded.

Together, they jumped off the ledge...

And Ere showed him how to fly.

*** *** *** ***

Later that night, Sorin felt the dragon's presence before Ere entered their cave.

He kept his eyes closed and evened his breathing, pretending to sleep.

Where had he been all this time? It was several hours after the congregation disbanded from the Great Hall. Sorin declined joining Rhys and other warriors for drinks, returning to his nest alone.

Unbidden, his mind filled with images of his dragon with the warrior who'd sat next to him. They knew each other well, Sorin could tell. There was a familiar ease, as if each always knew where the other was. As if they could communicate without words.

Sorin wondered who the male was to Ere. In his mindless jealousy, he couldn't tell if they were attracted to each other. If Ere had that sort of relationship with the male.

The dragon got into the nest, fully naked. He immediately tucked himself into Sorin's body, shivered as his cold skin adjusted to Sorin's blazing heat, his long limbs winding around Sorin like a possessive spider monkey.

Sorin sniffed surreptitiously.

His heart stuttered when he scented the other male on Ere's skin. Thankfully, it wasn't a sexual musk, but the smell of clean sweat from physical exertion.

But the fact that Ere carried the other male's scent meant that they'd been very close. Perhaps as close together as Sorin was with him now.

Ere pressed closer, squeezing their groins together and wrapping his legs around Sorin's hips, winding them around his calves.

"Missed you," the dragon murmured against his throat, already half asleep.

"Wish you could be with me always."

And with that, Ere sighed, his breath deepening in slumber.

Sorin waited until he was completely asleep before wrapping his arms around the male and unfurling his wings.

He held the dragon as close as he could. As close as he dared.

No matter what happened on the morrow, for tonight, Ere was his.

Chapter Nineteen

Pay attention.

Ere ignored Sorin's frustrated growl and soared directly into the gray clouds overhead, narrowly missing the torrent of flames that swept his way. They might have singed his tail, but the thorns were tough. Nothing like a good roasting to make them tougher.

Make me, he taunted, sneaking through the clouds and breathing more smoke to hide himself.

This is not a game, dragon. I almost killed you twice today.

Ere rolled over mid-flight and pretended to do the backstroke through the skies while waiting for Sorin to catch up with him.

I need an incentive. Maybe if you reward me a little now, then give me the big prize later (and by big, I mean BIG), I'll feel the urge to try harder.

Two massive claws came out of nowhere, gouging bloody grooves into his back from below, making him yelp and flip, flapping his wings to get away.

Avoiding mortal wounds, avoiding death, *is your incentive!*

Sorin finally lost his cool, digging those claws deeper into Ere's back, grappling enough scale, skin and muscle to gain leverage and throw him bodily across the sky, peeling off a whole strip of Ere's hide.

Gods damn it! Fucking OWW! Ere groused, trying to regain his bearings with a frantic flap of wings, tumbling head over claws through the clouds.

Must you take a pound of my flesh in every session?

Do you think the Hydra will go easy? She will rip you apart at the first opportunity. Fucking pay attention!

Ere landed on a jagged snow-capped peak to lick his scales.

He'd have several stripes of raw cuts in his back in humanoid form, but nothing that wouldn't heal with good food and a night's rest. Not when Sorin enfolded him in the healing cocoon of his flaming wings every night. Best medicine ever!

If only he'd heal him the way he used to on the inside.

Ere didn't need it. He was thoroughly put back together by now. Even the scars on his face had disappeared.

But he *wanted* it.

Sorin hadn't fucked him in *forever*!

Well, okay, forever might be a slight exaggeration. It had been five days and four nights. But it *felt* like forever.

At the enraged phoenix's approach, he scuttled away to make room, eyeing Sorin warily.

Were they done for the day yet? The sun was already setting. They'd been at this since dawn. Ere didn't even have luncheon yet. Never mind all the other non-culinary delights Sorin had forced him to do without.

The phoenix landed in the spot Ere vacated with supreme grace and regal poise.

Heaven and hell, but Sorin was a sight to behold.

It wasn't fair how beautiful he was. In any and every form, he was the most breathtaking vision Ere had ever seen. In comparison, Ere's scaly, black, overgrown lizard form might as well have been Quasimodo to Sorin's Esmeralda.

Give me something to look forward to, Ere wheedled.

He never thought he'd push and bargain for sex like some libidinous fiend. But here he was. Begging Sorin for scraps several times a day, to no avail. The man refused to play ball. Literally!

The phoenix narrowed his flaming gold eyes. Something like anger crackled within them, making Ere worried.

He folded one wing slightly over his head in case lightning was about to strike him where he squeezed himself against the mountainside.

That was one of Sorin's powers—the ability to shoot lightning from his eyes and turn his entire body into electricity that fried in radiating shockwaves, in addition to flames.

Ere had learned this the hard way.

That's your ambition after all this time? Just to fuck me?

Ere straightened a little and huffed smoke out of his nostrils, taking affront.

It's a lofty goal. Have you looked in a mirror lately? Who wouldn't *sell their soul to fuck you?*

Instead of preening under his praise (for he totally meant Sorin's eminent fuckability as a compliment), the male's hackles rose, the crown of feathers along his neck and head fanning forward like enemy spears about to punch holes into Ere for target practice.

I have every hope of reaching my ambitions, Ere continued, both scared and excited by the danger of Sorin's wrath.

But let's be clear. There's no "just" about fucking you. I have plans.

The phoenix's eyes blazed as he waited for Ere to expound as if daring him.

Big plans, he reiterated. *I want to fuck you against the wall, on the ground, on a bed (and who cares if we burn and break it). In the sky, in the sea, in the shower, in our nest. Pretty much fuck you anywhere I damn well please.*

Sorin was silent for a very long time, simply staring at him with those eerie flame-filled eyes.

Ere wondered whether he might have gone a little beyond the pale this time.

He did want all of those things. And *more*.

But he also wanted Sorin to hold him, kiss him, cuddle him. Pet his long, dark hair. Stroke those big manly hands over every inch of his skin.

He wanted Sorin to be inside him all the time. He missed the burn and the stretch, the ache and pressure. He missed feeling so full the word "empty" lost all meaning.

He missed hearing Sorin's raspy breaths and the deep, rumbly sounds he made when Ere brought him pleasure. Missed the way his musky scent infused the air with his sex, their sex, merged and blended together like a euphoric drug. Missed the taste of his sweet essence, and the spicy, salty cream of his seed.

He wanted to make love to Sorin. With Sorin. And he wanted Sorin to love him back.

He wanted Sorin to love him back.

Ere blinked in consternation and panic.

Holy shit! He loved Sorin!

Totally, irrevocably, incredibly in love, love, love!

It wasn't about sex at all.

Well, who was he kidding, it was.

But not entirely. He wanted Sorin desperately because he *loved* him. He wanted Sorin forever and ever, amen.

The flames suddenly extinguished from the phoenix's eyes, like a metal gate closing down over a furnace.

Survive the Hydra, and I'm all yours. Any way you want me. Not a moment before.

Wait.

Ere frowned.

That wasn't the deal. He said—

But the phoenix lifted with a great flap of those flaming wings, turned and shot through the sky like a streaking meteor. Within seconds, he disappeared through the clouds, probably camouflaging his body by turning the flames into smoke.

Ere kicked at the snow with a hind claw.

It was just like him to fall in love, or rather, come to the realization that he was in love, right before Armageddon.

With a front paw, he patted the feather that was embedded in his chest like a gem in dragon form. He felt like one of those medieval knights going into battle, wearing the favor of the fairest damsel in the kingdom. Sorin would kick his ass at the comparison, but Sorin wasn't here.

Maybe luck would be on his side this time. The odds of surviving the Hydra were slim to none, but even if there was just a split hair of a chance, Ere would take it. He hated dying as much as the next guy, but he wasn't going to cower from death if that was what it took so that those he cared about could live. He had no shortage of things worth dying for.

But for the first time...the *only* time across all of his existence and incarnations, he finally found the one thing in life worth living for.

*** *** *** ***

Sorin watched Ere interact with the other warriors readying for battle. They didn't know when the fight would come, but they were always ready, always alert.

In a few days, the Tiger King, with help from elite warriors from both the Pure and Dark contingents, had whipped his troops into shape. The once straggly band of Beasts and Lesser Beasts were now well-trained soldiers of war. Their coordination in the field was a thing of beauty, reminiscent of the Age of the Gods, when Sorin fought alongside Beasts of earth and sea.

Ere had clearly come into his own in a very short period of time, despite that Sorin never gave him an inch, never eased up on him enough to let him gloat over his progress.

This was life and death, no gloating allowed.

But...

Sorin was proud of his dragon.

Ere conversed with Tal, Gabriel, Inanna and Dalair on one side of the Great Hall, likely going over the defensive tactics again.

The Hydra was coming to them, after all. They had to split up the warriors to both defend and divert. They'd already determined which of them would draw Lilith away from this stronghold at the base of the mountain. And at all cost, they must keep her minions away from the human town.

Ere stood at least half a head taller than most of the other warriors, though almost everyone present was over six feet. The gods didn't make Immortals small; they were made in their image, after all.

He was no longer the broken man Sorin welded back together with his flames. He wasn't even the shaken man Sorin first met when he came here. Someone fragile and uncertain, hiding behind his disguises, too afraid to show the world his true self.

Now, Ere flaunted bravado like an armor, but beneath the veneer, there was solid strength. A quiet assurance and confidence. His back was straighter, his chin angled higher, his shoulders back. Poised and ready for anything that came his way.

Just then, Ere looked at Sorin, where he sat amongst the shadows of the hall.

The dragon's blue eyes glinted with promise. Of what, Sorin could not tell. Only that the look made Sorin's short hairs stand on end with awareness, as instant arousal electrified his veins.

Ere quirked his lips at one corner, as if he knew exactly how he affected Sorin.

He called it his "sexy quirk" or squirk. He said he was going to trademark or patent it to prevent the misuse of such devastating charm.

Ere said the damnest things.

Most of the time he didn't make sense to Sorin, who listened more for the tone of his voice, what he conveyed of his emotions, rather than the words themselves. In so many ways, he reminded Sorin of the Bane. But he was his own male, this was absolutely clear.

He was Erebu.

Who owned Sorin, body, heart and soul.

Even if he didn't know it.

A young raptor spirit drew Ere's attention away from his group. He went with the Beast to another circle of warriors who stood around the Tiger King and his son, Maximus, in deep discussion punctuated with growls, grunts, and other animal sounds. They communicated mostly telepathically, the intensity of their words revealed only briefly in their facial expressions.

Ere apparently jumped into the fray, for though he didn't speak out loud, he gestured animatedly with his hands.

The animal spirits listened and nodded, obviously finding merit in what he had to contribute. He didn't even realize how easily he assumed the role of leadership. But Sorin, and everyone around him, felt his charisma in spades.

It was his keen intelligence, cunning mind, and sly wit. He charmed and disarmed without trying. He drew people to him effortlessly, his self-deprecation endearing, his bravery and resolve heartening.

People followed him just like the raptors of old followed the Bane.

They forgave him for the bad things he once perpetrated. They recognized, as Sorin did, that fundamentally, he wanted to be good.

He wasn't always. He could be devious and petty and jealous and selfish. But it was in the desire and trying that mattered.

And when Ere made a real effort at anything, he excelled. Nothing could stop him.

The dragon's blue fire lit on Sorin once more, as it often did.

No matter if they were right next to each other or a good distance away, Ere's eyes were always drawn to him, as if tethered to his person by invisible strings.

He nodded to something Maximus said without looking at the male, already making his way to where Sorin sat against a wall. He straddled a chair right in front of Sorin and folded his arms across the back of it, propping his chin on his hands.

"What are you looking at, beautiful?" he greeted with his signature squirk.

"You," Sorin said simply, his expression as implacable as ever.

Ere casually looped a strand of silky black hair behind one ear with his little finger.

Did he know how gorgeous he was? How one little motion could set Sorin's entire body ablaze?

Did he realize the way he silently called to Sorin? His blue eyes begging, his full lips inviting, his body enticing Sorin to sink deep, *deep* inside.

Sorin spread his legs wider in an effort to ease the growing discomfort of his throbbing erection, trapped within the confines of his trousers. Thankfully, the table hid his lap from view. He did not want to have another discussion with Ere about fucking. He was already at the end of his dangerously frayed control as it was.

But he meant what he said.

Ere would have to come out of this alive if he wanted a piece of Sorin. Hell, he could have it all. He just had to *live* to claim it.

Ere's eyes dipped lower despite the table's obstruction of his view. The burn in his sapphire orbs told Sorin that he knew exactly what was hidden. It felt like he had X-ray vision and could see every veined ridge of Sorin's sex.

Sorin shuddered pre-cum through his swollen slit and just barely prevented himself from squeezing the aching head in desperate need.

Ere licked his lips slowly with his wet, pink tongue, his eyes still leveled on Sorin's groin.

"Did you miss me?"

We've been together all day, Sorin replied, not trusting his voice to speak out loud.

He could barely think for the fog of lust whenever Ere was near, never mind form coherent human words.

"But not *together*, together," Ere said in a sing-songy tone. "Just say the word, and I can rectify this gross oversight."

Sorin shook his head.

That's all you think about? Care about? Fucking?

"Not at all," Ere said gravely. "All I think about and care about is fucking *you*."

Sorin's cock jerked at this emphatic statement of ownership. His ass tightened in anticipation.

"There's a huge difference," Ere expounded. "And before you say I'm hornier than a teenager who recently discovered his first woody, I remind you that I have a lot of lost time to make up for. Millennia of it, in fact."

You're a pain in the ass.

"If only that were true!" Ere exclaimed with a hand to his heart, blinking with exaggerated innocence.

"I would love nothing better than to be a *thorough* pain in your ass. But you're locked up tighter than a virgin wearing a chastity belt. It's unfair to dangle such temptation before a starving man. I beg you to have mercy on my poor, sexually deprived soul."

Sorin snorted and rolled his eyes.

The dragon was never serious. But he was so *lovable* Sorin couldn't hold his annoyingness against him.

"Look," Ere said, no longer entirely teasing. "Our plans are set. We're as prepared for what's to come as we'll ever be. All we can do now is train harder, continue to fortify an already well-fortified...well, fortress."

He gestured to the warriors collected in their respective groups.

"Cloud expects that Lilith will launch her offensive any day now. He and Valerius have already evacuated as many of the humans as possible, sending them to the south. He even created ominous dark clouds over town to substantiate the threat of an advancing ice storm."

Here, Ere paused and tilted his head.

"By the way, I'm in awe of that Heavenly dragon, though he can no longer assume the form. He's my fucking hero. Maybe I'll learn how to command one of the Elements soon. Do you think that could be a Gift?"

Sorin gazed at him steadily.

There is no limit to your Gifts, dragon. You have only to discover them.

"Spoken like a true Jedi Master," Ere said, though Sorin didn't understand the reference.

"Gifts, you will find. Limits, there are none," the dragon intoned.

Sorin shook his head, biting the inside of his cheek to keep from smiling.

He didn't even know what was funny. But Ere always so effortlessly made him laugh.

You are the most annoying being I have ever met. You are such a child, he admonished with a frown, disguising his delight.

"'Truly wonderful, the mind of a child is,'" Ere quoted in a strange, nasally voice.

Then he switched back to his normal voice and added, "Mine is slightly more X-rated, however."

His gaze rivetted again on Sorin's groin beneath the table.

"Make that a *lot* more X-rated. Now can we please get out of here and put my imagination to good use? Maybe make a detour through the shower hall? I'll scrub your back if you scrub—"

The deafening boom that blasted through three-feet-thick solid rock cut off Ere's last words.

"We're under attack!" Maximus' shout could barely be heard amidst the ensuing chaos, as animals and warriors dove for cover, a couple of Lesser Beasts already buried under falling debris and broken beams.

Sorin and Ere shared one grim look before running for the nearest exit.

The end had begun.

*** *** *** ***

They had to draw their enemies away from the stronghold.

Even miles away from the edge of town, it was too close. When stealth fighter jets were deployed to bomb the mountain with the latest enhanced air-to-ground missiles to eviscerate everything within a seventy-yard radius, subtlety was obviously not on the top of Lilith's list.

No, she came to destroy. And to hell with anything or anyone that got in her way.

Something kicked into gear within Ere. Some long-forgotten instinct or training. He was stone-cold lucid, focused, his body fully amped up, adrenaline charging every vein.

"Raptors, with me!"

His voice could be heard over the din and pandemonium, less because of the volume, more because of the commanding tone.

Amazingly, the eagle spirits obeyed, flocking to his rear.

He bounded up the spiral stone staircase behind the Great Hall that led to the plateau, knowing that Sorin followed close on his heels.

That was their nearest exit point to take to the skies. There, they would lead the other raptors to take down enemy attack planes and draw the remaining troops toward the trap.

He and Sorin hadn't discussed the details. He knew the broad strokes from Goya and Maximus' plans.

A group of them would remain at the base of the mountain to engage enemy forces on the ground, keep them away from the human town, and push them into the canyons between the mountains. Cloud would provide...well, cloud coverage, to disorient their enemies and veil the lands as best as he could from targeted attacks. As well as to camouflage the awaiting guerilla fighters within the canyons.

Mother nature seemed willing to play ball this night, for a storm was already brewing on the horizon.

The raptors would fight off aerial attacks and scout ahead for signs of Lilith. Ideally, they would locate her before she could truly transform. If the stars aligned, they'd even exterminate her when she was still in her weakest form.

One could only hope.

And pray. And wish.

But Ere knew to prepare for the worst. Nothing came of wishes.

It was do or die.

They didn't discuss what Sorin's role would be. None of them took for granted that he would join their fight.

Ere never asked and he never would. He knew enough about Sorin to know that the male had fought more than his share of wars. He'd already gone above and beyond to rescue and heal Ere, make him strong enough to fight his own battles.

At the same time, when Sorin burst through the exit to the plateau and took to the air with one great leap right after him, he felt the rightness of having the warrior beside him in this final battle.

Like old times.

More bombs hailed from the skies, streaking in shrill whistles past them to explode the mountainside.

The animal spirit enclave was already completely decimated. But Ere could see from his aerial vantage point that most of the Tiger Kings' forces had escaped the onslaught, scattering like marbles in various directions.

Led by Maximus and Ariel, a large group moved under the cover Cloud provided between the canyons to take their positions. Another group led by Dalair and Valerius headed around the mountain by a separate route, advancing ahead to set a second trap.

He spotted no army leading the offensive on land. They must be parachuting the soldiers in by air.

He narrowed his eyes at the ominous shadows of fighter jets hidden in thick, dark clouds. There must be carrier planes behind them. The attack planes were simply out in front clearing the way.

Where was Lilith in all this? Was she in one of the planes?

Didn't matter. He'd take every single one of them down if he had to.

Target the F-35 Lightning and F-22 Raptors, he communicated to the few raptor spirits who joined them in the skies.

I'll go after the mothership.

What? Sorin called out in his mind, flying alongside him as they navigated bulky clouds and missile-locks.

The fast, small planes in front, Ere explained with a roll of his serpent eyes. *Take them down!*

Sorin veered left with a grunt of acknowledgement and promptly unleashed a crackle of lightning into the nearest cloud with his eyes.

The targeted fighter jet shook within its net of blazing electricity before all systems went out, and it took a sharp nosedive like a falling boulder from the sky.

Ere grinned a toothy grin at his big, gorgeous phoenix. This was going to be cake walk!

And then he saw the incoming squadron of at least two dozen fighter jets, with looming shadows of bigger aircrafts just behind them.

With implicit understanding, he left Sorin to lead a few of the raptors to take care of the closest jets, while he took the rest to attack the larger cargo planes.

A few of the planes were already opening their bloated bellies to release enemy soldiers that sprinkled from the sky like seeds of evil. There must have been hundreds of them. And more planes kept on coming.

The good guys on the ground numbered a few dozen at most. They weren't the best warriors. They were the sacrificial foot soldiers to give the illusion of critical mass, draw enemy eyes away from the troops that were making their way through the mountains toward the rendezvous point.

If the ground troops had belonged to Lilith, she'd treat all of them as dispensable collateral damage. But Ere couldn't, wouldn't, do the same.

He didn't know these animal spirits personally, but he wasn't going to leave them to fend for themselves, even if they were just the diversion. He couldn't let Lilith's sky-diving army reach the valley. He had to take out as many as he could mid-air.

Telepathically, he ordered the other raptors to deal with the planes, while he flew toward the parachuting enemy soldiers and sprayed them with white-hot flames the moment they were within reach.

Many of them disintegrated immediately into ashes or stardust; some of them simply burned to a crisp.

Looked like Lilith didn't hold back. All Kinds were represented here. Dark, Pure and human alike. Whether she'd turned them or whether they "worked" for her, Ere didn't have the luxury to dwell on it. He couldn't save any of them now. He could only protect the animal spirits below.

As he flew from plane to plane, raining fire through the skies, he caught most of the incoming army in his blasts, but there were too many. Soldiers still managed to land, armed with Immortal-killer weapons, amped up by Lilith's experiments. Stronger, deadlier. Fearless.

He could see the Tiger King's militia, led by Tal, Inanna and Gabriel, engage Lilith's minions on the ground. Rhys stayed with them to provide aerial support.

Goya himself must be with Eli. The two males were in charge of Lilith's "bait." Given the direction and speed of the wind, Eli should have spirited all three of them to the secret location by now. There, the other two contingents would meet up with them, hopefully after eliminating most of Lilith's minions along the way.

The General's ground forces were holding their position, keeping the mindless soldiers away from the human town. And when they fell back, it was to draw the enemies toward the canyons where more warriors lay in wait to ambush them.

Sorin and his raptors were doing a bang-up job of keeping the fighter jets in the lead too busy to fire their missiles, dismantling planes with claws and beak, engulfing them in flames. They were winning!

But where was Lilith?

Just as the thought entered his mind, an eerie, bone-chilling laugh echoed through the roiling skies, lit up with waves of flames and streaks of lightning, both natural and supernatural.

I come for a dragonling, maybe two. But I find the firebird I've been searching for instead. How convenient. How marvelous.

Shit.

Sorin.

Didn't Cloud say Lilith needed only one more ingredient to become a god? What were the chances that she knew that too?

Ere left the rest of the planes to the raptor spirits and doubled back toward the front of the pack. His haunted eyes searched for signs of Sorin's phoenix form.

Where were the flames? Where were the sparks?

Everything was eclipsed by dark, rolling clouds that rapidly spread across the skies like squid ink to enfold everything within them in total invisibility.

He couldn't see anything. Pitch black surrounded him. He could barely tell what was up or down.

He breathed a stream of flames to light the way, but the fire was put out as soon as it emerged from his jaws, dying rapidly in a sputter of harmless smoke.

He charged his eyes instead, harnessed the power of lightning within them, trying to see through the black fog of death. He could feel the unnatural mist settle on his scales like a plague. Like tar. Weighing him down. Making him lethargic.

What *was* this?

One of Lilith's tricks? A new "Gift"?

Fuck, what else did the she-demon have up her sleeves? As if a giant nine-headed Hydra wasn't bad enough?

The whistle of a missile was his only warning before he instinctively rolled and ducked, narrowly missing being hit.

As it was, the object still speared a bloody streak through his side, taking scales and hide off before exploding just a few yards away in the abyss.

The blast was swallowed within the mist as if it was trapped in water, preventing Ere from being caught in the explosion's radius. At the same time, the light from the detonation briefly illuminated the murky cloud he was wading through, revealing just a hint of flaming feathers in the distance.

As well as the dark, ominous object rapidly gaining upon them.

Ere flapped his wings as furiously as he could, trying to gain altitude and speed, aiming his flight path toward the flames.

It was getting harder and harder to breathe. What *were* these clouds? It felt like they sucked all the oxygen from his lungs, the strength from his body. Instead of lifting him, his wings felt like anvils that weighed him down.

Remember your training, Sorin's voice rumbled in his mind.

Fight fire with fire. Smoke with smoke.

Where the fuck are you! Ere shouted in their linked minds. This was not the time to give him a battle lesson!

Focus, the phoenix's deep voice commanded.

Don't let her distract you. I can handle myself.

Ere knew Sorin could, in fact, handle himself.

But this was the Hydra! And she was now focused on Sorin!

He had to find them.
He had to get to Sorin first.

Chapter Twenty

Sorin's words did manage to sink in, despite Ere's frantic fear.

He breathed smoke in great big gusts, his eyes widening when the inky cloud surrounding him began to dissipate as his own smoke took its place.

A menacing, thwarted growl shook through the air.

Lilith was obviously not expecting this comeback.

Soon, he could see enough to spot a flare of faint embers a good distance away, racing toward the rendezvous point—the barren death-valley within a circle of jagged peaks that he and Sorin had discovered before. Where they trained and mapped out every nook and cranny.

There was no water there, only unyielding earth and stone. Nothing to enhance Lilith's powers, for she was nigh indestructible in rivers, lakes and seas.

The plan was to draw her there and isolate her. Then unleash the full combination of all of their powers upon the Hydra to eradicate her once and for all.

It sounded good in theory. They just didn't know for certain it would work.

Well, no time to come up with a better plan. Better hustle to execute the one they had.

Close behind Sorin loomed a gigantic, nebulous darkness that moved through the clouds as fast as the wind.

Ere could see that a few inky curls reached toward Sorin's phoenix form as if trying to catch his tail feathers. Whenever they touched him, the flames would go out and the feather would blacken.

Merciless gods! So many of his tail feathers were already black. And a few along his wing tips too.

Ere huffed with exertion as he desperately tried to increase speed, but the phoenix was always faster. And the ominous cloud chasing him kept pace, while Ere struggled to keep them in his sights.

They were far enough away now that the battle at the Tiger King's stronghold could only be heard in distant roars and booms. The skies behind him occasionally lit up with missile fire or other explosions. But he couldn't afford to be distracted from his target ahead. His sole focus was on the Hydra, in what must be her nebulous, inky form, spreading through the night sky like a ravaging void.

Dark clouds shielded his view of the landscape below. He didn't know whether Maximus and Dalair's forces had made it through the canyon. He didn't know whether they were victorious against Lilith's minions that must have followed them into the traps. He could only trust that they were also moving toward the death-valley like they planned. And that most of their enemies had not survived the ambush.

So far, everything was going according to plan.

But they hadn't counted on Lilith's nebulous form. That she could move by herself, and at such alarming speed, through the skies.

They conceived the possibility that she would be airborne. It was the most expedient way to attack. Anything on the ground would give the Pure and Dark Ones more advantage. Anything by water would take too long.

She might even know that they had very few raptors in their group. Birds of prey didn't typically flock to Kings of Earth. It spoke to Goya's magnetism that he was able to recruit the eagle spirits he had. Lilith must have known that they were most vulnerable to aerial attacks.

Between himself, Sorin and Rhys, they thought they could fend her off. At least the flight squadron that she would likely bring with her. But they couldn't have possibly imagined this current form of hers, this burgeoning power that drew upon the moisture in the storm clouds.

As Ere used his full strength to chase after Lilith and Sorin, he felt suffocated again, enervated, as if he was slowly drowning.

Their plan had been to get her on the barren ground and surround her. Those with wings would still have the advantage of aerial attacks. But what if she engaged them in the skies instead? As she was doing now? What if only Sorin and Ere could fight her?

And what if they couldn't win against her almost godly powers without the others' help?

A couple more feathers went black, just before Sorin took a nosedive toward the valley below. The dark inky blob followed, pouring from the sky like spilled tar.

Ere dove as well, close on their heels. He couldn't think about what ifs. He could only *act*. Whatever happened, Lilith would get to Sorin and Benjamin over his dead body.

The phoenix shot down from the skies like a hurtling meteor, bright flames engulfing his entire body, blazing even through the murky, oily clouds that surrounded him.

Ere thought that nothing could catch him, he was going so fast. He was leading Lilith straight into the trap. And Ere was right on their tail. He'd fire upon Lilith from behind.

But just as he inhaled deeply to gather the firestorm within him for a monstrous release of pale blue flames, Lilith's inky blob gained speed.

All at once, the dark cloud behind the phoenix surged forward and enveloped him completely in its smothering darkness, banking the flames instantaneously.

No!

A bone-chilling, haunting laugh rolled across the skies.

In frenzied desperation, Ere unleashed his flames at the opaque, nebulous mass. But instead of dispersing Lilith's cloud form, or at least make it smaller, the flames simply died in harmless tendrils of smoke around her.

Fire needed oxygen to burn. She'd sucked all the air out of the blast as soon as it reached her.

Fuck!

Ere flapped his wings harder before tucking them close to his body to dive faster after the inky blob. It was too far away to unleash another torrent. Not that his flames did anything but tickle the monstrous thing.

Let's see what we have, Lilith's voice reverberated in Ere's mind, making his skull hurt.

Such a pretty, pretty bird. So many feathers to choose from...now where, oh, where is the one I want?

Before Ere's horrified eyes, the dark cloud began to rain feathers one by one like blackened snow from the skies.

Sorin didn't make any sounds, not even in his mind, but Ere could vicariously feel the male's agony as each feather was plucked by the root from his body, tearing bloody gouges into his flesh.

No, no, no! Not his beautiful Sorin!

The Hydra was breaking him, tearing him apart, literally feather by feather.

Ere tried but failed to harness lightning in his eyes, in his gullet, to hurl at the monstrous cloud. He couldn't focus when Sorin was slowly dying before his eyes. His own ragged breathing and building despair was all he knew.

Gods! Why couldn't he fly fast enough! Why couldn't he reach them!

Where were the others? The ground was visible through the mists now. They would hit earth soon.

Would Lilith take her Hydra form below? How could Ere possibly win against all nine of her dragon heads? He'd battled her before and failed. Sure, he had more powers now; he was stronger. But so was she.

And she had Sorin in her grasp. She was killing him by purposeful, meticulous, sadistic degree!

The inky cloud didn't settle upon the ground when it reached bottom like a soft mist or rolling fog. It rammed into the earth with a resounding boom that shook the barricade of mountains around it. Slowly, it took form. Massive tentacles unfurling from the nebula, long necks attached to those familiar monstrous serpent heads.

Even before one of the heads finished forming, it opened gigantic jaws and unleashed a blast of black fire directly at Ere, making him duck and roll at the last second to avoid its path.

The debilitating flames still caught the edge of one wing, immediately corroding through his scales, flaking the armor off and revealing raw, bloody flesh beneath.

More laughter echoed through the canyons as other dragon heads took shape.

You think I don't know your pathetic plans to trap me? You think you can draw me to this place and corner me? You can bring on all of your combined forces, en masse, and still you would never be able to defeat me.

I am a god! And you...

All of you will either kneel at, or perish beneath, my feet!

Ere swooped around to find a better angle for attack, but two of the other heads unleashed a spray of poison and a blast of black lightning his way to intercept his approach.

Fuck! He couldn't get close enough to even *try* to do damage, assuming that any of his own powers would have effect on the Hydra.

And where was Sorin? The black fog around the Hydra's base obscured everything from sight. He couldn't see any hint of the phoenix in her grasp.

She still had him, didn't she? Unless...

Looking for this?

Lilith seemed to read his thoughts, transforming one slimy tentacle into a giant claw, the inky fog dissipating enough from around the limb for Ere to see what she pinned beneath it.

Sorin in half-form on his stomach, on the ground.

The clothes had been burned away from his body. He was naked and bloody, his skin charred black in most places, his hair coated with that filthy tar, his wings totally black, no golden flame in sight.

She splayed his wings open under her claws, as other tentacles took the shape of legs as well, while the heel of her front paw held him immobile upon the ground. Like a moth pinned to a dissection board.

Ere roared in outrage and dove in a thoughtless, kamikaze move, releasing a shock of lightning from his eyes and jaws at the nearest Hydra head.

The head crackled with electricity in the onslaught, its serpent eyes rolling, tongue lolling. But it didn't go down. Only shaking off the lightning strike like a harmless buzz.

Nice try, the Hydra allowed, several of her other heads spreading their grisly maws in toothy grins.

A for effort.

Now pay attention while I show you how it's really done.

One of the heads dipped its long neck down to grip one of Sorin's wings by the top of the arch between its giant, shark-like teeth, punching through feathers, hide, muscle and bone.

Ere groaned as Sorin's unvoiced pain serrated like daggers through their linked minds.

No. Please... if there's anyone listening... please... Stars, heavens, Darkness and Light, the powers that be... don't do this! Ere screamed in his own head, praying to deities that no longer existed.

No one heard him. No one cared.

The Hydra whipped its head like Cerberus at the gates of hell and tore Sorin's wing from his back with a resounding crack and rip of bone and muscle.

"Noooooooo!"

Ere fought against the agony that washed through his own body like it was *his* wing being ripped out.

He dove again, heedless of the daunting heads, maneuvering past them by sheer force of will and luck to get to the claw that held Sorin down. He ripped at it with his own claws, breathed fire and lightning at it, and clamped down with his jaws.

The Hydra hissed as he managed to do some damage, but one of the heads caught Ere by the scruff of his neck and hurled him like a harmless stray dog nipping at the heels of an invincible giant several yards through the air.

He slammed into the mountainside with a resounding crash, jarring snow and rocks loose, and maybe a few of his own teeth.

Just for that, I won't be gentle with the other one.

Before Ere could blink, another Hydra head tore Sorin's remaining wing from his body, leaving gaping, bloody holes in his back as the shout of agony he tried unsuccessfully to hold back echoed in the merciless night.

Now where's my fucking feather! the monster roared, flipping Sorin onto his massacred back and digging one sharp claw straight into the left side of his chest.

Into his heart.

Ere recoiled and stumbled against the fallen debris, his own wings dragging uselessly on the ground as he watched his greatest nightmare unfold in mind-searing detail.

The Hydra seemed to have forgotten him in the moment, most of her heads focused on the broken male beneath her claw.

She sucked the tip of her claw into her mouth to take in the blood from Sorin's heart.

Nothing happened.

She growled with frustration and speared a forked tongue into Sorin's chest, licking away more blood.

Still, nothing happened.

It's gone.

Sorin's voice rasped in a weak whisper in their minds. Ere heard it clearly, just as the Hydra did.

I gave the feather away. The only one of its kind. You will never have it. You will never be a god. You are only an overgrown ugly fucker with nine too many heads. My dragon will avenge me when this is done. You should run for your life while you still can.

With those words, Sorin grabbed hold of the claw that pinned him with both his arms and opened his eyes wide.

White hot flames blazed through them, spreading over his face, his neck, his entire body, as his whole form became a nexus of crackling lightning. He opened his mouth on a silent scream, and flames poured out, engulfing the Hydra's claw.

The monster screeched shrilly with pain, lifting its leg to try to escape Sorin's blaze. But it kept traveling unrelentingly up the serpent's limb, until the entire claw and leg disintegrated into dirty ash.

Without its forepaw, the Hydra lost equilibrium, crashing clumsily to her chest, her many heads serving to unbalance her even more. They spewed poison, venom, fire and lightning aimlessly in the struggle, screaming with fury and perhaps a hint of fear.

Ere chose this moment to dive in again, shooting a stream of blue fire not at the heads but at the Hydra's torso, targeting the bloody, blackened hole where its limb used to be.

Lilith howled and writhed, obviously feeling the full force of Ere's attack.

This was it.

This was her weakness.

They had to exploit her wound to make it mortal. Before she could heal herself again.

The heads seemed to regain their bearings and launched a coordinated counter-offensive, keeping Ere from drawing close again with their blasts.

Before Ere's eyes, the wound from the missing leg was already starting to heal, the blood congealing as a thin layer of skin began to knit over it.

Fucking hell! He couldn't do this alone!

He'd never be able to take the Hydra down before she regained her strength.

Just when the thought crossed his mind, he saw the Pure and Dark warriors charge into the death-valley from surrounding mountain paths.

The Hydra shifted her three legs back into six tentacles for better balance, but the absence of her limb was obvious. It made her movements jerky and sluggish, clumsy.

Maximus and Ariel led the attack from her left side, their troops' smaller size and animal agility helping them to navigate the roiling tentacles. Without being directed, they went straight for her gaping wound with teeth and claws, making her howl anew.

Dalair and Valerius' forces charged from behind, distracting three of her heads as they gained ground, with Cloud providing a camouflaging mist to hide their advance.

The Hydra heads blindly tore through the fog not of her own making that covered her tentacles and half of her body. They dove one by one to chomp at the warriors that surrounded her, sometimes biting down on her own tentacles as a result.

The monster was starting to panic, Ere could tell. Wounded and grounded, surrounded on all sides.

And then, Lilith began to transform her physical body into a shapeless mass once more, preventing her attackers from gaining traction.

Ere inhaled deeply and unleashed a torrent of flames to prevent her shift, while there was still physical mass for his fire to burn.

Her transformation was stalled with a furious shriek, the nebulous cloud turning back into defined limbs and heads. Several of them opened fire back onto Ere at once, some of the poisonous sprays splattering onto his hind quarters, the acid eating through his flesh down to the bone.

He staggered mid-flight and pulled back, regrouping for another assault as the distracted heads struggled to defend the vulnerable body from the Pure and Dark Ones' concerted attack below.

Ere sensed but couldn't see Tal amongst the group, for the cover of Cloud's mist. Inanna, Gabriel and Rhys had all arrived. This must mean that they'd demolished Lilith's soldiers.

Were Goya and Eli here as well? What about Benjamin?

A flash of blazing red was all the warning anyone got before Tal's laser sword cut through another of Lilith's tentacles, making her scream and writhe, toppling to the side.

The enraged heads countered with more blasts in all directions, no longer aiming for accuracy, simply destroying everything within their range.

The Pure and Dark Ones had to leap out of the way or be caught in the ring of death that Lilith surrounded herself with.

You won't win, she cackled, though her breaths were belabored.

You can't win. I can do this all day and night. You'll never get close enough to do more damage. I'll heal myself in no time at all. You're only delaying the inevitable defeat!

Ere roared as he unleashed his own blast of blazing blue flames against two of the closest heads.

He was strong enough to push back the venomous black fire and sprays of acid. Strong enough to push Lilith's blasts all the way back to the mouths of the two serpent heads, into their gaping gullets and down their necks.

Both heads screeched and writhed, their flaming red eyes going dark, before the heads themselves blackened and stilled, frozen into charred stone upon their necks like dead, frost-bitten appendages.

That's it! Another weakness!

Cutting off her heads would enable the Hydra to grow new ones. But immobilizing them like this—turning them to stone—this was the way to destroy her once and for all.

Ere drew in another powerful breath, flying and dodging to aim at another head.

But before he could lock in on his next target, before the Pure and Dark Ones could advance upon Lilith from below, one of the Hydra's necks uncoiled, raising her head, her scaly, serpent lips peeled back to reveal the object she clamped between dagger-toothed jaws.

Nuh, uh uh, dragon, she hissed in their collective minds.

One more move from you and your friends and this tasty morsel gets crushed to smithereens.

Ere pulled back immediately, reflexively, seeing Sorin's lifeless body impaled upon the rows of gleaming teeth.

Merciless gods!

There was so much blood. He was covered with it, his wounds too many. It dripped slowly from his fingertips to the monster's thorned chin, where one of the other heads lapped the blood away with her disgusting forked tongue.

Sorin was still alive, Ere knew.

Barely.

He could feel the male's sluggish heartbeat within his own heart. He was unconscious but still breathing. His wounds might devastate him. The loss of his wings might destroy him. But he lived.

Ere would do everything in his power to keep it that way.

Wordlessly, he sent the same command to the Pure and Dark Ones on the ground, holding them back.

He refused to sacrifice Sorin in this battle. Nothing mattered but his male. Not even the end of the world if the Hydra survived.

I see you still have some shred of intelligence in that dense skull of yours, Lilith said, gloating confidence creeping back into her voice.

Now, I'm willing to call this a draw. I will give you back this broken pile of bones if you give me what I originally came here for.

Where is my favorite dragonling, hmm?

I can sense his nearness. You've brought him to me, haven't you? Even if it's to set this cunning little trap.

Before Ere could respond, Benjamin's boyish voice carried clearly in the canyon.

"Put Sorin down, Lily! I'm here. I'll go with you. Just leave my family and friends alone!"

Two of the Hydra heads immediately swiveled in the direction of the boy's voice, searching him out.

And there he stood. On a rocky plateau higher than the Hydra heads could reach. Eli and Goya standing guard behind him. But instead of protecting the boy, it looked more like they were trying to hold him back. Benjamin seemed poised to throw himself off the cliff at the Hydra to demand Sorin's release.

Come closer, little man, Lilith purred to her golden prize, one of her heads stretching toward Benjamin. Her tentacles were starting to lose shape again, lifting her higher like mushrooming clouds.

Ere tried to find the right angle of attack, but there was none. The head that held Sorin securely in her jaws was farthest away from the head that inched ever closer to Benjamin's ledge.

He could only choose one of them. And even then, keeping them from getting crushed or torched or poisoned in the process wasn't guaranteed.

Eli shifted to wind to push the Hydra's head back, stalling for time.

But the head that held Sorin in her jaws simply tightened until Ere heard bones break.

Stop! he roared in their minds.

Take me instead! I have what you want.

All eyes turned to him, including seven pairs from Lilith's Hydra heads.

Oh, you stupid dragon. Do you really think I have any use for you after what you did? You're beyond my control now. I'm not desperate enough to attempt another turning*. I learn from my mistakes.*

She turned back to Benjamin, and two more heads surged up to regard the boy as well.

Now this one, on the other hand, is still very malleable. So young.

The three heads licked their scaly maws at once.

So innocent and naïve, filled with untapped potential. He's like a blank canvas for me to paint on. He's the one I want.

Ere made his choice.

He flew to the rock overhang upon which Benjamin, Goya and Eli stood and planted himself firmly between his son and the towering, rising Hydra heads.

I have what you want, he repeated, inhaling deeply to puff out his chest.

Look closer.

One of the heads drew suspiciously near, narrowing her blood-red eyes.

When she finally realized what she was looking at—the glowing gem on Ere's scaly dragon chest, with its ruby tip—the mouth of the serpent spread in an avaricious grin.

Maniacal, cackling laughter rumbled through the valley, shrill enough to crumble loose rocks from the mountainsides.

The feather! The Eagle King's flame-tipped feather with his heart's blood! My missing ingredient!

Give it to me!

Six heads opened their jaws at once and screeched at Ere with enough force to almost make him lose his footing on the edge of the plateau.

He held his ground, his slitted eyes tracking the Pure and Dark warriors' movements below.

They were closing in on the Hydra. They couldn't make a move until she released Sorin, but they were taking their positions and readying for attack.

Eli's wind whistled through the valley, churning the mist that Cloud created. The animal spirits were poised to spring into battle. Pebbles and small rocks leapt on the ground to signal yet another presence that Ere felt but couldn't see.

Ramses, the Dark King.

He'd come.

All of the Elements were present now—Cloud's water, Eli's air, Ramses' earth, and Ere's fire. All of the Kinds were present as well, including a human boy.

And so was Lilith's missing ingredient.

Embedded in the middle of Ere's chest, as much a part of him as his own beating heart.

He knew what he had to do.

Finally, he recalled how the Bane, how *he,* and the other dragons and animal spirits had ended the gods millennia ago.

Let him go, and you can carve the feather right out of my chest, he told the Hydra.

He dies, you die. We all die. I don't give a fuck. Test me on this, I dare you.

Several of her heads considered him while the other ones kept an eye on the enemy forces that surrounded her.

Ere stepped off the ledge and flapped his wings to hover near the largest head. The one that breathed foul, rotting black flames. The one that looked upon him with the most cruelly cunning greed.

Whispers from his family and friends tried to gain his attention in his mind, but he ignored them. Most likely they were telling him not to do this. Probably thinking there was another way.

There wasn't. He knew.

He'd been here twice already. Once when he succeeded in destroying the gods as the Bane. And once when he'd been a newly formed dragon, failing to subdue the Hydra in her lake.

Put him down on that peak, he continued to instruct the Hydra. *He's too far away from others for them to steal him away. If you don't get what you want from me, you can always snatch him back.*

But do it now. My patience wears thin.

Lilith chafed at the order, growling in protest. But the head that held Sorin did as Ere commanded, spitting him out none too gently from her jaws. Then, she expelled a glob of slime on top of his body, trapping him within the viscous fluid.

In the same breath, the giant head closest to Ere suddenly attacked, sinking two long fangs into his chest, digging for the gemstone feather.

NOW! Ere roared in the collective minds of all those present.

As one, the Pure and Dark Ones, Elementals and Animal Spirits attacked.

The cats tore at Lilith's tentacles; the eagles gauged at her eyes. The Pure and Dark warriors focused on the wounds from her missing limbs, spearing into the exposed flesh with their weapons, making her shriek with agony.

Cloud conjured lightning in the stormy mists that surrounded her body, funneling debilitating shocks into her open wounds, making her shake and writhe. Ramses exploded boulders from the surrounding mountain peaks, raining them like missiles upon her many heads. Eli's wind kept her from drawing upon the clouds overhead for the water she needed to fuel her strength.

And Ere…

Ere's chest burned with acid, the Hydra's poison already seeping into his body, turning parts of him to ash.

He harnessed his strength and clawed his front paws into the serpent's eyes, rendering the head that held him completely blind.

Her jaw slacked slightly as she howled with pain, enough that he could have freed himself from her impaling fangs.

He didn't.

This was part of the plan, after all.

He had the final ingredient. The one that would make her a god. But before that unholy occurrence, it was the key to destroying her.

He closed his eyes and focused all of his energy and strength into the center of his chest. He recalled his training as the Bane. He recalled *everything*.

You are the fire, dragon. It is not simply a Gift. You are the lightning and the flames. The smoke and the ash. You are the rawest power in the universe. Stronger even than the gods. They made you. But you have the power to unmake them.

The holes in his chest from the Hydra's teeth began to radiate a bright white light, as if the sun was rising within him, his flesh and bone dissolving in the path of the expanding flames.

The Hydra tried to release him from her jaws, realizing too late what was happening. Her other heads flailed and twisted to avoid the nonstop bombardment of boulders and flaming rocks. The earth beneath her opened up to pull down her body like quicksand, her tentacles scrabbling desperately for purchase upon the fissuring ground.

The white-hot light that radiated from Ere's chest kept on burgeoning, like the nucleus of a newborn star. Soon, it engulfed the dragon's entire body and wings, then Lilith's main head, then a couple more heads, until it encapsulated her entire monstrous form.

No! her demonic voice howled like distant thunder.

The last ingredient! I have it! I can't be destroyed! I'm a g—

The pressure within the ball of flames finally reached its limit. It pulsed a warning before exploding outward in a deafening boom.

Everything that wasn't pinned down was hurled against the sides of the mountains surrounding the valley in the aftershock.

Pure and Dark Ones, animals alike—they all dove for cover at the last possible second, as Cloud, Eli and Ramses tried to protect as many as they could from the blast. Goya folded himself around Benjamin, using his own body as shelter for the boy, deflecting falling debris.

And then...

Silence.

As the skies showered all those below with incandescent sparks.

Everyone slowly straightened from their safe places, gathering in the center of the valley, standing on scorched and cracked earth, surrounded by boulders and rocks that had crumbled from the mountainsides.

Under the soft rain of stars.

At last, Sorin stirred from his lonely peak, turning his face toward the heavens. Taking a belabored, shuddering breath, his eyes too tired to open.

He felt the sparks upon his skin, melting away the slime that trapped him. Those same tiny flames licked at his countless wounds, trying to heal him.

It didn't matter.

He didn't care if he never opened his eyes again. Because he felt the hollowness within his soul. The spark of life that used to live there was no more.

Extinguished.

He knew that they were gone.

The Hydra.

Ere.

There was nothing left of them.

Chapter Twenty-One

Untold days later.

"He'll be back."

No, he wouldn't be.

"He has a Pure soul, after all. He's strong. The strongest of us all. He'll be back."

Even if that were true, the last time his soul was reincarnated, it had taken thousands of years. And then thousands more for Sorin to find him. After finding himself.

He wasn't coming back.

But Sorin didn't say so, as he sat at the dining table in Ere's parents' house.

He chewed and swallowed by rote, tasting nothing, his body on autopilot.

He'd been transported here...*after*. For several days and nights, he lay insensate on his stomach. On the new bed that Ere had ordered after they'd wrecked the last one. In Ere's room. Amongst his things, though there were few. Only clothes that smelled like him.

In moments of lucidity, Sorin wished he was strong enough to set the clothes on fire. He didn't want any more reminders of what was forever lost to him.

He lay on his stomach because his back was ripped to shreds. Though he bore puncture and slash wounds all over his body from the Hydra's teeth and claws, his back fared the worst. Great hunks of muscle and flesh missing completely. When the skin finally pulled itself together, there were two large craters on either side of his spine in his upper back.

Even in his humanoid form, he would forever bear the reminder of having his wings ripped out of his body. They would never grow back. He would never fly again. Never transform into either the half-form or animal.

A grounded raptor. Useless and weak. With a deadened soul to drag around for the rest of his immortal days.

He huffed a silent, humorless laugh.

Those days were numbered, if he had his druthers. He would make it happen. He was done with this shit.

Today was the day he was finally strong enough to get up off the bed. Finally steady enough to walk on his own two feet.

His body still felt like it was just pulled out of a blender, but the rest of him was numb. If he'd been stoic before, he was downright apathetic now. There were no more *feelings* broiling beneath the surface of his skin, no emotions to suppress or contain.

He might as well have been made of stone.

"Inanna, please."

It was "Mama Bear" who murmured the soft admonishment, her voice breaking, close to tears.

"*Ana* Ishtar..." the male called Tal-Telal rumbled, pulling her into his lap, enfolding her in his arms.

Sorin continued to chew and swallow his food, ignoring everything and everyone else around him.

"I can't believe he's gone," Ere's mother wailed quietly into her Mate's neck, making herself as small as possible, tucked into his body.

"Why don't I feel it? A mother should know, shouldn't she? Am I not a good mother? Is it because he was taken from me as a babe? I should know..."

She was sobbing in earnest now into the crook of the General's neck. Had she done this often over the past however many days? Seemed that way, for the blotchy coloring of her face, despite being Immortal and in her true form.

Inanna's face took on a stubborn, tight-lipped determination. As if she refused to accept reality. As if she could somehow bend the truth to her indomitable will. Her Mate, Gabriel, sat beside her on the wooden dining bench, one arm around her shoulder, quietly lending his strength. Holding her together.

Nobody sat next to Sorin. There was an obvious empty spot.

Though he could swear he heard the missing male's snarky remarks whispering in his ear. The faint touch of his hand sneaking onto Sorin's thigh in an exploratory, teasing caress.

He was tempted to turn and look at the empty seat. He didn't.

Only Benjamin was his normal, cheerful self, eating his breakfast with gusto, slurping the last of the milk from his cereal bowl.

"Sorin will bring Uncle Ere back, won't you, Sorin?" the boy looked at him with big, blue, angelic eyes.

There were no shadows in them from the harrowing ordeal he took part in. His face wasn't unnaturally pale, and there were no bruises under his eyes from lack of sleep due to nightmares. He seemed healthy, hearty and happy. As if his Uncle Ere might walk through the door at any moment.

Sorin didn't reply.

He finished the food put in front of him.

It was the first meal he had...*after.* His stomach cramped with the sudden influx, but he forcibly kept it down.

He needed fuel to get through today. He had things to do.

Destiny to kill.

He pushed away from the table without a word, without even a nod of thanks for the generous meal.

Everyone craned their necks to look up at him as he rose to his full height, though his shoulders were slightly hunched for the first time since he'd come into existence, for the barely healed wounds that painfully stretched the skin on his back.

He ignored it. Just like he ignored all the other unwanted sensations.

"Leaving."

It was the only word he'd uttered in all this time, but no one commented on his rudeness.

Tal gave him a brief nod and said, "Take care, warrior."

He didn't respond.

He was no longer a warrior. Just like he was no longer a raptor or anything else.

He was a dead man walking.

"Say hi to Uncle Ere when you see him, Sorin!" Benjamin called out as Sorin walked through the front door and into the cold.

"Tell him to visit us as soon as he can! We miss him!"

He walked away in ground-eating strides, never looking back. Away from the boy's hopeful, happy voice.

Away from hope, period.

It wasn't Sorin's problem. Benjamin was old enough that his parents should explain life and death to him. Some people simply weren't coming back. But Sorin wasn't going to be the one to destroy the boy's illusions.

He walked by the café *Drink of Me*. Out of habit, he looked toward the window in the back.

Someone seemed to peer out at him, but the winter sun glinting off the glass panes distorted the view.

Sorin squinted and slowed his steps without meaning to. It almost looked like Ere's ghost was staring back at him. And it looked like the blue-eyed man was smiling, tucking a strand of long, dark hair behind his ear. He looked as if he was waiting on Sorin to join him in their booth. Maybe he already ordered a hearty brunch with his favorite desserts and hot chocolate.

Sorin blinked, and the vision was gone.

There was nothing on the other side of that café window. Nothing but an empty table and deserted seats.

Sorin walked on.

Miles outside of town, he came to the rubble of what was once the Tiger King's stronghold at the base of the tallest mountain. Goya must have reorganized his animal spirits elsewhere. Perhaps they hunkered down temporarily in caves or lodgings on the outskirts of town.

Sorin didn't care. He wasn't here to find other warriors or the Tiger King himself. He was simply looking for a better pair of hiking boots that might fit him in the scattered remains of the enclave. A pair of thick gloves and some kind of climbing implement would come in handy as well. But weren't strictly necessary.

He'd use his bare hands and feet to scale the mountain if he had to. Nothing would prevent him from reaching the peak.

And thus, he began the climb.

He took the long route up the mountain. The "hiking" route. The one adventurous humans sometimes took in the summer season, or so Sorin had heard from random snippets of conversation during the times he'd waited for Ere in the café.

At the rate he was going, he might reach the top before sundown, as it was just an hour or so after dawn. If he still had his wings, he could have flown to the top within a few minutes. Even with the weight of another male, it wouldn't have been difficult.

Unbidden, he recalled the contours of Ere's body molding against his the first time he carried them both to the peak, on the North side of the mountain where he made his temporary nest. He recalled the male wrapping his arms tightly around Sorin's waist, tucking his cold face into Sorin's neck. Breathing in his scent.

He probably didn't realize how his body always melted against Sorin whenever he was close. He probably didn't know how the beat of his heart, the pulse in his throat, synchronized with Sorin's when they were together. Didn't realize that his scent changed to complement Sorin's musk. Mating with it to drug them both.

Sorin put one foot in front of the other and climbed.

His entire body was throbbing with agony from exhaustion and countless barely healed wounds at this point, the heat he always so effortlessly radiated receding as he reached higher altitudes. As the sub-zero air iced his veins, and the wind howled mercilessly, whipping his long hair around his face.

He wondered if it was still there. His nest.

He wondered if Lilith's air raid had destroyed it, the way her attack planes had destroyed the rest of the animal spirit enclave.

He looked up as he neared the peak. For the first time, he felt the cold. Icicles beaded his eyebrows and lashes, making his skin brittle, his lips chapped and blue.

He didn't care. He barely felt it. It was no surprise that the heat had died within him, like the rest of his fire. His body might still exist for some god-forsaken reason, but his heart and soul were already gone.

It must be the confounded runes tattooed into his left side. Though they were almost invisible by now, he could still feel the faint impression of the lines in his skin, like pinpricks in his flesh. Perhaps they were keeping this useless body in the mortal realm, while the rest of him had already departed. Curse the Gray Witch for doing this to him.

But it didn't matter. It would all be over soon.

He finally rounded the corner to the small plateau that hid the entrance to the cave.

The Labrador Tea bushes had completely withered, though they'd tenaciously withstood the unforgiving winter to date. The branches looked brittle as if burnt. Not a single leaf adorned them.

Sorin pushed the gnarled twigs aside and ducked into the cave.

The nest was still there, but it looked like the remains of a funeral pyre. Everything was charred black. All of the feathers were black. Like the ones the Hydra had plucked from Sorin's body one by one in search of the lone feather he no longer possessed.

He came to stand by the nest and swept a hand through the dead feathers. The moment he touched them, they turned to ash. Disintegrating into dirty flakes that the wind from the outside swept unceremoniously away.

Nothing remained but rubble and twigs.

Sorin turned around and walked back out.

It had begun to snow. A light flurry that floated wispy snowflakes like feathers or dandelion puffs in the icy air. The gray skies were almost completely swathed in puffy clouds and rolling mists.

Sorin could no longer see the ground he stood upon. He could barely make out the mountainside behind him. Barely see the other peaks that jutted past the sea of clouds.

But he knew where the edge of the ravine was. He knew it like the back of his hand.

He'd stood there often, surveying these mountains, these almost untouched lands that reminded him of a time before the advent of humans.

He'd never been afraid when he stood at the edge. Soaring through the skies was as natural to him as breathing. And despite the lack of wings now, he still wasn't afraid.

No. He looked forward to it.

The yawning unknown. The weightless fall. Most of all, he couldn't wait to embrace oblivion when everything crashed to an end.

He doffed the thin sweater and exposed his naked torso to the silent snow. His shoulders and back muscles tensed reflexively with the phantom echo of his missing wings. He couldn't wait to tumble through the clouds in this one last flight.

Freedom.

From pain. From heartache. From loss and despair.

He could taste it. It was finally within his reach.

His body leaned forward on its own accord.

And then—

"Whatcha doin'?"

*** *** *** ***

"Are those nipples getting frostbit or are they just happy to see me?"

Okay, that probably shouldn't have been the first thing that popped out of his mouth when Sorin slowly turned around, but he was *nervous*.

And his heart was trying to pound out of his chest. And his pulse was racing a thousand miles per hour. And he was hyperventilating from anticipation and expectation and *endless longing* for his male.

He was also instantly, ridiculously *horny*.

So, the first thing that popped into his high-altitude, oxygen-deprived brain at the sight of the most beautiful man in the whole universe, *his* man, was a morbid, sexual innuendo to camouflage the crazy explosions of fear, elation, lust and love within him.

Holy gods, but the male was a sight to behold!

Even when his face was a grim, emotionless mask. His skin deathly pale beneath the countless bruises and scars. His eyes a dull, opaque, muddy black. Even when his back looked like *The Texas Chainsaw Massacre*.

Sorin didn't speak as his lifeless eyes weighed upon him. They seemed unfocused, as if the male didn't really see him. As if he was looking through him.

He took one step closer, and immediately paused. Because Sorin took one step back, the heel of his right foot skidding off the edge of the ravine.

"Whoa," Ere said, putting his hands out in front of him.

"Easy."

He spoke to Sorin like the male was a spooked horse about to bolt. There was something terribly wrong here. This wasn't the welcome back he was expecting.

"Why are you standing there like that? Aren't you glad to see me?"

The male simply stared at him in that eerie, unfocused way of his.

For long moments, he didn't speak. Which wasn't unusual for him, so Ere patiently waited. He had a lot of explaining to do, he knew. He was going to tell Sorin everything soon. But for right now, he had more important priorities.

Like taking the male in his arms and never letting go.

You aren't real.

Ere jerked at the hollow sound of Sorin's deep voice in his mind.

There was no warmth in that voice, none of the smoky heat that Ere had grown used to. Addicted to.

There was no *life* in his voice.

"I am extremely present and real," he insisted immediately. "Come and see for yourself. Pinch me. Not too hard, mind you, I bruise easily."

A roiling darkness flashed in Sorin's eyes as his face contorted infinitesimally in excruciating pain before it settled into a ghastly smile, baring his teeth.

"Prove it."

Before Ere knew what he intended, the male pushed backwards off the ravine, taking the most gorgeous skydive to his death.

The fuck!

Ere took two giant leaps and dove off the peak right after him.

Where the fuck was he?!

He couldn't see anything!

The thick clouds and swirling mists completely blocked his view. There were endless layers of it.

He might have been able to catch a flicker of Sorin's flames if the male still had his feathers, but he didn't! His skin was as pale as the clouds, looked as cold as the snow. And his hair no longer shone like the sun. It had been a dark, dirty, blackish brown, straggly and limp down his shoulders and back.

Ere didn't unfurl his wings because they would slow his descent. He wished he was as heavy or heavier than the big, dumb bird so he could fall faster.

Gods!

When would these mists clear? When would these clouds separate? Visibility was impaired even further by the swirling snow.

Ere panicked in earnest. He couldn't see Sorin. Couldn't find his plummeting body.

And suddenly, he was furious. The immediacy of his wrath instantly transforming him into the obsidian dragon.

He kept his wings tucked close to his body and undulated his thorned tail to go faster. At the same time, he opened his great jaws and set the sky ablaze. Burning through the clouds, snow and mist.

There he was.

Ere's male.

Plummeting with his back towards the fast-approaching ground, his limbs spread apart, eyes closed.

Ere unleashed a resounding roar and dove for him.

A few seconds before he would have crashed into the jagged rocks below, Ere snatched him up in one gigantic dragon claw and shot back into the sky.

As he climbed higher, he switched his package from the hind claw to the front. Until he could hold the male in both paws right in front of his scaly face and shake the ever-loving shits out of him.

What the fuck is wrong with you! You have no wings! You could have died!

What if I hadn't reached you in time? What if I had no wings? Did you think of that?

No! Clearly, you didn't THINK!

What if I had chosen to be human instead of this particular monstrosity when the Pure Goddess gave me a choice?

What then, huh?

Shake.

Huh? You addlepated, suicidal maniac!

Shake, shake, shake.

Sorin's head lolled back on his shoulders like that of a lifeless doll in Ere's tight clutch, though he made sure not to squeeze the fragile humanoid body too hard.

The warrior's eyes finally opened a sliver. He regarded Ere wordlessly, unperturbed by the frantic rant.

It's you.

Was all he communicated, a soft amber igniting his gaze, like the dying embers of a bonfire being slowly fanned back to life by a gentle wind.

Of course it's fucking me, Ere growled. *How many other black dragons do you have in your vast acquaintance?*

One corner of Sorin's bluish-gray lips twitched.

Only one with your knack for barbed speech.

Ere rolled his serpent eyes.

Don't get me started. I could ream your ears til they're bleeding, but I won't. I'm just so fucking relieved I caught you in time.

Sorin seemed to settle more comfortably in Ere's grip, looking around him at the endless sea of clouds and mist.

I never thought I would soar again.

He swallowed visibly and looked into Ere's eyes.

Thank you, dragon.

Ere's heart cracked wide open then and there.

Oh gods...This male...

He'd do anything to bear Sorin's pain. He'd give everything to fan those sparks in his golden eyes into roaring flames once more.

And then, he remembered the words. He didn't know who whispered them in his ear when he needed them the most, and frankly, he didn't care. He only knew that he'd use them now to give back what the Hydra had taken away.

You are the fire, Sorin. You are the lightning and the flames. The smoke and the ash. You are the rawest power in the universe.

Sorin opened his eyes wider to spear into Ere.

Gold melding with sapphire blue.

It isn't the runes that kept you alive. It's your indomitable will and strength. Your purity of spirit and triumphant soul.

The dragon grinned his toothy, serpent grin, eyes crackling with blue lightning.

You're the fucking phoenix, man. Set the world on fire.

Let it burn.

In an instant, Sorin's body transformed as he unleashed a mighty roar.

Ere involuntarily loosed his grip, blinded by the bright blaze of the inferno where Sorin used to be. Clumsily, he grappled with the flames as they shot away, trying to hold onto his recently recovered treasure. But all he caught was a flaming tail feather in his claw.

With a grunt, he tucked the feather under a few scales near his heart. It was his to keep now. And he was going to collect them all.

With a crackling undulation of his serpent body and a couple flaps of his giant wings, he took off after the phoenix through the clouds, adrenaline and volcanic desire flooding his veins.

Yeah, you better run, pretty bird, he growled through their mind link.

Remember what I get when I catch you…

A few fiery flickers showed that the phoenix had banked left, turning sharply as he led Ere on a merry chase.

So, you think you're finally dragon enough to submit me? the gorgeous firebird rumbled, streaking through the skies like a shooting star.

Ere puffed up his substantial chest in a deep inhale, his tail wagging uncontrollably with anticipation and excitement.

Damn straight I am, he boasted. *You might wanna brace yourself.*

Sorin's husky deep laughter rolled through the skies like thunder, the sound pure sin, stroking along Ere's scales the way a lover's hand would stroke his cock.

I have many things yet to teach you about battle, dragon. You have a lot to learn.

Ere slowed his flight and hovered within the largest group of clouds. He breathed dragon smoke through his nostrils to conceal himself further, simply floating along with the rest of the mist.

I have a few new tricks up my sleeve too, he taunted the phoenix back. *I promise to make you like them.*

After a few minutes of hiding, his patience finally paid off.

Sorin flew closer, slower, sensing his nearness but not able to see where he was.

All at once he tackled the male, leading with a head butt, disorienting him. He grappled the phoenix' claws with his hind ones, locking them together, leaving his forepaws free. He beat his wings in counterpoint to Sorin's so that the male couldn't pull free no matter how he tried. He wound his tail tightly around Sorin's back to hold him close, practically squashing the other male against his scaly chest.

Let me have you, phoenix, he half ordered, half begged, wiping his serpent tongue up the firebird's neck and face.

Yuck, he grimaced. *Feathers. This tongue wasn't made for licking feathers.*

He used his greater strength and bulk in this form to squeeze Sorin tighter when the male squirmed to get free.

Please...beautiful warrior...let me have you, he coaxed without shame or pride, too desperate for his Mate.

Transform. I want to kiss you so bad. Don't make me wait any longer. We had a deal...you promised.

In the next blink, Sorin shifted into his half-form, and immediately, so did Ere.

They held each other as they synchronized their wings, hovering effortlessly, as if they were floating in a bed of clouds.

Ere gasped as if the breath had been knocked out of him as he regarded Sorin in all his original splendor.

Golden, smooth, satiny skin, glinting with the lightest sprinkling of hair, thicker across his massive pecs. Rays of sun lanced through his mane, long enough now to wave past his shoulders. His flame-filled eyes burning with life.

With love.

Ere saw it all. He didn't have to ask.

He *knew*.

In the roots of his soul, he knew this male and his endless, unconditional, unconquerable love for Ere.

You could use a shave, he said in their minds, instead of the poetic drivel he was just thinking.

Sorin's full lips spread in a smile within the bushiness of his whiskers, and Ere sighed like a swooning teenage girl.

You're wearing way too many clothes, was his next observation. Never mind that they were thousands of feet in the frigid, snow-filled air.

To which Sorin arched a golden brow.

Then, take them off me, dragon.

Ere was too impatient to rip Sorin's trousers off—they would have been hindered by his hiking boots in any case. So he shot one eager hand past the waistband and grabbed a handful of Sorin's hot, naked cock.

The other male groaned when Ere squeezed possessively, fisting the sensitive, swollen head. His wings flapped out of sync, throwing both of them off balance, sending them tumbling and rolling through the skies.

We need to land, Sorin rasped as Ere continued to clench and tighten his fist, spreading his slick along the heavy stalk.

You're going to get us killed. We're losing all sense of direction.

We're immortal, was Ere's unconcerned reply.

I love the feeling of falling with you. I want the world to be spinning around us when I come inside. When I make you lose your mind, and you plummet and soar to your little death, so I can revive you with my breath and start all over again.

Sorin exhaled sharply at Ere's words. Ere used his distraction to claw his other hand into Sorin's silky hair, bringing the male's face close to his.

Their wings synchronized again to lift them high. It should have been freezing; he should have been numb. But Ere's entire body was ablaze with want and incandescent heat. He knew that Sorin's was too. He could practically see the steam and smoke rising off of the male's golden skin.

He could feel the pulse of his hot blood in Sorin's veins. In his balls and cock, clutched covetously in Ere's hand.

He hovered his mouth close to Sorin's, brushing their lips together just barely, as he slicked his fingers in Sorin's essence below and probed between the tight, muscular globes.

So hot, he muttered against Sorin's mouth, the male's mustache and beard a tantalizing friction of silky bristles against his skin.

He stroked his longest finger with increasing pressure over Sorin's star, getting more and more desperate with each pass.

Wanting *in*.

Do it, dragon, the male rumbled through his mind, taking his mouth in a voracious kiss, plunging his tongue between Ere's lips.

Take what you want.

At last, Ere pushed his finger past the first ring of muscle into Sorin's utterly, unbelievably tight heat.

The male growled into his mouth and thrust his tongue deeper, making Ere devour it, suck on it mindlessly. Starved.

At the same time, Ere probed deeper, making Sorin hiss at the burn, a feeling Ere knew he'd never felt before. Because Sorin promised.

He would be the only one.

They kissed and clung to each other like there was no tomorrow. Like they were the only two beings in the world. Their wings flapped in a lazy rhythm, rocking their bodies together, pushing them closer.

Ere reached deeper, as deep as he could, curling his finger toward the front of Sorin's body instinctively.

The male shuddered all over when he rubbed against a hard knot. So he did it again and again and again, driving them both crazy with need.

Suddenly, he pulled free of Sorin's mouth, though he kept his finger exactly where it was, watching every contortion of pleasure on Sorin's face, blazing in his bright gold eyes.

Enough of games, he said with a close-lipped grin.

Time to land so I can fuck you properly. I have a hankering to split a few stones while I pound you into the ground. We'll save the aerial acrobatics for another time. Once I've had a few hundred rounds of "practice."

Sorin's eyes crackled with lightning as he gripped Ere's wrist and pulled his hand away from his prize.

Back at you, dragon.

With that, the male took off with a flap of his flaming wings, leaving Ere to pant in his dust.

Ere chuckled evilly, baring his fangs as he kept Sorin's feathers in his sights, before going after the male with a mighty surge.

Game fucking on.

Chapter Twenty-Two

Sorin wasn't going to make it easy.

He'd gone through an eternity of hell and back for this moment.

For this man.

The dragon could fucking work for it.

He flew faster, dodging jagged peaks that were hidden in the rolling clouds a moment before crashing, purposely going for the most difficult flight path. Egging Ere on.

The dragon was usually slower, but he was extremely motivated right now, and Sorin might have been slightly motivated to let him catch him too.

Ere didn't maneuver through the obstacle course of mountain peaks and the errant copses of trees as smoothly as Sorin did. He simply exploded the impediments that dared to get in his way with lightning from his eyes.

You're getting me all riled up making me chase you, the dragon said in a deeper voice than Sorin had ever heard him use before. As if it was wrapped in lust and tied up with hunger.

Not the best strategy for a blushing virgin, beautiful.

Sorin snorted a disbelieving laugh.

This was the broken shell he found at the bottom of a lake? *This* was the uncertain, self-hating, wounded soul who couldn't bear to be seen or touched?

He'd created a monster, obviously. A raging beast who was going to impale his ass on that dragon-sized cock and fuck him into the ground.

His chest puffed up with unseemly pride.

Sorin beat his wings faster as his body burned hotter, inflamed with desire and need, desperate for release from the volcanic pressure that burgeoned within.

The dragon kept pace. He could practically feel the male's hot breaths on his metaphorical tail.

By wordless agreement, they remained in their half-forms as they streaked through the sky. They were most equal in size and strength this way. If Ere wanted him, he could come and take him fair and square.

When I catch you, firebird, I'm not going to be gentle or patient, Ere threatened in his mind, his voice deceptively silky and low.

It'll be rough. It'll be hard. I'm gonna ride you long and deep. Fill you to overflowing with hot cum. The longer you make me chase you, the harder I'm going to nail you, baby. Even your healing powers won't let you sit down for a week.

Fuck.

Sorin lost his concentration for a split second, his wings stuttering mid stroke as his body clenched with an internal orgasm at Ere's words, though he prevented release just barely by fisting the head of his leaking cock through his trousers.

The dragon took full advantage of his momentary stall, hurtling into him from behind, crashing both of them onto the closest patch of earth and snow on a convenient plateau twenty yards below.

They rolled together on impact, the thick hides of their wings folded around them to protect their bodies.

Sorin got to his knees and started to push off the ground, but Ere grabbed his calf and tugged him down with a mighty pull. They grappled and rolled, fighting for dominance. Sorin gave him no quarter, using all of his training and battle-honed reflexes.

But Ere didn't play by the rules. And he learned fast. He transformed one hand into claws and ripped Sorin's pants to shreds, rendering him naked save for his boots. Ere himself was still fully clothed.

Sorin landed a solid punch to his side, but Ere tangled long legs with his and tightened them like screws, locking their lower bodies together.

They rolled again, each male trying his damnest to be on top.

Sorin was about to gain the upper hand when Ere reached between them to squeeze his balls in an illegal move. Sudden, unexpected pain exploded right between his eyes, making him gasp. Giving Ere just enough advantage to roll on top of him and stay on top with his full dragon weight.

You cheated, he gusted.

Even his telepathic voice sounded breathless.

As long as I win, anything goes, Ere returned without even a smidgeon of shame.

He had Sorin face down, flat on his stomach in the snow.
Naked and spread.

The fucker's voice was all smugness and giddy delight.

Sorin tried to get up, but the dragon simply added more weight, pressing so hard down on top of him his breath was squeezed out with a whoosh. He could barely breathe like this, and he certainly couldn't move. With Ere's hands pinning down his biceps, his knees gouging into the back of Sorin's open thighs.

Yield, phoenix, Ere commanded, his voice entirely serious this time, all teasing gone.

Let me have you. Just like this. Right here in the snow.

Sorin's heart thrashed. With exhilaration and the finest edge of fear.

He'd never made himself vulnerable like this before. Never let anyone inside him before. In every way another being could be inside him.

A part of him rebelled at the mere thought of being dominated. A very large part of him was poised to keep fighting.

But he calmed his breathing and his mind. Opened his heart and soul.

This was Ere. His dragon. Sorin promised him a reward.

And Sorin always kept his promises.

He relaxed his body and exhaled. The moment he did, the dragon's weight eased, and he could take in a lung-full of air again.

He turned his face to the side, looking back at his male.

His Mate.

And saw the rapturous need and desire on Ere's face, in his blazing blue eyes.

What are you waiting for? he murmured.

Take what you want. You've earned it.

I'm all yours.

*** *** *** ***

You've earned it.
Damn straight he had!

He was the badass that destroyed the Hydra. He'd died too many times to count and always found a way to claw back to life. Even when he hadn't wanted to. But now he understood.

Everything happened for a reason.

His whole existence, since being torn from his mother's arms in ancient Akkad during the Dark Ones' reign, he hadn't understood the reason.

Until now.

Until Sorin.

It had all been worth it to be here. With him. In this moment. In this new life that Ere chose.

He'd bargained and finagled with the Pure Goddess who seemed determined to put his beleaguered soul to rest. He threatened and raged. He charmed and cajoled her to give him one more chance. Just one.

To come back to this man.

To Claim his fucking reward!

And now Sorin was laid out beneath him like a pagan sacrifice. All golden-bronze, satiny skin over mounds upon mounds of steely muscle. The fire from his body radiated outward to melt the snow he lay upon. He was literally steaming hot.

That look he threw Ere over his shoulder. Daring Ere to do his worst.

Or his best, as the case might be.

Always egging him on. Pushing Ere to his boundaries and beyond.

No limits.

He'd never felt this free. This strong.

Despite his threat that he wouldn't be gentle, Ere couldn't help the reverent way he touched Sorin's skin. Reverent but demanding too, as his hands kneaded possessively from Sorin's shoulders to the healing scars on his upper back.

The male hissed softly at the lingering pain, every muscle delineating in stark relief.

Who knew there were so many muscles in the back? Ere didn't. He was quite certain he didn't have that many muscles in his own back. So, he traced each and every one of Sorin's with meticulous care, curious and exploring.

Soon, his wandering, worshipping hands arrived at the most magnificent pair of buttocks in the history of mankind. Two perfect globes of masculine power and grace.

Unable to help himself, he buried his face between the tight cheeks and moaned wantonly.

I want to live here forever, he declared. *And if I die, then I want to be asphyxiated between these stupendous spheres. I can't believe this is all mine.*

Only MINE.

Sorin's body shook with silent laughter, but the rumble abruptly cut off when Ere parted those miraculous mounds and licked his hot tongue through the secret valley between.

Sorin lifted his hips to give him better access, inviting him *in*, but Ere had other ideas.

He doubled back and kissed each cheek gently, lulling the male into a false sense of security. Then, he bit the left cheek like a savage little beast, sinking his fangs in the smooth flesh deep enough to draw blood.

Sorin growled, promising retribution.

But Ere was in charge here. He could do anything he damn well pleased!

He licked the small wound closed and dragged his tongue through the valley of Sorin's ass again, making him shudder. He then bit the other cheek, making him groan.

He pushed Sorin's heavy thighs farther apart, pulled them up to rest on his own as he knelt behind the male, and went to town on that gorgeous ass. He licked a strip from Sorin's scrotum to his taint. Licked around the shy, tightly shut entrance to his body, increasing pressure with every pass.

Dragon...

Sorin's guttural rasp was meant as a warning, but Ere ignored it.

This was his reward. He earned it. He wouldn't be rushed, even if the excruciating pressure in his balls killed him.

He tilted his face to get a better angle, zeroing in on that untapped bud. Every few laps he paused to suck the skin of Sorin's taint, dragging his fangs over the tender skin, pulling his ripe sac into his mouth and fondling it with his tongue.

The male was panting now, his big body shaking with need. His anus clenched every time Ere swiped it with the flat of his tongue, but it never opened.

Ere smiled with devilish intent, remembering his thoughts when he first met Sorin.

That this was a male who never got fucked. Who would always be the one doing the fucking. Alpha with a capital A. But he was submitting himself to Ere now.

Ere's chest felt full to bursting at the realization. Only he would ever see Sorin like this. Own him like this.

He used another trick he learned and transformed just one part of his body, his hands gripping Sorin's cheeks tightly, spreading them wide.

This time when he speared the tip of his tongue into Sorin's star, he kept right on going, extending the slippery muscle all the way inside, deeper than the reach of his longest finger, deeper than any human tongue could go.

Fuck, Dragon. What—

Whatever Sorin thought to say was cut off in a helpless groan as Ere tunneled his serpent tongue through the male's tight channel, curling it to rub against the walnut-sized gland with every thrust and retreat. He speared into Sorin relentlessly, glorying in his clean taste, his smoky musk, the mindless animal sounds he tried to hold back.

Ere was leaking pre-cum so copiously it felt like he'd already come. Impatiently, he ripped open his pants and took himself in hand.

He'd never been this hard in his entire existence. He'd never wanted anything this badly. He was desperate for it. Dying for it.

But it was more than simple release he chased. Nothing about this, with Sorin, was simple.

It was *everything*.

This was the Mate he'd been born to Claim.

He pulled his tongue out and licked the tight bud a few more times. Sorin wasn't remotely loosened, his inner muscles already locking again. But Ere couldn't wait any more. He couldn't even apologize in advance as he lined the weeping head of his cock to Sorin's hole and pushed.

There was no give. Not even a little. Ere would have to use force and hurt him. And a crazy, fiendish part of him wanted to.

Do it, Sorin rasped in their linked minds.

Hurt me. Fuck me.

I'm yours.

With a primal growl, Ere snapped his hips back. This time, when he surged forward, Sorin pushed back, swallowing the whole of his cock in one agonizing glide.

Ere might have blacked out for a moment from the indescribable pressure and pleasure in his reproductive organs. Without warning, his seed pulsed long and hard from the mouth of his cock, flooding Sorin's insides with liquid heat.

Merciful fucking gods! he exclaimed. Both hands clawed into Sorin's hips to hold him as close as possible. Like a lifeline.

He shuddered and quaked, released in endless, milky waves, holding still against Sorin but for the uncontrollable quivers of his body, succumbing totally to unimaginable ecstasy.

He came so hard, for so long, his cream overflowed the tight seal of their bodies until it dripped down Sorin's taint, stones and cock, making the male hiss and shiver, his own body straining for release.

But he didn't touch himself. Only braced his big body on his arms, taking both their weight. He was trusting Ere to take care of him. Pleasure or pain, Ere had absolute control.

The headiness of this knowledge almost eclipsed the euphoria melting through Ere's body like lava.

Gods! This male!

Now that he was finally inside Sorin, fisted in the hottest, tightest, silkiest channel on the face of the planet, and now that he'd lost his load most precipitously along with his marbles and every intelligent thought, Ere slumped bonelessly onto Sorin's back, shivering with electric aftershocks from his mind-blowing orgasm.

Sorry I hurt you, he had the wherewithal to mumble.

Didn't want to. But I also did. Need you too much.

His cock jerked and pulsed, making him sigh in wondrous bliss.

Does it make me evil if I revel in your pain? Drunk on the fact that you let me do this? That I'm the only one to ever be inside you.

Only I can give you pleasure and make you bleed.

Sorin was so silent and still beneath him, Ere began to worry. Was he all right? *Did* Ere make him bleed?

You talk too much, Dragon, the warrior rumbled in their minds. *Didn't you promise to pound me into the ground?*

Sorin undulated his hips and pushed his ass into Ere's groin, taking him all the way to the root with a pleasure-pained hiss.

Make it good. Make it hard. Then make me come until I see stars.

Well.

With poetry like that, how could Ere possibly refuse?

He braced himself up on one hand, grabbing onto Sorin's hip with the other, pulled out all the way to the tip, and slammed back in with a twisting lunge.

Sorin moaned and dropped his head forward while tensing his frame to take Ere's driving thrusts.

Ere had no finesse, no control, jackhammering into his male with delirious need. He took everything Sorin's body gave. And then he took some more. Lowering his mouth to the back of Sorin's neck to sink his fangs into succulent flesh.

Ah...*ambrosia.*

Sorin's hot blood was better than nectar from the gods. Ere was absolutely certain of it.

With every draw, his body tightened with increasing need, even as his movements slowed, the initial frantic edge to their mating subsiding.

He was acutely aware of every nerve ending in his body, as well as the minutest reaction from the man pinned beneath him.

How Sorin's breath faltered and hitched every time he pushed inside. How his pulse fluttered against Ere's fangs with every slow withdrawal. How his channel clenched and convulsed when Ere rubbed along that swollen gland. How his muscles quivered with stress every time Ere's heavy sac hit his perineum when he sank to the root.

Still hurt? Ere asked.

Sorin shook his head slowly from side to side like a mindless beast.

The motion could have meant no, it didn't hurt any more. Or no, he didn't care if it hurt. Whatever the meaning, Ere took it as a green light to continue. Which was serendipitous, because he wasn't sure he could stop.

Feel good?

Ere surged into him like a rolling wave, their bodies, minds, and hearts as one. Souls entangled, soaring higher.

And higher.

And higher still.

He pulled out of Sorin's neck and licked the puncture wounds closed. He angled both of their bodies up until their weight was on their knees. With one hand, he turned Sorin's head to the side, capturing the male's mouth in a searing, voluptuous kiss. He wrapped his other hand around Sorin's swollen cockhead and squeezed in time with the slow, impossibly deep, jolting thrusts into his body.

You're mine, firebird, he growled possessively.

Yours, his Mate replied.

Come for me, beautiful warrior.

He squeezed Sorin's stalk from root to tip. Once. Twice. And pushed into him as deep as he could go. Holding there. Holding them both at the precipice.

Now.

They climaxed as one, shouting their release. The sounds of their passion echoing through the night sky.

The stars looked down approvingly, as they entwined together, still locked as one, no telling where Sorin's body began and his ended. This time, when they fell into an exhausted sleep, it was Ere who spread his black wings around them both.

The dragon and his phoenix.

Together at last.

*** *** *** ***

You are a glutton, dragon. Haven't you had enough?

Ere was curled behind Sorin, lazily nudging his undying erection within the male's cum-slicked, clenching heat. Setting off rashes of euphoric sparks that radiated from the place they were joined throughout their bodies, to every extremity, until every cell felt like it was bursting in tiny, continuous, orgasmic fireworks.

Never, Ere replied fiercely. *If you could feel what I feel, you'd never want to stop either.*

Sorin turned his head to buss Ere's chin with his beard, rubbing their mouths together. Ere could almost taste his smile.

I know how it feels. I've been inside you too.

Ere shuddered at the reminder.

How could he possibly forget? His ass clenched with emptiness, wanting Sorin to fill him again. He didn't know what he loved more—fucking Sorin or getting fucked by Sorin. How would he ever choose?

Good thing he was in the most enviable position of being able to have his cake and eat it too.

How does it feel when I'm inside you? he asked, a thread of doubt in his voice.

Do you like it? Or are you just letting me have you because I won?

The male huffed what sounded like a snort. He wove the fingers of their left hands together and clasped them over his heart.

My coming countless times didn't give you a clue? he teased.

Ah, how Ere loved when his Solemnity teased.

Not countless, he argued. *You came eight times, if memory serves. I came more. I don't think I stopped coming since the moment I got inside you.*

Gods... You are so fucking tight.

To emphasize his point, he plowed hard and deep into the male, using more strength, snapping his hips.

Sorin grunted and pushed back into Ere's groin, clenching his channel with steely inner muscles, making Ere see stars.

Ere retaliated by stealing his right arm around Sorin's waist, wrapping his hand around the male's satiny erection and squeezing hard in rhythmic pulses in time with short, faster, sharper thrusts into the male's body.

You're killing me, Sorin rasped huskily.

Hurts…so good…

His head lolled to the side, exposing the long column of his throat, where his thick jugular vein pulsed in invitation.

Ere took full advantage, immediately sinking his fangs inside, swallowing Sorin's hot, sweet blood. As his cock plundered below. As his hand milked relentlessly. His left hand still clutched over Sorin's heart, as if he held the throbbing muscle directly in his palm.

Are you sore, beautiful? he taunted with an evil swivel of his hips, digging into Sorin's swollen gland, making his body jerk and shudder helplessly.

Do you love the burn? The way I wreck this gorgeous hole. The way I own every piece of you.

Sorin grunted incoherently, beyond words. His body so tight he was reinforced steel over molten lava. Lost to the inferno Ere stoked within him.

Come for me, firebird, he commanded. *I want to feel you come undone…it will never be enough…I'll never get enough…*

And Sorin came on a deep, guttural groan.

His hot cream spilling over Ere's fist, onto his chest and stomach, as his channel clenched tightly around Ere's cock, making him shout with his own release.

When they came back down from stratospheric heights, Ere sighed into Sorin's sweat-dampened nape, inhaling the drugging scent of his skin.

You've turned me into a sex fiend. I'll have you know I wasn't like this before. You've totally and irrevocably corrupted me.

Sorin didn't respond, but Ere could feel his satisfied smile even though he couldn't see it.

For a while they were still and silent, simply sharing breaths in the cozy cocoon of Ere's wings.

Until Sorin asked:

Isn't this what you came back for? To collect your reward?

Ere paused in the lazy stroking of Sorin's still hard cock. He suspected that neither of their bodies comprehended the phrase "stand down" when they were within ten feet of each other.

There was something in Sorin's tone that stabbed him a little in the heart. Could this stalwart warrior possibly have any doubts that he was eternally, ridiculously, stupidly loved by Ere?

Forever and ever, amen.

He eased out of Sorin with a wanton, insatiable, reluctant groan, and turned the male around.

Face to face, Ere missed being inside him, missed that ultimate, most intimate connection of their bodies. Instinctively, he reached down between them with one hand and inserted one, then two long fingers into Sorin's body, pushing the cream that leaked out back inside, rubbing it into Sorin's skin, caressing his pleasure knot with a curl of his fingers.

Sorin let him play with his hole, opening himself up to Ere in every way. Making himself vulnerable. Letting Ere *take* him.

His eyes were cast down, the thick fan of his lashes making crescent shadows on his color-darkened cheeks, perhaps equal parts from pleasure and reticence. His big body shivered uncontrollably as Ere stroked his secret gland, lubricated with the hot cum Ere had filled him with.

It was so dirty...wicked...primal and possessive. Ere loved it. It was almost as good as fucking Sorin with his cock. Almost.

But that wasn't why Ere turned him around. He needed to look into those intense, golden eyes. He needed Sorin to see his heart.

I came back for you, he said as plainly as he could, speaking slowly, because he wanted to get the words right. Nothing was more important.

I would die a thousand deaths to protect the people I love. But you're the one I live for, Sorin.

Only you.

The warrior was silent, not surprisingly, as he finally raised his eyes and stared back at Ere. His expression as implacable as ever.

I remember you, Ere whispered, cupping the side of Sorin's face in his other hand, stroking his thumb through the thick beard, across soft lips.

I remember being the Bane with you.

Sorin swallowed, his Adam's apple bobbing.

During the War of the Gods, the Bane found an Oracle. Just stumbled upon her one day in the mountains. She told him about the future the world was hurtling towards. About the deaths and destruction of everyone he loved. Including you.

Most of all, you.

Sorin lowered his lashes to veil part of his eyes, for they shimmered with an undefinable emotion. But he kept their gazes fused, unblinkingly intent as Ere continued the story.

The Oracle told him of a way to change the future. Gave him the secret to destroying the gods. The cost of his actions would be his life. And as a result, he'd also lose you.

It was an impossible choice. Because in both futures, he'd lose you. His Sol. His one and only Solemnity. But the path he chose held the smallest chance that he'd find you again. That your souls would remember each other in a distant, unknown future. While apart, you would both travel lonely paths, fraught with tribulations.

Ere's own eyes filled with tears, as his heart filled with the emotions that the Bane once felt.

He loved you so, Solemnity.

Sorin closed his eyes then, his whole body quaking.

Loved you more than life and death. But perhaps his greatest regret was...

Sorin raised his eyes, asking the unspoken question.

Ere smiled as a teasing glint entered his sapphire orbs. The same windows to his soul as the Bane's, for they shared the same soul.

He never got his "reward."

To punctuate his point, he pulled his fingers from Sorin's body and sucked them off in his mouth, waggling his brows wickedly all the while.

A surprised laugh burst out of Sorin at that, and he was so beautiful, Ere couldn't help but dive in for a hungry kiss, swallowing Sorin's joy and sadness into his own mouth, his hand trailing possessively to Sorin's ass to clutch and squeeze. Just because he could.

He could have this man whenever he wanted. And he *wanted* with every breath he took.

Before he lost his focus and his ever-loving mind to the all-consuming greed and need for his Mate, Ere pulled back and looked into Sorin's eyes again.

The Bane loved his Sol beyond all reason.

But Sorin...

Flames swirled in the male's beautiful golden eyes.

372

I love you infinitely more.

At last, those flames burst free. Engulfing them both. Remaking them. Binding their Destinies together.

Chest to chest, Sorin grasped Ere's outer thigh in one extra-large hand, lifted it over his hips and unerringly buried his swollen sex in Ere's clenching channel to the hilt.

Aaaaahhhhhhhh…

Ere's garbled groan at the fiery burn of Sorin's cock morphed into breathless moans when the male began to move.

So this was what it felt like. He was ever so grateful for the reminder.

The indescribable joy and freedom of being mastered. Being owned. The delicious ache and friction of the satiny glide. The clench of his hungry hole around that thick, hard, magnificent stalk. His most sensitive flesh stroked by the plump, meaty head.

He grabbed Sorin's face with both his hands and devoured the male's mouth with hot, voracious kisses. He pumped his hips in counterpoint to Sorin's thrusts, increasing the insane friction, the blistering heat. Fucking himself on that cannon cock. Fucking Sorin in equal measure.

Sorin's hands clutched his ass, squeezing his cheeks to the point of pain, pulling him in, and pushing him out. Driving his stupendous cock into Ere with increasing force. Manhandling him in the best possible way.

He'd wear those handprints for the rest of the day. He'd feel the possession of Sorin's cock for *all* his days.

Fill me, baby, he begged.

Demanded. Commanded. Then begged again.

Take me to heaven.

His crisis crashed upon him all at once, hot cream pulsing, tight hole convulsing, milking Sorin for his answering release.

His Mate didn't deny him. Holding his enraptured stare as he came apart. Letting Ere see what he couldn't put into words—

How devastatingly he loved him.

Take me…

Ere's soul begged of his glorious, golden warrior.

And he did.

To Eternity and beyond.

*** *** *** ***

At some point during the next day, Sorin and Ere finally made their way into town.

Their first stop was Tal and Ishtar's house. Fortunately, everyone was home, so Ere didn't have to suffer through more than one round of tears, kisses and excessive hugs. Also fortunately, the refrigerator and pantry were fully stocked, so they could celebrate his miraculous comeback with a hearty, home-cooked meal.

Everyone gathered around the dining area and kitchen so they could talk while Mama Bear cooked, the duties of sous chef falling to Gabriel, since Inanna barely knew how to boil an egg.

"I knew you'd bring him back, Sorin!" Benjamin practically bellowed in his boy-loud voice. "Sure took you long enough, though."

Ere eyed his male slyly, knowing exactly what caused the flush that darkened the golden-bronze complexion of his face and neck.

"Sorin is not to blame, dear boy," Ere said loftily, his voice conveying the utmost gravity. "I was the one who kept him too busy to think, much less move. The fault is mine."

Benjamin's big eyes blinked, as the adults coughed and cleared their throat.

Sorin shot daggers at Ere through narrowed eyes, but Ere blithely ignored him.

"In any case, we're here. Sorry to keep you waiting."

"How did you...come back?" Inanna asked, gesturing with a wave of her hand in Ere's general direction.

Her perplexity was understandable. The last time anyone saw him, he'd disappeared in an explosion of flames and a shower of stardust.

"Well, it wasn't easy," he shared. "The Goddess was quite adamant about keeping my unblemished soul from this cruel, harsh world."

"Indeed?" Tal put in with his signature "squirk."

He was the original, after all. Ere's would always just be an imitation.

Ere explained succinctly about his previous life as the Bane, with Sorin's previous incarnation as Sol. The Age of the Gods and the war that ended their reign.

Everyone looked at him with rounded, scarcely believing eyes, while he happily soaked in the avid attention.

"I reminded her that I'd only been reincarnated once in this current form. Yes, I died a couple times, or almost did. But she wasn't the one who revived me. I should still have one more chance before she struck me out. And besides, why did Sophia get more incarnations than me? Goddesses shouldn't play favorites. My soul is as Pure as any other. Possibly less deserving. But definitely more entertaining."

"You spoke to the Pure Goddess directly?" Gabriel asked, pausing in the dicing of vegetables.

"What was it like?"

Ere shrugged.

"I don't know if I spoke to her or her emissary. But you've been reborn too, so you should know. It's like a disembodied voice in a ball of light, sometimes formless, sometimes looking almost humanoid. I recall what the Twin Goddesses looked like eons ago. But they could take any shape or form. Who knows what their real forms are. But in essence, they are simply Darkness and Light. Raw power that shapes the universe."

Inanna and Gabriel shared a look, likely recalling the moment of their rebirth as well.

"Anyway, she didn't seem terribly moved by that argument. So, I reminded her that I accomplished a great feat, defeating the Hydra and restoring the all-important Balance. I should be rewarded."

Sorin made a strange sound beside him, but Ere paid him no mind.

"She retorted that I just killed her sister, *again*. Why should I get anything?"

Everyone around the table gaped with shock at this particular revelation. Ere continued on.

"And I replied quite reasonably that she should thank me for returning the Dark Goddess to her bosom at last. They are sisters, after all. It's time they kissed and made up. If anyone should be kept from the world, it's the both of them."

Ere waited for the simple truth of this statement to settle upon his listeners. Once upon a time, and even in the modern era, what he said would be considered blasphemy.

But he was a god-killer. Blasphemy was the least of his sins.

"The Pure Goddess grew a soul before the end of the gods when she saved Goya's life. But Lilith never 'got it,' if you know what I mean. I don't know her whole story, but I didn't get the sense she cared about anything but power even in the end. The Pure Goddess should show her the way, now that they are together again. I advised strongly that she doesn't send her twin back to earth to learn the hard way. *That* was a spectacular failure for everyone involved."

"And she listened to you?" Inanna said with brows raised.

Ere shrugged modestly.

"Why not? I am eminently logical and terrifyingly convincing."

Disbelieving eyes regarded him.

"In any case, I suspect it was the fact that I threatened to rip out every star in the heavens, curse every soul on earth, and plague her immortal consciousness with everlasting migraines, if I don't get what I want—that she finally capitulated in the end."

"You threatened a goddess," Mama Bear said rather breathlessly.

"Or her emissary," Ere demurred. "I got what I wanted. That's all that matters."

"Just like that?" Inanna asked doubtfully.

"Well…" Ere hesitated.

Everyone waited for his next words with baited breath.

"She might have given me some duties to fulfill in exchange for keeping my body and Gifts. Apparently, you can't be a dragon, Mated to a phoenix, and shirk the responsibilities of having so much power."

"What duties?" Benjamin asked excitedly.

Ere grinned, a devilish, mischievous glint entering his lightning-blue eyes.

"That, my dear boy, is a story for another day."

Epilogue

We lived happily ever after.

The End.

=)

That's what you want to hear right?

Well...

You're not wrong.

I don't know about ever after, but I do know that, ten years after Medusa and the Hydra were destroyed, my family and friends have done extremely well.

Not to say there haven't been ups and downs. The Universe is always struggling for Balance, which means there will always be galactic battles between "good" and "evil." But honestly, if there's one thing I've learned, one thing I *know*, is that nothing is black and white. Only a kaleidoscope of colors and shades in between.

We split our time between the Yukon Territory and NYC.

It's the perfect balance of city life and wilderness retreat for Uncle Tal and Aunt Ishtar, who still keeps her all-things shop *Dark Dreams*. As Mama Bear, she doles out love as generously as she gifts her desserts and the carvings that Tal makes to strangers who need them.

Just as she once did for a man called Binu. A man who turned out to be her long-lost son.

With administrative and monetary aid from the Shield, Tal and Ishtar also took over the Little Flower Orphanage close to her shop. It's one of the many "experimental sites" that Medusa and Lilith spawned around the world, as we learned through clues left by an insider that once infiltrated enemy ranks. Over the years, the Pure and Dark Ones have gained control of several of the orphanages. And more importantly, taken the children under our wing.

We believe these children have supernatural powers. Some of them have already exhibited Gifts, while others seem dormant.

Ava Monroe, a brilliant superhuman geneticist, and Rain, the Pure Ones' Healer, are working together to better understand the magic in these children's genes. In Ava and Ryu's own son's genes, for Kane is a rare combination of vampire and human.

The orphans who are old enough, who possess the desire, joined the ranks of Chevaliers, the first line of Pure and human defense against supernatural or Immortal threats that could upset the Universal Balance. They call themselves the Dandelions.

Mom and Dad spend most of their time at the Shield, given their role as Elite warriors in Sophia's guard. They are famous, or infamous, depending on your perspective, as the only Dark Ones to serve the Pure Queen.

Similarly, Eveline Marceau, the Pure Ones' Seer and Scribe, is also the New England vampire hive's Keeper. Legendarily, she is also known as the Keeper of the Dark King Ramses' heart.

They officially Mated before a joint congregation of Dark and Pure Ones, animal spirits and Elementals alike. A few trusted humans were also invited and present, including yours truly. It was the first ever such high-profile, public Mating between these two Kinds.

Things turned rather bloody before the honeymoon, however, though it was not unexpected. The Elite and Chosen worked together to subdue vampire revolts and just barely averted civil war.

On the bright side, the happy couple openly enjoy their notoriety, and have plenty of powerful allies to support their union. Including Queen Jade of the Great Plains hive and her Pure Consort, Seth Tremaine. (Theirs was the second high-profile, official Mating between a Pure and a Dark One).

Times have certainly changed. So much for the better, if you ask me.

In other news, Sophia didn't like the idea of being "Queen," it turns out; she felt the idea was too Medieval. She decided to let the Pure Ones elect their leader by popular vote. I, for one, wasn't at all surprised when she retained her metaphorical crown.

Apparently, being voted into office made her take the role that much more seriously. She is working closely with the Dozen and her Dark allies to establish peace amongst the Immortals, while maintaining secrecy from humankind.

Dalair remains one of her Elite guards, though they are Mated. Given Tal's focus with orphanages, and raising as many orphans as he can, together with Ishtar, Dalair has taken the official role of General of the Pure Ones. Seth remains the Consul, though he splits his duties between Sophia and Jade's new hive as her Consort.

Goya, the Tiger King, and his animal spirits are a crucial part of the Immortal Pact, though they remain at their base in the Yukon Territory. They provide aid to the Pure and Dark Ones whenever they are called upon to do so. After all, the Chosen's Commander, and the Dark King's right hand, Maximus, is Goya's son.

Meanwhile, King Ramses continues his search for long-lost Elementals like himself, the rarest of all Immortals. Eveline helps him in this endeavor through her diligent research and interpretation of ancient texts and oral histories. Whenever I'm in NYC, I try to help as well, for I love soaking up knowledge and exploring this fantastical world in which I live.

Just when you think you're starting to figure it out, new mysterious arise.

I am certain we haven't peeled away the endless layers of truth and lies. Some mysteries remain unsolved, unknown or unacknowledged. If you're looking for closure, I have to warn you: there's no such thing.

There are only stories heaped upon myths, wrapped in legends, and gilded with interpretation.

The only truths are the ones we believe in.

We do know that some of the Dandelions have Elemental Gifts. While others have hints of animal spirits or Pure and Dark tendencies. There are many orphanages we still haven't found. Many more "children" who don't realize the powers they might possess.

A very few of them could even have all of the "ingredients" that make up the magic of bygone gods.

Like me.

Well, technically, I'm not an orphan. I have two of the most amazing parents on earth! They are super badass cool. If they weren't simply Mom and Dad, I'd totally be in awe.

But I don't actually have their genes. At least not directly.

Yeah, I know who my biological father is—my mother's twin brother. Uncle Tal and Aunt Ishtar's son.

My Uncle Erebu.

He and I had a sit-down, man-to-man conversation back when I turned ten.

I still can't believe how nervous he was. He stuttered so bad and had so many false starts I thought he was going to tell me something dire. Like maybe he's the first-ever Immortal to have a terminal illness that also impacted his ability to speak. (If you knew Uncle Ere, you'd understand what I mean. No one beats his snark, glibness and sarcasm).

At the end of his speech, I told him the simple truth: I am the luckiest boy in the world to have not one, but *two* great men who love me. Who set the example of what men ought to be.

Gabriel. Ere.

And don't forget my "grandpa" Tal-Telal, the mythical General of the Pure Ones.

Plus Sorin, Uncle Ere's Destined Mate.

On top of which, I'm also surrounded by loving, mighty, brilliant women—Inanna, Ishtar, Sophia...

What more could a boy ask for?

Uncle Ere simply stared at me with saucer-like eyes after that impassioned reply, and said, "Well, that's that."

Speaking of awe-inspiring men, I'm due to meet a heavenly jade-green dragon by the name of Cloud (though he can only take that form in dreams) on the tallest mountain peak. I'm currently in the Yukon to start my training. It's never too early, even if I'm just a human.

My constant companion flutters his wings beside my ear as he perches on my left shoulder. A white dragonfly I call Opal, just to pull his leg.

Sorin and Ere are already waiting for me at the edge of town.

"Ready for your ride?" Uncle Ere asks, smiling with his bright blue eyes.

"Born ready," I reply.

He gives me his famous "squirk," and says, "What'll it be? Dragon or phoenix?"

"Can I just say—told you so."

He rolls his eyes heavenward, his mouth forming silent prayers for patience, no doubt, as I emphasize my point.

"I *told* you, you were destined for a phoenix mate," I say smugly.

"Yes, dear boy, this might be the thousandth time you've mentioned it."

"And yet I never tire of being right."

"Honestly, where *do* you get such big-headedness?"

"Must be in the genes," I quip. "Because you're similarly afflicted."

"Choose," Sorin broke in with his usual succinctness.

"We're late."

I pretend to waffle between them, looking from one tall male to the other. Golden warrior or black-maned assassin. Good thing I'm almost as tall now. I might even grow a couple more inches before my twentieth birthday and eek out half an inch over my old man.

As I say, all in the genes.

"Dragon," I finally announce.

Because, come on. Like there's a real choice.

Ere immediately transforms into an obsidian dragon, a fiery jewel blazing in his massive, black chest, as Sorin leaps into flight as a flaming phoenix.

Okay, so the phoenix is pretty fucking awesome too.

I climb onto the dragon's back and hold onto one of his thorns as he takes off with a mighty flap of those gigantic wings.

As we soar through summer blue skies, the wind in my face, adrenaline in my veins, I whoop with pure joy and boundless hope.

Ere roars with the echoing boom of thunder, and the phoenix's screech answers his call, as he leads us on a hell of a chase through a sea of clouds rolling across jagged mountain peaks.

Ultimate freedom. Nothing like it.

One day soon, when my powers Awaken, I'll be flying alongside the obsidian dragon and his phoenix Mate.

Hurrah!

Let the Age of Dragons begin!

*** *** *** ***

Series Finis.

*** *** *** ***

Other Books in the Pure/ Dark Ones series**:**

Book 1, *Pure Healing*
Book 2, *Dark Longing*
Book 3, *Dark Desires*
Book 4, *Dark Pleasures*
Book 5, *Pure Rapture*
Book 6, *Dark Redemption*
Book 6.5, *Pure Awakening*
Book 7, *Pure Ecstasy*
Book 8, *Dark Obsession*
Book 8.5, *Pure Providence*
Book 9, *Pure Magnetism*
Book 10, *Pure Surrender*
Book 10.5, *Pure Darkness*
Book 11, *Dark Possession*
Book 11.5, *Pure Requiem*
Book 12, *Pure Destiny*

And don't miss Aja James' new series Dragon Tails:
Book 1, *Dream of Dragons*
Book 2, *Song of Dragons*
Book 1, *Wish of Dragons*

Preview for Dream of Dragons

Every lore of every clan, across time and space, dreamed of dragons. Did you ever wonder why?

Erebu and Sorin fought through countless lifetimes of trials and tribulations to find one another again. They even conquered death.

But Ere's rebirth requires a price: he must answer the Celestial Summons when it comes and faithfully complete each task the Jade Emperor sets before him.

On the bright side, he doesn't have to perform miracles alone. Sorin will be right there with him. One the not so bright side, his Fate, the Fate of all dragon Kind, and by extension, the Universal Balance, depend on the successful execution of each quest.

No pressure.

His first task is find and retrieve the **Jewel of Dreams.**

Location: Unknown. Time travel will be required.
Clues: Too few. But there may be a dragon-slayer, a king, a wizard, and a few mythical monsters along the way.
Accompaniments: His beloved Sorin (who is all he needs!) A humorless, anti-social female dragon (who he doesn't need). Though her kickass fighting skills do come in handy in a pinch.
Timing: ASAP. Determined by an arbitrary Sandglass in the Jade Emperor's possession.

The end of the world may be just around the corner. Along the way, *enemies may become lovers, reluctant friendships may form, and lots of hot, desperate, this-may-be-the-last-time-we-have-sex sex will definitely be had.*

And who knows, you may never want to wake up from this...

DREAM OF DRAGONS.

Glossary of Characters

Alend Ramses: The reigning Dark King of the New England vampire hive, formerly one of the Chosen. Gift(s): ability to command the Element earth, the most powerful telekinetic in existence. Weapon of choice: scimitar.

Elementals: Immortals who can command Earth, Water, Air, or Fire.

The Chosen: The Dark King's personal guards and advisors.

> **Maximus Justus Copernicus**: The Commander. Leader of the Chosen. Known Gift(s): ability to transform into a giant white tiger.

> **Ariel Kyles**: Maximus's Mate. Known Gift(s): ability to transform into a giant black panther.

> **Rhys Evans**: Call sign to be designated. Previously Goya's right hand. Now a member of the Chosen. Known Gift(s): ability to transform into a giant Golden Eagle.

> **Ryu Takamura**: The Assassin. Executes special, often covert missions for the King. Known Gift(s): ability to turn to shadow. Weapon of choice: Ninja blade or ninjaken.

> **Devlin Sinclair**: The Hunter. Hunts down and eliminates vampire rogues. Ensures security of the New England hive's borders. Known Gift(s): photographic memory. Weapon of choice: varies, but usually a saber or gun.

> **Anastasia Zima**: The Phoenix. The Dark King's head of security, ensures safety of the King and assists Maximus with affairs of state. Known Gift(s): telekinesis. Weapon of choice: varies, as a lover and expert in all manner of weapons. Soft spot for daggers.

388

Enlil Naram-Anu/ Eli Scott: Formerly the Blooded Mate of Anunit Salamu and leader of the shadow warriors in Ancient Akkad. Known Gift(s): the ability to turn into air or wind, as well as shadows.

Ava Monroe Takamura: Ryu's human wife and mate. Brilliant geneticist who developed and took a serum that makes her uniquely super-human, with the Pure Ones' ability to heal, the source of their eternal youth and apparent immortality.

Kane (pronounced Kah-Nay) Takamura: Ryu and Ava's son.

Grace Darling: Devlin's Blooded Mate. Cyber genius who used to work unwittingly for Medusa's empire.

Clara Scott: Eli's human wife.

Annie (Annabelle) Scott: Eli and Clara's adopted daughter.

Sophia Victoria St. James: Queen of the Pure Ones. Known in her past life as Ninti in her original Pure One incarnation during the Akkadian Empire. Known as Kira in her past life as an Egyptian princess who married the Crown Prince Cambyses of Persia. Known Gift(s): the ability to see and influence Pure souls; the ability to see the true intentions of all beings. The ability to turn into the Destroyer and eradicate souls en masse, as well as the ability to inspire and strengthen souls.

The Circlet: The Pure Queen's royal advisors. Part of the Dozen or Royal Zodiac.

> **Seth Tremaine**: The Consul. Handles the Pure Ones' diplomatic affairs. Talented negotiator. Known Gift(s): the ability to project a spiritual version of his physical self anytime, anywhere.

Ayelet Baltazar: The Guardian. Main responsibility is to guide and educate the Pure Queen, caretaker and mother figure. Known Gift(s): the ability to feel and experience what others feel using a physical artifact of the individual or direct touch; deep empathy.

Eveline Marceau: The Seer, Scribe and Keeper. Ramses' Destined Mate: Records and interprets Pure Ones' potential future in the Zodiac Prophesies. Known Gift(s): spells, some telepathy.

Rain: The Healer: Ensures the health and vitality of Pure Ones, especially members of the Royal Zodiac. Known Gift(s): used to have the ability to absorb pain and poison from severe wounds using the needles of her hair, called *zhen*. Since she gave up her Gift for her Eternal Mate, Valerius, her *zhen* acts more as acupuncture needles, and occasionally used as weapons.

The Elite: The Pure Queen's personal guards. Part of the Dozen or Royal Zodiac.

Dalair Al Amirah: Paladin of the Pure Ones, now the General. Leads the Elite. Recruits humans and Pure Ones to their cause. Sophia's Destined Mate. Known Gift(s): hyper-developed senses. Strength and endurance beyond average Immortals. Weapon of choice: Twin Dragon Blades or two half-moon crescent blades that can be combined into a disc.

Valerius Marcus Ambrosius: The Protector. Hunts down rogue vampires who hurt humans. Known Gift(s): fast healing, beyond even the typical Pure Ones' ability to heal. Weapon of choice: Chained scythe.

Tristan du Lac: The Champion. Historically, he is the first warrior to be dispatched against enemies in one-on-one combat. In modern times, he helps train human Chevaliers. Known Gift(s): none. Weapon of choice: Excalibur or long sword.

Aella Alexander: The Strategist. Mated to Cloud. Plans all manner of defense and attack vs. enemies and threats. Known Gift(s): speed. Weapon of choice: three chakrams, which can link together and stiffen into a longer-range hand-to-hand weapon or be thrown individually.

Cloud Drako: The Valiant. Trains Pure Ones and humans in combat. Known Gift(s): ability to exert strong compulsion on anyone who stares into his eyes. Ability to command the Element water. Weapon of choice: long spear.

Inanna: The ex-Angel of Death or Angel of the New England vampire hive under Jade Cicada, used to be a member of the Chosen. After discovering her Pure Soul as the daughter of a Pure and Dark One and having her Awakening, she is known as the Light Bringer. Human alias: Nana Chastain. Now a member of the Elite. Known Gift(s): the ability to see through any material and zoom in and out like a telescope or microscope. Weapon of choice: chained whip.

Gabriel D'Angelo: Inanna's Blooded Mate. Used to be known as Alad Da-an-nim, born a Pure One, died and reincarnated as a human. Turned into a vampire by Inanna but retains his Pure Soul. Gift(s): none, but is a skilled martial artist as a human and was one of the fiercest Pure warriors in ancient Akkad.

Jade Cicada: Former Queen of the New England vampire hive, now Queen of the Great Plains hive. Mated to Seth Tremaine. Known Gift(s): Ability to draw others' life force through touch and sexual intercourse; ability to heal or take life through touch.

Benjamin Larkin D'Angelo: Inanna and Gabriel's adopted son. Known Gift(s): the ability to see people's true selves. Destined to become an earth-bound dragon.

Tal-Telal: The General who led the Pure Ones to victory in the Great War. Inanna's and Ere's father. Known Gift(s): used to have the ability to see possible futures, now with the Gift of anticipation.

Ishtar Anshar: Once a Dark Princess when Dark Ones ruled the earth. Tal's Destined Mate, Eternal and Blooded. Inanna's and Ere's mother. Human alias: Estelle Martin or "Mama Bear," owns all-things and pastry shop called Dark Dreams. Known Gift(s): the ability to transform into a giant snow leopard.

Medusa: Anunit Salamu (the Dark Star). The arch nemesis of the Pure and Dark Ones, as well as humans. Known Gift(s): used to have telepathy and telekinesis. Now, the ability to transform into the Hydra. (Shared form with Wan'er).

Wan'er: Used to be the Pure Healer, Rain's, handmaiden. Head researcher for Medusa. Also known as Lilith. Known Gift(s): a fox spirit who has one life for each of its nine tails. Ability to extend life indefinitely by shifting into another "skin," but limited to nine skins. Ability to transform into the Hydra, and at least one other form. (Shared form with Medusa, but no longer).

Lilith: See also Wan'er. Ninti's mother.

Ere: Sophia's ex-teaching assistant and brief love interest. Also known as the Creature, Erebu, Cambyses and Binu. He is the lost son of Tal and Ishtar, twin brother of Inanna, biological father of Benjamin. Known Gift(s): ability to transform into any humanoid form. Ability to transform into a black, flying dragon that can harness the power of flames, smoke and lightning, among other Gifts.

Sorin: Ere's Destined Mate. Born during the Age of the Gods as the Eagle King. Reborn as the Phoenix. Known Gift(s): ability to transform into a giant phoenix, almost the size of a dragon, that can turn its entire body into flames or just certain feathers, as well as harness lightning, among other Gifts.

Goya: the Tiger King. Maximus's sire. Mostly animal. Known Gift(s): ability to transform into humanoid form. Natural form is a giant Siberian tiger.

Madison Jane Peterson (Maddie): Goya's Eternal Mate. Human single mother of son, Logan, and marketing executive.

Animal spirits: Goya's kinsmen. Pure, Dark Ones, and humans who can transform into animals, as well as animals who can take humanoid forms.

Character Relationships and Timeline

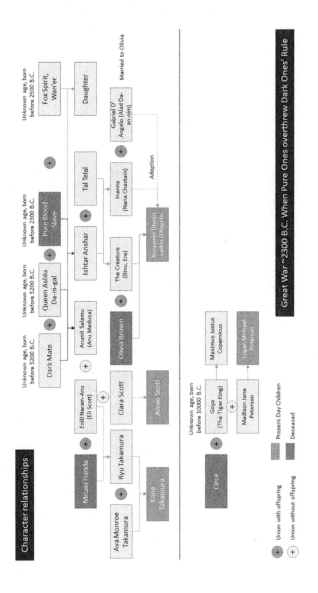

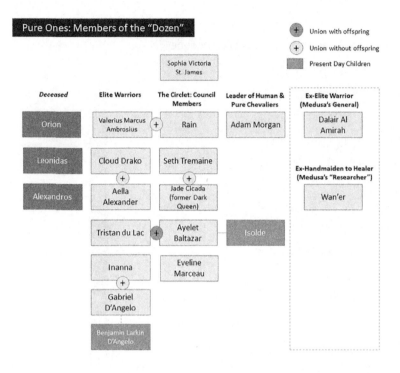

Pure Ones: Members of the "Dozen"

Union with offspring
Union without offspring
Present Day Children

Sophia Victoria St. James

Deceased — **Elite Warriors** — **The Circlet: Council Members** — **Leader of Human & Pure Chevaliers** — **Ex-Elite Warrior (Medusa's General)**

Orion | Valerius Marcus Ambrosius (+) Rain | Adam Morgan | Dalair Al Amirah

Leonidas | Cloud Drako | Seth Tremaine

Ex-Handmaiden to Healer (Medusa's "Researcher")

Alexandros | (+) Aella Alexander | (+) Jade Cicada (former Dark Queen) | Wan'er

Tristan du Lac (+) Ayelet Baltazar | Isolde

Inanna | Eveline Marceau

(+) Gabriel D'Angelo

Benjamin Larkin D'Angelo

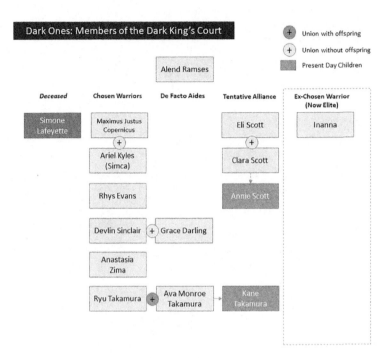

Dark Ones: Members of the Dark King's Court

⊕ Union with offspring

⊕ Union without offspring

▢ Present Day Children

Alend Ramses

Deceased	Chosen Warriors	De Facto Aides	Tentative Alliance	Ex-Chosen Warrior (Now Elite)
Simone Lafeyette	Maximus Justus Copernicus ⊕ Ariel Kyles (Simca)		Eli Scott ⊕ Clara Scott → Annie Scott	Inanna
	Rhys Evans			
	Devlin Sinclair ⊕ Grace Darling			
	Anastasia Zima			
	Ryu Takamura ⊕ Ava Monroe Takamura → Kane Takamura			

396

Historical Timeline

Mentioned in Which Book

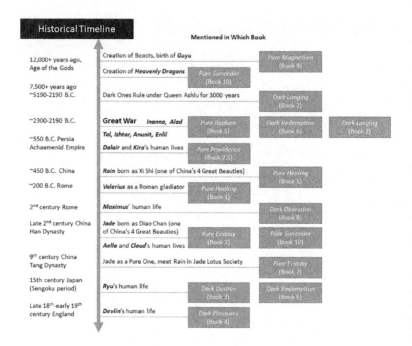

12,000+ years ago, Age of the Gods	Creation of Beasts, birth of *Goya* — *Pure Magnetism* (Book 9)
	Creation of *Heavenly Dragons* — *Pure Surrender* (Book 10)
7,500+ years ago ~5190-2190 B.C.	Dark Ones Rule under Queen Ashlu for 3000 years — *Dark Longing* (Book 2)
~2300-2190 B.C.	**Great War** *Inanna, Alad* — *Pure Rapture* (Book 5), *Dark Redemption* (Book 6), *Dark Longing* (Book 2)
	Tal, Ishtar, Anunit, Enlil
~550 B.C. Persia Achaemenid Empire	*Dalair* and *Kira*'s human lives — *Pure Providence* (Book 7.5)
~450 B.C. China	*Rain* born as Xi Shi (one of China's 4 Great Beauties) — *Pure Healing* (Book 1)
~200 B.C. Rome	*Valerius* as a Roman gladiator — *Pure Healing* (Book 1)
2nd century Rome	*Maximus*' human life — *Dark Obsession* (Book 8)
Late 2nd century China Han Dynasty	*Jade* born as Diao Chan (one of China's 4 Great Beauties) — *Pure Ecstasy* (Book 7), *Pure Surrender* (Book 10)
	Aella and *Cloud*'s human lives
9th century China Tang Dynasty	Jade as a Pure One, meet Rain in Jade Lotus Society — *Pure Ecstasy* (Book 7)
15th century Japan (Sengoku period)	*Ryu*'s human life — *Dark Desires* (Book 3), *Dark Redemption* (Book 6)
Late 18th-early 19th century England	*Devlin*'s human life — *Dark Pleasures* (Book 4)

Printed in Great Britain
by Amazon

18257205R10231